T·HE HIDDEN STARS

THE
HIDDEN
STARS

BOOK ONE OF THE
RUNE OF UNMAKING

MADELINE HOWARD

An Imprint of HarperCollinsPublishers

THE HIDDEN STARS. Copyright © 2004 by Madeline Howard. All rights reserved. Printed in the United States of America. No part of this book may be used or reproduced in any manner whatsoever without written permission except in the case of brief quotations embodied in critical articles and reviews. For information address HarperCollins Publishers Inc., 10 East 53rd Street, New York, NY 10022.

HarperCollins books may be purchased for educational, business, or sales promotional use. For information please write: Special Markets Department, HarperCollins Publishers Inc., 10 East 53rd Street, New York, NY 10022.

FIRST EDITION

Designed by Renato Stanisic

EOS is a federally registered trademark of HarperCollins Publishers.

Library of Congress Cataloging-in-Publication Data has been applied for.

ISBN 0-06-057587-5

04 05 06 07 08 DIX/RRD 10 9 8 7 6 5 4 3 2 1

✳ BOOK ONE ✳

1

✳

On the great isle of Thäerie, there is a region north of the Siobhagh River where the barley fields and apple orchards of the south, the prosperous farms and the ancient many-towered cities, gleaming white and gold, give way to bleak dun-colored moorland, sullen hills, and rocky upland valleys. They call this country the Mointeach. Long ago, it was a land much plagued by warlocks, black bards, and cunning-men, but many perished at the Changing of the World, and many more fled at the coming of the High King. His allies were the mighty wizards of Leal, whose powers were far too great for these rustic necromancers and petty spell-casters to withstand—and there were still, in those days, many wild, uncivilized places in the world where those who made their living raising ghosts and cursing cattle might flourish unmolested. Yet they left a number of strange customs and beliefs behind them on the Mointeach, and there was hardly a house to be found there without a rune-wand or a bundle of bones buried under the doorsill, some half-understood charm scratched upon the hearthstone.

The land remained much as it had always been. Villages

wére few, and divided by vast tracts of wilderness, while the little stormy bays and inlets were treacherous and difficult to navigate. No visitor ever came there traveling for pleasure, and few of any sort came there at all.

Yet it happened, one dreary day on the cusp of winter, in the time of the High King, that a trio of wizards trudged through the Mointeach. They were on their way to witness a birth and (it might be) a death, and a great sense of urgency and dread was on them.

For hours they walked through country wild and trackless, while a lonely wind whistled in the rocky defiles, and hawks and gulls circled overhead. Late in the day, they finally came upon a road. Little more than a footpath it was, and very rough and stony, but quite unmistakable, cut deep into the earth and running on for mile upon mile. They had seen no other signs of human habitation since landing their boat on one of the pebbly beaches to the northeast, and it seemed to the wizard Faolein and his two companions that this road must lead to the town of Cuirglaes. They decided to follow it.

After skirting the hills for an hour or two, the track began to climb. The wizards kilted up their long robes and continued on. The road wound uphill between shadowy stands of pine and spruce. Every now and then the forest grew thinner, and Faolein could see all the way to the top of the hill, could just make out in the failing light a huddle of ancient buildings made of stacked stone.

Could this be Cuirglaes? he asked himself. They had been expecting a town of moderate size, at the very least a great seaside fortress, not this tiny isolated settlement. Sudden panic clutched at his throat. If they had missed their true road, gone somehow astray—

A scattering of big wet snowflakes drifted down, melting

as soon as they touched the ground. Faolein tripped over a knotted root, barked his shin on a tree stump, righted himself, and continued on, trying to ignore the sting where his skin had been scraped raw. Clumsy. Clumsy he was and always had been, especially when he allowed his thoughts to wander, when he failed to use all six senses to observe his surroundings.

The forest closed in again. Under the trees the air was damp and cool, heavy with the sharp scent of pine.

He considered the possibility that a mistake had been made. The sky had been overcast since morning, with not a single gleam of sunlight the whole grey day. Nevertheless, his own sense of direction was good, and Éireamhóine's was even better. He thought: *If we've gone astray, it is the curse at work. It must be. Mother and child will both die, and with them all our hope.*

Another bend in the road brought the village back into view, this time from the west. And now, partly screened from the road by a ragged line of beanpoles and skeletal dried cornstalks, Faolein spotted a cluster of buildings larger and more solidly built than the rest, and in their midst, thrusting upward, a round tower some thirty or forty feet high, with narrow windows set into the thickness of the walls.

"Perhaps Cuirglaes after all," said Éireamhóine. His pale, perfect face was impassive in the gathering gloom, the deep-set dark eyes without expression; only his words betrayed his fear. "May the Fates grant that we come in time to save two lives and foil our enemy's schemes."

Even as he spoke, the wind came up and scattered the clouds. The stone buildings on the summit stood silhouetted against a bloody sunset sky and the immense yellow moon, like a rotten pumpkin, just then rising behind the tor. As one man, the three wizards stopped where they stood, and Curóide flung up his yew-wood staff like a barrier against the ill omen, muttering a *béanath,* a charm of blessing, under his breath.

Then, carried on the wind, thin but unmistakable, came the anguished cries of a woman suffering a difficult labor.

It was Éireamhóine who first shook off the fey mood that held them rooted in place. He left the track and the shelter of the trees for a more direct route: up an uneven slope of gravelly shingle, then across a dry streambed. Recovering, Faolein and Curóide scrambled up the scarp behind him, then pushed their way through a mazy thicket of thorny cat's-whiskers and yorrel growing between outcrops of weathered granite.

As they entered the village, a door at the base of the tower flew open, and a tall woman appeared backlit on the threshold, beckoning them on.

"We had almost given up hope," she said, at the wizards' approach. Ushering them inside, into a low, round, firelit chamber, she closed the door behind them. "But the Princess sensed you were drawing near; she has that much power left to her at least."

From a room up above came a despairing wail. Momentarily distracted, the woman stood with her hand still on the door, frowning up at the rough plank ceiling. She turned back toward the wizards just as they began to remove their cloaks.

"But you are none of you healers!" she protested, taking in at a glance their long woolen robes: deep purple for Éireamhóine and Faolein, sage-green for Curóide.

"There were no healers to send. As here on Thäerie, so it is on Leal," said Éireamhóine. "When we left the Scholia, the healers were all bedridden—without strength, without power, many of them almost lifeless."

"But then *what good* are you?" the woman asked bitterly. Her dark hair was disheveled and her face deeply marked with signs of weariness and strain. Into the mind of Faolein, who had a gift for names, came one that seemed to belong to that face: Rionnagh.

Her thin, nervous hands clasped and unclasped. "Why have you even come here?"

"We believe," said Faolein gently, "it can be no coincidence: our healers all helpless just when the Princess has such need of them. It is Ouriána's doing—her malice made manifest."

Rionnagh made a sign to ward off evil. Her hard grey eyes traveled to each of their faces in turn, challenging them. She knew, as they knew, how hopeless it all was. .

Éireamhóine bowed his head; the other men did likewise. "We will try once more to remove the *aniffath*."

———

Left to themselves in the firelit room a short while later, the wizards set their wards with runes of protection, secrecy, and silence; they sketched a magic circle on the packed earth floor. Stepping inside the circle, Éireamhóine began to trace a glimmering figure on the air. Shaping energies like filaments of starlight, he drew them out with his lean, strong hands, forming an image of the vast, complicated pattern of time and chance and circumstance that was the *aniffath*—the Empress Ouriána's curse on the woman upstairs.

Taking seats by the fire, on two stools and a chair they had previously arranged facing north, west, and east around the central hearthstone, the three wizards closed their eyes and began to chant.

The magic came, as it always did for Faolein, like liquid fire, like molten gold running through his veins. It burned through him, consuming, refining, reducing thought and intention to a pure, vital essence. Then came the familiar disorientation, a spinning vertigo as mind separated from body. He felt himself sailing, bodiless, through infinite regions of wind and darkness.

Suddenly, he was there: within the *aniffath*. It surrounded him on all sides, a silvery network so intricate and involved that it bewildered him. The thing had been growing in complexity over the years. How could it be the product of a single mind? He began to fear that there were other forces at work here, beyond the one he knew.

Somewhere in the distance, someone was speaking, reciting a spell in a harsh, grinding voice. It filled him with dismay, that voice, it was so pitiless, so impersonal, like stones rubbing together under the earth, like cold water seeping down and down, eating away at the roots of mountains. It was, he realized, a Hymn of Unmaking, the Dark whispering to the Dark; if he listened to it very long, he would go mad.

With the greatest care, Faolein began to explore the patterns of the curse, moving from thread to thread as delicately as a spider traversing her web, following each glittering strand to its ultimate conclusion. From path to path he followed, as one possibility led to the next. But in every situation, in every circumstance, the end was the same: Death.

Faolein came slowly back to an awareness of who he was, and where and when.

With his eyes still closed, the otherworldly image lingered behind his eyelids. He took a deep breath, then released it. At the same time, he felt the power flow out of him like water from a cracked jar, leaving him dull and heavy, mired in the flesh, a creature subject to the eight elements rather than their master. There was a stabbing pain in his right shoulder, an ache in the small of his back, and a cramp in his left foot.

He opened his eyes and glanced around the shadowy chamber. He was alone. The others, wiser than he, or perhaps less patient, had abandoned the attempt long before Faolein was willing to admit defeat, and had apparently gone upstairs to pay their last respects to the dying Princess.

Flexing muscles grown stiff after so many hours in one position, the wizard rose from his uncomfortable seat. The room was chilly and damp; the fire had burned down to a handful of glowing embers. Bending with an effort, Faolein selected a block of dried peat from a pile on the floor near the hearth, placed it on the ashes, and spoke a simple spell: *"Hanemh féalen, perifehlim éma üli."*

The peat ignited with a white flash, and the flames rose high momentarily, illuminating the entire room with an unnatural brightness until the fire died back again.

But in that moment of uncanny clarity, the wizard had spotted a childish figure, huddled disconsolately on a low rough bench in a niche in the wall. Drawing his stool up closer to the fire, he sat down, tugged at his beard, and nodded in her direction. "Sindérian, is that you?"

"Yes, Father," a small voice answered.

"Then come here, my child, and let me look at you."

With a sigh, she pulled herself up from the bench and crossed the floor with a dragging step. Though he knew what to expect, her waxen pallor and alarming thinness shocked him.

He reached out with a trembling hand to stroke her long dark hair. "You have grown so tall, so womanly. How many years has it been? One year? Two?"

"Almost three," she answered softly.

He made a swift mental calculation: she would be eleven, no, twelve years old—tall for her age, as he had already noted, growing swiftly, he supposed, and changing from day to day. And he, Faolein, had missed it all. *Old fool,* he thought, *old fool—did you think she would stay a child forever? You ought to know by now, they never do.*

"I asked after you when I arrived. They told me you were sleeping. As indeed you should be," he added, groping for the proper note of paternal authority. "You ought to be resting."

Sindérian blinked back tears, shrugged a thin, angular shoulder under her gown of apprentice healer's russet. "How could I sleep, when I could hear her screaming? And she needs me, Father. *Why* won't they allow me to go to her?"

Faolein ran his fingers through his neat black beard, obscurely embarrassed. A woman would know what to say, how to comfort her, but the women were all occupied in the room above.

"There is nothing that you can do. If there *were* anything, you would certainly be there," he managed at last. "As it is, there are far too many in attendance already—too much noise, too much confusion. It's always so at a royal birth, I am afraid, even when all goes well."

"But the Princess is in pain, terrible pain."

He nodded solemnly. "But pain is a natural part of childbirth. Our philosophers say that is the price we pay for a new life."

"But she ought not to suffer like *this,*" said Sindérian, as he drew her down to sit on his bony knees. "*I know,* Father. Something is very, very wrong. Will the Princess die?"

Again he hesitated. But, after all, Sindérian was no ordinary little girl. She was wizard-born and showed promise of extraordinary talents. These three years just past, she had been training as a healer, under the guidance of the Princess Nimenoë. Still too young to work the greater spells of mending and healing even before this mysterious malady sapped her strength, she could no doubt make a simple sleep charm, or dull the edge of pain—which meant that her work would often take her to the bedsides of the dying, that she would be called upon again and again to ease the passing of those too ill or injured for the older healers to save.

It was a harsh beginning young healers experienced, harder than anything faced by apprentice wizards in the other disciplines, but it was necessary. Healers must be strong, or the work would break them; any weakness was best discovered early. Faolein could only imagine the things she had seen, the heartbreak she had witnessed. Yet how to explain to this child—as precocious as she was—that her friend, her teacher, her foster mother, the most powerful healer on Thäerie—perhaps the most powerful healer anywhere, ever—was dying in childbed?

Surely not, her father decided, by any evasion of the truth, by an attempt to conceal from her things that Sindérian probably understood a great deal better than he did.

"There is something wrong with the way the infant is placed; the midwives tried to shift it, but without success. A healer might have done it with magic; the Princess herself might have done this thing, at any other time; but you know that all of the healers on Thäerie and Leal, from the Princess on down to the youngest apprentice, are helpless and ill, many of them unable to rise from their beds. They may yet recover, just as you seem to be recovering, but it will be too late to help Nimenoë."

Sindérian brushed away tears with the back of her hand. "I heard someone say—one of the midwives—the Princess is under a curse."

"An *aniffath*, yes. There is a prophecy, which has come again and again to our seers: *'Not by the will of any wizard of Leal, or by the hand of any warrior of Thäerie, shall the Dark Lady of Phaôrax be driven from her throne and her temple, but only by the power of one who comes of her own house and blood.'* The wording changes, but the meaning is always the same. It's Ouriána's plan to twist this prophecy to her own uses by crowning her son Guindeluc as her successor during her own lifetime. But she fears above all that a child or a grandchild of her sister will someday grow powerful enough to challenge and defeat her. And so, when Nimenoë and Eldori were wed, Ouriána cursed their union. That was before the old Queen, Prince Eldori's kinswoman, died and her magic ring passed to the Princess," Faolein explained. "Had Nimenoë been wearing the ivory ring at the time, the curse would never have touched her. As it was, the Princess was barren for many, many years. When she finally conceived, she thought, we all thought—we who knew of it—that the curse had been lifted. But we were wrong: Ouriána's spell had merely assumed another shape. First it took Eldori, and now it is taking the Princess."

Sindérian drew in a long shaky breath. "But if it's a spell, can't you and the other Master Wizards banish it?"

"We have tried. Again and again we have tried. You know that Ouriána claims divinity, that she calls herself a goddess. It's not true, of course, but there is no denying that her spells are very, very strong. And the fact that she was carrying a child at the time made this particular spell . . . extraordinarily power-ful."

Faolein put an arm around her shoulders, dropped a self-conscious kiss on the top of her head, where the dark hair parted. Thyssop, pennymint, and other bitter herbs, that was what she smelled of, reminding him of his own mother, a no-table healer, dead these ninety years.

He was not a demonstrative man, the wizard Faolein, being of a mild disposition and temperate in all things; he had suffered few pangs on parting with his daughter, had been so busy dur-ing her absence he had rarely remembered her existence. Yet she was his, the last of his children living, almost certainly the last that he would ever father, and the affection he felt for her, if sometimes awkwardly expressed, was deep and genuine.

Most often, it took the form of a lesson, a lecture, for as he valued knowledge so highly himself, he truly believed it was the best thing he had to offer. He had a dim realization that she needed something more, something his other children had never seemed to lack, being blessed or afflicted with his same placid disposition, but he had lived too many years as he was to change now. He gave her what he could.

"You know how dangerous it is to kill a wizard with magic. It can—it almost certainly will—have unforeseen conse-quences, unless done very carefully. But an *aniffath* is not like any other curse or spell. It is more . . . insidious. It can take years and years to work itself out, it may manifest in entirely unexpected ways, and it can even use natural means to achieve its purpose. Because of all this, and its complexity, a curse of this sort can be difficult to unravel. Three of us, most skilled in these matters, set out to unravel this one, to follow the threads of all the myriad possibilities down through the years, to untie all the knots. We thought that we had succeeded, but we were wrong.

"We tried again tonight," he added under his breath, "and again we failed."

"Will the baby die, too?" asked Sindérian, very low. Slipping off his lap, she sank down by the fire, hugging her knees to her chest, resting one cheek against the thick russet wool of her skirt.

"It is possible. But the Princess has vowed that her child will be born alive. I'm inclined to believe her. Those on the threshold of death sometimes see the future with amazing clarity."

Abandoning his stool, he knelt on the hard earth floor beside her. Reminded of the herbs he carried in a pouch of tooled leather over his left hip, he worked the catch and extracted a handful of dried chamfrey. "There is also this to consider: Ouriána may not even know that the child exists. The Princess has lived in this isolated spot all of these months, concealing her name and rank from the village folk—"

From the room above came a horrible keening, like an animal caught in a trap. Then hurried footsteps crashed across the floor, a babble of voices rose and fell and rose again. At length, there came the shrill but welcome cries of a newborn infant.

In the brief silence that followed, the wizard and Sindérian listened breathlessly. Then one of the midwives spoke. "Lady, you have a daughter. She is perfectly formed: beautiful and strong."

"She must needs be strong," answered the Princess, weakly. "Neither I nor her father will be there to protect her."

"She has powerful kinsmen; they will make it their business to protect her," said Éireamhóine, in his deep, resonant voice, and there was a low murmur of assent.

But even as the other wizard spoke, Faolein felt a shiver of apprehension pass through his entire body. For a timeless instant he hovered on the brink of some revelation, but the revelation eluded him, and the cold thrill passed.

Tossing his handful of herbs into the fire, he peered into its glowing heart, searching for portents. The flames turned from gold to green, figures began to form and to move about: tiny men and women flickering into a brief, bright existence, along with their fiery miniature castles, and cities, and towns, then gone again with another motion of the flames. His eyes must be tired; he could not see any of them clearly enough to know who they were or to guess what they were doing.

Faolein sat back on his heels, looked to his daughter to see her reaction. She had raised her head from her knees and was gazing intently at the changing colors of the fire. Knowing she had gifts in that direction as well, he asked her: "What do you see?"

Her lips moved, but she spoke so softly, he had to lean closer before he could hear her. "A woman in a casket made of ice. An oak with the moon in her branches. What does it mean?"

"It is *your* vision," said Faolein. "Therefore, it is yours to interpret." Yet again came that pulse of fear.

And he knew, as he sometimes knew things without knowing how he knew them—with a clear sight that owed nothing to the fire, or the crystal, or to any other means of divination—that the destiny of the infant just born would not be here on Thäerie, and not on Leal, the isle of the wizards.

It would be complicated, dangerous: more tangled than a curse.

2

*

At *malanëos,* the hour of utter darkness, the Princess died. From one moment to the next she simply stopped breathing; the white face on the pillow went utterly still.

Yet the death of any great wizard before his or her time is no small event. It shatters the pattern of cause and effect, it alters the flow of time and sends shock after shock through the world of matter, subtly changing all things so they can never again be what they were before. The three wizards standing vigil at Nimenoë's bedside felt her passing as a disturbance in the air, a voiceless wind that swept through the chamber, circled the room a dozen times, and then escaped through one of the arrow-slit windows. Over their heads, right under the rugged roof beams, a series of discordant notes split the air like a jangling of harp strings as Nimenoë's bindings broke, one after the other.

But other magicians, in far-distant places, experienced her death, too. In the High King's great house at Pentheirie, the wizard Elidûc felt the marble floor buckling and sliding beneath his feet, as if in an earthquake. At the Scholia on Leal, spells that warded the college fragmented in rainbow bursts of color, startling apprentices, journeymen, and Masters alike. In the underground realm of Nederhemlichreisch, a Dwarf alchemist watched the gold he had spent seven years transmuting change back into base metal; and in the groves of a fairy queen, far to the south, all the swallows and starlings she had raised to speak prophecy, as one bird gave a single heartrending shriek, then fell silent forever. Spaewives on Erios, runestone readers on Skyrra, astrologers in Nephuar and Mirizandi, half a world away, paused in the midst of their divinations, dazed, uncertain.

In Apharos on Phaôrax, two priests of the Devouring Moon saw the sacred fire on their altar go out as they performed their abominable rites. A violent pulse of energy passed through the entire temple edifice, rattling the carven doors, causing hundreds of brass oil lamps to swing on their chains, but the foundations held. And in her palace across the city, the Empress Ouriána, self-proclaimed goddess, was shocked out of sleep and into the knowledge that her twin sister was dead. She rolled out of bed and sprang to her feet, sweating and shivering. She had not expected this; the *aniffath* was more than a decade old, and Nimenoë's death had been no part of her intention.

Moving lightly in her white silk bedgown, she stepped into a pool of wan moonlight, shook back her long, auburn hair, and sent her thoughts questing across the miles, searching for answers: Why and how? But everywhere there was chaos, confusion. Magic mirrors cracked, stone circles danced, enchanted sleepers woke momentarily, looked around them with bewildered eyes, then slid back into slumber.

Running barefoot across cold tiles, Ouriána left her bedchamber, surprising the two sleepy guards keeping watch by her door when she erupted into the corridor. With a Word, she lit a dozen torches in ornate iron sconces along one wall; with another, she roused every slave and servant in the palace. They all came running: with wine, with embroidered slippers, with velvet robes and fur-lined mantles to stop her convulsive shivering. She scarcely noticed. Her mind still reeled with questions, and the answers were nowhere to be found.

⊷—⊶

But in the tower of Cuirglaes, a thick cloak of silence enveloped the upstairs bedchamber, heavy with portent. Stationed at the foot of the high oak bedstead where the body of the Princess rested, Faolein waited. Beside him, Curóide waited, his fair broad face and his light blue eyes intent, watchful. To their left, Éireamhóine stood alert, anxious, listening. For this was the moment, as the soul takes flight, when inspiration descends on those who watch; when prophecies blossom in the mind like rare, brilliant flowers unfurling their petals and revelation strikes like lightning from a clear sky.

Nothing happened. The thoughts of the three wizards remained dark, unenlightened. With a sigh and a small impatient gesture, Éireamhóine brought Faolein and Curóide back to the present. Making the sign of the Seven Fates over the body, he began to chant an *eirias,* a prayer to the Light, and the others joined in.

While the wizards chanted, a pale wraith in an earth-colored gown crept into the room and stationed herself across from Éireamhóine. Bending to impress a final kiss on one colorless long-fingered hand, Sindérian dropped bitter tears on the clay-cold flesh, on the linen bedsheets.

As the last mournful phrase trembled in the air, there rose, as if in counterpoint, a high, tuneless wailing from the motherless infant.

"Sindérian," said Faolein gently, "look to your foster sister. She has need of you."

The child nodded, scrubbed at her eyes with one rough woolen sleeve, and turned away from the bed. Crossing to the wicker basket where the swaddled infant lay whimpering, she bent down, lifted the baby in her thin, wiry arms, and cradled it competently against her narrow chest. Her father could not repress a faint smile at her obvious expertise.

Éireamhóine's voice spoke in his mind: *The infant is in deadly danger. We must reset the wards around the tower. And even then—*

Together, the two Master Wizards wove a spell of binding and blinding; they cast a charm of silence, so that no word thought or spoken within those walls of stacked stone could be carried on the wind or travel the ley lines under the earth to be detected by their enemy.

Éireamhóine knelt by the bed and took the Princess's hand in his for the last time. A wide ivory band that she wore as a thumb-ring passed from her hand to his. He held it in his palm for a moment, then closed his fingers around the ring and rose to his feet. Leaving Rionnagh and the two midwives to wash and prepare the body for burial, the men slipped quietly out of the room and took the steep circular stone staircase down to the ground floor. Sindérian and the now peaceful infant followed close behind them.

Once downstairs, Faolein threw open the door and stood on the threshold under the weathered lintel, scanning the heavens for portents. They were not long in coming. A comet streaked across the sky, trailing glory. To his wizard's sight, the very firmament seemed to reel, planets and constellations invisible to ordinary eyes to dance madly. *Nydra* the dragon rose in the east, a red star shining in his forehead like a jewel; across the sky, *Qwilidan* the watchman passed over the western horizon, swinging his starry lantern. *Thaga* the bat, *Brüac* the badger spun in place, and the swan plucked at her breast until feathers flew across the sky and the heavens ran crimson with blood. If the signs had been ambiguous when Faolein looked for them before, they were dangerously obvious now.

He heard a sharp intake of breath behind him, and half turned. Curóide had joined him at the door. Peering over Faolein's shoulder, the younger wizard watched the giddy revolution of the stars. "It's no wonder the Princess was so fatally weary. She must have deranged the whole course of nature to keep her secret all these months."

Faolein nodded, stepped back inside the room, and Éireamhóine took his place under the lintel. "A tremendous effort to conceal the truth from any astrologer able to read a message in the stars—how much greater an effort to deceive the woman who commands the Dragonstones, the *Talir en Nydra.*"

He sat down again on the three-legged stool he had used earlier, rubbed his eyes with the heels of his hands. "But what Ouriána did not know before, she surely knows now. Her sister has just given birth to a prodigy, a child of prophecy. Can anyone question what she will do next?"

"There is no doubt at all," said Éireamhóine, gazing into the night. "Even now, across the miles, Ouriána will be plotting the infant's death."

———

A distant rumor of men and horses announced the coming of the High King. Éireamhóine's message, sent arrowing through the night on wings of starlight to Eliduc at the palace, shortly after sunset, had alerted King Réodan to Nimenoë's peril. Assembling a troop of trusted warriors to serve as his escort, he had traveled at great speed, changing horses often, and arrived at Cuirglaes much sooner than anyone expected to see him.

Riding into the village on a damp predawn wind, Réodan and his men clattered up the street and dismounted outside the tower.

The battered oak door flew open; Curóide appeared on the threshold, bowing low before the King. Réodan left orders for his men to walk and water the horses, then followed the wizard inside.

He entered the building in a swirl of sky-blue cloak, a tall, vigorous man, though no longer young, broad-shouldered and tawny-haired. His gaze swept the room, taking in everything at once: the disordered furnishings and smoldering fire; the stumps of yellow candles, standing in pools of melted wax; a scattering of broken crusts and empty wine cups—all evidence of a long night's vigil.

One glance at the weary, grief-stricken faces of the three wizards, and Réodan's first question was answered before he spoke it aloud. "She is gone, then?"

Éireamhóine bowed his head.

"And her child?"

"A princess, Lord King," said Faolein, indicating with a gesture the bench in the wall, where a sleepy Sindérian sat rocking the baby.

Réodan crossed the floor with a jingling of spurs and the faint *ching, ching* of chain mail against plate armor. There was not much of the infant to be seen: just a tiny wrinkled face and a fuzz of pale reddish hair, inside a nest of wool and linen and squirrel-skin blankets. But the light eyes blinked at him; the tiny mouth moved, soundlessly, and that was enough to reassure him.

"I will take her back to Pentheirie with me," he said heavily.

He felt a sudden constriction in his throat; for a moment, his sight blurred. He was only just beginning to comprehend Nimenoë's loss. They had been allies more than friends, distant cousins raised side by side but never playfellows—for even as a child her gifts had set her apart—yet for as long as he could remember he had relied on her strength. It was, he realized now, the rock on which his own granite determination and stubborn will had been built. And had it never occurred to him—not once, in all his long years—that the woman who had remained beautiful, vital, ageless, while streaks of silver appeared in his own hair and beard, and his eyesight dimmed, could possibly die before him, could leave him as he was now, so terribly and shockingly bereft?

"The daughter of the woman who warded this island for so many years, who fought our battles against the Dark, deserves all that we have to give," said Réodan, turning abruptly to face the other men. "She will live in the Great House with me, share the same nurses and tutors as my own grandchildren."

There was a faint stir of protest from the wizards. "But can you keep her safe?" asked Faolein. "Among the hundreds who live at the palace, the hundreds more who visit there every day, it would take but one traitor, one act of betrayal, to endanger her life."

For a moment, indignation flared in Réodan's heavy-lidded hazel eyes. Stripping off his soft leather gloves and thrusting them into his belt, his hard swordsman's hands clenched and unclenched. "*What would you have me do?* If she will not be safe in *my* house, then where can she be safe at all?"

"In utter anonymity," said Curóide, "and as far from any place where Ouriána will be looking for her as it is possible to take her."

There was a tense, waiting silence in the room while Réodan considered the wizard's words. Faolein trimmed the candles, which were beginning to smoke; Curóide knelt by the hearth in his sage-green robe and mended the fire; Éireamhóine stood quietly with his arms crossed and his hands inside his dusky purple sleeves, watching the King with his night-dark eyes.

Very softly, under her breath, Sindérian began to sing to the baby, a lullaby in the Old Tongue, the language of magic:

> *Shenana, beichlin*
> *Shenana, beich ilthanen*
> *Shenana, beich-sin*
> *Shenanar uiléthani sillüer.*

At last Réodan spoke. "You have already discussed this, the three of you. You have reached a decision without me."

"Any decision must be yours, Lord King," said Éireamhóine, shaking his head. "With your permission, I will take the infant to some distant part of the world and raise her there in secret. No one will know where I am headed; I'll send no word when I arrive. But when she is old enough, when she has grown strong enough and wise enough to claim whatever power is in her, I will bring her back to you here on Thäerie, to fulfill her destiny."

There was a murmur of approbation and assent from the other wizards. Still, Réodan hesitated. "*Even from me* you intend to keep your destination a secret? Even from these, your fellow wizards?"

Faolein took a step in his direction, made a half bow of deference. "Lord King," he said, "we have warded this tower: ringed it round with powerful runes and spells. What we say here remains private among us. But we none of us live our entire lives in warded rooms. One slip, one careless speech could prove fatal to the little princess's chances." He made a weary gesture. "It will be far better for her if we all remain ignorant."

Réodan began to pace the floor, causing the candles to flicker, the coarse wall hangings to stir faintly as he passed. Three times he circled the room, then stopped and whirled around to face the wizards. "Be it so, then. Take the infant, Éireamhóine, but if you're unable to keep her safe—" He passed a hand over his eyes. "What am I saying? If *you* can't protect her, then no one can."

"And yet your fears are reasonable," answered Éireamhóine, reaching out to touch him lightly. Some of the wizard's serenity, his calm acceptance of the world in all its troublesome complexity, seemed to flow into Réodan with that touch, though his words were far from reassuring. "It may be there is no place of safety for this child, not in all the world. I will do what I can . . . but it may not be enough."

"We are forgetting something," Curóide said quietly. "Protect her he may, but Éircamhóine can hardly care for an infant himself. It requires a woman: a wet nurse."

There followed several moments of baffled silence, as the four men wrestled with this intractable fact.

"I suppose," said Réodan, his broad forehead creased in thought, "there is no other way to provide for her nourishment?"

"No way that lends itself to a difficult and possibly dangerous journey," answered Faolein. "Moreover, a man *and* a

woman traveling with a newborn child will be far less conspicuous than the man and the infant alone."

In the end, they decided to send for Rionnagh. Knowing
her to be devoted to the Princess, the King confided the plan to
her, presented their dilemma. She listened patiently, standing
with her hands clasped in front of her, her head tilted to one
side. But there was a faint curl to her lips, a look of cool amusement in her grey eyes, and Faolein had an idea she had recognized the problem long before Réodan explained it.

When he had finished, she shook her head, as though wondering at the opacity of the male mind. "You would need a wet
nurse in any case. There is a girl in the village who gave birth to
a stillborn child seven days ago. According to one of the midwives, she still has milk."

Réodan frowned, as though doubting so easy a solution
could possibly exist. "There would be more required of her
than just suckling the young princess. She must abandon her
home and all her family, undertake a perilous journey into foreign lands. I wonder if she would even understand—"

"Luenil is no simple village maiden," said Rionnagh, with a
small, tight smile. "She arrived in Cuirglaes only six weeks ago,
a young widow with a tragic past. I think she would be willing
to begin her life over again in a far country. I suggest that you
speak to her, Lord King, Master Wizards. I think you'll find
she is exactly what you need."

"Whatever we decide," said Faolein, "it must be *soon*."

3

✳

Dawn came, grey and chilly, with a driving sleety rain. King Réodan's escort took refuge down in the pinewood, out of the wind and the worst of the weather. From her vantage point at one of the arrow-slit windows, Sindérian could see a line of smoky small campfires glowing red between the trees, and hear the stamping and *whuffling* of horses.

A short time later, when the King walked downhill to join them, the men all saddled up and rode away. By then, Sindérian had retreated to her own little bed under the roof, curled up with the baby in a cozy nest of rough woolen blankets and sheepskin rugs. But she heard them go, and the sound of hoofbeats on the stony road entered her dreams.

———

She dreamed of a scouring wind in rocky high places, of snow as fine and hard and sharp as diamond dust. There was a fortress built in the heights, of smooth white stone, with towers high and fair and banners bright as jewels. A proud, cruel, sorcerous people lived there, and into the castle from distant lands came many beautiful and magical things: starry crowns and crystal harps; caskets of ivory, ebony, and pearl; wands made of lignum vitae; enchantments written on lambskin parchments and tablets of stone and leaves of gold.

The name of the lord who ruled that people was known and feared throughout the north. The King of the Dwarves sent him tribute; Shadows and Shapechangers served in his bodyguard. If he sent a message to the Gnomes or the Sea-People requesting any favor, that favor was granted without hesitation.

His fortress was strong and ringed with such spells of power that none might breach the walls from without. But there was treachery within. Lured by the promise of greater riches, greater power, the sorcerer-lord betrayed his people. Death walked through the castle then, sparing no one, not even the one who summoned him.

For long years the fortress lay deserted, open to the sky and the bitter weather. Hawks came and built nests on ledges and in empty tower windows; snow-cats laired in the overgrown courtyards among the bones of the dead.

Then a small party of horsemen came pounding up the long white road to the fortress, leaving tracks in the snow. They came seeking the treasure waiting in the ruins: chalices of silver and gold; bowls set with amethyst, tourmaline, and owl's-eye agate; beads of honey-colored amber, each one enclosing a perfect dragonfly or a tiny frond of fossilized fern. But something else waited in the castle. As the men filled their saddlebags with precious things, a dispute broke out over a necklace of diamonds as clear as dewdrops. They drew their swords; the stones of the fortress were stained with their blood. Only one man left the castle alive, and he was crippled and mad and blind.

Now ghosts walked in the empty halls, haunted the treasuries, counting old coins with their bony fingers; they wore crowns

and rings and armbands, bright with gemstones, but their eyes
were hollow; they had crystal harps and silver flutes, but their
voices were gone. Only the wind had a voice in that lonely land.

While Sindérian slept, and her elders made preparations for
travel, the storm passed, and the sky gradually brightened.
Later, a thin fog crept in, followed by a drizzly rain.

At moonrise, when frost lay hard and cold on the ground,
the first party set out: Faolein, Sindérian, and Rionnagh, riding
sturdy grey cart horses, purchased with silver coins from a man
who lived in the village. Sindérian rode pillion behind her
father, with her arms clasped around his waist. She wore a
sheepskin cloak over her woolen gown, and sturdy boots and
fur-lined mittens; but he could feel her teeth chattering and
tremors pass over her slight body.

"We will take it in easy stages to Pentheirie," he said, when
Curóide came out of the tower to bid father and daughter a safe
journey. As always, when forcibly reminded of his duties as a
parent, Faolein was chastened and ashamed, regretting his own
negligence—and determined to do better. "She is still very
weak, and these last few days of worry and grief have done her
no good."

Curóide stood at the base of the tower, his fair hair lifted
by a slight breeze, and watched them go.

The ruddy sunset faded to grey, and then to black; stars appeared in the sky like tiny jewels of fire and ice. Then the second party set out: the two wizards walking, and the girl,
Luenil, mounted on a shaggy black pony, holding the newborn
princess in her arms. They followed the road to the foot of the
hill, then turned northeast, heading straight for the coast,

where the boat that had carried the wizards from Leal to Thäerie awaited their return.

East of the hills, they came upon a forest of pine and spruce and oak, silvered with frost and moonlight. Éireamhóine and Curóide walked in silence for many miles, before the younger wizard spoke. "I had a word with the High King, before he left us this morning. He plans a diversion—an attack on Phaôrax. By now, I suppose, he will be provisioning his ships, mustering his troops."

Éireamhóine frowned. "A *diversion* you call it—but it sounds like suicidal *folly* to me. What can Réodan be thinking, to take such a reckless step?"

The pony shied at something moving in the shadows under the trees, and Curóide dropped a square, blunt-fingered hand on her neck to calm her. "For twenty-two years we have been fighting this war, ever since the smoke of sacrifice first rose over Apharos, and our enemy laid claim to all of the former Empire lands. In Rhuaddlyn, Malindor, Brielliend, we've fought battle after battle in defense of our allies. There are cities on the coast that have changed hands a half-dozen times—and the slaughter every time has been tremendous—but always, in the end, our armies fall back, and Ouriána's generals move in to conquer new territories."

His fair bright face, with its broad cheekbones, clear blue eyes, and spurious look of youthful innocence, was uncharacteristically grim. "Those are our former allies rowing in her slave ships. And woman and children go hungry all through the south, while the first fruits and the pick of every flock go to be sacrificed in her temples. Last year, she invaded Rheithûn. Now, Réodan believes, it is time to wage war on Phaôrax directly. If nothing else, it will distract Ouriána, engage her attention while you are going—wherever it is that you are going.

And perhaps he will even take her by surprise, this attack is so unprecedented."

"There are reasons," said Éireamhóine, evenly, "that we have never tried anything of the sort before. Ouriána will be terrible defending her own land. The Isle of Phaôrax is surrounded by a triple wall of magical protection; Réodan can never hope to pierce it. Unless . . . unless he plans to take wizards with him, and even then—"

The baby began to whimper, and the wet nurse hushed her. Éireamhóine tried to quiet the infant with his mind, but met with a surprising resistance. Her will was unformed but already very strong. It came to him then that the next fifteen or twenty years of his life were likely to prove interesting ones.

"*I* intend to go with Réodan, others may follow," said Curóide. He threw back his long yellow hair, and his jaw set in a hard line.

Éireamhóine sighed. "I had hoped you would return to Leal and fill my place on the Council. Take my advice and leave Réodan to his folly—he will come to nothing but grief!"

An owl hooted somewhere in the woods; dried oak leaves crunched underfoot. The night was growing steadily colder, and their breath came out like smoke as they walked.

"Nevertheless," said Curóide, "I think *your* journey is likely to prove more perilous than mine."

Something in his voice troubled Éireamhóine; he flashed his companion a quick, apprehensive glance. "Have you seen something? Is this meant as a warning?"

Curóide shrugged a burly shoulder under his wooly cloak. "I have seen many things—a hundred different possibilities, from the downfall of all our hopes to our ultimate triumph. But when the mind is anxious and overwrought, it's best not to rely on the Sight. Then we can only fall back on those things we know for certain—and on common sense.

"You taught me that," he added, with a slight smile, "sixty years ago, when I was a very young wizard and your student."

"You are still a young wizard," said Éireamhóine, shaking his head. "At eighty, you are only just beginning. May we both live to see two hundred . . . and better times."

She was just such a boat as the fisherman of Thäerie and the Lesser Isles rely on to make their living: clinker-built, sturdy, with a stout mast and a square sail of weathered canvas. She had seen Éireamhóine through many a perilous adventure and across many heavy seas.

He took her out with the tide, then set the sail. Making all fast, he took his place at the tiller and glanced over at the girl, Luenil. She sat on the thwart, shielding the infant as best she could from the biting wind, under her fur-lined cloak.

The hood of that cloak was pulled forward to shadow her face, and her features were only a pale blur in the silvery moonlight. "It will be colder," she said, "when we leave the bay and go out on the open sea before the sun rises. The little princess—"

"We will do all that we can to keep her warm," answered Éireamhóine.

He could see nothing of the child from where he sat. The girl had her bundled up safe in skins and blankets, and the little white face was turned away from him, out of the wind. But when he closed his eyes, he could sense her: Nimenoë's daughter, a tiny spark of life but a steady one, burning with a clear, fierce light in the darkness. "There is a power inside this child, raw and unformed as it is. I think she'll be at home in the elements and likely to weather this voyage much better than you or I will."

They sailed out beyond the breakwater, and the boat danced on the choppy waves, keeping the wizard busy for a time, with the sail, with the rudder. When he resumed his seat, he said to Luenil: "The child has a name chosen by her mother just before she died: Guenloie. It's best that we use it and never refer to her rank, ever. There is no telling how far the wind may carry our words over the water."

Dawn came at last, a faint rosy light growing in the east, a tinge of gold on the crests of the waves. Gradually, the light broadened, until a cloudless blue sky stretched from horizon to horizon. Éireamhóine felt an uneasy mixture of relief and apprehension. In spite of what he had said to Luenil, he feared for the infant if the weather turned foul—yet he felt vulnerable, exposed, out on the open waters of the Thäerian Sea while the light was so clear and revealing. Between sea and sky, there was no place to hide.

He considered, briefly, a spell of concealment, a charm to call up a favorable wind—and rejected that thought almost immediately. If he was forced to rely on his ordinary seamanship, the voyage was certain to last for several days, but by using magic he risked drawing attention from the very quarter where he feared it most. He had provisioned the boat before sailing from Leal with ample supplies: dried fish, fresh water, winter apples, and hard ship's biscuit, sufficient to keep himself and the girl while the voyage lasted. Yet every day was a day during which they might somehow attract Ouriána's notice, as she sat in her tower searching land and sea with the farseeing power of the Dragonstones.

And whenever a gull sailed overhead, its white wings catching the light, the wizard said to himself: *Is this one of my enemy's spies?* Crows, ravens, jackdaws, magpies, wyvaerun, they all served her, and he knew that her influence was growing daily. Perhaps she had already corrupted the gulls, the sea hawks. Many hundreds of miles of ocean divided him from Phaôrax, but for the birds of the air that was no great distance.

⸻

That day passed, and a clear, starry night. Other days followed: days of cold autumn sunlight and sea spray, or of thin fog and gusty rain. Luenil proved a surprisingly pleasant companion, a handy and cooperative shipmate.

When he first spoke to her, back at Cuirglaes, Éireamhóine had thought her sullen, guarded, even hostile, but it was very different now. On fair days, she sat on the thwart with her hood thrown back and her rich brown hair blowing in the breeze. And if she was not suckling the infant, she sang, or spoke nonsense, that secret language between mother and child which is older than time.

But then, watching her one day, Éireamhóine felt a shadow darken his heart, a little chill of doubt crept over him. It was good that Luenil seemed fond of the little Guenloie, but if she began to regard the child as her own—

The girl glanced up suddenly, caught him looking at her, and spoke as though reading his thoughts. "She is nothing at all like the infant I lost. That was a son, and small—so small. I wasn't supposed to see him before they buried him, but I insisted." As she spoke, a fierce light came into her eyes, and Éireamhóine sensed the slow-burning anger that was in her before, at Cuirglaes.

They had dressed her in clothing belonging to the Princess; her own things had been too poor and too scanty, unsuitable for a journey on the threshold of winter. Gown, cloak, boots, gloves, all were the dull black of mourning. But she wore, as well, something that must be her own: a brooch of base metal, with a lock of wheat-colored hair set behind glass. The materials ought to be finer, thought Éireamhóine—silver and quartz, or platinum and rock crystal—for her accent, her manners, were not those of a country village or of the lowest class. She had been born to a life of ease and luxury, he was very certain of that.

"You are estranged from your family," he said. "So Rionnagh told me."

The color went out of her face; her lips compressed in a thin hard line. It seemed she was reluctant to speak—but then it all came out in a rush. "I displeased my father, my grandfather, when I married. They had intended me for a great merchant prince, a dealer in brocades and satins and rare orient silks. It was to be an *alliance of families,* you understand, rather than a love match. But I—I was determined to choose for myself." She closed her hand in a sudden fierce gesture, and her voice grew husky with repressed emotion. "The man that I chose was strong and brave and honorable, but he was only the son of a poor tradesman. He went for a soldier in the war, and died at Quirfaimre with Prince Eldori. When word of his death arrived, my father might *then* have welcomed me back into the family . . . had I not been with child by the man he despised."

She looked down at the infant lying across her lap. Freed of her swaddling bands but still loosely wrapped in warm woolen blankets, the baby blinked in the sunlight, waved her tiny white fists. "I lived," said Luenil, "as best I could by the charity of my neighbors, who had little enough for themselves. But when I grew ill there was no money for medicine, and my father was deaf to all my pleas."

She took a deep breath of the salt air, reached out absently to stroke the infant's downy hair. "I set out walking—I don't know why. My mind was hazy, feverish. How many days I walked, I can't even tell you. I walked out of the town where my family lived and into the countryside. At last the Fates led me to Cuirglaes and to the Lady you know. She told me . . . she told me my little son had already been dead in the womb for many weeks, there was nothing that she or anyone could do. Yet for all the difference in rank and age between us, she spoke to me like a sister, and she seemed to share my grief. The Lady said to me, *'We are both widows, estranged from our families. We have much in common.'* I didn't know what she meant at the time, but when I heard of her death, I knew I was destined to care for her child."

The wind died, the sail went slack, and the wizard was briefly occupied, pulling out the oars he had stowed in the bottom of the boat and fitting them into their locks. "After all," he said at last, "you were the logical choice. The village was small—"

"No," she protested, "it was more than that." The color came back into her face as she spoke, and her eyes glowed. "I knew that I would be chosen, but not in any *ordinary* way."

He sat silent for many minutes, considering her words. Waves slapped against the side; the little boat rocked. "You are gifted with Foresight?"

Luenil shook her head. "Not as you mean it, I think. Or only a little. I was told when I was small that any talent I possessed was too slight, too ordinary, to interest the great wizards of Leal. There are children in every village and town who have what I had," she added bitterly, "but they have too little of it to merit training them."

What she said was unanswerable, being all too true; but there was something in the way that she said it that he found moving. "I am sorry," he said, "that you were disappointed. In this, as in so much else."

She surprised him by laughing: an unexpectedly bright sound out in that vast grey wilderness of wind and wave. "Why should you be sorry? It was no doing of yours. I'm the one who should apologize if I sounded resentful."

He searched him mind for something he could offer, some words of comfort. "I have lived in this world for much more than a century," he said at last, "and I don't pretend to understand the will of the Fates. Yet this much I know: they can be cruelest when they seem kind, and kindest when they seem cruel."

Again Luenil laughed, but then she grew sober. "If that should be true, then they must have something extraordinarily pleasant in mind for me."

"Be it so," said the wizard, sketching a powerful rune on the air.

4

✴

They landed on a grey day of sleet and snow, near the town of Povey in Hythe. Of two minds about taking his companions into town with him, Éireamhóine chose, in the end, to lead them to a little sheltered woodland about a mile from the nearest houses. There he left Luenil rocking the baby to sleep and singing one of her incomprehensible nonsense songs.

He remained wary of using any magic, but people knew him all up and down this coast, from Weye in the north to Rheithûn in the south, and his greatest fear was that someone might recognize him and speak of it later. So he wove a little spell of illusion, a harmless *shibéath,* to disguise his face and his purple robe. Then he went into Povey.

Situated near the mouth of the placid river Brae, Povey is a town of bridges and rowboats, of little whitewashed shops and houses, where the blue smoke of hearthfires hovers over steep-pointed roofs of slate or thatch. Pelicans and herons fish in the river; ducks and skrinks and other small fowl paddle in the shallows. Great clattering flocks of skua-gulls wheel overhead, and all the narrow cobblestone streets smell of fish—wherever one goes in the town there is the smell of fish. On this day, Éireamhóine passed open stalls selling oysters and roasted chestnuts and tiny flaky pies stuffed with crabmeat or mushrooms, all smoking hot. The town had a wholesome feel. No servants of the enemy lurked there to sense his magic, Éireamhóine felt certain of that, and he began to wish he had brought Luenil and the little Princess Guenloie with him.

Moving quickly past the houses, the inns, and the market stalls, he headed toward the south side of town, where most of the shops and stables congregated. There, he bought horses, and supplies, and a mule to carry what the horses could not, and for himself a pair of leather breeches and a rich woolen tunic lined with otter skins. In this new dress, he felt confident no one would recognize him for a wizard of Leal, once he left the coast and the towns where he was known.

Then, on an impulse, just before leaving the last of the shops, he bought a handful of lavender hair ribbons for Luenil. She was, he thought, much too young, and far too pretty, to wear such deep, unrelieved mourning. He returned to the wood to find nursemaid and infant sleeping peacefully, curled up on a pile of dry autumn leaves.

They rode east, through Hythe, heading for the Cadmin Aernan, the high range of mountains that divides the coastal realms of Mere, Hythe, and Weye from the interior. They passed through easy, rolling country, through tiny villages and lonely farmsteads. A thin blanket of snow lay gently on the land. The baby traveled in a wicker basket, lashed to the back of the mule, while Luenil rode a pretty grey mare, and Éireamhóine a bay gelding. Their pace was slow; those who might follow in pursuit would be looking for signs of a wizard traveling in haste, at great speed, not for a man and a woman riding peacefully through the countryside. As they continued inland, the roads grew worse and were often nonexistent; rivers were too icy-cold to be forded; again and again they were forced to turn aside and find some other way.

In his tunic and cross-gartered trousers, Éireamhóine thought he might easily be mistaken for a prosperous farmer or ordinary merchant. He wore his long hair braided back in a fishtail plait, and (because he had always gone smooth-shaven before) allowed a rough dark stubble to grow along his jawline, hoping a beard would disguise his face.

Luenil, as he soon discovered, had lived her entire life in the islands. Up until now, she told him, one brief voyage to Leal and twice to Nimhelli had been the extent of her travels. She was accustomed to the sea—its vast size, its many moods—but here on the edge of the great continent she seemed overwhelmed by the immensity, the extent of the *land*.

"And you tell me," she said, "that it goes on like this for *thousands of miles*, with forests and mountains and cities—and people! I never imagined the world was so populous. There must be as many as there are fish in the sea."

"No," said Éireamhóine, suppressing a smile. "This land is vast, but the sea is still greater. Nobody knows how far it continues."

She would not, as yet, wear the lavender hair ribbons, but her mood was lighter; she never spoke with the same bitterness he had heard in her voice before. And she was interested in everything she saw: a flock of blackbirds in the bare white branches of a birch, a herd of spotted deer grazing in a snowy wood.

"When my son died," she said to Éireamhóine one day, "I

thought that I would soon die, too. And I was glad to think so. But now—" Her voice faded away, the sentence unfinished.

"The young are resilient," said the wizard.

For a moment, her eyebrows came together in a frown, as though she resented the implication. But then Luenil laughed, her clear bright laugh. "I must seem little older than this infant to *you*!"

She looked around her, with wonder in her eyes. "After all, I am only seventeen," she said softly. "And my heart is mending."

But one day, at the back of his mind, Éireamhóine felt a nudge of fear.

They had stopped early, when the weather turned bitter, with snow and lashing winds, and taken shelter in a barn, which the farmer was willing they should do in return for a few small coins.

An entire month had passed since they left Thäerie, and the moon waxed full again. Éireamhóine could sense it, brooding and malignant behind the overcast; he could feel a series of tiny quakes and jolts pass through the earth. And somehow, sitting beside the small crackling fire of sticks he had built in the middle of the packed-earth floor, the wizard found himself telling Luenil something of his long life and of the world that he remembered, the world that was gone.

"I was born," he said, "only a few years before the Change. As now, there was always the threat of war. And I have a dim memory of the full moon, high and cold and distant as we never see her now. The moon was always so, from phase to phase: remote, benign. No one dreaded her influence. It was our fellow men we doubted."

He picked up a bit of straw from the floor, held it between his thumb and forefinger, before feeding it to the fire. But his mind was elsewhere, remembering the great kingdom that was—Alluinn of the Bright Towers. As a provincial youth from Thäerie, visiting the mighty seat of Empire in the train of the wizard prince to whom he had recently been apprenticed, how she had dazzled him, with her palaces, her pageantry, her ancientry and pride! Every hour he could spare from his studies, he spent wandering the streets, marveling at the statues, the gardens, the tall, fortified houses. Each morning, he woke with the same thought, the same little thrill of delight: *I am here at the very heart of the world.* But that idyll was to prove as brief as it was precious. A great company of warriors and wizards marched out through the gates of the capital, going to do battle with the legions of the Otöwan Sorcerer-King far to the south. Vast armies met and clashed; while ordinary men fought, wizards and mages engaged in a cataclysmic battle. The wizards were victorious, and Otöi was reduced to ashes. But the death of a thousand magicians sent a shock through the entire world of matter, changing the path of the moon, the courses of rivers, the face of the land and the sea. A great wave of destruction passed over Alluinn. Even now, much more than a century later, Éireamhóine could still remember it vividly. The beautiful old cities leveled: the great temples and houses; libraries, universities, schools of magic, astronomy, and healing; inns, shops, shipyards, and playhouses, all gone in an instant. And the white towers falling, falling, as great kings and princes; courtiers, heralds, pages, cooks, grooms, seamstresses, and gardeners; hawks, horses, greyhounds, and all—all went down to dust.

He came back to a realization of where he was and who was with him, with a start. Luenil sat nursing the baby, humming a tune under her breath. A blast of wind rattled the walls of the barn, and the cattle and horses stirred uneasily in their narrow stalls. He saw that the fire was burning low, reached out for another handful of sticks to replenish it—

And it was then that he felt the first twinge of apprehension. He scolded himself, silently, for speaking of things that were best left unmentioned—but still, he discounted the warning, believed it was only the return of his own natural caution, which had somehow slipped away during the uneventful journey.

Yet the fear was with him all through the night, and the next day. As they packed up to leave in the morning, as he helped Luenil to mount and swung up into the saddle, he experienced a rising sense of panic, most uncharacteristic, and a desire to urge the gelding into a canter that was almost overwhelming.

He began to suspect that his mind had been touched from the outside, that a trap had been prepared, and they had only to give in to the fear in order for it to close on them. *If we run,* he told himself, *it will be easier to spot us.*

A new day dawned, the clouds parted, and Éireamhóine was able to point out the gaunt snowy peaks of the Cadmin Aernan marching along the horizon, sharp and distinct against a blue winter sky. Yet he knew that the distances were deceptive; the mountains were still a long way off.

He felt a constant pressure on his mind. *We are moving too slow, too slow,* he thought, in a near panic. *Taking it too easy for the sake of the girl, the infant, the horses.* And that was true: some days they had not traveled at all because of the weather, and some days for an hour or two only.

But at last the weather relented, and they made good progress. A faint breeze came fresh and sweet down from the north, and the fields sparkled in the mild light of a winter day. The horses plodded on through the powdery snow, moving between milestones of weathered granite that marked what remained of an ancient road. It was possible to make out the tumbled shapes of the foothills, rising ridge upon ridge, smoke-blue and smoke-grey, until they met the great needle-sharp pillars and spires, precipices, stacks, chimneys, and towers of the snowy mountains. Yet still the voice in his head said, *Hurry— hurry!*

They stopped in the afternoon, to rest the horses, and to allow Luenil to feed the baby. Éircamhóine built a fire, to warm some wine and cook some food. He had only just begun to eat when he felt a prickling all down his spine, and knew it for a true warning. He sprang to his feet, kicked out the fire, and scanned the land, the sky, in all directions.

Then he spotted them: far across the snowy landscape, a blur of red and brown and grey—horses, and men in scarlet cloaks riding them, still distant but closing rapidly.

He snatched the infant out of Luenil's arms. *"Furiádhin!* Six of them, I think."

Éireamhóine saw her eyes dilate, the blood drain out of her face as the name shocked through her. *"They will kill Guenloie."*

"They will try," he answered, with a hard look, slipping

the baby into the basket, and quickly and deftly fastening the straps over her blankets to keep her securely in place. "But first they must catch us!"

Luenil had already mounted, and the wizard flung himself into the saddle atop the bay. Then they were off: the mare and the mule running flat out, but Éireamhóine was obliged to hold the gelding back, just a little, to keep from outdistancing the young woman and the child.

It was, he reflected as they went hurtling down the road, in some ways a relief to run at last, to know the danger, even if that danger consisted of Ouriána's most feared servants. Yet he shuddered at the memory of cold, inhuman faces, and of a pain past bearing, pain unremitting.

Behind him he cast an illusion: a long line of trees in full leaf, a phantom forest of oak, ash, and hawthorn, separating those who fled from those who followed. It would not deceive the Furiádhin, but it would confuse the horses and serve as a blind between him and the men while Éireamhóine urged the bay to a faster pace, briefly surging ahead of his companions, to lead them off in a new direction, cross-country: north this time, parallel to the mountains. Then he drew down a storm from the peaks to cover their tracks.

As he dropped back to keep an eye on the others, the clouds he had summoned came streaming on the wind like dark flags over head, and flurries of snow fell all around him.

———

They rode until their mounts were stumbling with exhaustion. Looking back over his shoulder, the way they had come, Éireamhóine could see no signs of pursuit. They were in the foothills, where a little stream came clattering down from the heights. Though they had run a straight course all afternoon, heading north, true north the whole time, they had reached a place where the mountain range veered toward the sea. The storm clouds broke, and the sky overhead was a dull gold, shading to grey over the Cadmin Aernan, to crimson in the west.

Because it seemed safe, as much as for pity of the horses and the mule, he finally called a halt by a thin line of trees, evergreens and hollies and cowan, straggling along beside the stream. He climbed wearily down from the saddle, then forced his legs to move, to take a few steps, his aching arms to reach out and assist Luenil as she dismounted. The hand that she put in his was icy-cold, and trembling; her eyes were glazed with fear and fatigue. But she made a valiant attempt at a smile as she dropped to the ground and stood on unsteady legs.

The baby began to fuss and whimper in her nest of blankets. She had been quiet all the time they were running, perhaps sensing their danger, perhaps lulled to sleep by the rocking gait of the mule.

"Feed her; then take something for yourself," said the wizard. "I will do what I can for these poor beasts."

While he made himself busy, he continued to talk, more to himself than to the girl. "King Réodan's diversion has gained us this much: there were only six of them, not the full twelve. It seems that Ouriána holds something back to defend the island. And—thank the Fates!—Camhóinhann wasn't with those we saw."

"But how can you tell?" asked Luenil, behind him. She sounded tired and ill, her voice hoarse and faintly querulous. "They all looked the same to me."

"That is *how* I can tell. It would be impossible to mistake Camhóinhann, even at a distance. There is that about him—a power, a brilliance—that makes him stand out among the others like a giant among pygmies."

Later on, while they rested, all huddled together, wizard, nursemaid, and baby, under the trees and out of the wind, Éireamhóine said to Luenil: "We should be safe for the night. They don't see in the dark any better than we do; neither can their horses run any longer than ours can. But if we can only reach the mountains! I know them well: all the high roads and passes, which ones will be open this time of year. We'll have the advantage there. Unless—

"Unless Guirion should chance to be with them," he finished under his breath. "For of all her servants, he knows that country the best."

5

✳

They made their way slowly through the rumpled foothills, by way of hidden paths and narrow, shadowed
ravines, and a week later they began the arduous climb up the
rugged wooded slopes of the Cadmin Aernan. Deep winter had
gained an iron-grip on all the land, and the air had an edge as
keen as a knife. The mule trudged along with her head down,
and the horses' breath rose in great silvery white clouds.

As they left the dark fir-woods and ascended the bare
windy flanks of the mountains, the wind blew increasingly
colder, under a sky the color of burnished pewter. Luenil felt
fear catch at her heart, not for herself, but for the little Guenloie.

"What does it matter whether those creatures following us
catch up to us or not, if she freezes to death first?" she asked Éireamhóine, her teeth rattling in her head. Frost glittered on her
woolen cloak, silver against black, and there was frost in the
wizard's beard.

"She will not freeze; I won't let her." Reaching out to
touch the infant, Éireamhóine fed a little of the heat from his
own body into hers. It was such a small, intimate spell, he did
not think it would be detected.

This is how you do it, he said, speaking mind to mind. *This is how you stay alive.* And he felt that tiny spark of power within her flare up in response. He knew the child was too young, her mind too unformed, to understand him; she still lived by instinct only, like a little animal. But he hoped that instinct would teach her to seek the warmth—to draw it out of him, Luenil, the horses, the earth and the sky, wherever she might find it—as instinct prompted her to turn toward food and comfort at her nurse's breast.

Climbing from the boulder-strewn middle slopes to the high passes, sheer precipices, and arid bony shoulders of the mountains, it became harder and harder to breathe, the air was so thin and bitterly cold. Éireamhóine's ears turned red and tingling inside his hooded cloak; ice crystals formed on his eyelashes. Winds shrilled and moaned between the great steeples and chimneys of stone, and the track often rose so steep and dangerous it became necessary to dismount and lead the horses, wading through thick powdery snow or slipping and sliding where the rocks were bare and icy.

There were glaciers, slow-moving leviathans of rock and snow, carving out gullies and valleys with their patient millennia-long advance. Éireamhóine heard Luenil catch her breath, saw her face grow strained with shock as she spied a vast shape caged in the ice: a magnificent golden griffon, suspended as it seemed in the midst of some terrifying action, with wings outstretched and beak wide-open, caught like a bubble in glass or a fly in amber. Farther on, they passed other tremendous figures prisoned in the glacier: a stone giant, a winged serpent, a manticore captured in midpounce.

"You need not fear them," said Éireamhóine. "Most of them are dead; the rest have been sleeping for a thousand years. As they didn't wake when the mountains danced, they're not likely to wake for our passing."

———

At night, he and Luenil slept as close to the fire as they dared, with the baby between them, in whatever cave or sheltered hollow they had set up camp. Even so, the wizard, his teeth chattering, spent many long hours shivering under his blankets, unwilling to draw more than his share of the heat. Whenever he woke, he could hear Luenil's restless movements a few feet away, her sobbing breaths, and knew she was just as sleepless and miserable as he was.

Fool, he said to himself, striding along in the weak daylight with the snow crunching beneath his feet. *Idiot. I accused Réodan of suicidal folly, but have my own decisions been any better? The child might have been safe on Thäerie, at least until spring.* He began to wonder: how many disastrous choices had he made along the way? There was no knowing, there was never a way to know. The best he could do was carry on and try to make the best of the decisions and the mistakes he had made so far. This much he did know: with the Furiádhin following somewhere behind, it would be folly to turn back.

"*Do* what you can," that is what his teachers used to tell him. "*Do* as conscience and experience dictate, and leave the outcome in the hands of the Fates." A wizard—most of all a seer—could go mad, could drive *himself* unreasoning mad, asking himself too many questions. Or he could flounder forever, paralyzed and impotent, in a swamp of possibilities, of half-perceived outcomes and alternatives, and never accomplish anything at all.

Become a vessel for the Light and allow it to work through you, that was another thing his teachers had taught him, what he told his own apprentices and journeymen. Give yourself wholly up to the Light, without reservation, without trying to make bargains with the Incomprehensible. But also: the Fates help those who help themselves, they have little patience and less charity with cowards and weaklings. It was important to *do* something, to struggle on, no matter how hopeless things might appear.

One day, as he toiled up an ice-slicked trail, Éireamhóine again felt that prickle of warning. He glanced back and saw a flash of red on the snowy slope below.

The Furiádhin were ascending rapidly, striding along and leading their horses. Scarlet robes and crimson cloaks fluttered, white hair whipped in the wind. Éireamhóine recognized Guirion moving a little ahead of the others: Guirion, who knew these mountains almost as intimately as he did.

Perhaps Ouriána's servants had never been far behind, perhaps they had only waited to show themselves, choosing the time and the place carefully: there on a trail so slippery and treacherous it was impossible to mount up and flee. And the way that the path switched back and forth across the face of the mountain, there was no use running, anyway. However great the distance between the two parties on foot or ahorse, the distance as the spell flies would continue to narrow.

"We will stop here and make a stand," said Éireamhóine to Luenil. "We have no choice. I must try and fight them."

"*Fight them?*" said the girl, turning to face him, wild-eyed and incredulous, forcing the words out between cracked lips. The wind caught up her protest and tore it to shreds, forcing her to raise her voice almost to a shriek. "What chance have you against *six* of Ouriána's warrior-priests? Are they not powerful? Are they not terrible?"

"Nevertheless," he answered grimly, "against six I have some small chance of prevailing, however desperate. Against one—and that one Camhóinhann—our case might be hopeless, but by chance or good fortune he's not here." As he spoke, Éireamhóine loosened the straps that held the infant in place. Removing her from the basket, he thrust her into Luenil's arms. "Stay just behind me, *whatever happens*. I'll do all I can to protect you."

———

The wizard forced himself to stand still and silent, his thoughts and senses turning inward. Now that the time for action had come, the time for second-guessing himself had passed, he felt a surge of confidence. This was how it *was* to be a wizard: not the endless weighing and measuring, but a way of experiencing the world and acting within it. He searched his mind for ancient names; for runes and charms; for spells of power and might; for patterns, symbols, riddles, and strictures; for all the knowledge of the eight great elemental forces he had been acquiring from his first lessons as a youth through all the long years of his maturity.

Then he began to gather those forces to him. Drawing energies up out of the soil, the rocks, the hidden veins of metal and the secret springs and rivers under the snow-covered mountains, he reached deeper and deeper still, groping in the dark, dredging up every vestige of power that he could. He knew that the battle before him would be a terrible one.

Meanwhile, the six Furiádhin proceeded inexorably up the icy trail. They were not so much hideous as grotesque, unnatural, these Priests of the Incarnated Devouring Moon; the dark magics they practiced, the debased rites they performed in Ouriána's name, had withered them and changed them, until they were no longer human.

Their faces were stern, bloodless, framed by fine, flowing hair the color of moonlight. Their eyes glinted silver, gold, or bronze, without white or pupil, giving to their faces the flat, expressionless gaze of beasts or statues.

One gripped the reins with a hand covered in silvery fish scales. Another had a pair of ragged and leathery wings sprouting from his shoulders and trailing behind him, pale and leprous. A third had a face of singular beauty but for the mouth: a thin, lipless slit that opened on sharp, fanged teeth as deadly as knives. So each of Ouriána's priests, as well as the strangeness he shared with the others, had his own particular and unique deformity, and so they had come by the name by which they were known: the *Furiádhin*, the furies, the Mutated Ones.

—◆—

But all the time his enemies were approaching, the wizard prepared for battle. Out of a small hidden pocket inside the breast of his tunic, Éireamhóine drew something he had carried with him, secretly, all the way from Thäerie: Nimenoë's ring. He had intended to pass it on to the little princess, an inheritance from her mother, when she had wisdom and strength enough to use it: for there was no one, now, on Thäerie or Leal, capable of commanding its full powers.

The history of Nimenoë's ring was clouded, there were many different tales of its origin and how it had become an heirloom of the Pendawer house. It was made of a substance much like ivory, polished to a milky sheen—the knucklebone of a giant, according to most accounts, an elemental creature with power over earth, wind, and storm; a Shapechanger who often took the form of a great wingless and fireless dragon, a horrific and hungry cold-wyrm—an ancient and evil thing that ring, until the Fates took it and blessed it, in years long past when they still walked among men, setting five runes into the band as a sign of their hallowing.

First came the runes *duenin* and *güwelan,* protection and healing. Then came *theroghal* and *désedh,* transformation and making. The last rune was the dark rune whose name the wizards never spoke aloud, though they carried the knowledge of its name always in their hearts. For to use any smallest part of that power, even at greatest need, might be presumption, while to misuse it was anathema, abomination.

In the days when Nimenoë wore the ring, she had employed it most often for warding and healing. Éireamhóine was no healer, but he had performed many marvels in his time, and he hoped to accomplish even more through the power of the ring. But on the fifth rune, the dark rune, he was determined not to call.

As he slipped the wide band onto his smallest finger, the world seemed to change around him. He could see the energies he had summoned, glowing in jewel-bright colors: a pure, bright, living green; a deep and thunderous purple; a hungry red that consumed and devoured; a rich blue, constantly mutating, like the changing colors of the sea.

With the power of *duenin* he drew a fiery circle of protection around Luenil and Guenloie; while Éireamhóine lived, no evil thing would cross that boundary, no spell would touch them.

Then, calling on *theroghal* and *désedh*, he took the shimmering rainbow energies and began to mold them, crafting them into weapons: spears and arrows tipped with fire; swords of light and daggers of pure living flame; maces and hammers with the weight of stones and the crushing power of mountains; bolts of raw energy that sizzled like lightning and roared like thunder.

One after another, he made them, and cast them at his enemies. But the Furiádhin were powerful, too. They threw up invisible barriers, exploded his weapons in the air, and not one missile hit its mark.

Then Éireamhóine took the swift-rushing force of a river in full flood, and he made it into a wall of sound and fury to batter his enemies. He drew geysers of boiling water up out of the depths of the earth. Snow melted and steam rose in thick clouds, obscuring the sun. He wove illusions which he animated with his own life and substance: a cloud of stinging insects to torment his foes; a flock of great raptors to dive at them and tear them with beaks and talons; a vast army of rats and mice and creeping vermin that swept down the mountain like a flood.

So the battle continued for hours. The sun dipped toward the western horizon, and night gathered on the eastern slopes of the mountains. Éireamhóine inflicted great pain on the Furiádhin, he blinded them, confused them, lashed them to fury—but he could not break them, he could not destroy them.

And he realized that he was growing weary, that his powers waned. Even were it otherwise, he knew he must eventually pay a price for this profligate use of forces and energies; the violence, the turmoil, had created stresses, oppositions, antipathies. He knew, too, that his enemies had all this time held something in reserve; they had only defended themselves, they had yet to attack him. They waited for his powers to fail, then they would strike, strike hard, without mercy or ruth. For a moment, he considered the power of the fifth rune, but his heart quailed at the thought of using it.

So he made a final effort, and called up the winds, out of the north, east, south, and west. It is no small thing to summon the winds, for they are willful, capricious, and impatient of control, particularly for a wizard who feels the strength draining out of him like blood from a wound. But the image of the dark rune was still in his thoughts, and that hardened his resolve.

He called out a *lledrion,* an elemental spell, to the winds:

> Nésadach anadi duidon!
> Nésadach anadi galadon!
> Nésadach óni anadi ellidon ei odeidon,
> ei deinach óni uilé piholadem éipeamhóinen!

And powerful and wild and lawless as they were, they came at his command. Winds out of the desert, dry and burning; winds from the sea, laden with salt; rough inclement winds, filled with rain, snow, and sleet; turbulent winds; winds that came roaring and rioting—monsoons, cyclones, and hurricanes.

He took them and fashioned them into a weapon greater and more terrible than any he had shaped before, and he sent them, raging and railing and shrieking, straight at the Furiádhin.

But Guirion raised his hand, and cried out in his turn:

> Anadi! omach nad!
> Émipas deinna né nelo navüs, bas oma nad.

There was a mighty clash of wills; intention met resistance, and resistance met a relentless opposition. The destinies of all hung in the balance.

And in that moment, nature herself, thrown out of equilibrium by the tumults of the battle, responded with a convulsion, a violent upheaval of her own. Thunder crashed, the mountains reverberated, and a mighty avalanche came roaring down from the heights.

Horses screamed, the priests turned to flee; Éireamhóine had only enough time to wrest the infant from her nurse's arms, to shout an unintelligible word in Luenil's ear, before the great wave of snow and ice and earth and stones came sweeping down. It caught them all, it crushed them, tumbled them, stifled them, buried them in chaos. Bones broke; eyes and ears and mouths filled with snow; spirits went shrieking off into the night.

Then there was only a long white silence.

✻ BOOK TWO ✻
(NINETEEN YEARS LATER)

1

*

The air reeked of blood and smoke and heated iron. Sindérian made her way slowly but deliberately across the courtyard, through the confusion of men and warhorses, wading ankle deep in the dirt, snow, straw, and horse urine they had churned into mud. As tall as any of the men, she moved easily and fearlessly among them. This turmoil was nothing new.

In a long, low hut built of stacked flint, she could hear the smiths at work: beating dents out of plate armor, mending helms and shields, repairing broken links of mail, as they always did after a battle. Sometimes, the incessant clang, clang, clang of hammer against metal, of metal against anvil, was almost too much to bear.

Meanwhile, more men kept pouring in through the gate: some riding, some walking, some carried in by their comrades—slung across a saddle, or on an improvised litter. They were returning from a skirmish to the east. Everyone said that Cailltin and his men had been victorious, and Sindérian supposed that it was true, though by the number of the dead and wounded she knew they could not afford many such victories.

Wherever she went, faces turned her way. Recognizing

her for a healer by the grey woolen tabard she wore over her long, homespun gown, many cried out, begging her assistance, for themselves, for their friends. Wherever she could, Sindérian stopped to help: setting a bone or weaving a charm to stop the flow of blood. Traveling from battlefield to battlefield these last five years, she rarely had a chance to work a real healing.

On Leal, she would have had the entire pharmacopoeia at her command: wormwood and spermaceti for bruises; boneset for fractures; basilicon and mithridate to draw poisons out of a wound; verjuice and mustard seed for children with scurvy; purges of clavendar and stag's-foot for anyone sinking into a melancholy humor. But just as with so many other things needed in this war-ravaged land, there were no medicines; Sindérian and the other healers were forced to rely on their own native talents, and on a smattering of spells and charms they held in common. It was wasteful and stupid to do things that way, drawing on power that ought to be tapped only in an emergency, kept in reserve for the more desperate cases—but it was all they could do, else hundreds, perhaps thousands would have died who might otherwise have lived.

And sometimes, it was the wizard-physician who died instead. There were always so many in need that a healer might drain herself to the point of exhaustion, to the point of death, and still there would be those who required her attention. So now Sindérian gave as much as she could—all that prudence dictated and perhaps a bit more—enough to keep a man on the verge of death alive, in the hope that she might return to him later, enough, where the damage was less serious, to start the healing process and leave the rest to nature.

She was kneeling in the muck, removing an arrow from a young warrior's shoulder, when Lord Duillig found her.

"Eiarann is dead. But perhaps you knew?"

Sindérian glanced up briefly, nodded, and went back to work, murmuring a shibéath *to dull the pain, beginning to ease the arrow out of the bone.*

"I did—I did feel a wizard die last night." Her voice shook, but she kept her hands steady. *"I thought it must be someone at Cuirarthéros, or Dunnardeth, it seemed so remote. How did it happen?"*

"He rode out with some of the men just after nightfall, and they met an enemy party much larger than theirs was. He kept so busy helping his companions, he left his own healing too late and bled to death."

She caught her breath, and for a moment she forgot what she was doing. Healers were sometimes killed in the war—in a rain of arrows, or a fall of stones when the enemy brought in a siege engine, and they all knew the danger. But for anyone to strike deliberately at an unarmed man in healer's grey—*"The moon was full last night; it was almost as bright as day. Are our enemies barbarians?"*

"He wore a dark cloak," replied Duillig. *"And in all fairness to the men of Phaôrax and Rhuaddlyn, Eiarann had no right to a healer's protection. He went out with a scouting party, and he was helping them."*

Sindérian felt a jolt of outrage at such unmitigated folly. *"He had no right to endanger himself that way! There are scouts enough, but we've a shortage of healers."* Still, she was hardly surprised. Desperation grew, day by day, and reckless acts by the fighting men, the wizards, even the civilians, were all too common.

"I understood he was supposed to go with the wagons today, to escort the women and children to Thäerie." She braced herself, tightened her grip on the shaft of the arrow, and gave it

another pull. The point came grating out of the bone, slid through muscle and skin, past broken metal links, and a moment later she had it in her hand.

"Yes," said Duillig. "He meant to go with the refugees. That is why I've come to you."

Sindérian scarcely heard him. She sat staring down at the broken shaft lying across her palm, at the cruel bodkin point, glistening with blood. It might have been cast right there at Gilaefri. Both sides gleaned arrows after a battle, for reuse later. In the forge at that very moment the smiths were making more heads, exactly like it.

A slight restless movement by Duillig reminded her of his presence. She dropped the arrow into the mud, gathered up the heavy folds of her skirt, and rose to her feet. "You can't mean that I should go in Eiarann's place. I am needed here."

"As you say," Duillig admitted, with a sigh. "But the refugees need you, too. Many of the women are ill, many of the children, also. Without a healer, few can expect to survive the journey."

"They will still have Bainné, or has that plan changed?" Without waiting for his answer, Sindérian walked across the yard, knelt by a redheaded boy who sat, or had been propped up, with his back against a rough stone wall.

An ugly bruise covered the entire left side of his face. His auburn hair was clotted with blood, and his wide blue eyes stared vacant, unseeing. The moment she touched him, she could sense internal bleeding: in his brain, in his chest, in his belly. Her stomach clenched, and her heart gave a painful thud as she realized the truth. The boy was past saving. All she could grant him was sleep, sleep and sweet dreams till the end, which could hardly be long in coming.

She wove the charm—by now it was second nature—then

*made the sign of the Fates and whispered a prayer to the Light.
Her own faith was in crisis, but the boy and his family might still
be devout. The brother or friend who had carried him home—
still daring to hope, though his wounds were so grievous—might
care for such things. For their sake, she recited the eirias and tried
to mean it.*

*Meanwhile, Duillig came limping up to join her. A wound
too long untended, half a year ago, had left him unable to sit a
horse, forced him to use a stick when he walked. On Leal, there
might be someone with the time and the ability to make him
whole again; but here, in his own country, he was doomed to remain a cripple.*

*"Bainné is only an apprentice. And the journey could be a
dangerous one. It may take someone with Foresight to guide
them safely." He ran a hand through his greying hair. "That
was why we chose Eiarann to go."*

"It would seem that Eiarann's Foresight failed him."

*A troop of horsemen came clattering through the gate, forc-
ing Duillig to raise his voice in order to be heard. "Perhaps it did
fail him. Perhaps not."*

*Sindérian sat back on her heels, suddenly feeling drained.
Almost too tired to think, certainly too tired to argue. She knew
what he meant, and what he meant was undeniable.*

*All the healers wrestled with despair from time to time, es-
pecially those who had served long on the battlefield, as Eiarann
had, as she had. The empathy required of a healer, these oceans
of human blood, this vast tide of suffering: it could be a lethal
combination. She wondered, suddenly, if she had been chosen to
replace Eiarann because somebody thought she needed to go
home, because someone imagined she was on the verge of doing
herself an injury.*

But she quickly dismissed the idea. The lives of many were at stake here, and it did not make sense that Duillig would put the safety of his women and children in the hands of a suicidal seer.

"I will make you a bargain," she said. "I will go with the refugees . . . if you go with me to the Scholia on Leal for healing."

Glancing up, Sindérian saw the sudden flare of hope in his eyes, as he considered what he would do if whole and strong again. But then it died, and his eyes went dull, his expression hopeless again. "No, I can still be of some use here. I may not be able to ride into battle, but if these walls are breached, I can still swing a sword. It would be wrong for me to go."

"And yet you suggest that I go."

"That is entirely different," he insisted. "You may save lives by going, I by staying."

Unspoken between them was the fact that she had a home to return to, while Duillig had only this, this time, this place, this losing battle. "Very well," she said with a sigh. "When do I leave?"

"You leave at midday. That should give you just enough time to gather your things—and say your good-byes."

———

She could not find Cailltin until the very end. He and some of his captains appeared by the stables just as the women and children came out of the keep and headed toward the wagons. When Sindérian ran to meet him, he caught her up in a hard embrace. "They told me you were going."

He had cleaned up after the battle, but he still smelled of blood and sweat. As his arms encircled her, a cold edge of metal from one of his vambraces cut into her back. Sindérian hardly noticed. She leaned into the embrace and buried her face against his neck. "I didn't want—"

"No. But you couldn't refuse to go where you are needed."

She drew away, a new suspicion forming in her mind. She felt her throat close, so that it was difficult to force out the words. "Cailltin. Was this your idea? You were not the one who suggested that I—"

"How can you think it?" He took her hand and raised it to his lips. "We vowed to face all chances and mischances together—as duty and honor allowed. *Now it seems that your duty calls you elsewhere."*

Sindérian studied his face. He had changed since first she met him—why had she never before noticed, until now, how great the change? Though she was two or three years older than he, time had already touched him as it would not touch her for another century. There were silver threads in his fair hair and fine lines around the eyes.

But those who live their entire lives in the shadow of war lose their youth early, *she thought.*

"I will come back," she said, "as soon as ever I can. On the very first ship."

Cailltin did not answer, in words, but in his silence, in the sudden droop of his shoulders, she read all his meaning. "You think it will all be over by the time I can return!"

He made a faint helpless gesture. "We have been losing this war for the last nine years; they now lay claim to more of this kingdom than we do. The end is very near, Sindérian. Oh, not for you and your people, or for our allies to the north, but certainly for my people, here. And most of all for me and those like me: the fighting men of Rheithûn."

"For all that, I am coming back," she insisted. "I swear a most solemn oath—" Her voice faltered, then failed.

*He put up a hand to cover her mouth. "Don't make a vow
that you may not be able to keep." His fingers moved lightly
over her lips, trailed around to the back of her neck, under the
heavy fall of dark hair. "And don't poison the memory of our
time together with regret for an oath, which, in the end, you
might find you should never have sworn."*

*"I don't understand you," she said. The color had drained
out of his face, the light of youth and hope had gone from his
eyes; he looked suddenly old, and haggard, and ill. Yet still
Sindérian struggled against despair with all her remaining
strength. "How could any memories of our loving be poi-
soned?"*

*He pulled her closer, so that their foreheads touched. She
heard the sudden intake and release of his breath before he
spoke. "If the Fates are kind, you never will understand," he answered softly.*

*The road to the coast was long and cold and windswept. Sin-
dérian went on foot between the wagons, moving from one to
the next, looking in, meeting the hopeless stares of the women
and children, then moving on. All of the faces had a white,
pinched look; the old and the young, the sick and the well,
famine and grief had marked them, everyone alike. There had
been no harvest, not even a meager one, this last season. How
could there be, when all of the fields were battlefields and all of
the men and half-grown boys gone for soldiers? And the promised supplies of wheat, apples, beer, and cabbages from Hythe
and Mere had never arrived.*

*Some of the children began to whimper. Too cold to sleep,
Sindérian guessed, too distracted by the* bump, bump, bump of

cart wheels over ruts to take any comfort from their mothers' weary attempts to soothe them. She began to croon a lullaby:

Shenana, beichlin,
Shenana, beich ilthanen—

Then she remembered the last time she had whispered those words in an infant's ear, and the breath caught in her throat and she could not go on.

The wind had scoured the road clear of snow, but dark clouds gathered overhead, promising a blizzard by sunset. Where in all this vacant stretch of country, she wondered, was shelter for so many to be found? Surely not in any of the burnt-out farmsteads they had already passed along the way.

She was still trying to think of someplace where they could wait out the storm, when a current of force passed under her feet, a thrill of power that burned right through her, then was gone. She felt all of the fine, invisible hairs at the back of her neck stir; gooseflesh prickled on her back and her arms.

Instinctively, Sindérian looked to the south. Over the town of Cuirarthéros—where Cuirarthéros ought to be—a great smoky cloud was rising. At such a distance, she could not hear the stones crack, the walls come tumbling down, but she felt it all: as though her own bones crumbled, and the world around her shattered like glass, as though her eyes and nose and throat were full of smoke and powdered stone and mortar ground to dust, as if all the deaths of men and wizards up on the walls were her own death, experienced again and again and again—

She came back to herself, down on her hands and knees in the road, blind and sick, with the sound of Bainné's voice in her head, repeating her name over and over. She struggled to catch her breath, but she could not get enough air, could not get enough; the world went briefly grey, then came back into focus. Sindérian sat back on her heels, panting and sweating. There was grit in the palms of her hands, which she wiped on the full skirts of her gown.

As her mind cleared, as her awareness of her immediate surroundings grew sharper, she saw that the wagons were no longer moving; the women and children huddled together, their eyes wide with unspoken questions. Bainné knelt in the road beside her, pale but composed, yet behind that composure Sindérian could sense a confusion to match that of the refugees. What had been so intensely real and immediate for her *could be nothing more than a passing shadow over the mind of the young apprentice. Bainné's powers were as yet (and mercifully) undeveloped.*

"The Furiádhin have thrown down the walls of Cuirartchéros." Bile burned in Sindérian's throat, and her stomach continued to heave. *"All along the eastern and western side—there is nothing left but rubble."* And dead men, and men who are still dying, *she added to herself. She swallowed hard several times, but the sickness stayed with her.*

"But how—?" whispered Bainné. "Goezenou and Ganhardin have been laying siege to the town for almost a month. If they had the power to—to do that, to topple the walls, why not do it before this?"

"There may be more of them now. Dyonas, Náoiss, they were a hundred miles to the south a month ago. Perhaps they've come north to lend their strength." With an effort, she climbed back to her feet, but the world turned dark again, and she swayed where she stood as the truth shocked through her . . . "Gilaefri will fall next, then Dunnardeth. *Everyone we know, everyone we left behind—"*

The caravan started to move again. The wagon wheels creaked. The burning taste of acid was still in Sindérian's mouth, in her throat, as she continued, half-blind with fear and grief, down the road. It was all too familiar, this heartbreak, this frustration. She thought, They always die. I am sent away, and the people that I love are left to die.

Somewhere along the way, she had turned her ankle. Every step she took brought a jolt of pain, but she lacked the will or the energy to do anything about it.

In the nearest wagon, one of the children began to cry, and others joined in. The wind caught up their shrill voices, wove them into a melody, into a dirge, and carried them away, across the barren fields of Rheithûn.

———

She woke to the sound of her own name, and a light shining in the darkness. Sindérian sat up in bed, feeling the cold sweat slide over her skin under the linen nightdress. She struggled to regulate her ragged breathing, the wild pounding of her heart. She was at home surrounded on all sides by peace and safety, in her tiny whitewashed cell-like room at the Scholia on Leal, the room that had been hers on and off since childhood. What time was it? It must still be very early.

Níone stood by the door, holding a honey-scented beeswax candle and shielding the flame with her other hand. Her lovely ageless face was serene, but her hand shook, holding the candle. "Are you ill? You cried out in your sleep; then I heard you weeping."

"No—no, I'm not ill." Sindérian pushed back a damp strand of dark hair. Her voice sounded hoarse in her own ears;

she wondered how she must look, how she must sound, to frighten a healer as experienced as Níone. "I'm sorry if I disturbed you. It was only a dream."

Floorboards worn smooth after countless years creaked as Níone crossed the room. Setting her candle down on a little iron stand near the bed, she turned to face her onetime pupil. "The same dream that has tormented you every night for the last three weeks? Isn't it enough that you had to live through these things once? Must you relive them each night in your sleep?"

Sindérian felt the hot color flood into her face. "You think that I bring these nightmares on myself!"

Níone sat down on the thick wool blanket and folded her hands in her lap. "This house is warded, as you know quite well. Every stone, every beam, every board, peg, and nail, woven round with spells. No dream ever comes here uninvited."

Sindérian was silent, biting her lip at the gentle reproof.

"My dear child," said her friend and teacher, "can you not forget?" Glancing around the room, Níone's gaze came to rest briefly on a little shrine in a niche in the wall, on the earthenware oil lamp with seven wicks, which had not been lighted since Sindérian returned from Rheithûn. "Can you not *permit* yourself to forget?"

"Men that I knew—friends that I loved—died." Sindérian's voice shook; her eyes stung with tears. "Not in battle, as they had long since resigned themselves to die, but executed like criminals, *slaughtered like beasts*—"

Níone reached out, touched one burning cheek with her long cool fingers. "That was no fault of yours—nothing you could have prevented by remaining. And it was no fault of yours, either, that you were sent home, to live, while others died."

"And yet I *remain* at home," said Sindérian, in a stifled voice. In all truth, sometimes the peace of the Scholia felt more like suffocation, sometimes this weight of pain around her heart threatened to crush her. "The war continues: in Gonlündor, on Erios. What use am I to *anyone* here?"

The older woman drew back, her softly arched eyebrows coming together in a slight, perplexed frown. "You think that the work you do here is worthless? The training of young healers?"

"No, no." Sindérian's hands closed around the heavy blanket. Like everything else in the room, it was simple, well made, practical, yet there was something of wizardry about it, too. The wool had been mixed with flax and milkweed, then woven with charms for sleep and healing, with a single red thread running through for protection. It seemed that everything at the Scholia had its place, its uses—except for her. "The work is necessary, the work is vital. If one could do it well . . . but I don't! I lack the patience." On the stand by her bed, the candle flickered and almost went out with the vehemence of her protest. Instinctively, she steadied the flame with her mind.

"You might learn patience, if you applied yourself," Níone suggested. "You might learn it in time."

"So I might. But what would my *students* be learning, while I am about it?"

Níone shook her head. One eyebrow went up, one corner of her mouth twitched—perhaps in memory of a certain headstrong, homesick twelve-year-old newly arrived from Tháerie—yet she answered blandly enough: "Who can say? Duty perhaps. Or acceptance. There is always something to be learned by a willing mind."

Rising to her feet in one swift graceful movement, Níone picked up her light again and glided toward the door. But she paused on the threshold, turning back toward the room. "Try to rest, Sindérian. Try not to dream." Her eyes flickered, momentarily, back to the dark, neglected shrine. "Pray, if you can. And in the meantime—"

Her gentle face was all compassion as she stood cupping the candle flame with her hand. "In the meantime, I'll apply myself to finding you some new task. One better suited to your talents."

2

✴

Baillébachlain on the Isle of Leal, is a port of some consequence: an ancient town, solidly built of slate and limestone, half-timber, oak, and cobble, with shops, inns, houses, taverns, and a fine old harbor whose quays and warehouses, made of the native stone, are as weathered and enduring as the town itself. Ships from every allied nation drop anchor at Baillébachlain, and traders from countries as far distant as Pehlidor and Oméïä stop there to barter goods. In every season, the narrow streets are crowded with wagons and oxcarts, and with men and women on horseback, afoot, or riding the sturdy island ponies. A hundred different languages and dialects can be heard along the waterfront, and anything from furs, to salt, to blocks of tin, lumps of ambergris, and copper beads may be purchased at a reasonable price.

Above the beehive of the town, remote but watchful, stands the famous Scholia of the wizards: an immense block of building with a great central dome, perched on a rocky eminence overlooking the sea.

On a day in spring, travelers began to converge on the Scholia. Ships carrying grim-faced warlords in silver mail and surcoats embroidered with marvelous devices of birds and beasts sailed into the harbor, startling the merchants. The Prince of Weye rode up the hill on a mettlesome grey stallion and with him, on foot, came a company of archers and pikemen, dusty and travel-stained after walking the length of the island, under his standard of the silver elk. Wizards and swordsmen appeared out of the east, west, and south.

King Réodan, who had summoned them all, watched them arrive from a vantage point in one of the square corner towers.

"There were many I expected to see who haven't yet come," he said on the third day. "I begin to wonder if we will even see them." Turning away from the window, he met an unexpected challenge in the steady hazel eyes of his young kinsman Gwynnek of Weye.

"Men who don't have wizards at their beck and call may find themselves at the mercy of contrary winds . . . or of no winds at all," said Prince Gwynnek. "My own ship was becalmed two days on the Thäerian Sea. Depend on it: our cousins have suffered a similar delay."

"But *what news* will they bring when they do come?" asked a soft, melodious voice. It was the wizard Elidûc, who had been sitting unnoticed in a corner of the room, as silent and unobtrusive as any of the simple furnishings. "We have heard nothing so far but the very worst news that could possibly be. The tides of war are turning against us."

"If that is so, the time has come for a change of tactics," Gwynnek replied, thrusting out his chin. "A bold stroke is needed—we have been too cautious."

Elidûc rose from his seat. He was a man of average height, average looks; he had hair and eyes of no particular color. In his plain long robes, with his short, neatly trimmed beard, he might easily have been mistaken for some minor court official, rather than a mighty wizard, a great king's friend and advisor. When silent, he was easily overlooked. Yet there was a quality in his musical voice, even when he spoke as quietly as he did now, that commanded attention. "And you would suggest?"

The Prince of Weye was silent a moment, as though measuring his words. But then he burst out: "An attack on Phaôrax—why not? We've tried nothing of the sort for almost twenty years. She would never expect it."

"No, our enemy would never expect anything so foolhardy; not after the resounding defeat we suffered the last time." This came, not from the wizard or the King, but from a slender, fair-haired youth who had just entered the room. He stood in the doorway, lithe and graceful in a sky-blue surcoat emblazoned with the screaming Thäerian eagle differenced by a pattern of three stars, and he surveyed the others with an expression that was difficult to fathom. "More than a hundred ships lost, more than two thousand men, and we never even came in sight of the island."

"You speak as though you were there!" exclaimed Gwynnek, though he eyed the newcomer warily, as if uncertain how to react in his presence, uncertain what he might say or do. But then, even Elidûc (who knew Prince Ruan as well as anyone did) did not always know what to make of King Réodan's uncanny half-blood grandson.

"No," said Ruan, smiling slightly. "I wasn't there. My nursemaids and tutors forbade it." On the word *tutors* he glanced briefly in the wizard's direction; then his bright inhuman gaze turned back toward Prince Gwynnek. "And you, as I recall, were still a sucking infant."

Gwynnek gnawed on his lower lip; his hand twitched in

the direction of the sword he wore on his hip, but the movement was arrested. There were few men, perhaps, from whom he would brook such disrespect, but this distant cousin was apparently one of them. Stronger than he looked, and deceptively quick, Ruan had a formidable reputation as a swordsman. Now, though he did not seem to move with any haste, he was suddenly there across the room, standing beside Eliduc.

"Well then," said Gwynnek. "Perhaps the time has come to seek new allies. Your own kinsmen among the Ni-Féa Faey—" He bit off the sentence, unfinished, at the sudden fierce glow in Prince Ruan's eyes.

"Our wars, our policies, our sufferings are *as nothing* to the Ni-Féa. No more to them than the politics of fleas and gnats are to us. And if you were about to suggest that they might take an interest for my sake—" Ruan's teeth flashed white in something that was not a smile. "My kinsmen among the Faey, if they bothered to consider my existence—which we may count ourselves fortunate they can't and don't—would be far more likely to rain down curses on our heads."

There was a brief, silent struggle between the two young princes, though all of the effort seemed to be on Gwynnek's side. Eliduc watched, fascinated, as they stood facing each other: the Prince of Weye, solid and ordinary, with straw-colored hair and eyes of a clear golden brown, like a good homely ale; and Ruan, light-boned, fair-skinned, silvery-haired, with nothing ordinary or comfortable about him. Finally, Gwynnek accepted defeat. With a glance of pure dislike for his cousin and another for the wizard, he jerked a bow to the King and strode out of the room. With a slight shrug of his shoulders, Ruan bowed, too, and followed lightly after him.

As they left, Eliduc thought he saw something, some scrap of darkness, some fragment of shadow denser than any of the shadows in the room, clinging to the folds of Prince Gwynnek's cloak. But all that he said to the King was, "They are growing restless, some of the younger men. Restless and reckless. They would buy peace, I think, at practically any price."

"I know it," answered Réodan, grimly. "It becomes harder and harder to make them see reason." He stepped aside, and the wizard took his place at the window.

As he stood gazing out, over land and sea, Eliduc sensed the presence of six Master Wizards in a room directly above, mind-linked, hovering over a smoking brazier and breathing in the fumes of a fire made of nine aromatic woods. He joined his mind to theirs, and gradually his sight grew sharper, his ears keener; he became aware of many things from afar.

The war continued on many fronts. Men died; women wept for them, then picked up their children and their belongings and carried on, following first one army, then another. Crops were burning, cities were razed to the ground. A great naval battle raged somewhere to the south, between ships flying the eagle standard of Thäerie and a fleet of black galleys. And there was turmoil everywhere, even among those who played no part in the war. He sensed dark forces at work in the realm of the Dwarves; doubt and fear among the Gnomes, and the Seal-Folk. Things were beginning to awake, creatures of an older world, bound fast by the spells of ancient wizards. The Change had not aroused them, but something did so now, causing them to stir, to stretch, to struggle to break free from their prisons under the earth, under the sea. *Is this Ouriána's doing?* Eliduc wondered.

But when he shifted his sight in her direction, all he could see was the usual barrier around Phaôrax, a blankness, a vacancy that frustrated all attempts to see through it or beyond it. Ouriána warded her island well.

"What do you see?" asked the King, bringing him back to that austere tower chamber, with its spare furnishings and bare stone walls.

"I see a world in grave peril," answered the wizard. "I see despair spreading like a disease." He blinked, to bring his surroundings back into focus, and found that his hands were trembling, his palms clammy with sweat. "I have an idea that all the ill news we've received so far is only the beginning."

Meanwhile, lords and warriors continued to arrive at the Scholia. They shattered the serenity of the ancient college. In the narrow corridors—once the domain of soft-footed students in robes of sky-blue, russet, and saffron, and of wizards impenetrably serene in colors signifying the various ranks and disciplines—now there was a clatter of arms and the clink of chain mail, and the long staircases resounded with the thud and echo of booted feet ascending and descending. The visitors broke the peace, and continued to do so for three long days, waiting for the latecomers, the Prince of Hythe and the Duke of Mere, and speculating loudly over the delay.

Hythe finally came—a black-browed, broad-shouldered youth, who arrived like a storm cloud, full of bad news—but Mere did not, and Réodan left off waiting and called for his Council of War to assemble.

They met in the Hall of Winds under the dome. That was and is a high, spacious chamber, with tall, arched windows on all four sides, unglazed, and open to every wind that blows. The floor is a mosaic swirling with all the colors of the ocean, and the dome is painted with golden stars on a dark blue ground, so that to enter that room is to feel suspended between sea and sky. In those days, it was triple-warded so the airs that passed through might carry away no hint or rumor of anything said there.

For this occasion, chairs, benches, and stools were brought in for the King, the Masters of the Scholia, and the other great men. While the warriors and men-at-arms took up positions by the windows and by the great double doors, a handful of the younger wizards and a half-dozen students of the college sat down cross-legged on the cool tile floor.

Faolein came in late. Making his way slowly across the crowded room, he tripped over a young healer and bit his tongue, and continued on with his eyes watering, until he found a place for himself among the other Master Wizards—Tuilach, Ariéneil, Níone, Cathaoch, Curóide, Draithleann, Melliéne, and Feneilas—and sat down.

Motioning the assembly to remain seated, the King rose to his feet, stood tall and grave to address them all. "We have come together," he said, "in a time of great trouble. These may be the last days of Thäerie and of the Alliance. But if, by wisdom, sacrifice, foresight, and courage, we may still find a way to live on as a free people, then let us find that way. For this war we fight, however long, bloody, and cruel, is but a single battle in a much greater war, *and that is one in which surrender is unthinkable.*"

He spoke, then, of the Black Years, a time when men had neither peace nor rest, nor safety, being perpetually at war with hags and wraiths, demons, dragons, basilisks, and other such creatures of Night and Unlife. While some men defied the Dark, others yielded, becoming thereafter tyrants and oppressors and black magicians. Yet, through the intervention of the

Fates, chief servants of the Light, a new race of men arose—
a race of healers, prophets, heroes, and wizards. After many
years, they succeeded in building first a city, then a kingdom,
then a mighty Empire.

While the Empire of Alluinn flourished, a rival power far
to the south and east also grew mighty, but Otöi was a realm
founded on slavery and piracy, on every form of rapine and
cruelty, maintaining a covenant with the Dark through blood
sacrifices and other rituals too terrible to mention.

He would not, said Réodan, speak of the inevitable clash
between those two great powers. It was enough to say that, in
the end, the world was cleansed of a great evil, but at a cost
nearly beyond comprehension.

Yet the battle between *Erüi*, which is the Light, and *Nëos*,
which is Darkness, is as old as time itself—in all ages of the
world it must be fought and refought again. One hundred years
after the fall of Otöi, Ouriána of Phaôrax had revived in her
own person all the black sorceries of the Otöwan mages. With
power came pride and vaunting ambition. She established a
new cult, proclaiming her own status as an object of worship.
When even that proved insufficient to sate her ambition, she set
out to conquer what remained of the Empire. Those who did
not wish to accept Ouriána's rule resisted under the leadership
of the Pendawer Kings on Thäerie. So events had come full circle, with north and south again at war. That war had dragged on
for decades.

"But of our most recent battles, our most recent losses,
I will not speak," said Réodan. "There are others here more
qualified to do so than I. Let each tell his own tale, then we will
decide what is to be done for the future."

The High King sat down in his carven chair. His two eldest grandsons, Ailbhan and Ruan, leaned forward in their seats, as though they were disposed to speak, but at a signal from Réodan, so slight that Faolein almost missed it, they subsided.

There was movement among the men-at-arms, a clash of iron rings. Finally, a warrior with a grim, weary face left his place by the doors and approached the King with a heavy step. "I will speak next, with your permission."

One of the nobles whispered something in Réodan's ear, and the King nodded. "Llio of Cuirquorno, you are welcome here. We are ready to hear you."

Llio half turned, so that his words might carry to all parts of the room. "No one here can be ignorant of the evil and tragic events of the last days of Rheithûn, but with your leave I'll tell something of what occurred at Gilaefri, for I was there at the very end."

Faolein leaned forward in his seat, intent on Llio's words—hoping, for Sindérian's sake, that the story about to unfold would not bring further grief.

"It would be impossible to describe the horror," said Llio, "or the confusion, when the Furiádhin threw down the walls: the choking dust, the terrible noise. The maimed and the dying were lying in the rubble, crying out for help, and our healers were few, too few. And when the smoke cleared, when it was possible to see the ruin of our defenses, our leaders surrendered at once, rather than spend more lives in useless resistance.

"Men of Phaôrax and of Rhuaddlyn took them, and bound them, and led them away. I can see our lords now: how Cailltin looked so pale, and so sick at heart—yet he never flinched as they tied his wrists. Briac and Coall—those noble youths, treated like felons. And Lord Duillig—grey-haired and leaning on his crutch—"

Llio slammed a meaty fist into the palm of his hand, and his voice grew hoarse with emotion. "*What need to bind ANY of them,* who were men of honor, and had already given their parole? That was what we all wondered, and accounted it a very shameful thing. A short while later, one of the Furiádhin came and spoke to us. For their rebellion against the rightful rule of their undoubted Empress, he told us, our leaders had earned the lingering death reserved for traitors. Yet, as Ouriána was *merciful,* they had not suffered *'according to their deserts'* and death had come swiftly. So said the furiádh Goezenou, branding as renegades men who died as patriots and heroes. Though we were not allowed to witness the executions, we did see the bodies later. They had been badly mutilated. I hope it was done after they were dead, as the Pharaxions told us."

Faolein sat back, shielding his eyes with one hand. For, of course, Sindérian would hear of this; the story of the mutilations would run through the Scholia. It would be far, far better if the news were broken to her gently by her own father, than carelessly by any of the students, or roughly by the men-at-arms. Yet he shrank from the task, fearing he would do it badly.

"No act so vile was ever committed when Prince Guindeluc was her Captain-General," Llio was saying. "Nor would Prince Cuillioc have permitted such a thing. But the one is dead and the other recalled to Apharos, and the Dark Lady has placed the command of her armies solely in the hands of the Furiádhin.

"It was intended, maybe, to bring shame and despair to the living, to crush any thought we might have of escape or resistance. But as we were marched south, some of us *did* resist. We overpowered our guards, made our way north, and crossed safely into Mere." His big fists clenched again. "Yes, we escaped—but our kingdom of Rheithûn no longer exists. We are homeless, leaderless, hopeless—"

"You will not be homeless," said Réodan, reaching out to touch Llio lightly on the arm. "A place will be found for you, *all of you*. I know it's small recompense for what you have lost, but all that can be done *will* be done."

Next came a man of Gonlündor to speak. His clothing was rough, made of sheepskin and leather, worn and patched, but there was dignity in his glance, and his speech was not unmannerly. "It may be that few here know much of my homeland. It's a desolate region, very wild and largely unsettled since the fall of the Empire—for, being then a principality of Alluinn, we were caught in the backwash of her destruction. Though we live in a land once famed for poets and minstrels, for men of high learning, we are, in these latter days, farmers and herdsmen and nomadic hunters, a simple and rustic folk. Yet we, too, have resisted Ouriána. We may lack the numbers to muster a great army of our own, but many of our sons have joined your companies, fought side by side with the men of Thäerie and other western lands. Over the years, we have served as your scouts in Rhuaddlyn, Rheithûn, and Malindor. But now she has answered our little defiance with a devastating blow.

"Five weeks ago, a thick yellow fog came creeping over our land. It was no natural fog, no weather of this world. Horses and cattle ran mad. Strong men, women in their prime, healthy young children, fell down in fits." He shuddered at the memory. "Fully a third of our people died overnight. Why has she done this thing, you may ask, sent forth this mighty sorcery merely to bring such an insignificant number of us to our knees—"

"If we ask," interrupted a richly dressed nobleman seated by the King, "the answer is not long in coming. It was meant as an example to the rest of us, a demonstration of her power. She means to dishearten the allies of Thäerie, to make them question their allegiance to our cause."

"I fear that some have already done so," said Réodan, exchanging a glance with Elidûc across the room. "The Duke of Mere promised to send someone to take part in our council, but no one has come."

At this, Bael of Hythe—he that had arrived so late—sprang to his feet, a great hobbledehoy youth half a head taller than anyone else in the room, still growing by the evidence of clothing that did not quite fit him. "Mere has deserted us." Then, remembering himself, he swept a bow to the King, to the other princes. "Let it be my turn to speak. I was delayed in coming because my cousin of Mere was to have sailed with me. I waited on the coast for three days. At last a messenger came. *The Duke has withdrawn from the Alliance.* He vows not to take up arms against any of his kinsmen, any of his former allies, but neither will he—in his own words—'*continue to conspire against the Empress Ouriána.*' "

"I think this is no new decision on his part," muttered Llio. "This is why the promised supplies of beer and grain never came, why our women and children starved, why so much of the strength went out of our fighting men and our wizards. Not take up arms against us? He's already betrayed us!"

"If he were a traitor," said Réodan, frowning thoughtfully, "I think he would be here listening to our plans, carrying everything we say directly to our enemy. Though whether he will be *permitted* to remain neutral is another matter. Pharaxion armies are massed on his borders. Will Ouriána and her Furiádhin accept this tepid attempt at conciliation and turn their attention elsewhere?"

"She would be wise to pretend that she *does* accept it," said Tuilach. The oldest of the Nine Masters, he had long white hair falling past his knees, and a thin, high voice. He looked bleached and frail, but his mind remained sharp, and Faolein and the other wizards had the habit of deferring to him. He had seen more than two hundred years, and his knowledge of the world was very great. "I think she will hold her hand, though Mere is within her reach, in the hope that she might encourage Weye and Hythe to follow his example."

"*We will never do so!*" cried Prince Gwynnek, surging to his feet to stand, sturdy and truculent, by his cousin of Hythe. "If she knows us at all, she knows we won't turn coward as our kinsman has done."

"But, in fact, she doesn't know much about either of you, Lord Prince," returned Tuilach mildly. "You have both so recently come to rule. Your late fathers she *did* know—or at least, she knew what they might do in any given circumstance. But sons are not always like their fathers. She may hope to see you follow the example of your cousin the Duke."

"We will speak more of this later," said Réodan, gesturing to the two young princes to return to their seats. They obeyed, but reluctantly, and sat glaring defiantly at the assembly, their faces flushed and their eyes very bright as if some doubt had been cast on their courage or their honor.

⊢———⊣

"For now," said the High King, "let us hear from Gearhan of Erios."

Gearhan was a small man, in armor of black leather stamped with the spiraling maelstrom badge of the island; he wore also a long, dark cloak, which swept the floor as he crossed the room and bowed low before the King. "What I have to say makes ill telling. Ouriána has reclaimed Erios. For ten years we managed to hold the island against her, despite many determined assaults, but in the end she conquered us by magic and trickery.

"You mustn't think that she found us careless or idling," Gearhan went on. "The Isle of Erios is small but mountainous, and we had watchmen and seers in all the high places, gazing out to sea. We had boats patrolling the waters. My grief that we should be defeated by something so insubstantial as an illusion! One moment, our watchers were staring out to sea, where they saw nothing more dangerous than a flock of seagulls. The next, a great fleet of black ships with sails of crimson and purple came sailing into the harbor at Sgeirre, at the southern tip of the island. The very magic that created the illusion should have forewarned our seers, but the magic itself was somehow disguised. The enemy was upon us before we had time to board our own ships, before we could organize our forces on land.

"We fought hard to defend our city. From street to street they harried us, then uphill, to the fortress of Dunsgeirre, where many of our people had gathered. I think we might have held the fortress, too, had we not been suddenly attacked from the east *by wyvaerun*. The smallest were as large and as fierce as eagles, and some were many times larger. They came at us without warning, and tore a dozen men to shreds with their beaks and claws before we had time to react."

There were gasps of surprise and dismay throughout the room. All knew of the wyvaerun: hybrid creatures, part bird, part serpent, originally bred for the Otöwan nobility, who had

flown them like kestrels. After the world Changed the creatures reverted to the wild, until Ouriána somehow contrived to
win their allegiance, employing the hybrids as spies and messengers, for their sight and hearing were very keen. She had
also, apparently, been selectively breeding them larger and
larger, but no one had imagined they could reach such an enormous size, or that the wyvaerun were dangerous.

"So we're now to be attacked from the air, as well as by
land and sea," growled Bael of Hythe.

"We have archers," answered Réodan. "And more of
those, perhaps, than Ouriána has giant wyvaerun."

* * *

The late-afternoon sunshine poured into the great chamber
through the high western windows; wherever it touched the
mosaic floor the variegated blue tiles gleamed like water. Here
and there, sunlight glanced off armor, off a crimson jewel set in
the hilt of a sword, off silver-and-gold embroideries on lordly
surcoats and banners. The Master Wizards sat silent and medi-
tative in their twilight-purple robes. It was very still in that
bright room: everyone felt weighted with knowledge, and the
burden of the choices before them seemed almost too much to
bear.

Then Prince Bael left his seat again. His dark eyes swept
the room, and his voice took on a challenging note. "Archers
are all very well, but they are only men. *What do the wizards of
Leal have to say to us?* For in all that has been said here today,
we've heard much of our fighting men, but very little of our
magicians."

"We will do what we have always done," said Faolein quietly. "We will heal. We will advise. We will foresee—where

we are able. We will counter Ouriána's spells, as and when we may."

"And that is *all* you will do? In truth, *you'll not act at all*—you will merely react, and that, as often as not, too late!"

There was an angry stir among the Nine Masters, a low protest from the lesser wizards and from the students of the Scholia. In the sudden agitation that moved through their ranks, no one noticed a shabby figure, dressed for travel in high boots and weather-stained cloak, slip into the room and take a seat on the floor with the young wizards.

"I take it," said Curóide, crossing his arms across his broad chest, "that you would have us attack Ouriána directly, with all of the spells at our command—the wizards of Leal against Ouriána, her magicians, and her priests, in one great arcane battle?"

"Why not?" said Prince Bael. "We have been at war more than forty years, but you might end it overnight."

Curóide's light eyes narrowed, his square jaw set. Yet it was Tuilach who spoke, gently scolding, in his thin, high voice. "Lord Prince, no good thing could possibly come from such a battle. When the wizards of Alluinn fought the mages of Otöi, both sides lost. A thousand magicians died, all told, many thousands of others died, too, and the world was Changed. There was—"

"There was *a century of peace* that followed after," Bael interrupted him. "Evil was defeated, virtue triumphed, and men built a better world out of the ashes of two fallen civilizations." Then remembering to whom he spoke—or perhaps ashamed of his own discourtesy—the Prince flushed painfully, and sat down in his chair, dropping his face into his hands.

"I think we need not lesson Tuilach on an era he remembers very well," said Faolein, with a slight, ironic smile. "Yes, there was a time of peace—between nations, because men were too much at war with their changed world to fight among themselves. New species arose—plants and animals, birds and fish—some of them dangerous. Runes that magicians had relied on for centuries lost their potency, and wizards labored for decades discovering new ones. And later, when we came to know our world and how to live in it, it did seem we had finally grown too wise ever again to yield to the temptations of the Dark. We did, then, believe that the world was perfected, but we were wrong. For evil was *not* defeated. It merely found a new vessel in Ouriána of Phaôrax."

Prince Bael lifted his face. "And you would not risk yourselves for the sake of another century of peace, perhaps even longer?"

"Our fear," said Curóide, "is that we might sacrifice everything—our own lives and the lives of countless innocents, too—and there would be no peace. Ouriána would not be defeated."

A brief, meaningful glance passed between the two princes, Hythe and Weye. Then Weye spoke, drumming his fingers against the arm of his chair. "She calls herself a goddess, but I, for one, have never believed her. Yet it seems that our Master Wizards do. Is she, then, truly invincible?"

"No," said Draithleann. Next in age and wisdom to Tuilach, she had long, braided hair the color of old ivory, and clear grey eyes brimming with light, which seemed to see everything and nothing—for Draithleann was a blind seer. "But we do believe in our own prophecy: that the Dark Lady of Phaôrax will not be defeated by the men of Thäerie, and not by the wizards of Leal. She will yield—if ever she does yield—only before the power of one of her own blood."

"But there is no magician, no wizard of the house of

Phaôrax capable of challenging her," Prince Bael protested. "Those who *might* have done so are dead. Years may pass, *decades may pass,* before another is born to take the place of the child who was lost. By then it may be too late."

The burning color came back into his face as he spoke, and his dark brows came together in a fierce scowl. "Will there be blood sacrifices on Leal, on the very steps of the Scholia? Slave ships in the harbor at Penthéirie? Will we see all the world in thrall to the overmastering pride of this one woman steeped in black magics?"

At these words, many in the hall blessed themselves— some openly, some furtively, as though by doing so they betrayed some doubt or distrust of the King or the wizards.

But then Tuilach rose, and he, too, signed a *béanath* against the ill omen, with a sweeping gesture that took in the whole room. "We will do all that we can to prevent it," he answered quietly, "each according to the dictates of his own conscience. No man, and certainly no wizard, should ever do more."

"And so," said Prince Gwynnek, with a bitter laugh, "the soldiers and sailors of Thäeric, the fighting men of Weye, Hythe, Rheithûn, Malindor, Erios, Gonlündor—they have all spilled out their blood *for nothing,* for a hope that may never materialize?"

"We must not forget that Leal has also known losses," the High King reminded him sternly.

"More than a hundred wizards have died in this war," said Níone, her cool grey eyes moving from one flushed and angry young face to the other. "That hundred may seem a trifle to you, but it was almost half our number. And those who live are not unscathed; our healers, most of all, have suffered greatly. The despair, the inner turmoil of those who have returned from the battlefield is like a cry of agony in our minds at all times. What then? Would you have us forget the lessons of the past, adopt a course so dangerous and so unthinkable that even Ouriána, in all her ruthless arrogance, would shrink from attempting it?"

"Then what hope have any of us?" asked Bael, sliding down in his chair, giving the wizards a black look under his heavy eyebrows. "Our list of allies grows shorter and shorter. Our wizards are afraid to act. Should we sue for peace? The recent atrocities in Rheithûn should be warning enough—will our enemy be any more merciful to any of us, once she has us in her power?"

"No," answered Réodan, wearily. "We will not treat with her, and we won't surrender. We continue to fight her as best we may—*with hope or without it.*"

It was then that the traveler seated on the floor with the young wizards rose to his feet and threw back his hood, revealing a head of shaggy brown hair and a lean, scarred face. "Not entirely without hope," he said in a clear voice. "For one that we all thought lost has been found, and the tide of battle may still turn our way."

In the sudden uproar that followed, the King barked out an uncharacteristic demand for silence. The noise died; all faces turned his way, startled to hear him speak so roughly. But he was intent now on the weather-beaten figure in the worn green cloak and high boots. "*Who is this man?* How did he come here?"

"It is Aethon of Sibri," answered Tuilach. "Once a student at the Scholia, a wanderer since. I can vouch for him myself. He was my own apprentice."

"Then," said the King, "I will hear him speak. But what he

has to say may not be a matter for open discussion. Master Wizards, Aethon, my kinsmen of Hythe and Weye, Eliduc; lords of my own household, you may all stay." As he spoke, his glance passed over each one that he named.

Then he made a broad gesture of dismissal. "All the rest have my leave to depart."

3

✦

There was silence in the room, a great silence made up of many little silences. Only those the King had invited to stay remained; the massive doors had been closed and locked, the wards reset. This done, no one spoke, no one moved, waiting for the King to speak. Sitting among the other wizards and struggling to maintain his outward composure, Faolein felt a little sickly thrill of expectation.

"And now," Réodan said to the wanderer, "I would have you explain yourself." His words echoed through the vast chamber.

"I have been to Skyrra," replied Aethon. "Where I spent a fortnight at the court of King Ristil at Lückenbörg. While I was there, I saw a wonder: men brought back to life, who appeared to be dead, and Nimenoë's ring on a lady's hand."

There was an explosion of tiny sounds as wizards and noblemen shifted forward in their seats: a rustle of cloth, a hiss of indrawn breath, a scrape of spurs on the tile floor.

"On whose hand?" asked Réodan. His tawny hazel eyes glittered with excitement, but his voice remained calm, measured.

"On the hand of the youngest princess. But perhaps I should tell you my story from the very beginning."

The King nodded, and the wanderer began his tale:

"For the benefit of those who know little of Skyrra, I will tell you that it's an open country of grassy plains and rolling hills. Across the wide channel known as the Necke are the nations of Arkenfell and Mistlewald—friendly and kindred folk—to the east lies Eisenlonde. Ever since the Change, the men of the north have returned to an older way of life, abandoned their cities, turned their backs on book learning, wizardry, and the greater world, growing insular and clannish. But although they are unlettered, the men of Skyrra, Arkenfell, and Mistlewald are a brave and generous and honorable people. The Eisenlonders, on the other hand, are much as they always were: savage and cruel. They pledged their fealty to the Dark long ages ago, and there's no reason to suppose that their allegiance has shifted.

"For many years, a threat has been growing throughout the north. Skinchangers—werewolves and werebears—attack isolated villages in Arkenfell, Skyrra, and Mistlewald, and there have been occasional armed clashes between the men of Skyrra and the barbarians of Eisenlonde. Lesser evils, these skinchangers and berserker warriors may seem to us, who have been at war with Ouriána of Phaôrax for all these long years, but a village raided, a farmstead burned, a family killed and eaten—these are no small matters when they take place just over the next hill, or in the next valley.

"One day while I was at Lückenbörg, a host of King Ristil's men rode in, wounded and bloody after a skirmish to the east. They had been victorious, but the battle was a very close thing, for all that their numbers were so much greater.

The barbarians have apparently revived one of the ancient ice giants. An—"

He was interrupted by a brief sensation following this news, a barrage of questions. Aethon waited patiently while their voices battered him, and answered not a word. Only when the noise died down did he continue:

"An immense dark figure fights in their ranks, wielding a mighty war hammer scrolled with runes and strange devices. Where that dread weapon strikes, it crushes, but even those who feel the wind of its passing fall, and are rendered as cold and still as death. Several of the bodies were carried to Lücken-börg and laid at King Ristil's feet. I saw them myself, touched them, and there was not a doubt in my mind: they were dead. *Even the Skyrran healers* thought they were dead. Yet almost a week had passed, and the bodies were still fresh.

"Then Ristil sent for his niece, the Lady Winloki. The princess moved among the fallen, spoke words over them, and—it was a marvel!—the color came back into their faces, the air rushed into their lungs. All but one revived." Aethon's eyes glowed with the memory. "I was close enough while the lady was tending them to see the band that she wore on her hand, and to recognize it as Nimenoë's runic ring. But after the men were healed, the lady apparently put the ring aside, as though she understood it was dangerous to be seen wearing it—for I never saw it again while I was there."

There followed another little stir among the nobles of the King's household, a ripple of excited speculation. The wizards were silent, but they exchanged speaking glances, which were more than sufficient.

Réodan received the news quietly. He ran a thumb along the line of his jaw, and his thoughts seemed to turn inward.

"The ring may have come to this lady by mere chance," he said at last. "Nor is her ability to make use of it proof of anything. Wizards are few in the north, but healers are not. How old is this Lady Winloki, and does she resemble Nimenoë?"

"She is nineteen years old," replied Aethon. "Which you'll admit is exactly the right age. She resembles Nimenoë only a little, but she has Eldori's eyes and hair, a certain look of him about the mouth."

Faolein rose from his place among the Master Wizards. "Many of you will remember, I always doubted the child was dead. The portents surrounding her birth were unmistakable. And I read the signs on her hand when she was an hour old. The lifeline, in particular, was strongly marked."

Curóide shifted in his seat, turned his pale blue-eyed gaze on the traveler. "But did you see *Éireamhóine* at Lückenbörg?" he asked eagerly.

When Aethon shook his head, his glance darkened. "Even if Éireamhóine and the infant survived that cataclysmic battle in the Cadmin Aernan—the repercussions of which we felt even here—I can't believe that he would abandon her later. And certainly not on the plains of Skyrra, among such simple, unmagical folk!"

"It is possible," suggested Tuilach, "that he had very little choice in the matter. We don't know what his circumstances were; they may have been desperate. Or it may have been the nurse who survived, and carried the infant to Skyrra."

The King turned to Prince Gwynnek. "You have been to Skyrra. What do you say?"

"I don't remember seeing this girl Winloki, if that is what you mean. But there are dozens of young princes and princesses at King Ristil's court: his own sons and daughters, his younger brothers and sisters, and any number of nieces, nephews, and more distant relations he has chosen to foster. There was no making them out one from the other they were so very numerous." A brief, condescending smile flickered across his face. "Though I will say the girls were comely enough, and some quite pretty."

Ignoring this last remark, Draithleann said, "And where better, Lord King, to hide an infant than in a house already swarming with children? For who, outside the house, would notice the addition of a single child more?"

Réodan nodded slowly. "And it was not as though she was left—if she *was* left—in a peasant's cot. In the house of a king she would be nobly reared. Yes, in even so simple and rustic a court as King Ristil's."

The wanderer, Aethon, cleared his throat. "I have a tale to tell, which may make the matter . . . somewhat less ambiguous. A story that I heard at Lückenbörg.

"In the very same year and season that Éireamhóine was lost, King Ristil's sister, the Lady Elfhael, gave birth to a pair of twins: a fine strong boy, and a healthy girl. The lady was young, her labor not difficult, and all seemed well. Yet the next morning, as she sat up in her bed to receive visitors, without any warning she gave a great cry, the visitors were ushered out of the room, and the midwives shortly announced that *a third child* was born, all unexpected, almost an entire day after the others. That infant, a girl, was given the name Winloki."

Réodan looked to Níone, as the one healer present; others turned to watch her as well, awaiting her reaction. "It might have happened exactly that way," she said, hesitantly. "And yet—"

"And yet," Réodan finished for her, "it seems altogether more likely that someone arrived with a child shortly after the others were born, and Ristil and his sister contrived this mummery to account for her sudden appearance in the King's household."

Faces began to brighten around the room; hope blazed up in a dozen pairs of eyes at once. Faolein took in a deep breath, then released it. "It would seem she's been safe in Skyrra all of these years, our lost princess, our child of prophecy. But perhaps safe no more. What Aethon has seen and guessed may have also been seen by less friendly eyes."

"There can be no doubt," said Curóide, "that Ouriána has spies in the north, as she has spies everywhere. The princess ought to come home at once. She must be convinced to come home. Not only for her own safety, but the better to be trained in the use of her gifts, whatever they may be. There will be no one among the healers and runestone readers of Skyrra capable of teaching her."

"We should not speak of *convincing* her, when so much is at stake," cried out one of the noblemen in the King's entourage. "Let us send an army to escort this lady to Thäerie, whether she wishes to come or not! Time enough, then, to *convince* her, when we have her *safe*."

Réodan shook his head slowly from side to side. "No, no, my good Lord Daómhóine. If our enemy doesn't know yet that the princess still lives, we would only draw her attention by sending an army where no army of ours would ordinarily go."

There rose a murmur of agreement from the wizards, a faint movement among the other noble lords, though whether of protest or assent Faolein could not tell.

"And as for storming into Skyrra with force of arms," Réodan continued, "King Ristil would take that ill, very ill, and who could blame him? We would have a fight on our hands before we had time for explanations."

"Yet if she refuses to come, we are all lost," said Lord Daómhóine.

"That is a risk we must take. Even if she does prove to be the child of the prophecy, her friendship, her assistance, these are not things we can claim as a *right*. She must come willingly or not at all—else we are no better than Ouriána, and so the princess might well think us. We should send an embassy, to present our respects, inform the lady of her true origins, and bring her home, *if she will come*. A small but carefully chosen party, it should be, able to go swiftly and secretly, and to return the same way."

"I will go," said Bael of Hythe, grudgingly, as though conferring a gift. "There ought to be someone of suitable rank to treat with King Ristil, if he is reluctant to let her go."

"And I will accompany him," volunteered Prince Gwynnek. "After all, they know me in Skyrra. My presence, if nothing else, will assure King Ristil of our goodwill."

Faolein felt a jolt of dismay pass through the ranks of his fellow wizards; he saw that same dismay mirrored on faces around the room. To trust so delicate, so vital a mission to this hotheaded pair was clearly unthinkable, but none of them seemed willing to speak and so draw the fire of the two young princes.

The King, however, proved equal to the task. "I hardly think," he said evenly, "that either of you can be spared from the defense of the coast. If Ouriána's forces don't strike at Mere, they may take advantage of the Duke's declared neutrality to sail on past his seaside fortresses, his ships of war, and land in Hythe."

Prince Bael expelled a long breath. "I never thought—But of course you are right. I ought to go home and see to my own defenses." He sat back in his chair, his dark brows drawn together, obviously contemplating the worst that might happen.

"I will send one of my own grandsons, either Ailbhan or Ruan," said Réodan, glancing to either side of him at the two just named: the one tawny-haired, muscular, a typical Pendawer; the other slight and inhumanly fair. "He can carry my greetings to King Ristil, speak in my name. And whichever I choose, he can take three or four of his own men with him, ostensibly as an honor guard."

He turned, then, to the Nine Masters. "But who will go for Leal? For it's certain that wizards should also go, as we have no way of knowing what challenges, what dangers, may be met with along the way."

The wizards gave no immediate answer, awaiting some sign, some revelation. Faolein returned to his seat, sat with his head bowed, as mute as any of the others, but he felt an increasing pressure on his mind, which made his head throb and his thoughts race around and around without arriving anywhere. It seemed there was something he was *supposed* to say, yet there was nothing he *wanted* to say.

At last the pressure became too great. "I will go, if it pleases the King," he heard himself declare. "Anyone will tell you: I am no diplomat. But I was there at the very beginning, when the princess was born, and I may be able to, well, answer some of her questions."

Even as he spoke, he fully expected the others to object, the King to refuse him. The truth was, he had very good reasons to stay at home. But all around him heads nodded, the other Masters murmured their approval. He felt his heart sink.

"Faolein should certainly go," said Draithleann, turning her blind eyes in his direction. "With his gift for naming, he will know at once if she is . . . who we have very good reason to suppose she is. And as he says, she may have questions that he can answer: about her birth, about the decision to hide her away."

"And for that same reason, Sindérian should go with him," Níone suggested quietly.

Startled, Faolein turned to look at her, his pulse jumping, his mouth suddenly gone dry with fear. But it was not Níone that he was seeing: a dizzy array of possible futures whirled through his mind. He opened his mouth to speak, but this time the words would not come.

In any case, the other Masters had already begun to react.

"Too young," said Melliéne, with an emphatic shake of her golden head.

"That Sindérian is gifted none can deny," Cathaoch put in, a doubtful look on his shrewd square face. "But she remains largely untested. I see no reason why she should be chosen."

"Indeed," said Tuilach, in his high, unsteady voice. "This is a task, I think, for one much older and wiser. Let Melliéne go, or Feneilas, for there should certainly be a woman present."

Curóide snorted something unintelligible under his breath. "No one protests that our healers are *too young* when we send them off to battlefields and into cities under siege," he growled. "After six years of horror and heartbreak in Rheithûn, I think Sindérian is wise enough!"

Níone put a hand on his arm to quiet him. "In fact, her age might work to our advantage," she stated calmly. "What years and wisdom can't accomplish, youth and eloquence may. And who better to win the princess's trust than one much like herself: a young woman and a healer?"

Her words made an impression. And suddenly, Faolein felt himself the center of everyone's attention, even more than he had been before, when his own name was mentioned.

"What does Sindérian's father say?" asked the King.

The wizard tugged at his beard, as he always did when perplexed. But as he hesitated, the myriad possibilities resolved in his mind to a single vision of remarkable clarity, to one inevitable, inescapable conclusion.

"I think . . . I think that my daughter would choose to be one of the party." The words slipped out before he could catch them. "More than that, I think she is *meant* to go."

"Then," said the King, "it is decided: Faolein and his daughter will represent Leal."

───

It was that time when *yffarian*, the day's waning, passed into *anoë*, the twilight hour. The light coming in through the deep windows on the west was tinted a sunset orange; the starry dome overhead was lost in shadows. A cold wind passed through the vast airy chamber. Réodan dismissed the council, rose from his chair, and headed for the doors. Others followed after him. This was a time reserved for prayer, for meditation, for setting one's mind and house in order before the evening meal.

Only Faolein remained in his seat, his shoulders hunched and his brow furrowed in thought. After a time, he realized that he was not alone. A shadow fell across the floor at his feet, and he could smell the herb scent clinging to Níone's violet silk gown.

He looked up, met a questioning gleam in her mist-colored eyes. "You did not say so, but you were reluctant to take Sindérian with you."

Faolein's hands gripped at his knees through the heavy folds of purple cloth. His moment of clarity past, the memory fading, he was left only with a sense of impending grief, the conviction that something very precious to him would be lost. What had he chosen for Sindérian, and why? Suddenly, he felt his years, as he had never experienced them before. The wind seemed to pass right through him; he felt chilled and empty.

"The truth is, I fear for Sindérian whether she goes or stays. And yet, if we are at least together—" He lost the thread of his thought; as he groped for it, the end of his sentence continued to elude him.

He shook his head. "I sometimes wonder if I did right, all those years ago, allowing her to be trained as a healer. What Curóide said troubles me more than anything: What *right* have we to expose our children to so much, so young, simply because they show the gift of empathy? Sindérian has other talents as well—why did we not choose to develop those instead? If she had spent the last six years studying at the Scholia, instead of breaking her heart on the battlefields of Rheithûn . . ."

Selfish, he thought. Selfish is what they had been, he and Shionneth, getting a child (not entirely by natural means) at such an advanced age. A wizard child, likely to outlive them both, that was the lure, one who would not grow up, grow old, and die, while an absentminded parent was occupied elsewhere. But who would have supposed such a placid elderly pair could produce such a vivid, passionate, empathetic child? They had been like two drab brown moths watching a brilliant butterfly emerge from its chrysalis, with no idea what to do next or how to do it. Selfish and heedless, that was how they began it, which was unforgivable in the so-called wise, and he, left alone to raise the child after Shionneth died: a well-meaning fool, but a fool nonetheless. He had allowed Sindérian to put herself in harm's way with scarcely a second thought.

"My dear old friend," said Níone, with a little laugh, her

fair face bright with amusement, "what else could you have possibly done? It is many years since Sindérian was a child by anyone's reckoning, and it was her *own wish* to go to Rheithûn. There is something in what you say—perhaps some aspects of her education have been neglected, but those talents are still there and can still be developed. And she would have become a healer in any case. A gift like hers is not to be denied. The only difference is that without the proper training she would have killed more than she cured, at least at the beginning."

He knew they had had this conversation before, or one very like it, and just as he always did, he was forced to yield to her gentle certainty. "Perhaps you're right. It was never for me to choose; it was always Sindérian. And however that might be, it is too late, now, to repine." Faolein rose heavily from his chair and headed for the door, Níone gliding along beside him.

"I can only hope," he said under his breath, "that we have chosen better for her today, you and I."

4

＊

The hour was very early, the air damp and utterly still, dawn no more than a faint white line along the eastern horizon. In the harbor at Baillébachlein, a small rowboat carrying four silent passengers slid out from a long, low boathouse, slipped between the dark hulks of ships massed along the docks, and headed out into deeper water, moving swiftly with the tide.

No one had seen them go. They had chosen this hour of uttermost secrecy so that none should mark the time of their departure. Oars creaked, the weathered hull dipped and bobbed in the water, but those in the boat remained silent until half a mile of water lay between them and the docks. Then Curóide grunted a few words to Cathaoch, the other oarsman.

"No, I don't see anything," said Cathaoch, speaking in short bursts between oar strokes. "But that's as we arranged it. They'll keep themselves dark until we hail them."

To the east, a fragile seashell-pink spread slowly across the sky. The sea was the color of opals and amethysts; but the west still blazed with stars. A stiff breeze sprang up, blowing off the land, scented with apple blossom and freshly tilled earth.

Sindérian crouched in the bottom of the rowboat, cloaked and hooded against the early-morning chill, trailing one hand in the sea and watching the glittering foam fly off her fingertips. Because she barely listened, conversation between Faolein and the other two wizards came to her in fragments.

"... we can hardly expect this Winloki to change our fortunes in the war *overnight*. What will she know of wizardry, or the battles we've fought?"

"—too many were there to hear the plan. The High King erred. Hythe and Weye—"

"If *something* isn't done, it will be Alluinn and Otöi all over again. I've seen portents in the fire, in the wind and the sky—"

None of this made more than a passing impression on Sindérian. She was intent on the opalescent water sliding under the bow, on the starry ocean, on everything she could sense below the surface. She thought, *Something has changed. It wasn't like this when I sailed from Rheithûn—was it only three months ago?*

A school of young herring passed under the boat; she could see them in her mind—tiny flickering lights moving in the darkness—and she felt their confusion. A hundred yards away, she detected a shark, its slow, savage, pitiless mind troubled, uneasy. She sent her thoughts deeper and deeper still, down to a place where long, sinuous shadows moved in the deep.

The moon, Ouriána's ally, was still young, yet Sindérian could feel her influence, her pull on the tides, like a great slow heartbeat. And she sensed something more, profoundly disturbing, a steady vibration under the water as though something down there, something beneath the sandy floor of the bay, struggled to be free.

Then it seemed to her, for a moment, that she could hear faint music coming to her over the water, across the years and centuries, music as of reed pipes, and wooden flutes, and sistrums. She heard women wailing, priests chanting, the dull boom of drums.

Lifting her hand, she tasted the water, and a cold chill snaked down her spine. *It tastes of blood,* she thought, *blood and death.* Words in a language she did not know came unbidden into her mind: *Hanòg domendeth amissa abhoran vòragol. Ephësien! Ephësien!*

"I see a ship," said Cathaoch. The sound of his voice, so familiar and ordinary, brought Sindérian out of her trance, into the present.

She sat back on her heels, breathing hard. What was it that had spoken to her and through her, out of the past? Already, the strange words faded from her mind. *Hano? Hanam?* No, it was all gone.

But all the time she had been dreaming, Cathaoch and Curóide kept steadily rowing. Now they had reached the mouth of the bay, and the long waves and deep waters of the open sea lay before them. About fifty yards ahead, a dark indeterminate shape rose up against the deep lavender sky, blotting out the last dim stars.

Faolein rose awkwardly to his feet and called out a greeting. There was a sudden blaze of torchlight ahead, and the shadowy bulk took on the lines of a ship, one of the light, fleet caravels of the Thäerian navy. Gold glistened on her prow, but the customary line of shields along her bulwarks had been stripped away, her figurehead removed.

Someone on board returned his hail. "Is that you, Master Wizard?"

"It is," said Faolein, his voice sounding thin and shrill against the wind.

With a dozen strokes of the oars, Curóide and Cathaoch brought the rowboat in close beside the hull. Someone tossed a rope ladder down the side, and the wizard reached out and caught it. Sindérian watched her father ascend into the torchlight. Then it was her turn.

"Go safely," she heard Curóide say behind her, as she took the prickly salt-crusted ropes between her two hands, put a foot on the first rung, and pulled herself up. Her legs tangled in her long cloak and full skirts, impeding her progress, but just as her fingers fastened on the top rung, a pale, delicate-looking hand reached out from above, grasped her by the wrist, and heaved her up and over the side with surprising strength.

A thin, hard arm came out to steady her as she landed feet-first on the deck; then arm and hand withdrew. She stood blinking like an owl in the glare of the torches, waiting for her eyes to adjust, while indistinct shapes milled around her, dark against the light. Gradually, those figures grew sharper, took on recognizable human features, so that she was able to identify them: some weather-beaten sailors in rough clothing, three men-at-arms in glittering mail, and a slender youth in a long velvet cloak, his silvery-fair hair held back by a golden circlet.

"We had expected to see your cousin: Prince Ailbhan," Faolein was saying. He wrinkled his narrow brow, cast uneasy sidelong glances both left and right. "No one told us of this change in plans."

The answer came in a musical baritone, unexpectedly rich and deep. "It was my grandfather's decision that I should come in Ailbhan's place. Though, in truth, I believe the suggestion came from Elidûc. He had a dream, or a premonition, I know not what."

The frown between Faolein's eyes smoothed out. "Well, then, perhaps it's a good sign, after all. If a seer so wise and farseeing as Eliduc chooses you for this task—"

"I fear it was very much otherwise. That is, the wizard had no clear idea who *ought* to go, he was merely quite certain that my kinsman *should not*."

All during this exchange, the fair-haired stranger looked not at the father but at the daughter, examining her face, and what could be seen of her figure under the long black cloak, with a bold direct gaze that Sindérian thought insolent and impertinent.

Perhaps becoming aware of the Prince's interest—perhaps just remembering what was due to the High King's grandson— Faolein made the belated introduction. "My daughter, Sindérian Faellanëos, Lord Prince. My dear, they have sent Prince Ruan in his cousin's place."

"So I see," replied Sindérian, making a slight curtsy, then looking away. Of Prince Ruan she knew very little, aside from a reputation for reckless courage and the curious circumstances surrounding his birth. Yet nothing, she thought, could have possibly prepared her for his pale unearthly beauty—or for the bright, disturbing arrogance of his glance.

"And the other ships?" said Faolein, squinting and peering out to sea. "What has become of the escort we were promised as far as Hythe?"

"Unfortunately, there will be no escort," said Ruan, shifting his attention to the wizard. "Just before we parted company, my grandfather received word of a fleet of Pharaxion galleys spotted off Nimhelli. Every available ship but this one has gone to the defense of the island."

Faolein looked more and more dismayed. "The entire plan made so hastily and with so little forethought," he muttered into his beard, "and already it has gone astray!" Watching him, Sindérian felt a twinge of foreboding.

"We might have waited for the other ships, but already Ouriána's messengers may be ahead of us. If we don't hurry, they might arrive in Lückenbörg long before we do, do the Lady some harm, or woo her away with their lying words." The Prince shrugged. "These are my grandfather's thoughts I give you, not my own. Even if our enemy knows nothing of this Lady Winloki, Skyrra and Eisenlonde are on the brink of war—may *be* at war now, for all that we know. There's no longer any safety in the north."

"Nor anywhere else," said Sindérian, under her breath. Though she did not mean to be heard, Prince Ruan, apparently, had keen ears. His eyes flickered back in her direction, a faint smile played about the corners of his mouth.

"No, my Lady Healer, nor anywhere else," he answered softly. "What hope we have is all in haste . . . and perhaps not even there."

The white rim of the sun rose above the horizon; light broadened on the face of the water. With a stiff breeze filling her sails and a bright sky arching overhead, the caravel *Balaquendor* coasted around the Isle of Leal, now running before the wind, now beating against it. Reaching the northeastern tip of the island, she headed out into those vast watery expanses known as the Thäerian Sea. For two days and nights, by sunlight and moonlight, she skimmed like a white gull over the waves.

But the winds of that sea are capricious and fitful; they are never to be relied on. On the third day, *Balanquendor* was becalmed on a sea as smooth and clear and motionless as glass. The air lay heavy and still, the canvas hung slack.

Late in the afternoon, when the helmsman sat drowsing in the sunlight at the tiller, Faolein and Sindérian appeared from below: he in a drab wool cloak over his purple robes, she in a long black gown of some rich, heavy material. A dusky silken veil, so light, even that breathless air might lift it, floated behind as she walked. While the wizard paced the deck with slow, even steps, her movements were restless and a little erratic. And there was a visible constraint, on her part at least, a series of indirect glances so that their eyes never quite met, which seemed to indicate a continuing dispute, some matter unresolved between them.

After a time, Faolein turned toward his daughter and spoke, in his gentle, absent voice. "There is no use making yourself ill with anticipation. Even with favorable winds, we'll not see Skyrra for many weeks."

Sindérian released her breath in a long explosive sigh. "I know it," she said. "I know that very well." Yet her pale face and her dark eyes, glowing with impatience, gave the lie to her words.

They continued to walk, he calmly and deliberately; she with an energy barely contained. Clouds hung motionless in the sky overhead; the sun stood fixed in place with a dull sheen like brass. It seemed as if time itself had been suspended. In that great stillness, Sindérian felt all her conflicting desires rise up clamorous inside of her.

At last she burst out: "It is true. I *am* half-sick with excitement, at the prospect of seeing my little Guenloie—my sister that should have been! I've thought of her so often over the years: where she might be and what she might be like, if she survived. Sometimes I think that I meet her in my dreams, but in the morning I can't remember what I said to her, or if she even knew me." Sindérian stopped walking and whirled around to face her father. "But the sooner we complete our business in Skyrra, the sooner *I* can return to the work I am meant for."

The wizard drew back, his usual air of vague bemusement giving way to a vague alarm. "I was certain you would wish to make this voyage. Níone and I both thought—"

"I *do want* to go; there is no question of *that*." She made a wide gesture, as though casting aside any attempt to make him understand her. "But what I wish and where I should be—what I should be doing!—are very different things."

Faolein bowed his head. "No doubt I am being obtuse again. You must bear with me, my child. I mean well."

"No, no!" Sindérian felt a pang of guilt wrench at her heart. She reached out impulsively with both of her hands, took one of his, and pressed it between them. "You are always so patient, so good. Much more forbearing with me than I ever am with you."

No one, she thought, *could ask for a kinder father—or a more difficult, ungrateful daughter.* That he loved her she could not doubt, for all his reserve, in spite of his occasional clumsiness. But the differences between them—of sympathy, of temperament—seemed to be growing as the years passed by. The gap had became so great that she began to fear that no amount of love and goodwill would ever be enough to bridge it. Sincerely grieved at having wounded him, Sindérian lifted his hand to her lips and kissed it remorsefully.

"I think you would prefer a father less patient, but with greater feeling and a stronger understanding," he said humbly.

Tears burned in her eyes; a lump rose in her throat. But before she could make any coherent reply, there came an interruption: a *clink* of armor and a low rumble of masculine voices as Prince Ruan and his "honor guard" of three appeared from below and moved toward the two wizards.

Dropping her father's hand, Sindérian turned away, unwilling to allow the newcomers to witness her discomposure.

"It would seem that the wind has failed us, Master Wizard," said the Prince, crossing the deck with his light step. The three men-at-arms—Aell, Tuillo, and Jago—followed just behind him, their bootheels striking heavily against the weathered planks. "Is there nothing that you can do?"

"There is a time for wizardry, Lord Prince, and a time for caution," Faolein replied. "*'Go swiftly and secretly.'* That is what the High King told us, and I can think of no better way to announce our presence out on the water than to summon a wind from some other quarter."

"Far be it from me to lesson a wizard in his own arts," said Ruan. "Yet it seems to me, we could hardly give a clearer sign that we've something to hide than to sit here helpless while two powerful magicians do nothing at all."

His words came out on a light, even breath; it would have been easy to miss the challenge in them. If Faolein did, Sindérian did not. She felt a rush of indignation. Casting the twilight-colored veil over her face, she turned around and stared at the Prince through the thin silken folds, wondering if the challenge had been a serious one.

But Faolein was already speaking, gravely and quietly. "Perhaps there is something in what you say. Yet *any* weather-worker would be slow to meddle with the natural order, when he had only been becalmed for half a day."

The Prince inclined his head, whether in mockery or deference it was impossible to say. He moved past Sindérian, stood gazing out across the still water. "I sometimes think," he said, after a time, "we are not wise to depend so much on these caravels and carracks. If we were on a great Pharaxion galley, with two banks of oars—"

"We are a *free* people," answered Faolein. "Without slaves to power her, a galley is just as dependent on the wind as we are now."

The Prince half turned, gave the wizard a slanting look. "Free men can row as well as slaves. And with the proper incentive—" But then he smiled and shrugged; something in his face relaxed. "I suppose you are right. The *symbolic* value of a navy such as ours is beyond calculation."

"Galleys do well enough hopping from island to island in the southern archipelagoes," volunteered Aell. He spoke with the accent of Erios; like many who hailed from the Lesser Isles, he was short and slight, with rough dark hair and clear, farseeing eyes. For twenty years he had fought in the wars. Before that he had been a fisherman. "But ships of that sort were never meant for our wide northern seas."

At this, a lively discussion sprang up between the five men. Listening to them speak—hearing them argue the relative merits of cogs, caravels, dromonds, lymphads, naus, and galleasses; debate the advantages of lateen versus square sails, the rudder over the steering oar; and then go on to dissect every naval battle of the last two decades—Sindérian soon grew bored. Seeking distraction, she took a seat on a bale of canvas and continued to watch Prince Ruan through her veil.

That he was beautiful she could not deny—but what was

he, or any handsome youth, to a woman still in mourning? Her
first unfavorable impression remained, and she thought he was
likely to prove an uncomfortable traveling companion, an uncertain ally. Still he intrigued her, this half-blood son of a
Thäerian prince and a Ni-Féa princess, and she studied him for
signs of his fairy heritage.

Though he had a Man's height and something over, his
figure was that of a Faey: slender, wiry, and agile. From his
mother's people, too, came his triangular face, luminous fair
skin, and silver-gilt hair—but the strange turquoise eyes were
entirely anomalous in their shape and coloring. Trying to make
sense of him, she found that she could not. Though he spoke
easily and well, without affectation, there was, at times, a faint,
contemptuous undertone in his voice—and always a discon-
certing directness in his gaze—which seemed to set him apart
and at odds with those around him. Did he, she wondered,
have the keen eyes and ears of his fairy kindred, the other
heightened senses? If so, that would go far to explain his manner, his air of disdain. This ship must smell like a stable to him,
and some of the Men on it worse than beasts.

For the rest, she detected in his posture, in his movements,
a tension, an intensity, the promise of an extreme volatility, that
was both like and unlike her own.

So absorbed was Sindérian in studying the Prince, that
what happened next came without warning. It was not so with
Faolein. His sudden indrawn breath, his cry of warning, came
just before the whole ship shuddered from end to end, and a
shock of danger thrilled right through both wizards at once. A
puff of sulfurous air momentarily filled the sails; then the canvas hung slack again.

Springing to her feet, Sindérian threw back her veil and ran
to the side. She leaned over the rail, scanning the sea from hori-

zon to horizon. There was nothing to be seen, only a slow, heavy swell, which lifted the ship without breaking the surface of the water. Yet every nerve in her body tingled, and her breath came hard and fast.

Meanwhile, there was activity all around her, as sailors came boiling up from below, and the Master of the *Balaquendor* emerged from his cabin. Their voices rose and fell, now questioning, now exclaiming, so shrill with confusion they sounded like a colony of gulls.

Sindérian scarcely heeded them. The swell had subsided, but faint silvery ripples moved across the surface of the water. For all the heat of the afternoon, a creeping sensation passed over her skin, a piercing cold shot through to the marrow of her bones.

Suddenly aware of Faolein standing beside her, she linked minds with him. Together, they sent their thoughts out over the sea for mile upon empty mile; then down through the crystal waters, past great silvery shoals of fish, mackerels, and tunnies, and eels, like veins of rich ores under the earth; and on to the colder blue of the middle waters, where pods of whales passed to and fro, ponderous and graceful at the same time.

Where the seabed rose to an underwater ridge, they spied a lost mermaid city deserted since the Change: a maze of broken walls, fallen columns, and empty arches, of streets paved with agate and jade, all crusted over with barnacles or disappearing beneath overgrown seaweed gardens. A little farther, on another plateau, a hippocampus grazed on sea-wrack and sea lilies, its dark, iridescent mane streaming in an unseen current, black, blue-black, violet, and silver, and a gigantic green turtle, greater than any beast that lived on land, swam through an undulating forest of giant kelp with a ruined castle on its back.

Deeper and deeper still the two wizards sent their thoughts, until they reached a place where no light was, where they were forced to make their own. There are lines on the floor of the ocean, like the ley lines upon the earth, by which currents of power are endlessly generated, along which power flows freely. They followed one of these lines until it met with another, where two mighty forces of nature met and merged at the juncture. And there they found what they were looking for, what they had feared to find, at the foot of a range of underwater mountains: a hole in the bottom of the ocean, darker than the darkness in those sunless depths.

A hundred yards deep and twice that distance across, it gaped like a mouth with stony teeth. Shards of some clear crystalline substance were scattered over the floor of the crater. Something had been imprisoned there, bound to the rocks with chains of adamant, by the spells of ancient wizards. Something had slumbered there, unable to wake, unable to move for more than a millennium, but once again it was free.

"What is it you see?" Prince Ruan's strong, musical voice brought Sindérian back to herself, back to the bright world of light and air under the sky, and broke her link with her father. She realized that her hands were gripping the wood at the top of the bulwarks, and her palms stung where tiny splinters had worked their way in.

While Faolein went up to the quarterdeck to summon a wind, Sindérian explained to the Prince what they had found. "That is what we felt just a little while ago: when it broke free from its prison. It will be many miles away by now—it must be, or we would certainly have sensed it. But it may come back this way, and they can move very fast, some of them. To call a wind seems the lesser danger now; these waters have become more perilous still, and we dare not remain."

"*They* move very quickly?" said Ruan. "But you haven't told me, yet, *what was imprisoned down there.*"

Sindérian shook her head, blew on her tingling hands to ease the pain. "A kraken, perhaps, or a sea serpent, or a great water dragon. There were many monstrous things that lived in the sea a thousand years ago. Men used to make sacrifices of young boys and maidens in an attempt to placate them, before the wizards of Alluinn killed all those they could and put bindings on the rest."

"And how did this one break free?"

She shrugged, pretending to make light of her own fears. "After all, the spell had lasted for more than ten centuries. It's not to be supposed that it would hold forever."

"Nevertheless, you have an idea, and it isn't a pleasant one," the Prince persisted. And again she wondered how much he sensed: did he perceive the world as an ordinary Man did, or as a wizard, or as something entirely other?

Up on the quarterdeck, Faolein's chanting had ceased; the wind he had summoned out of the west came with a shriek and a moan and filled up the sails. It sent *Balaquendor* scudding across the water, toward the great continent. Now that they were moving again, Sindérian felt her spirits momentarily rise; but they sank again, dismally, with the answer to Ruan's question.

"The wizards of Leal have known for some time that something is coming—some danger, some disruption in the natural flow of time and circumstance."

"And this is Ouriána's doing?"

"Not, not something she has done deliberately, we think.

She's been tampering for a long time with things better left alone—has been so very reckless in her use of magic—there is some fear that the Walls of the World are beginning to fray, and the Darkness outside is finding more and more ways to slip through the cracks. Wherever it does so, ancient bindings may lose their strength, many of them may already be failing.

"Runes—" She caught her breath at the thought. "The names and forms of powerful runes may fade from wizards' minds. For all intents and purposes, those runes and the magic associated with them would cease to exist."

"Then what," said Ruan, "do the wizards of Leal propose to do, if this should prove to be so?"

Sindérian shook her head. "You must understand, where these bindings are concerned, we won't do anything to strengthen those spells—*we don't work those magics anymore.* The binding or enslavement of a sentient creature is—"

"Is a *waethas,* a very dubious sorcery, if not outright black magic," the Prince finished for her. And then, at her look of surprise, he smiled and shrugged. "I *was* tutored for many years by a wizard."

She nodded, determined to remember this. "Well then, you will see why we don't wish to emulate those ancient wizards. They were desperate in those days, of course, and it's difficult to condemn them, besieged as they were. They had a choice between imprisoning *themselves* and all they wished to protect, narrowly confined behind powerful wards, or they could imprison the monsters of the sea and the earth instead, and continue to move freely themselves."

"And they chose to work *waethassi.*"

"Yes," said Sindérian, with a thin smile and a lift of her eyebrows. "They chose that path. But *we* account ourselves wiser now . . . at least more aware of the consequences of our acts. We learned a hard lesson in Otöi. No wizard of the present age would make that same choice."

"And so?" asked the Prince, continuing to watch her with that assured ironical gaze of his. She found herself blushing under his scrutiny, though she did not know why she should.

"And so . . . We are doing the only thing that we can do. We are trying to put an end to Ouriána's dangerous meddling before whatever it is she's accidentally begun proceeds so far there will be no halting it."

5

*

In the great city of Apharos, inside the brass wall and more than a mile from the gates of ivory and pearl, there once lived a magician who had fallen on hard times. Maelor the Astromancer he was called, more familiarly, Maelor the Mountebank, the Drunkard, the Mad. A ragtag, threadbare, makeshift creature, he was a familiar sight in his dusty robes, shuffling through the narrow lanes and alleys of Ouriána's capital city, muttering to himself or making signs on the air like a lunatic.

Yet there were times when something seemed to ignite behind his dull eyes, a flash of sorcery, a glimpse of power debased or diminished, that caused his neighbors to treat the magician with a grudging respect, and the more imaginative to invent for him a glamorous history of palaces and temples, of mastery over wind, wave, earth, and fire, before a life of riotous excess brought him so low. For all that, no one knew very much about him, and least of all what his past had truly been.

Ostensibly, he made his living casting horoscopes, scratching out charts on scraps of dirty parchment for anyone willing to pay the price of three coppers, but his clients were few. He made ends meet by performing as a conjurer in the busy market squares down by the docks: simple tricks and sleights for the most part, as any true power he retained was unreliable, and such vanishments and conjurations as depended on it were only successful half of the time.

After a day spent juggling wooden balls and making small coins disappear, he would wander over to one of the humbler stalls, purchase a morsel of supper with his meager earnings—a withered turnip, a whiskery onion, a day-old fish wrapped up in brown paper—then amble homeward. He was often distracted: by an angular formation of birds passing overhead, by the last light of sunset burning on a puddle of stagnant water. Then he would stand, transfixed, absorbed in some waking dream for minutes or hours, until someone hurrying by elbowed him aside, jolting him out of his dream. Sometimes, he grew weary of the steep uphill climb and sat down on a crumbling doorstep to munch on a stale heel of bread or a bit of rancid cheese, and there he remained, until some household servant came along to send him off in a shower of hard words and kicks and blows. These the old man accepted meekly, without resentment, and continued on his erratic way.

He lived in the attic of a dreary old house perched high above the city. When the magician threw open the battered shutters on his one hexagonal window, he could see the headless statue of a winged Fate on the roof next door, and an iron drainpipe shaped like a crested serpent winding down one side of another building. The rusty pipe was broken in several places, as was the copper cistern it was meant to fill, but when spring came Maelor was pleased to see that the head of the snake still served a useful function: a pair of ravens had built their nest inside its open mouth and were raising a family of raucous black chicks, well out of reach of the hundreds of lean, hungry cats prowling the alleys below.

Ravens, as everyone knew, were Ouriána's spies and messengers, but he bore the creatures no ill will. This pair seemed
far too busy meeting the needs of their increasingly demanding
brood to carry any tales to the palace—and besides, it had been
a long time since he had anything to hide.

From his window looking east, Maelor could see most of
the capital spread out before him: a fantastical vista of crooked
tall houses, towers, steeples, gargoyles, and spiky obelisks,
all in dark granite, black marble, and obsidian, like a city in
sackcloth and ashes, perpetually doing penance for some un-
named sin.

Twice every fortnight, a pall of black smoke rose from the
New Temple, where the acolytes built great bonfires in the
courtyard, and the bloody-handed Furiádhin consigned offerings of wine and grain, fur and feathers and flesh to the flames.

One evening early in the year, the old man sat dozing by a tiny
hearthfire, while his supper boiled in a dented iron pot. Past
and present merged in his mind, dim memories mingled with
dreams and visions.

How long he sat there he did not know. When he came out
of his reverie, the room was thick with moving shadows, darkness that ebbed and flowed with the flickering of his fire.
Through the open window, he could see a crown of pale stars
over the building next door. While he was dreaming, most of
the water in his stewpot had boiled away, and all that remained
of his supper was a dark sludgy mass in the bottom of the
vessel.

Using a rag to shield his hands from the heat, he removed
the pot from the fire, set it down on the hearth to cool. Then,

very carefully, so as not to burn his long, thin fingers, he began to fish out tiny bits of bone and lay them out on the sooty bricks.

Like this, he thought. *No, like this.* His high forehead furrowed in a deep frown as he arranged and rearranged the delicate pieces of bone: the head, the tail, the long spine. Tentatively, he spoke a Word of Power. Nothing happened. He moved the bones around on the bricks again, spoke another Word, more potent than the first. Something started to happen, something struggled to take form. Breathlessly, he watched a ghostly image of the fish tremble on the verge of being, a bare hint of what it had been in life be—

But a sharp, impatient rapping at his chamber door shattered his concentration and severed the thread of his spell.

With a sigh, the magician rose. Lighting the stub of a greasy tallow candle, he padded in his stocking feet across the room and lifted the latch. Then, cautiously, he eased the low wooden door open, a fraction of an inch at a time, and peered out.

On the dark landing outside stood a tall figure swathed from head to toe in a voluminous velvet cloak. Man or woman he could not tell, for the hood was pulled forward to obscure the face.

"Is this the home of Maelor the Astromancer?" The clear, masculine voice issuing from the shadowy cowl had an unmistakable note of command. And from the stairwell below came sounds of movement: a scuffling of feet, a *clink* of metal— whoever he was, he had not come alone.

A tremor passed over Maelor from head to foot; he felt a heavy weight pressing on his chest, the same pain that came increasingly, these days, with any exertion or agitation. *Be calm,* he told himself, *be at peace. Let the world flow past you; do not fight what must be.*

"I have paid my tithe to the temple," he said in a shrill voice. "It may seem very little to the priests, but it was my full share and even something ov—

"I come from the palace, not the temple. And I've no wish to communicate my business to every cutpurse and footpad in the house. Will you or will you not let me in?"

Wordlessly, Maelor stepped aside. As his visitor crossed the threshold, ducking his head to avoid the lintel, there was a flash and glitter of gemstones and gilded armor under the heavy velvet cloak.

The magician bowed so low that his head nearly touched his feet. "Pardon me for asking, Great Lord, but— Do I know you?"

For answer, the visitor threw back his hood, revealing a pale face, green eyes, and thick red-gold hair drawn back and plaited in a warrior's braid. Maelor caught his breath sharply; another convulsive movement passed over his skeletal frame. The profile he saw before him, with its prominent cheekbones, long, tense mouth, and aquiline nose, had been etched on Pharaxion coins of silver and gold for the last two decades; but the man on the coins had died ten months ago.

The old man quickly recovered. Though Prince Guindeluc had been dead for almost a year, his younger brothers were said to resemble him closely. Rumor had it that Meriasec was with the fleet to the north, and that left . . . "Prince Cuillioc," said the magician, raking his fingers through his long, straggling hair, his thin grey beard. "You are welcome to visit my house at any time. Nevertheless, I am at a loss to understand—"

The Prince silenced him with an abrupt gesture. He was

not, after all, so very like his brother. His face conveyed both wit and intelligence, but also a deep reserve; he had the look of a man who was always questioning himself, weighing his every thought and action, and too often finding himself wanting, some essential quality lacking. "I want you to cast my horoscope. One of the servants at the palace spoke of you. He said that your talents far exceeded your miserable circumstances. Did the man lie?"

Maelor tugged at his tattered and dirty robes. "No, he didn't lie. What you see before you is only the result of folly and pride. I have lost much, but I can still read the stars.

"In truth," he added, under his breath, as he lit more of the stubby candles, made futile attempts to tidy up the room, "some things I see more clearly now than I ever did before."

"Then tell me what the stars reveal about my proposed expedition to Mirizandi." Moving with a stiff grace, the Prince took several steps away from the door. "The Court Astrologer tells me that great danger awaits me there: danger and betrayal, disgrace, perhaps even death."

Maelor whisked some dirty dishes off a table, stacked them on the floor in a dark corner of the room. "Pardon me," he said, the ragged grey tufts of his eyebrows coming together in a puzzled frown. "But if the great Lailoken—an astromancer of the highest competence—has already advised you, I can't help wondering why you should come to me for a second opinion." Again, fear washed over him, the pain in his chest tightened like a vise. His recent activities had been innocent enough, but what did that signify? If he had somehow attracted the attention of the palace or the temple . . . "And why you should come to someone like *me,* in this great city of seers and astrologers—"

"It's not Lailoken's competence I question," said Prince

Cuillioc. "But he owes his position at court to my younger brother, and therefore I question the accuracy and honesty of his interpretation. And it seemed to me—*in this great city of seers and astrologers*—that I would do well to consult someone with no possible ties to the court. Will you serve me in this, or shall I go elsewhere?"

The magician stopped with a crystal orb balanced in one hand. The center of the globe was clouded, and the surface covered with a network of tiny cracks. "I will serve you, my Prince, as well as I am able," he murmured. But a momentary confusion came over him, as he stood there in his threadbare stockings and scarecrow robes. His thoughts all jumbled together in a senseless muddle, his voice died, and his eyes glazed over.

"Is there something amiss?" asked Prince Cuillioc, when the old man continued dumb and bewildered for several minutes. With surprising gentleness, he reached out and touched Maelor softly on the arm. Almost immediately, he seemed to regret the gesture; he drew back, and said with a little barking, contemptuous laugh: "Or is it that I'm expected to cross your palm with silver in advance?"

At the sound of his voice, Maelor revived. He passed an unsteady hand across his eyes. "When you have seen the value of my advice, Lord Prince, then you must pay me whatever you think it is worth."

⁂

Stowing the crystal ball and some other oddments under his bed, the magician began to assemble books, paper, goose quill, and ink, carrying them over to a scarred and stained table near the open window. Then he pulled up a battered oak chest to serve as his seat, sat down, and began to make the necessary calculations.

Looking up only once—in order to ask the exact hour of his visitor's birth—the old man hunched over his books, turning over a leaf every now and then, running a grimy finger down a long column of numbers, or scribbling arcane figures on an ancient piece of vellum. Meanwhile, Cuillioc paced the room with long, restless strides, his velvet cloak flowing behind him.

The narrow room was as shabby and unkempt as its occupant; it smelled of mildew, tallow, mouse droppings, old boots, and decaying scholarship. Knots of brittle herbs dangled from the slanted beams overhead: Cuillioc recognized moly and witch's-knot, sarrow, dragon's-tongue, and thyssop—the rest he could not name. In a tall oak cabinet with a half-open door sagging on its hinges, he saw retorts, flasks, green glass bottles, and stoneware jars, along with other more curious vessels, harder to identify. On a shelf to themselves were five or six ancient books, scaled with wax seals or bound shut with iron chains.

Scattered across the bed among the dirty linens, piled on the floor—which was otherwise littered with nutshells, bread crumbs, and greasy parchment playing cards—were still more books, less magical perhaps, but rather more exotic in appearance: books bound in sharkskin, snake, and seal; crocodile, ibex, and zebra. One lay open at a map of the moon, another had strange tinted woodcuts of mermaids, sirens, sea unicorns, and whales.

And on a long table, a seemingly random collection of splintered glass and rough shards of broken crockery gradually resolved into a pattern so complex and involved that it dazed his mind to look on it. Continuing to pace, the Prince began to see more and more of these convoluted patterns: around the fireplace, the floor, and the ceiling, where the old man had sketched diagrams in chalk, charcoal, and ochre; carved on the inside of the door; in an arrangement of frail small skeletons, moles and lizards and tiny songbirds, up on the mantelpiece. Everywhere he looked, there were polygons, spirals, mazes, constellations, augeries—the strange geometries of a troubled mind. Over everything hung veils of cobweb grown furry with dust.

Even something about the shadows in the room worried him: the way they seemed to congregate in the center of the floor, to flow into each other, then separate into smaller shadows, scatter, and come together again. Darkness—darkness was an element, inanimate and benign. So the lessons he had studied as a boy informed him. But there was that other Darkness, both like and unlike, which was infinitely greater. His mother, the Empress, had claimed it for her ally; she had taught her sons to respect it, but not to fear it, nor to fear the shadows. Yet he did fear them, in this place.

He began to experience an unreasoning panic. A sickness rose in his throat. What was he doing here? What impulse, what folly, had inspired him to take such an ill-considered step? Had the old man's madness infected him? If this Maelor was not brain-sick and wandering, he, Cuillioc, was very much mistaken.

Yet pride forbade him to run away; pride, most of all, would not allow him to be intimidated by such a preposterous figure of a befuddled old man. So the Prince stayed on, listening to the magician mutter to himself, the sound of his goose quill moving across parchment, like the scratching of tiny mice feet behind ancient wainscoting.

"And so, what do you see?" said Cuillioc eagerly, when the old man finally glanced up.

Maelor did not reply immediately. He rose from his seat, drew up a chair with a cracked leather seat and one broken arm, and offered it to the Prince, then resumed his place on the oak chest. Even when Cuillioc sat down facing him across the table, the magician hesitated, picking up the blotched and inky chart, squinting at it, putting it down, then repeating the action a second and even a third time, before the Prince—all alive with curiosity and forgetting his recent doubts about the astrologer's sanity—burst out: "Speak, man, and do not fear the consequences. I wish to know *the truth*, no matter how dire."

Maelor frowned, ran his fingers again through his scanty grey beard, coughed once to clear his throat. "Pardon my seeming reluctance. But it seems to me that my esteemed colleague, the great Lailoken, could not possibly have your best interests at heart if he tried to discourage you from sailing to Mirizandi."

The Prince leaned forward, his forearms on the table, and fixed the magician with a glittering green glance. "But why do you say so?"

"Prince Cuillioc, you have always lived in the shadow of your elder brother. Even now that he is gone, relations between you and the Empress are far from cordial. You have always felt that she does not value you as she ought; you would do anything in your power to gain her favor. Anything, that is, a great prince such as yourself might do without compromising his honor.

"I will not deceive you," the old man added, with a faint insinuating smile, spreading out his hands, palms upward. "All of these things are a matter of public knowledge. I speak of them not to impress you, but so you will understand how it is that I interpret your chart. There is an art to these things as well as a science. Two men might make the very same calculations and read the aspects very differently. A truly gifted astromancer can detect patterns that escape an ordinary man, and even an ordinary astrologer. Moreover, there are bodies in the heavens, which wizards and great mages call the Hidden Stars, whose movements are unpredictable, whose patterns are constantly changing, not with the years or the seasons, but as harbingers of events below." He made a deprecating gesture. "But I should not lecture the son of the Goddess Ouriána. These stars, which it is not given to all men to see—"

"I understand you, I think," said Cuillioc, his eyes narrowing, the muscles in his jaws tightening. "And no doubt you will come to the point in your own good time."

Maelor took a deep breath; his thin frame seemed to expand with the intake of air. "If you go to Mirizandi, I see danger, it is true. There will be battle by land and by sea, and the slaughter will be tremendous. Also, there will be treachery. Look for a knife in every hand, for poison in every cup." As he continued to speak, a gradual change came over him. His dark eyes kindled; his face took on a new animation, and his voice grew stronger, deeper, filled with a strange music. He seemed many years younger, a vigorous man, confident in his powers.

"But after all these things have come to pass, I see for you a hero's ovation. I see a procession winding through the streets of Apharos, with many wagons draped in scarlet and gold. I see torches blazing, banners waving. Medals will be struck in your honor, bearing your likeness. The Empress, your divine mother, will stand on the steps of the Temple of the Moon and—"

"You might just easily be describing my funeral as my triumphant return," the Prince interrupted him. *"But which one is it?"*

Before his eyes, the magician seemed to dwindle, to grow dusty and vague again, a dim grey ghost of a man, as insubstantial as a dream or memory. The face fell in on itself, the cheeks hollowed, the grim line of the mouth grew softer. Only the glowing dark eyes remained the same, and the quiet, cold, powerful voice. "Do you truly care, Prince Cuillioc, whether it be the one or the other?"

Cuillioc sat back in his chair. He considered a moment; then he shook his head. "No, I don't believe that I *do* care," he said, surprising himself. His strong, nervous hands relaxed; some of the tension drained out of his face. He felt, somehow, curiously at peace. "So long as I return from Mirizandi a hero, it is all the same to me."

6

✳

All day, the two wizards lived with a prickly sensation across the skin, a persistent warning of present danger. Again and again, Sindérian's restless pacing took her up to the quarterdeck, where she scanned the ocean from horizon to horizon. Though her heart said danger, eyes and ears could perceive no threat; extend her senses as she might, there was never anything there to be seen but endless miles of bright blue water, and the V-shaped wake of the ship, like curdled buttermilk.

At sunset, they decided to take it in turns to keep watch through the night. While Faolein went below, Sindérian stood the first vigil, holding her father's wayward little wind on a tight leash, but otherwise passing the dark hours uneventfully. A little before dawn, Faolein reappeared, and together they watched a flush of color spread across the sky, the pale rim of the sun rise at the edge of the world. Then she went down to the cabin they shared in the hold of the ship, and tried to fall asleep.

Yet Sindérian found that she could not rest. Even after the long, quiet night, she felt threatened, uneasy. Whenever she closed her eyes, she saw other eyes looking back at her: sea-green and deadly cold, like pale, venomous moons. And every time she began to drift off, she startled back awake at the imagined sound of heavy breathing: a vast windy exhalation within the tiny confines of the cabin, smelling of dead fish and rotting seaweed.

Finally, she slid into a deep, oppressive sleep filled with unpleasant dreams.

———

Hours later, she woke in the dark with Faolein's shout echoing in her mind. Drowsy and disoriented, she levered herself into a sitting position. Somewhere up above, men were screaming, footsteps clattered across the deck. On all sides of her, timbers creaked and groaned, while the hull of the ship vibrated as though it must surely burst apart. And again—even more imperative than before—came the wizard's mind-shout: *Sindérian! We are under attack.*

She threw her legs over the side of the bunk, and, with her heart rattling in her chest, she groped her way across the cabin in the dark, pushed open the door, and entered the crew's quarters. There at least there was light, thanks to a half-burnt candle in a hanging tin lantern. An overturned bench, a tankard lying on its side in a pool of ale, a sea chest thrown open and its contents scattered across the floor, all spoke of a sudden alarm, followed by a hasty departure.

Weaving a hurried path through kegs, boxes, bales, and hammocks, Sindérian finally reached the ladder. A babble of voices—screams, shouts, frantic orders being relayed from man to man—came down the hatchway as she kilted up her skirts and scrambled from rung to rung. Even before she reached the top, she had an idea of what she would find. The air stank of blood and panic and the rank stench of some deep-sea creature.

She came out into the blazing midafternoon sunlight to find the decks awash with blood and broken bodies everywhere she looked.

———

Despite the wizard's vigilance, a great water dragon with eyes and horns of crystal had taken *Balaquendor* by surprise, rising from the depths, slithering up one side of the ship, and looping a section of its long, flexible body around the hull, almost before anyone had time to react. Men had scattered in search of weapons, calling out to their mates below, and Faolein's mind-shout sounded like a clap of thunder in his daughter's head. Then, constricting its snakelike body, the dragon began to squeeze the vessel until boards cracked, and the sea came rushing in. Sindérian arrived just in time to see the monster throw another coil around the ship.

It was nothing like she had dreamed it, being at once more beautiful and more deadly. Sun reflected off hard, glittering scales: steel-blue, amethyst, and silver, shading to mother-of-pearl below. Light dazzled off the pronounced ridges of its immense rib cage, shone through thin membranous fins all down its spine. It had pointed fishlike teeth, the color of old ivory, the smallest as long as Sindérian's hand, and a pale tongue that flickered in and out like a green flame. Around its neck, ancient wizards had placed a wide metal band, a collar forged of iron and bronze, etched with runes of power to keep it spellbound—but the runes had failed.

The ship gave another violent shudder. While Faolein frantically wove spells to keep the hull together, the water out, and the caravel from sinking, two men up on the quarterdeck armed themselves with bows and sent down a rain of arrows.

At the same time, Prince Ruan, his guards, and the remaining sailors attacked the monster with swords, knives, axes, clubs— anything that came to hand.

Linking minds with her father, Sindérian felt his *lledrion* take hold: shining strands of light and energy drew the broken timbers together and held them, slowing the leaks in the side to a mere trickle. Yet it took all of his thought and will to keep the ship from breaking apart faster than he could repair the damage; if he shifted his attention for even a moment, his spell would fail. Rather than distract him, Sindérian withdrew.

Dropping to her knees beside one of the bodies on the deck, running her hands hastily over him, she sensed a broken arm, a concussion, and massive internal injuries. The spark of life had been so nearly extinguished, for a moment she thought that he was gone. But dead men don't *bleed*, she reminded herself. And probing a little deeper she was able to detect an almost imperceptible flicker.

There was no time for the delicate joining of broken blood vessels, the careful knitting of flesh and bone; what Sindérian did instead was simple, crude, and temporary—but under her hands the life force flared up, the sailor groaned, blinked his eyes, and mumbled a question.

"Stay there. Don't move, or you'll begin to bleed again," she tossed over her shoulder as she stumbled to her feet and staggered for balance. "I'll come back to you when I can."

The dragon's wedge-shaped head was weaving from side to side on its long, sinewy neck, and the great tail lashed back and forth across the deck between the masts, making it dangerous to cross. The boards under her feet were slick with blood and seawater. At the sight of a man sprawled unconscious or lifeless on the planks only a dozen feet from the place where she stood, Sindérian felt caution fall away. With reckless determination, she made up her mind that she would somehow find a way to reach him. She waited until one of the Prince's guards engaged the monster's attention by slashing at its head in a blur of motion, then she ducked under the thick muscular tail and flung herself down beside the man on the deck.

He was already dead—had almost certainly died instantly, for his neck had snapped, and his head was battered beyond recognition.

Sindérian felt a sickening sensation of guilt wash over her. *I wished to go back into battle,* she reflected bitterly, *but a wizard should* always *be careful of her thoughts. Did I, somehow, cause this to happen?*

Yet she knew that to entertain these fears was worse than futile. Let a wizard start blaming herself for everything wrong that happened in her vicinity, and she soon became useless, too frightened to do anything at all, and ultimately a danger to herself. So she had been taught by her masters at the Scholia, and so experience had taught her since.

She rose to her feet, scolding herself for her momentary weakness. *The monsters of the deep don't come at your beck and call, Sindérian, nor the Tides of Fortune flow at your command. Don't make yourself more* important *than you are.* Still, the impression that she was to blame lingered like a thorn beneath the flesh, too painful to be ignored.

Over by the mainmast, a sailor failed to move quickly enough. The mighty tail swept him across the deck and crushed him against the bulwarks.

Meanwhile, Prince Ruan and the guardsman Tuillo were in the very thick of the battle. As the dragon's head weaved from side to side, jaws snapping, they both rushed in with their broadswords.

Grasping the hilt of his sword with both hands, Ruan slashed downward, felt the blade connect and cut through the glittering hide, only to glance off the bone below. The huge head recoiled, laid back its ears, and hissed, then came hurtling down in his direction. He threw himself back and to the left, just in time to avoid being gutted by the jagged ivory teeth. Beside him, Tuillo swung an overhead cut at the extended neck, striking just behind the skull; there was a trickle of dark red blood, smelling strongly of seawater, but nothing more. Ruan realized they were doing the monster little damage, and only dulling their swords.

"The eyes," he shouted over the din. *"Try for the eyes."*

Tuillo nodded grimly and reached for his dagger, just as the Prince reached for his. They sprang from either side at the same moment, stabbing at the crystalline eyes. Ruan felt his dagger connect; there was a sound like shattering glass, and his blade broke, but the eye went dark, and more of the thick red blood came dribbling out.

Tuillo was less fortunate. His stroke just missed, his dagger skidded off the slick, scaly hide, and his own impetus continued to carry him forward. Trying to recover his balance, he slipped in someone's blood, fell to the deck and hit his head, and lay there stunned.

Even as Ruan rushed to his defense, the dragon's head came down, and its wide mouth closed around Tuillo's armored torso. There was a horrid sound of teeth grinding against metal links as the monster lifted the guardsman off the slippery boards, whipped him through the air like a terrier worrying a rat, and flung him against one of the masts. His body hit the oaken spar with bone-crushing force, then slid down to the deck.

In the moment of shock that followed, Ruan heard Sindérian's voice speaking urgently behind him. "Behind the ear. There is an old story: Prince Revin of Alluinn killed a water dragon once, by driving his spear into a soft spot behind the ear. I don't know if the story is true, but—"

The Prince had already heard enough, and he knew what he must do. Dropping his dagger, he caught one of the ratlines and pulled himself up. Climbing swiftly and agilely, he went halfway up the rigging, then was forced to hang there while the battle continued below, waiting for just the right moment to jump.

Seeing his chance at last, he leapt from the ropes and landed soft-footed on the broad triangular head, reaching out to grasp one of the curved horns just in time to keep from being thrown off. Then, tossing his sword into the air to reverse his grip, he caught the hilt and drove the point downward, just behind the dragon's fan-shaped ear. The blade went in only an inch or two, then stuck fast, and would go no farther.

Shifting his footing, Ruan released his grip on the horn, took his sword in both hands, and threw the full weight of his body forward, driving the blade in all the way to the hilt. The monster bellowed, flung its head back, and Ruan felt himself flying through the air.

He hit the water with a loud splash some twenty yards from the ship and only narrowly missed being caught by the lashing tail as the dragon lost its grip on *Balaquendor* and landed in the ocean beside him.

Though a strong swimmer, the Prince was barely able to stay afloat as the monster beat the water into a bloody froth with its convulsions, then sank beneath the waves.

The tumult of battle was over, but the air rang with the sound of hammers, and the smell of burning pitch was everywhere, as the men made temporary repairs to the ship.

Sindérian knelt on the deck beside the battered body of the guardsman Tuillo, desperately trying to stop the bleeding. For every blood vessel she repaired there was always another and another requiring her attention, and despite her increasingly frantic exertions the life went leaking out of him so quickly she could not keep up. At last his heart gave a final, feeble flutter and stopped beating altogether.

Why she should doggedly keep on after all hope faded, she did not know. Perhaps it was a lingering sense of guilt and shame, the fear that some careless wish of hers had brought this thing about. When a light hand fell on her shoulder, a quiet voice spoke in her ear, it was a long time before the meaning of Prince Ruan's words finally penetrated.

"You can't call back the dead. You have labored most heroically on his behalf, but there is no use going on."

Looking up at him, Sindérian drew in her breath; a flush of anger passed over her. She had blood on her hands and on her gown; her dark hair was sticky with it; she was weary, sweating, bedraggled. Yet the Prince had somehow found the time to remove his wet tunic and braid back his damp hair; in shirt, hose, long cloak, and high boots, he looked none the worse for his dip in the ocean.

"This man's life may mean little to you," she said, in a voice shaking with anger. "There will be others, I suppose, eager to take his place in your Honor Guard, men of no name or importance ready to serve the High King's grandson—"

"You are mistaken," Ruan answered softly. "I knew this

man's name very well and what his life was. He had a wife and a family, and a farm near Pentheirie. His oldest daughter is named Fearn, and she's to be married this summer at Hafentide. Tuillo hoped to return in time to see her wed, and I promised him—" For a moment, the Prince's voice wavered, then it and his jewel-bright gaze steadied. "But dead is dead, and there are others here who have need of your skills."

One of the two surviving guardsmen, the one called Aell, offered her a rough, callused hand. Sindérian took it, rose stiffly to her feet, and looked around her with dull eyes. At least a dozen men with bruised and broken limbs were lying on the deck or sitting propped up against the masts; everywhere she looked she saw faces sick with horror or drawn with pain.

She tried to swallow, but her mouth was dry, tried to stop the shaking of her own limbs, but found that she could not. It was true: she had drained herself to no good purpose, and now she had less than enough to give to those still in need. *Did I learn nothing at all in Rheithûn?* she wondered.

An unreasoning resentment flared up inside of her: against the world at large, against herself—most of all, and by far the least reasonable—against the silver-haired young man standing before her, flanked by his guardsmen.

Sindérian swept him an unsteady curtsy, spoke to him between clenched teeth. "I thank you, Prince Ruan, for teaching me my duty."

They prepared the dead for burial at sea, after the custom of Thäerie and the Lesser Isles: bathing them first with sweet waters, placing packets of silk-wrapped earth next to their hearts, then sewing the bodies up in canvas shrouds.

Sindérian took no part in these rituals. She went below to wash off the blood and change her gown, and returned in time for the funeral, standing stiff-shouldered and mute while the Master spoke solemn words over his own men, the Prince over Tuillo. She did not join in the *eirias* after, and turned abruptly aside and went back down to her cabin as the bodies were tipped over the rail and consigned to the deep.

After the funeral was over, the Prince and Faolein climbed the ladder up to the quarterdeck and spoke for a long time apart from the others.

"We will never make it as far as Skyrra," said Ruan. "Can we even make it as far as Hythe?" Though outwardly cool and composed, he could feel his heart still beating strongly, his nerves tightly strung, like those of a man on the verge of battle. But where was the threat? Not anywhere that he could see.

"We will land at Tregna, in Mere," the wizard answered. "It is the nearest port. In a storm, these makeshift repairs would never hold, nor could my daughter and I work the weather and keep the hull together with our spells at the same time."

It was a bright blue afternoon of sun and soft wind. The deck swayed gently under their feet; a cloudless sky tilted overhead. It was hard to imagine a spell of bad weather on such a day, but the Thäerian Sea was prone to freakish gales, as Ruan knew very well.

He made a wry face. "And so we are forced to land in Mere—where the Duke keeps faith with no one and plays all sides at once—where otherwise we should never have ventured at all." He felt an uneasy stir of suspicion; his frown deepened. "It seems to me that the sudden appearance of this water dragon was almost too convenient. Can we really be certain that our enemy didn't free the creature, break the spell that held it sleeping, and send it to follow and attack our ship?"

"Sea serpents and water dragons and all such creatures are utterly lawless. No one can tame them, no one can predict where they will go or what they will do," Faolein replied in his calm, gentle voice. But a fine line appeared on his high white forehead: there was something tense and watchful in his lean, stooped figure. "Phaôrax is an island the same as Thäerie, the same as Leal. Ouriána has no more desire to fill the seas with monsters than we do."

Ruan pondered that for several minutes—a loose strand of silver hair blowing across his face, his turquoise eyes narrowed against the light—considering all the implications. "*To fill the seas with monsters.*" He repeated the words slowly, thoughtfully. "But how *many* such creatures could there possibly be?"

"According to legend, the greatest of all wizards, Mallion Penn, bound six hundred and ten dragons to the ocean floor with his spells. His brother Coall accounted for one hundred sea serpents, as well as nearly a dozen great monsters that even his fellow magicians did not know how to name. Meanwhile, the other wizards of Alluinn—"

But then (remembering, perhaps, that these were only the tales of minstrels and storytellers, not written histories) Faolein shrugged. "It's likely the numbers have been exaggerated over the years. And though the creatures live longer than wizards, longer even than your kinsmen among the Faey, they are not immortal. Some of them *must* have died during the long years of their captivity.

"For all that," he said, sliding his hands into the sleeves of his long purple robe, gazing out across the water, "there could be hundreds of them, even thousands of them."

7

✳

Two days later, they limped into the harbor at Tregna and docked at a weather-beaten pier south of the port, where the waves broke white against massive piles of rotting oak.

Those on deck had already spied three sleek black galleys of thirty or more oars, ominous with red sails and banners of crimson and sable, in among the great merchant cogs and carracks and three-masted round ships at the busier quays to the north. They might not have docked at all, but for the fear they had already been spotted entering the mouth of the bay. To turn back *then* would have aroused suspicion, and battered and patched as she was, *Balaquendor* had no hope of escape if the galleys pursued her.

Ruan and the two wizards met by lanternlight in his cabin to discuss their situation. Sindérian sat on the bed, wrapped up in her cloak against the dank chill of the leaky hold, while Faolein and the Prince studied a map spread out on a chest between them. It was a rough map of the coastal duchies and principalities, sketched out by the wizard from memory—not to be absolutely relied on, he said, for he had last traveled in these realms as a young man more than a hundred years ago.

"Repairs to the ship will take too long, and we dare not sit here waiting to be noticed by those on the Pharaxion galleys," said Faolein. "We never intended an overland journey, but it seems we have little choice now. It will be lengthy and arduous, no doubt, and not without danger, perhaps. Yet the sooner begun the sooner ended."

The Prince nodded grimly. He slid his dagger from its sheath, traced out a route on Faolein's map with the point. "It will be at least a four days' ride north to the border—and that's with good roads and good weather. Then, I suppose, we turn immediately east and head across Hythe to the Cadmin Aernan."

In the passage outside, there was a stir of movement. Faolein's gaze flickered briefly in that direction, but it was only the two guardsmen keeping watch against any intrusion. "I had far rather head east from Tregna, and so come sooner to the mountains. There could be some delay crossing the border into Hythe, and even if not—" He hesitated, then went on with a faint air of apology, "Even if not, I do not quite like the idea of putting ourselves in the hands of your kinsman, Prince Bael."

Ruan's strange eyes widened in surprise. "Bael is a fool, but he holds to the Alliance. Whereas the Duke of Mere—"

"The Duke of Mere knows nothing of where we are going or what we intend to do there. Hythe *does know,* and may even await our coming, hoping some mischance will bring us his way. Mere with his uncertain loyalties worries me less than Hythe and Weye in their reckless zeal. A man may serve the Dark, Prince Ruan, and never suspect that he does so."

An incredulous smile played across Ruan's face; he looked at the wizard, at Sindérian, then back at Faolein. "What is it you imagine that Bael would do to us? Or, more to the point, I suppose, *try to make us do,* if we were in his power?"

"There is no saying what Prince Bael might expect of us. It is bad enough when our enemies take us by surprise, but when it is our friends who prove unpredictable and untrustworthy—" He shook his head dolefully. "It seems that we can't avoid a journey across Mere, either north or east, but we *can* choose not to risk Hythe as well, and that is what I advise."

Though still unconvinced, Ruan declined to argue more. He had not spent much of his youth under Eliduc's tutelage without learning that a wizard's instincts sometimes took him where reason might not follow: nevertheless, those instincts were not to be ignored, nor a wizard's words lightly set aside.

In the morning, they prepared to go ashore.

"It would be better," said Faolein to the Prince, "if until we reach Skyrra you went by some other name, or by one of your lesser titles." He had already discarded his purple robes, replacing them with nondescript garments of earth-brown and russet; now he traded his long carven staff of yew wood banded with silver for a shorter one of oak with a bone handle, such as any old man might carry.

"I shall be the Lord of Penraeth," said Ruan, after a moment of thought. "That's a small holding on the west of Thäerie, which nobody here will know anything about."

In leather breeches and silver mail, with his long fair hair hanging loose behind and braided in front, warrior fashion, there was little in his dress to set him apart from the guardsmen Aell and Jago, except for a cloak of fine soft wool dyed the brilliant blue of a summer sky and a slender golden torc that he wore on his neck. Just before they had parted, his grandfather had provided him with a heavy purse filled with gold and silver, and the amber and ivory used as money in the north, for there was no telling what expenses they might meet with along the way. This purse he gave into the wizard's keeping before he left the cabin.

———

Tregna, in Mere, is a grey old town, crouched behind massive dikes and breakwaters of stone and clay, which hold back the sea during a high tide. Yet it is nearly impossible to pass through Tregna dry-shod: water wells up between cobbles in the streets, makes brackish rills of all the gutters, trickles under wooden walkways. Along the noisy waterfront, peddlers hawk boning knives, fishhooks, and string; scrimshaw, trinkets made of whalebone and shell; and baskets of clams or live eels. The houses are built of sun-bleached planks, and the nets of the fishermen make a canopy of light and shadow overhead, where the fishwives string them from house to house to dry.

In those days, Tregna, like other towns in Mere, had a mixed population: Men in great numbers; tiny, claw-footed Gnomes; and a thriving colony of full- and half-blooded Faey. Sinderian saw many of these Faey as she crossed the slippery stones down by the breakwaters, heading for the town: white-skinned and yellow-eyed, with fine, flowing hair of ivory or silver gilt, and delicate, birdlike bones. Few even of the half-bloods were as tall as Prince Ruan. He walked right past them as if unseeing, and none of them looked at him.

While Faolein, Jago, and Aell went off to buy horses, waterskins, saddles, and all of the other things they would need, Sindérian and the Prince stopped in one of the fishy dockside taverns to gather what news they could.

In the low-ceilinged taproom, windowless and smoky, Sindérian sat down on a narrow bench scarred with the names and initials of previous visitors, and glanced around her. Already, the tavern was crowded, though the hour was still early. The air reeked of herring, onions, pipeweed, and unwashed bodies, but under all else she detected the unmistakable stench of fear. The conversation on every side of her was loud and profane, with much laughter, yet the laughter was false and much too shrill— and if nobody mentioned the Pharaxion galleys at rest by the quays, Sindérian guessed there was not a man present but knew they were there.

Loudest of all was a group of Men by the bar, in shabby cloaks, out-at-elbow tunics, and worn-looking boots. They wore random bits of armor, unpolished and beginning to show rust, and some had great swords hanging from belts or leather baldrics marked with the Duke's badge of the armored fist.

Soldiers, she thought, *recently released from their lord's service, with no place to go and no way to keep themselves.* Their faces were lean and hungry, the bones too prominent, and the eyes wary; though their part in the war was apparently over, nobody seemed to know what would happen next.

Over oatcakes, green pears, and a thin young wine, Sindérian asked Prince Ruan if he had kinsmen in the town. "Is there anyone here," she asked, lowering her voice, "who might possibly know you?"

His face hardened; he linked his fingers around the stem of his cup, and his knuckles showed pale in the gloom. "The Faey you see here are Ni-Ferys—they have *nothing* to do with me," he answered coldly. "My mother is of the Ni-Féa."

A short while later, when one of the Merian Faeys chanced to pass too close on his way to the bar, there was an immediate and instinctive reaction on both sides—a flaring of nostrils, a flash of bared teeth—so that Sindérian was reminded of two lean white cats, bristling and spitting their defiance.

Just after *erién,* the noon hour, Faolein pushed his way through the crowd and came to their table. Supplies, he told them, had been easily if not cheaply obtained. "Whether there are shortages or not I can't say, but prices are so inflated that few can buy, and our Thäerian gold was readily accepted." When Sindérian and the Prince followed him outside, they found Aell and Jago minding five good horses and a pair of pack mules.

For Sindérian, her father had purchased a bay mare and a lady's sidesaddle. Gathering up her heavy dark skirts, she was preparing to mount, when Prince Ruan appeared at her side, holding out a hand sheathed in a grey leather gauntlet.

"I know that you have often traveled with an army," he said, as he helped her into the saddle. "But here there will be no wagons—no other women—not any of the things to which you are accustomed. I wonder," he added, with a glinting smile, "if you regret that you came?"

She gave him a sparkling glance of defiance under her dusky veil. "I am not so poor a creature as you seem to think," she said, taking up the reins. "And if you, Lord, can put aside your titles and your silks and velvets, and take no harm from it, it is likely that *I* can survive as well."

On the outskirts of town, they rode past a large and prosperous-looking inn, three stories high with stables and a garden, behind low stone walls. The yard was full of stamping horses under the lime trees; men in black armor with traceries of silver and bronze stood in a knot by the door; and a troop of harried, baggage-laden servants ran back and forth between the horses and the covered porch. It was, to all appearances, a nobleman's party, about to embark on a long journey.

But riding past the gateway, Faolein felt a chill pass over his skin. He reached out and touched Sindérian lightly on the arm, directing her attention to a gaunt white-haired figure, booted and spurred and cloaked for travel, who was just crossing the yard and moving toward the stables. A vagrant gust of wind billowed the cloak of rich wine-colored brocade; there was a flash of scarlet beneath, and a thin hand covered with shining silver scales reached out to grasp an edge of cloth and pull it back again. On every knuckle of that hand were rings of hard metal.

Very slowly, and apparently without seeing them, the head turned their way. Faolein knew that dead white face, with its heavy jaw, hawk nose, and barren eyes—and Sindérian knew it, too. He heard her sudden harsh intake of breath; saw her hands tighten convulsively on the reins; but she said nothing. Nor did Faolein, until they had pounded over an arched wooden bridge and left the town behind.

Then, just out of sight of the houses, if not of the smoke that hovered over the rooftops, he called a brief halt. The other men drew up their horses in a circle around him, while he told them what he and his daughter had seen. "One of the Furiádhin, in Tregna. Whether he is on the way to Skyrra as we are it is impossible to say. But if he is . . . we are only a little ahead of him."

Sindérian had gone as pale as wax; her voice trembled with anger and loathing. "It was Goezenou—little chance that I wouldn't recognize him, having seen him lead armies so often in Rheithûn. They say he is the cruelest of all the Furiádhin, and that he was the one who ordered the slaughter at Gilaefri."

Ruan and the men-at-arms exchanged fierce, eager glances. The horses, scenting their excitement, danced in place. "How many with him?" asked the Prince, only just managing to keep his restive roan stallion under control.

"Some eight or ten that I saw in the yard," answered Faolein. "Perhaps more inside the stable or the inn. And I caution you, Lord, that we are not at home here. We have no right to break the Duke's peace without provocation."

The guards looked crestfallen, and the Prince gave an angry laugh as he tugged at the reins.

"Then let us go swiftly," he said, wheeling the stallion about, casting a savage look back the way they had come. "If we are not to fight them, let us at least make haste to reach Skyrra first."

They rode all through that afternoon, in the soft light of a fine spring day. The sky overhead was high and cloudless, but there was a thin haze to the west, turning the sun the color of a ripe apricot. Because nothing further happened to threaten or disturb them, they camped that night under the stars, continuing the next day at a more comfortable pace.

On either side of the road there were wet green fields; little rills and streamlets, waterways choked with reeds; ditches alive with muskrats and voles; and silver pools and lakes, scattered like coins across the countryside. Sometimes, the level of the land sank beneath the water into marshland, then the road continued as a mighty stone causeway. Frogs sang in the bulrushes; great flocks of white birds startled up out of the high grasses as the horses passed by.

Wherever there was higher ground—a steep embankment, an upswelling hillside—there always seemed to be a tiny village or isolated manor house, seldom more than a handful of buildings, a garden patch, and some pens for the animals. The country folk of Mere, said Faolein, lived largely by fishing and fowling. This was not good country for farming.

Occasionally, they passed, off in the distance, a shapeless heap of stone and rubble, marking some ruined city or castle. Many had fallen during the Change, the wizard explained, but no few had been destroyed by the earthquakes that rocked this region at every full moon.

In the early evening, they stopped to rest and water the horses by a narrow stream running swift between large mossy stones. Some old bent trees, willows and alders, grew on the bank, trailing their hair in the water, and there Sindérian threw off her veil and knelt in the green shade to wash the dust from her face and hands.

With the others, she made a cold supper of bread and cheese, washed down with water from the brook. Aell and Jago sat a little apart, keeping watch on the road. By the time they had finished eating, the shadows of the trees lay long on the grass, and the sun had disappeared behind a hill to the west.

"It will soon be night," said Ruan. "But the moon is already up, and waxing near to full. Surely after the horses have rested we can keep on for several hours more."

Yet the hour was so peaceful, no one felt inclined to move. Sindérian wondered if the others felt as miserably stiff and sore as she did, after such a long ride yesterday, a longer ride today. As she sat trying to knead the pain out of a muscle in her calf through the folds of her skirt, she could not even remember the last time she had spent so many hours in the saddle. However long it was, she thought glumly, she paid a heavy toll now in aches and pains.

A flock of birds flew overhead, dark against the reddening

sky, and as the shadow of their wings passed over, two of the horses squealed and pulled at their pickets.

Ruan's head came suddenly up; his nose wrinkled, and his lip curled as though he, like the horses, caught a whiff of some unpleasant odor that eluded the others. The flock wheeled in a great circle, hanging briefly silhouetted against the round yellow face of the moon, and the Prince sprang to his feet, calling out a warning. "Wyvaerun—*and they have seen us!*"

He and his guards all drew steel; the wizard reached for his staff. The horses stamped and whinnied their alarm. Sindérian darted looks in all directions, seeking some weapon with which to arm herself, something more effective than her small ivory-handled eating knife.

But it was already too late. With thin piercing shrieks, the wyvaerun descended: black wings beating, iron beaks and claws slashing, scaly tails glittering in the ruddy light of sunset. A creature the size of an eagle died on the point of Acll's blade; Jago beheaded another. Prince Ruan's sword flashed in the dusky air, accounting for two with a single stroke, and Faolein's staff burst into flame. For a moment, the wyvaerun bated and rose, hovering overhead, but then they attacked with redoubled fury.

Raking talons struck at Sindérian's face; she ducked to avoid them, and flung up her knife to ward off the next attack. But somehow, Prince Ruan and his sword were between her and the wyvaerun, reducing the creature to a heap of oily feathers and bloody scales. "For the Light's sake, keep *down,*" he hissed at her furiously. "A blade that size is no use at all." Then he turned his back on her and killed two more of the hybrids.

Remembering, suddenly, the stream nearby, Sindérian slid down the grassy bank to the water's edge. Bending low, she snatched up small stones from the shallow streambed, sent them whistling through the air with a spell of true-aiming. Four of her missiles struck home, killing two wyvaerun, and disabling two more.

But as she reached for another stone, there was a storm of wings overhead, and steely claws fastened in her hair and cloak. Struggling to pull herself free, she felt herself lifted off the grass and into the air. And there she hung suspended, panic drumming in her blood, for what seemed like hours—six feet—eight feet—a dozen feet above the ground, with wings beating like thunder all around her, the musty serpentine odor of the hybrid filling her throat and lungs, and the wyvaerun, laboring under her added weight, striving to rise higher and still higher—

Until Faolein's flaming staff flew like a meteor through the night air and struck the creature dead. Sindérian heard the creature's dying shriek, like rending metal, at the same moment the claws lost their grip; and she felt herself falling, helpless to stop her sudden descent.

Then she hit the earth with such bruising force that the wind was knocked out of her and the world went dark.

8

✳

On the night before the day he was to sail for Mirizandi, Prince Cuillioc was vexed and troubled by a remarkably vivid and unpleasing dream.

For it seemed to him, as he drifted off to sleep in his great silver bed, that a nightmare—a little wizened bat-winged creature with basilisk eyes and tiny wrinkled hands—flew in through a high, arched window and sat gibbering atop one of the bedposts for all the long hours between midnight and dawn.

There was little of sense to be gained from its rambling discourse, which climbed the scale from hysteria to delirium. Yet every now and again, as it chattered and stammered, while Cuillioc lay helpless and motionless under the brocade coverings and the silken canopy—unable to speak, to stir, to wake— he seemed to divine some secret, sinister meaning mixed in with all the nonsense. At cockcrow, the creature vanished. Released from its spell, the Prince sat up in bed, all quaking and sweating, threw off the bedclothes, and called for light.

The house slaves came in, soft-footed across the tile floors, bearing flaming torches dipped in scented oils to perfume the air. They offered him potions and cordials to drive off the night-fears, brought him heated water in a malachite bowl. He sent them all away, muffled himself up in a great cloak, and went out to the balcony that opened from his bedchamber, to watch the sun rise over Apharos.

The air was cool and very clear; as intoxicating sweet as wine. This was the one time of day when Ouriána's capital was touched by beauty: the thorny towers and dagger-pointed obelisks burning crimson and gold, the tangled maze of lanes and alleys flooded with a warm orange light. On the rooftops and upper ledges of the great houses the stone monsters stretched their gilded wings as if poised to take flight; and, a mile to the south, that greater monstrosity which was the New Temple glittered with rare jewel-like colors. It was as though a kindly spell lay, however briefly, over Apharos—a transformation that seldom failed to raise Prince Cuillioc's spirits. But the horror of the dream was still on him, cold serpents of fear still writhed in his belly, and it would have taken more than the sight of his city flaming into sudden beauty to raise the oppression that weighed on him.

It was more than a hundred feet from the balcony where Cuillioc watched the sunrise to the hard dark stones of the courtyard below—and another hundred to a grove of wind-bent olives and plane trees below that—and a hundred more to the base of the cliffs, where the sea boiled white between jagged rocks. For the palace at Apharos is built upon a rocky spit of land, surrounded on three sides by water during a high tide. Nine great towers of rough-hewn dark marble perch on the heights, with gardens and orchards, groves, fountains, vine-yards, and bowers descending in terraces on the south, east, and west, all enclosed within a mighty curtain wall shimmering with plates of beaten gold. It was built (some say) in imitation of that ancient citadel, now in ruins, which once stood at Ceir Eldig, the City of Princes, in Alluinn.

At that hour, every sound seemed magnified: the pounding of the surf, the beating of his own blood, the shrill morning chorus of blackbirds in the grove below. Then a party of horsemen came riding round the curve of the bay from the harbor, passed through the gate of ivory and horn, and clattered through the stony streets. From Cuillioc's vantage point on the balcony, he could just make out their colors of lavender and purple, though he was unable to recognize the devices. Nevertheless, their very haste was ominous. Remembering his dream, he felt another stir of apprehension; his hand closed hard on the marble railing.

They disappeared from view behind the bulk of the hill; moments later, he heard armored fists hammering on the palace gate. Someone replied faintly from within. While the Prince strained to hear, words were exchanged, questions asked and answered. Then he heard timbers scraping, iron hinges creaking as the gate swung open, followed by the clamor of ironshod hooves on flagstones as the men rode through.

He was eating a halfhearted breakfast—spiced wine and honeycakes and small yellow grapes—when the summons arrived. A page in Ouriána's livery stumbled through the doorway and out onto the balcony, breathless after the climb. The boy wheezed out a message: the Empress would see Prince Cuillioc.

Springing up from his seat, Cuillioc brushed past the messenger. He entered his torchlit bedchamber, calling out for shaving water, his sword, his boots— He dressed swiftly, turning aside all offers of assistance. There was no time for ceremony. This early audience was almost without precedent, and he feared that something had occurred to arouse his mother's displeasure.

Buckling on his sword belt, he left the room, took the long spiral staircase to the ground floor, and emerged in a shadowy courtyard. The walls were so high, there were places where the sun rarely came; aconite, toadstool, mousefoot, and other strange funguses flourished in the damp shade. He followed a mossy pathway, passed through an avenue of yew and dark cypress struggling toward the sunlight, and came at last to the massive block of the central tower, which he entered through a high, narrow door.

Despite the early hour, large groups of courtiers and officials had gathered in the wide corridors, looking interested and excited. Their garments, of silk and cloth of silver, of velvets cunningly embroidered, displayed the new heraldry that honored the Empress, and was therefore watery and lunar: crabs, crayfish, clamshells, lymphads, the moon in all her phases, fish, eels, crocodiles. The hues were reds and purples, golds and oranges, sable and grey, a heraldry of subtle shadings, of intricate devices displayed on seal rings and brooches, on the borders of garments, stitched color on color—a heraldry of the court, meant to be appreciated at close quarters, not for the battlefield, where they all wore Ouriána's colors and fought under her banner.

As Cuillioc strode past, he heard voices rise to a greater pitch of excitement, saw faces avid with curiosity turn his way. He did not stop to learn what it was all about—yet again his stomach clenched tight with apprehension; a cold sweat came out on his skin.

Outside the audience chamber, he paused for a moment to catch his breath and steady himself. If something had occurred to make his sailing impossible—if the Empress had decided to replace him as commander of the expedition—but no, he had done *nothing* these last weeks that could have possibly displeased her; there was no way he could have fallen even further from favor than he already was. Yet his pulse pounded, and his palms grew slick with sweat as he entered the immense chamber, walked past the guards, and passed between long rows of pearl-encrusted pillars leading up to the dais.

Ouriána's lovely face was blank, unreadable, as Cuillioc threw himself down kneeling on the top step, and she gave him, at arm's length, her cool white hand.

"Empress and Goddess," he whispered, around the constriction in his throat. He pressed her long, smooth fingers reverently to his lips, then released them. "Have I offended?"

There was a pause before she answered—hardly more than the pause between breath and breath, though it seemed to Cuillioc to last an age. As always, he was tremulous and amazed, as men must be in the presence of a goddess, even her own sons— almost afraid to look at her, for the dread of what he might see. It was a fearful thing to be the son of a divinity and mere mortal clay himself.

At last, turning away with a little disdainful shrug, she said, "Your brother Guindeluc conquered nine cities for me before he died, but what have *you* done? *You have lost me Quirabon!*"

Cuillioc's head came up abruptly. His eyes met hers: greener than his own, with golden lights, and velvety-dark lashes. Not a line, not a blemish marred the smooth perfection of her skin, which glowed faintly in the dim chamber; yet looking into those eyes one could guess at her age; they held too much knowledge, too much experience. Oceans existed in her gaze, vast seas filled with living things: fish and whales, turtles, porpoises, eels, rays, and sinuous sea worms.

"It was I who *took* Quirabon," he said, stumbling over the words, though at last he understood what news the horsemen brought with them at dawn: the great city he had gained after a long, bitter siege seven months ago had changed hands once more. He felt himself go cold with shame at the realization he had disappointed her again.

Ouriána sat down on her throne, which was decorated with seashells and coral, with bits of carved whalebone and silvery freshwater pearls. Her gown was of velvet, the luminous yellow-gold of the harvest moon; and gemstones—opals and moonstones and pearls—glittered in the heavy coils of her rich auburn hair. There was a sweet, almost cloying scent about her, which dizzied and confused him, making him think of strange hothouse flowers opening their white fleshy petals, or of bright many-tentacled anemones swaying in mermaid gardens under the sea.

And just as it always did, her beauty wounded him like a knife, but crueler still was the edged contempt in her voice, in her words. "It was because you gave too easy terms when Lord Deryx surrendered that he and his men were able to take the city back."

Where he had been cold before, the Prince felt himself blushing hotly. And the words came tumbling out before he could stop them. "They were *honorable* terms. If we expect our foes to deal honorably with us—"

"They were *generous* terms. You must learn, my son, that there is no place for generosity in war. Had Deryx and his sons been executed—or sent here to Phaôrax prisoners, as Guindeluc might have done it—we should have avoided another long, bloody, and wasteful battle. And so, for that matter, had the unfortunate people of Quirabon. Sometimes, one must be cruel to be kind."

Cuillioc felt himself flushing even more painfully than before; he started to speak, but the words withered on his tongue. There was nothing that he *could* say, for he knew that she spoke the truth: Guindeluc had had his chivalrous impulses, too—all the world spoke of his magnanimity, his open-handed noble courtesy—but he had always tempered that with wisdom and foresight. Lacking these qualities, Cuillioc's attempts to emulate the brother he worshiped almost invariably fell short and produced some disaster.

He remained on his knees, heartsick and shaken, waiting for his mother to speak the words that would crush his hopes. And he was suddenly aware that they were not alone. Two Furiádhin stood about twenty feet from the dais, grim, ghostly, and powerful in their crimson robes, flanked by a half-dozen acolytes in sooty black cloaks. They had not been there when he first entered the room.

Ouriána raised her hand, and one of the priests mounted the steps with a rustle of scarlet silk. There were those who could hardly tell the creatures apart, who found them, in spite of their deformities, confusingly identical, with their bone-white faces and cloudy hair. But Cuillioc was not of that number, he knew them each one. He knew *this* one particularly well, one who dogged his mother's footsteps on all occasions.

"If you are an *honorable fool,* you brother Meriasec is an overconfident one," the Empress told her son coldly. "There is not much to choose between you, if the truth were known. But now that Guindeluc is gone, you are the eldest—therefore my heir. It would not be wise to show a lack of faith in you; that might give our enemies too much to hope for. You will go to

Mirizandi as I had originally planned, and you will retain the command. However, I am going to send an . . . advisor . . . with you. One on whom you may utterly rely for wise counsel, given without flattery or fear." She turned, then, toward the priest. "Can you be ready to sail at the change of the tide this evening?"

The furiádh prostrated himself before the throne. Cuillioc jumped to his feet and stood scowling down at him. "*Iobhar?* If you must send someone, why not Camhóinhann?"

"Camhóinhann serves me best where he is. Should I recall him from his vital work elsewhere to suit your whim?" she said. As the priest rose gracefully to his feet, between Ouriána and her votary there passed a look, sudden, then gone; but Cuillioc saw it, and his heart sank. "Surely you can have no objection to Iobhar . . . or to *anyone else* I might decide to send with you."

The Prince could only bow his head, biting his lip almost until the blood came, for it was plain that the matter had already been settled.

⁂

In the late afternoon, the Prince and his household went down to the courtyard outside the stables, where their horses were saddled and waiting. A pair of glossy black ravens settled on an archway, and watched with wicked yellow eyes as they rode out the gate.

On his high-mettled silver stallion, Cuillioc moved through the complex maze of the city, going by chosen byways and streets less crowded and dirty. He rode in a brooding silence, looking neither to left or right, his mind much occupied with his dream. Some instinct told him there was a connection between his nightmare and the ambiguous prophecies of the old madman, Maelor.

Look for a knife in every hand, poison in every cup, so said Maelor. Such were the stock phrases of the mountebank, as the Prince knew very well, trite and familiar. In this case, however, they rang true.

Many of the lords who would sail with the fleet were men whom he could not trust. But that was nothing. There were only a handful in all Apharos that he *did* trust, and all were members of his own household. Men of honor, men of courage, men of integrity, the war had claimed far too many of them over the years, and those few who had survived were scattered across the map, fighting Ouriána's battles, governing conquered cities. And from the horde of petty schemers who made up her court, men of large ambitions and small talents, the Empress had chosen a half dozen, no better or worse than the rest, to accompany her son. Knowing them for what they were, he would be on his guard: but he did not fear any of them as he feared the priest, Iobhar.

The Furiádhin had strange powers. Riding toward the harbor, under the baleful gaze of snakes and gargoyles, Cuillioc considered what he knew of Ouriána's warrior-priests. They were no longer quite human. For the lame, the sick, the deformed, a man ought to feel compassion, but the Furiádhin had *chosen* to be as they were, had *made* themselves monstrous.

Yet, the Prince thought confusedly, by doing so they served the Empress. Certain magics had their price, and her priests paid that price so that Ouriána—goddess though she was, imprisoned in a mortal body—need not pay it, ever.

But, he reminded himself, *they also served their* own *ambitions, their own hunger for power.* Only Camhóinhann, the High Priest, was free of that taint, and over the years Cuillioc's boyhood infatuation, his admiration for that great and tragic figure, had gradually waned. Camhóinhann, too, was a monster, though a splendid one, a glorious one. The other eight—those of the original twelve who were left after the disaster in the Cadmin Aernan nineteen years ago—they were simply loathsome.

———

When Cuillioc reached the harbor, it was all hustle and bustle: wagons and oxcarts, barrows and pushcarts, went in and out, bringing supplies for the fleet. The Prince's flagship, already provisioned, rode at anchor out in the bay, her scarlet sails furled and her sixty pair of oars at rest, and another galley of similar size was just being towed with much labor clear of the docks, by two small rowboats.

When Cuillioc dismounted, handing the reins over to one of his grooms, he saw a sudden flurry of movement on the ceremonial barge that was to take him out to his ship. Apparently, no one had told them he was on his way. Waiting for all to be made ready, he glanced around him, and despite everything he felt his mood lighten, for the brawling life of the docks never failed to interest him.

There were men rolling barrels—casks of wine, tuns of salt, kegs of oil for light and for cooking—longshoremen moving crates of oranges or baskets of figs and raisins and sugared dates; merchants in rich brocades come down to supervise the loading or unloading of their goods, peddlers singing out, fishwives wrangling and cursing. Gulls screamed overhead; parrots and peacocks screeched in their wicker cages; and a sailor played on a whalebone flute, while one of his shipmates danced a hornpipe. Beyond them all surged the restless blue waters of the bay, crowned with whitecaps.

But there was one sight in which the Prince took no pleasure at all. On the next quay but one, a gang of dirty and emaciated prisoners, chained together in a long line with heavy iron fetters, were being herded toward a galley of thirty oars. Catching sight of one of the prisoners, a small boy of no more than eight or nine, so thin and weak that he could scarcely stand, Cuillioc felt an uncomfortable jolt of surprise. Disturbed and not a little curious, the Prince sent his guard captain to fetch the overseer.

The slave driver arrived, bowing and scraping, darting sidelong glances. "Pardon, Great Prince," he said with a cringe. "Had I known you'd be boarding just now, I'd never have offended your eyes with this filth from the prisons."

"I have seen uglier sights in the war," Cuillioc answered shortly. The wind had changed, blowing off the land, bringing with it the stench of the city. He felt his gorge rise, as much from the brute's servility as the reek of sewage and rotting fruit. "But how is this? The laws have grown harsh indeed if mere infants are now being sent to the galleys."

" 'The law is stern, but the law is just,' " the overseer quoted. He jerked his head in the direction of the prisoners. "That boy over there is a sneak thief, Lord Prince."

Cuillioc frowned, for this could mean almost anything. "A cutpurse?"

"Most like. They train these young rogues to a variety of trades, as you might say: to cut purses, snatch cloaks, filch goods from the marketplace. This lad, now, he was caught where he'd no business to be, holding what he'd no business to have. Entirely wicked and unrepentant, too."

"He doesn't look *strong enough* to pull an oar!" blurted out one of the Prince's companions. "Poor little gutter rat."

"No more he does, Great Lord. They use little 'uns like him to beat the drum. That frees one of the men to take up an oar."

"By the look of him, he won't last many days even at that," said Cuillioc, with a measuring glance. "He will be shark bait inside a week." That the boy was shiftless, dishonest, as unrepentant as the slave driver painted him, he did not doubt. He tried to convince himself that the young thief's fate was no concern of his. And yet—and yet the thought of a child, any child, being chained belowdecks with those rough, violent men was simply intolerable.

Cuillioc gave up the struggle with his too-tender conscience. *Cruel to be kind,* said the Empress, and *stern but just,* said the slave driver—but the Prince only knew that he was already tormented by too many nightmares, and he had no wish to make them worse. "My page is ill with a fever and can't sail," he said with a sigh. "This boy will take his place. You may turn him over to the Captain here, then go on boarding your other prisoners."

The overseer gaped, at a loss for words. Then he became flustered, stammering out a protest. "Great Prince, I haven't the authority. It's as much as my position is worth. And the boy— *the boy was sentenced to the galleys.*"

"He will *be* on a galley. What becomes of him there is no concern of yours. Or do you—" Cuillioc asked, with a glinting smile in his long, green eyes "—do you question *my authority* to do as I wish with your prisoner?"

To this the slave driver had no ready answer. He merely cringed, abased himself, and hurried off to loose the young thief from his chains.

Satisfied, Cuillioc nodded, turned to his guard-captain, and instructed him to have the boy made presentable before bringing him on board, and immediately lost interest in his new acquisition.

⊢————⊣

An hour later, in his luxurious cabin on the galley, the Prince surveyed the newly scrubbed and more or less decently clad urchin with a mixture of humor and dismay.

"You are scarcely prepossessing, are you?" he said, with a rueful glance.

Lamps had been lit, and the cabin was bright, if a little close and stuffy. It was plain to see that the boy had not been improved much by washing and dressing. His mouse-colored hair stuck up in tufts and cowlicks; at least half of his teeth were missing. He had eyes like two grey pebbles in a thin, pale face, and the dirt in the creases of his neck and his hands was apparently ineradicable—though the Captain had assured Cuillioc that he did his best.

The retreating tide tugged at the galley, so that she strained at her anchor. It was a warm, windless evening, and Cuillioc heard a clatter down below as oars slipped into their locks, a murmur and a groan as slaves took their places on the benches and prepared themselves for the long hours of labor ahead. "I wonder if you have any least idea what I have saved you from?"

The urchin muttered something unintelligible in response. He would, Cuillioc supposed, have the accent of the stews and a foul tongue besides. And thinking of his former page, left behind at the palace—a handy, well-trained, efficient lad from an excellent family—he expelled a deep sigh.

The Prince sat down on his bed, linked his fingers together, and rested his chin on them. "I would imagine the qualities of a sneak thief are much the same as those of a spy," he said, more to himself than to the boy. "To move silently and unobtrusively. To listen and to observe the movements of others while remaining unseen yourself. Perhaps, occasionally, to obtain by stealth letters I might wish to look at."

Opening a small gilded casket by his bed, Cuillioc extracted a sweetmeat: a dried apricot dipped in honey, then rolled in nutmeg and cassia. He tossed it to the boy, carelessly, as he might throw a scrap to a dog. There was a movement so swift as to be almost imperceptible—the urchin caught the sweet in midair and popped it into his mouth.

The Prince reached into the coffer again and produced another sugarplum, which he offered this time on the palm of his hand. It disappeared even more quickly than the first.

"I don't expect you to be grateful, that much is certain," he said, with a grimace. "You could hardly have studied gratitude, the life you have led until now. But I *do* expect you to be useful—I hope that you may be."

9

✳

The air reeked of blood and sweat and burning feathers, rang with the harsh metallic cries of wyvaerun. Sindérian did not want to wake. There was a pounding inside her skull, her head ached intolerably, and she did not want to open her eyes, but she knew that she must. When she finally forced her eyelids open, the sunset sky blurred overhead, then gradually came back into focus. She rolled over on her side, put her hands to the ground, and pushed herself into a sitting position.

The grass around her was littered with black-feathered bodies, but the battle raged on. Faolein's flaming staff barely glowed; it gave off puffs of dirty white smoke. The wizard's movements were stiff and slow—he looked, Sindérian thought, as though he were fighting underwater. The guardsmen, Jago and Aell, fought on, their faces pale and streaked with sweat; it was evident that they, too, were tiring. Even Prince Ruan moved more clumsily, his lithe body less quick and agile as he avoided the strike of an iron beak. They had killed dozens of the wyvaerun between them, but they were still outnumbered. It was a question, she realized, of how long their strength would last.

I ought to help them, Sindérian thought. *If I don't do something, we will all die.* Yet a great weariness was on her, a heaviness weighed on her limbs, on her will. Halfheartedly, she scrambled to her knees, fumbled in the grass for more stones that she could throw. She picked one up, aimed, searched her mind for the same spell she had used before. Her lips moved but she could not form the words, could not even remember them—and her head ached so, she thought that perhaps she might not mind dying after all, just to be quit of the pain.

Then, unexpectedly, the surviving wyvaerun all rose simultaneously high into the air, and, as if in response to some unheard command, went winging off toward the south.

In the sudden silence that followed, Sindérian's companions gathered around her. Speaking in low, tense voices, they took stock of their situation.

The men had sustained only minor injuries: scratched hands and faces; a deep cut over Aell's left eye, which bled and bled as head wounds will, but did not look serious. Sindérian realized she was by far the worst. Feeling under the hair at the back of her head she found a lump the size of a pigeon's egg, and when she tried to stand her knees buckled; the ground tilted beneath her. The dark sky was not where it should be; constellations danced, stars burst into rainbow showers around her, and a pain like red-hot iron shot down her neck to the base of her spine. Faolein threw out a bony arm to catch her and carefully lowered her to a seat on the grass.

Sindérian put her head down on her knees, drew several long, deep breaths. *I will* not *be sick,* she told herself fiercely. Yet her stomach continued to heave, the world refused to settle into place around her. She felt sticky with sweat and as weak as a kitten. Might it be a concussion? She struggled to remember the symptoms, but it was agony even to think. If she could not help herself, how could she possibly hope to help anyone else?

Then she felt Faolein's hand laid gently on her shoulder. The life force surged in her veins, and a little clarity returned to her. Her father was aiding her in the best way he could. He could not work a healing spell, lacking the requisite fineness of touch, the trained mental reflexes, but he was pouring some of his own strength into Sindérian, so that she could heal herself.

"Enough," she whispered after a moment, when she felt his power begin to flag. Looking up, she saw that his face had gone grey with fatigue. Out of concern for her, he had given more than he ought to have spared. She removed his hand from her shoulder, took it between both of hers, held it for a moment to her lips. "I will be entirely myself in another moment or two."

It was a lie, and they both knew it, but he wisely withdrew. The danger might not be over; one of them had to remain as strong and alert as possible.

She dropped her head back down on her knees and allowed herself to drift off into a waking dream.

Finally, Sindérian felt well enough to stand. Shaking her hair out of her eyes, she gathered the long dark weight of it up in a knot on the top of her head, picked up the silken veil, which had fallen to the ground, and pinned it securely in place. Then she joined the men in the deep shadows under the trees, where they had begun to discuss what they ought to do next.

Their faces were grim in that failing light, and the eyes of the men-at-arms wary and a little wild.

"This was no chance attack," Prince Ruan said, as she walked up. "That creature you saw back in Tregna, the way the wyvaerun swooped down on us without provocation. *It is too much coincidence.*"

"I think you must be right," she said unsteadily. "It was the abominable Goezenou who sent the wyvaerun. And he may not be done with us."

The men exchanged glances; their faces grew grimmer still. "You think that he saw you and knew you, that he guessed where we are heading?" asked the Prince.

Sindérian shook her head and regretted it; the motion made her so wretchedly ill. "He recognized something; he recognized one of us. I don't flatter myself it was I. What was one more healer on the battlefield to Goezenou?"

"It is likely that *I* am the one the furiádh recognized," Faolein admitted with a sigh. "It was so long ago that we met on Phaôrax, and we have both changed so much, I never thought he would see me to know me again."

The horses and pack mules had bolted during the attack, and had yet to return. Faolein sent out a spell to call them back, but soon realized they were still too agitated to respond. "They have run so far and in such a panic, they may not return at all," he told his companions. "It is hard to speak to them at this distance. And impossible to calm them."

"We would be fools to walk back the same way we came, with our enemy, very likely, on the road following us," said Ruan, speaking between clenched teeth. "So long as we are afoot and he and his men are mounted, the advantage will all be theirs."

Faolein nodded wearily. "Speaking for myself, I don't fear Goezenou very much. But I think of those other galleys we saw, and I wonder who else came with him into Mere. To meet two or three Furiádhin in this lonely place—I must admit that I dread the outcome if that was to happen."

"We are five days' march from the fortress at Saer," said Ruan, apparently retaining a clear mental picture of Faolein's map. "Perhaps less, if we leave the road and cut across country."

"That would be best in any case. On the road, we are too exposed."

All their food and supplies, all their bedding and extra clothes, had been lost with the horses and mules, except for some leather flasks that Jago had filled at the stream shortly before the wyvaerun attacked. Fortune, or the Fates, had been with them in that much. Otherwise, they had only those things they carried on them: armor and weapons for the Prince and his men, Faolein's staff and the contents of his pouch, some packets of medicinal herbs that Sindérian kept in a pocket of her cloak. They had also the Prince's heavy purse, still weighted with the High King's gold—but much good that was likely to do them, without a town in sight. If they wished to eat, they would have to forage, and so early in the year the land would not have much to offer.

Before they set out, they each knelt on the bank by the stream and took a long drink. There was no saying how soon or how often they would be able to refill the flasks. The country they were about to travel, the sparsely wooded hills to the northeast, was higher and drier than the marshy ground they were leaving behind.

They abandoned the road, scrambled up a slope where the scree slipped and slid dangerously underfoot, pushed through scrubby bushes of heather and broom until they found what looked like a path. A game trail it might be, for it was very narrow and rough, winding through the trees and the waist-high brush; and once, bending low in a patch of moonlight between the trees, Sindérian spotted the hoofprints of a deer pressed into the earth.

Faolein called up a tiny breeze to cover their tracks; he would not keep it up long, for the *lledrion* itself might also betray them—magic left its own trail, even if that trail was difficult to detect. "It is possible," he said, "that Goezenou and his men will be distracted for a time following our horses."

"If they bother with us any further at all," said Sindérian, putting a hand to her head, which still ached fiercely. "It is one thing to call up a flock of wyvaerun to harry us, another to turn aside from their own road—particularly if they are in any sort of hurry to go somewhere."

"Somewhere meaning Skyrra, seemingly," muttered Jago, under his breath, trudging along just ahead of her. "But what if they are heading for Saer the same as we are?"

Faolein considered that in silence for several minutes before he spoke. Glancing back over her shoulder, Sindérian saw him rake his fingers through his beard, then shake his head. "It is the next large settlement, yet I hardly think they will choose to go there. Or that they would be welcomed inside if they did. Where the loyalties of our sometime ally the Duke of Mere lie now is a matter for debate, but the same can hardly be said of his liege man Goslin of Saer. He'll have no dealings with Ouriána or her Furiádhin. He lost his two sons and all three of his brothers in the war.

"And Saer," he added, "is a place they would find it difficult to enter without an invitation."

Letting his breeze die down, the wizard went ahead of the rest, edging past Sindérian, Jago, Aell, and the Prince, who had been in the lead before. Ruan fell back without demur, and took a place at the rear of the party, behind Sindérian.

She tried to ignore his presence, though he walked so close behind her. He moved so lightly, she could not even hear his booted feet striking the hard earth, but she was keenly aware of him all the same: his bright eyes and glittering golden torc, his watchful posture, the way he kept his hand on the hilt of his sword. She was as sure of those things as if she could see him, flowing like quicksilver through the dappled moonlight.

She pulled the black veil down over her face, lowered her head, set her jaw, and forced herself to concentrate on the uneven path before her.

For many hours they kept on moving, plodding through that stony, slanted country—always, it seemed, uphill. At last, in the cold dark time between midnight and dawn, they came to a hollow sheltered on all sides, where Faolein thought they might safely camp for what remained of the night.

Aell and Jago and the Prince threw themselves down on the ground. Sindérian wrapped herself up in her cloak, stretched out with a sigh on the coarse, moon-silvered grass, and was almost immediately asleep.

Faolein made a small smokeless fire. While his companions slept, he kept watch, his staff at his side, feeding his fire with twigs and bits of bark and dried moss.

It was a clear, starry night, and the wizard was very much aware of the immense waxing moon overhead—westering by then, but not to set for another hour. It was a weight upon the sky, upon the hills. Under its influence, the earth rumbled from time to time; only the smallest tremors for the moment, but as the moon continued to grow these would increase in power and frequency. In another day or two, when it was quite full, there might be earthquakes, this whole region was so un-stable.

Sitting cross-legged by his fire, Faolein felt himself drifting off, despite his best efforts to stay awake, and caught himself just before he slipped away. He was unutterably weary; age, it seemed, was finally catching up with him. He could remember a time, eighty years ago when he was in his prime, when he could walk all day without fatigue, when sleep was a mere dis-traction, and one that he could, as often as not, easily dispense with. He ached to the very bone; if he could only lay his head down, close his eyes, and rest for a moment—

As the darkness swept over him he felt it: a light touch at first, then a deeper and more insidious probing by another mind. He struggled against it, fought his way free, came up out of that bottomless well of sleep and black magic gasping and fighting for air like a drowning man.

Then he sat by the fire, trembling with reaction and horror. When at last he felt strong enough, he left his seat, crept past the others where they slept, and bent over to wake Sindérian.

It took no more than his dry fingertips brushing her face. She sat up at once, muzzy with sleep but obedient to his word, gazing up at her father with bruised dark eyes. It cut him to the heart to have to disturb her when she so clearly needed rest and healing, but the danger was simply too great.

"We ought to set wards with our enemies so near," said Faolein, very low. "He—they—whoever is on the road—he hasn't forgotten us. He is seeking us through the night."

"Who? Who was it you felt, out there in the darkness?" she whispered back. Gathering her feet under her, she clasped the hand that he was offering her, letting him pull her up so that they stood shoulder to shoulder. "It was never Goezenou who frightened you so. Who else is there?"

Remembering that brief, terrifying contact with a clear, cold, powerful intelligence, Faolein shook his head. "I would rather not say, rather not guess. To say or even think the name when he is trying to find us—" As his voice trailed off, he saw the pupils of her eyes grow large with fear and speculation; reflexively, she signed a *béanath*. "Turn your thoughts in some other direction . . . but don't let down your guard for a single instant."

———

While Faolein wove ropes out of grass and used them to bind sheaves of heather into a kind of primitive lintel, Sindérian gathered sticks and placed them on the ground around the campsite so that they formed a perfect square. Then she hunted up a large flat rock to serve as the *corridrüis*, the door-stone, or threshold.

Hallowing these structures with fire and with water, with herbs of great virtue and protection, they set the charm with care. But it was only makeshift, and the boundary they had established would only continue to exist because they *willed* it so. Whether or not it could withstand a determined assault by a mind as powerful as the one that Faolein had detected earlier— that was by no means certain.

And when the wards were in place, when Faolein resumed his seat by the fire, and Sindérian cast herself down in her former spot on the ground and tried to rest, the most she could achieve—the most she would allow herself—was a light, fitful doze.

In dreams one was vulnerable. So long as they remained under threat from without she dared not give herself up wholly to sleep.

The moon set. In another hour, the fabric of night began to fray, and a pale-hued light shone through. The tops of the trees on the crests of the hills turned to fallow gold; dew glistened like drops of silver in the grass. Faolein woke the Prince and his men. Breakfast was water and a handful of sloes, not quite ripe, which Sindérian gathered from bushes on the slopes of the hollow. Then they set off walking again.

Midmorning found them in country more heavily wooded than before; the trees drew together in thickets, birch and cowan and ash, their branches tangling overhead. The ground underfoot was thick and fragrant with fallen leaves. There were broad pathways weaving between the trees, and the occasional scent of woodsmoke, as plain a sign as they could ask for that the land was inhabited. But whenever Faolein smelled smoke he turned aside to lead his companions down some other pathway. He had no wish, he told them, to approach any village or settlement, to meet *anyone* before they came to Saer, where they might be sure of finding allies.

As he walked, staff in hand, Faolein let his senses go wide: sight, hearing, scent, touch, and that other, extra sense. He moved through the world as only a wizard can, in communion with rocks and hills, wind and water, trees and grass, yet always apart from them, uniquely himself. Squirrels chattered in the branches overhead; tiny brown field mice and shrew mice went scurrying for their nests under the roots. Red foxes in their dens peered out with bright, inquiring eyes. Nowhere could he detect any threat. He could almost believe that they had eluded their enemies, that they were not being followed, had it not been for that stealthy touch he felt in the night.

Sindérian walked a little apart, her head still aching. At times, she felt muddled and stupid, and there was an occasional giddiness, when the landscape reeled—though whether that was lack of sleep or the head injury she could not be certain. Such injuries were difficult to heal, and dangerous work for a healer not in full command of her faculties. She had done all that it was safe to do under the circumstances; nature must do the rest.

Her feet hurt. Her boots had never been meant for walking; she could feel every rock, every pebble, through the thin leather soles, bruising the flesh. Her pulse beat with a sullen, irregular beat, and there was a stitch in her side, a sharp, tearing pain, which grew steadily worse the longer she walked.

She gritted her teeth. *All those weeks of soft living on Leal, and I'm fit for nothing. Prince Ruan was right, though I'd die before I told him so: I bitterly regret embarking on this hopeless enterprise, this journey where things have gone wrong from the very beginning.*

They took a path leading downhill, where the trees grew denser. Sindérian began to smell water, and soon they came upon a trail—scarcely worth the name, it was so steep and treacherous—where a damp trickle began to follow their course down the slope.

The trickle met other rills, and finally became a stream at the bottom of the hill. Ferns grew there under the trees, along with hart's-tongue, pennymint, and stinging nettle. White-flag, spiky purple iris, and golden marsh marigold sprang up where the ground was boggy along the margin.

"This will be Ceriolle, which flows into the Saille," said Faolein. "If we follow its course, it will lead us to Saer."

Little fat silvery fish, no greater than the palm of a hand, swam in the shallows, and Prince Ruan proved surprisingly adept at catching them with his bare hands. "They make poor eating," he said, passing one over to Aell, who wrapped it in green leaves to keep it fresh, "but I fear we can't afford to be too dainty in our tastes." Sindérian wondered, absently, where he had lived that he had eaten such fish before.

In another hour, they came to a place where a mossy stone bridge curved over the stream. The stonework was very old, the weathered granite of the balustrades crumbling away, but the bridge was solid underfoot, and they crossed over safely in a single file. Higher up the hill, the Prince spied the evidence of some ancient delvings.

"There will be Gnomes living somewhere hereabout," he said. "They are a peaceable, hospitable people—"

"Too peaceable," replied Faolein, with a worried frown. "I would not expose those kindly little folk to the furiádh and his men—not for the sake of hospitality we can live without."

At *erién*, when the sun sent shafts of golden light down between the trees, the wizard suggested that they stop and rest. Without waiting for a further invitation, Sindérian sank down where she was, leaned her back against the trunk of a tree, and closed her eyes to shut out the light.

She listened to the sounds of the others setting up camp: gathering firewood, preparing Prince Ruan's fish and some edible roots for cooking. She felt utterly dislocated from her surroundings, floating like a soap bubble on the wind, sick and bodiless. But she came back to earth at the Prince's approach, the crackling of leaves underfoot, the soft sigh of his breath as he sat down near her. When she opened her eyes again, he was perched on a fallen log about three feet way, watching her intently.

Avoiding that arrogant gaze of his, her glance fell, as if for the first time, on the silver brooch fastening his cloak. It was simple and well made, set with gems of no great value, and its design contained two of the ordinary runes used in writing: the Tree Runes these were called, to distinguish them from the Wizard's Runes, which contained so much power. The runes on the brooch were *aethin* and *piridwen*—furze and spruce— set side by side as if it were a monogram or cypher.

"*A* and *P,*" she said aloud, without even thinking. "Was it a gift?"

The Prince smiled slightly. "If you mean was this brooch a lady's favor, no," he replied coolly. And realizing that her question *had* implied something of the sort—and therefore suggested rather too much interest in his affairs of the heart— Sindérian felt the heat rise in her face.

"As for the initials, they are my own," he went on. "My mother, who is of the Ni-Féa Faey, named me 'Anerüian' for the hour at which I was born. It is a common practice among the Faey, to name their children for seasons and hours. But when I went to live with my father's people on Thäerie, they thought it strange that one so pale-skinned and light-haired should be called 'Midnight.' And so, to make more sense of it and me, they shortened the name by degrees: first to 'Rüian,' then to 'Ruan.' I've long since learned to answer to that name, but I could hardly mark my things with an *R* and a *P,* which is my grandfather's cypher.

"And now," he said, as Sindérian sat sifting leaves through her fingers, "now that I have told you so much about myself, may I ask you a question?"

She nodded reluctantly, having an idea what he would ask. But it was only a fair exchange; she could not, in courtesy, refuse him, having asked her question first.

"I see that you wear the color of mourning, though your father does not. Have you suffered a personal loss, or do you wear it as certain warriors I know—because they served at one time in Rheithûn—in memory of a valiant people now enslaved?"

Because she was so very tired—surely that, for the pain was an old one—she felt the salt tears scalding her eyes. Resolutely, she blinked them back. "For both reasons. I did serve as a healer six years in Rheithûn, and I was betrothed to Cailltin of Aefri. We intended to be married if"—her voice broke momentarily; she took several deep breaths, then went on—"when the war ends. But he died along with so many other brave men when the last fortress fell."

"*You were there?*" asked the Prince, leaning forward in his interest. "You saw the fall of Gilaefri—the executions after?"

Sindérian felt her face grow stiff, her throat go dry. "No," she whispered, feeling the old sickness, the old shame. She crushed a handful of leaves between her fingers, watched them crumble. "No, I wasn't there. I was on my way to the coast, shepherding a party of women and children."

The Prince sat back. "You have no reason to reproach yourself," he said, speaking more gently than she had ever heard him. "You couldn't have saved him. When the Furiádhin threw down the walls, when they put all the commanders to the sword, what could you have done, then, for Cailltin of Aefri—or anyone?"

She swallowed the hot retort that rose to her lips at the familiar platitude. She only answered, in a stifled voice: "I could have died with him."

"Which would have been some comfort to *you* perhaps, but none at all to the noble Cailltin. Whereas now you can live to avenge him."

Sindérian sighed and gave a dreary little laugh. "You would say so, of course. I've heard the Ni-Féa believe in revenge—that they will pursue a grudge as long as seven generations. Wizards, however, live by a different rule. To seek after vengeance goes against everything they teach us at the Scholia."

His strange eyes glittered in the shadows under the trees. "The Ni-Féa believe in justice," he said, with a light emphasis on the last word. "Though to those raised as you and I were, their ideas of gratitude, fair recompense, and injury may seem exaggerated. But the desire for revenge in the face of some insult or injury—real or imagined—is no mere article of faith, no quaint cultural artifact. It is an *inborn hunger,* a fierce compulsion, the consummation of which may be postponed for a day, or a year, or even a decade, but never completely denied."

Sindérian bit her lip. She was tired and cross and on the defensive, as it seemed she always was in his presence. And she was not really interested, just at that moment, in the ways of the Ni-Féa, though she might have been curious any other time. Yet she was glad enough for the change of subject.

"And do you share that compulsion, Prince Ruan?" she asked, in her most offhand manner.

His face went very still. For a moment, his eyes were veiled by his silvery eyelashes, then a fierce emotion shone out. He was remembering something or remembering somebody. He spoke very quietly. "Half-blood that I am, I find the compulsion *much less insistent,* more easily suppressed, but it is still *far* from absent."

IO

*

It was a dusty, weary, and footsore party that came to Saer
four days later. Emerging from densely forested country,
they found themselves looking down on a pleasant valley and
across a stretch of cultivated farmland, to the sprawling stone
fortress built on and into rocky cliffs on the farther side.

Parts of Saer are old, very old, its ancient crumbling towers
rooted in the native stone, castle and hill both weathered alike,
so that even with the Sight it is difficult to see where the towers
end and the unshaped rock begins. But there is more to the
fortress at Saer than age. Faolein had said this was a place that
Ouriána's servants would have difficulty entering without an
invitation, and it was equally true for him and Sindérian. Before the present fortress, old as it is, a primitive hill fort stood
where it stands now. Before the Empire of Alluinn, before Alluinn was even a kingdom, before wizards like Mallion Penn
worked their wonders, there were those who practiced older
magics, belonging neither to the Dark nor to the Light, but
wholly dedicated to the Earth. These magics had their origin at
certain powerful sites, and Saer is one of those places, where ley
lines meet.

By the time Faolein and his companions came down the last rough slope to the valley floor, the sun had already set, and an immense hag-faced moon hung in the sky between two of the towers. Little grey bats flitted overhead; owls began to awake in the woods, filling the dusky air with their eerie, plaintive cries. The silver waters of the Ceriolle meandered across the bowl of the valley and disappeared in a slot between the hills to the south.

The wizard took a more direct route, when the path they had been following became a wide, smooth road, well marked with granite milestones. For all that, twilight had faded into night, the first stars had come out, before Faolein and the others finally stood in a circle of torchlight below the gatehouse, and he lifted his staff to knock on the stout oak planks.

But then he stopped, his movement arrested. Sindérian, who had walked at his side for the last mile, turned a worried glance his way, wondering what made him hesitate.

Half of his face was in shadow, and the lurid yellow torchlight on the other side emphasized every wrinkle and hollow. His shoulders were stooped and his back bent, as if in intolerable pain. But she knew without being told that it was no bodily hurt that troubled him now. His brow was furrowed, and his dark eyes gazed inward, as if he were caught in some terrifying dream.

She put out a hand to touch him, to share his thought, but he flinched away, a violent shrinking, which shocked her as nothing else could. Her father was a man of great reserve, shy and undemonstrative, but he had *never* in all the years of Sindérian's life rejected her own more ready displays of emotion and affection.

He had flinched from the mind-touch, too, as though what he saw was too terrible to share.

"What is it?" she whispered, the words catching in her throat. "What is it you sense here?"

Faolein shuddered from head to toe, took several harsh scraping breaths. Then, abruptly, he was himself again: he stood a little straighter; the look of horror was wiped away. When he turned his eyes in her direction, she knew that he was seeing her now.

"It would be well," he said softly, though loud enough that the Prince and the men-at-arms might also hear him, "if we did not reveal too much of ourselves or our business while we are here. Only enough to convince them to provide us with horses and the other things we need."

He lifted his staff again, preparing to knock, but this time he stopped when a voice hailed them from the walls. "Who comes at this late hour—and why should we admit you?"

"It is Faolein of Leal who asks to be admitted. Send word to your Lord. He knows me; he would not see his friend of so many years turned away at the gate."

There were sounds of movement up on the walls, a buzz of voices, a consultation too low to be rightly heard. Then the same voice that had addressed them before spoke: "We will send word as you suggest. Pardon us, Lord Wizard, if we keep you waiting a little longer."

It seemed a long wait to those standing famished and exhausted outside, but perhaps it was only minutes before chains rattled and they heard the sound of a wooden bar sliding to the ground. The gate swung inward, and a tall sallow man in robes of tattered brown silk stood within the firelit guardroom, bowing and welcoming them inside.

Faolein was the first to step across the threshold. "My daughter Sindérian," he said, beginning the introductions. "The Lord of Penraeth and members of his household," he went on, using the title they had agreed on for the Prince. "We had the misfortune to lose our horses, or we would never have arrived at Saer like beggars."

The tall man in ragged silk sketched another bow. His dark hair was shorn straight across the shoulders, except at the very front, where it was longer and tied up in charm knots like a village witch or warlock. He wore a gold ring in his left ear. There was something indefinably foreign about him, though he spoke the local dialect without an accent. "Lord Saer greets you and welcomes you through me. As for myself, I am—"

"—Thaga," said Faolein, startling the man so that his head came suddenly up, and his face went from sallow to bloodless white.

Yet he quickly recovered himself. "Yes, I am Thaga," he agreed, with an ingratiating smile. "Sorcerer to the Lord of Saer. Not of your order on Leal, alas. I was trained . . . in a smaller school to the east, no longer in existence."

Liar and braggart, thought Sindérian. *He wishes us to think that he studied in Alluinn, but he is by no means old enough. Either that, or he is wonderfully well preserved—but we would know if any wizard of great age and power had survived the disaster. The Masters at the Scholia would know.*

For all that, he was no mountebank; he did have a gift; she could smell it and feel it. Her own power Sindérian drew into herself, kept it secret and close.

Thaga led them out of the gatehouse and into an unpaved courtyard with an odor of hay and stables, the scent of cooking. Goats bleated inside a wattle fence; cattle lowed in the shadows. Windows glowed with yellow firelight higher up. The sorcerer led the way up a wooden staircase, through a pair of high double doors, and along a passage that took them inside the hill.

But Sindérian's attention was all on her father. What had disturbed him outside the gate? Whatever it was, it had passed and gone. There was nothing in his face, in his movements, but what she had seen there her entire life. Climbing the steps, he had even tripped on the hem of his long cloak, but caught himself just short of a fall and continued on with unruffled serenity. Had she imagined what she saw by the gate? Or had she exaggerated what she did see?

For a wizard's Foresight is an odd, unpredictable thing. Ordinary people, even wizards without that particular gift, rarely understand how it can come and go, in bits and flashes, now muddled and unclear, now vivid but fleeting. Sometimes not remembered after, and sometimes more a hindrance than a help. Whatever it was that had troubled Faolein earlier, Sindérian knew it might not have anything to do with the here and now; it might be a warning of things days, weeks, or even months in the future.

As if to reassure her this indeed was the case, he gave her one of his rare, sweet smiles, reached out, and patted her hand with his thin dry one. One thing at least Sindérian knew: her father would never knowingly lead her into deadly danger.

———

They moved through a series of wide corridors and narrow passageways. Sometimes they met people rushing about at various tasks: carrying trays of food, or tall white candles, or firewood. When they spotted Thaga, these people ducked and bowed and drew back—more in fear than respect, it seemed to Sindérian.

Following after the sorcerer, she and her companions entered an immense, cavernous chamber carved out of the living rock, the distant ceiling upheld by pillars greater in girth than the tallest trees. The torchlit corridor behind them receded to a tiny speck of light; there was no illumination ahead of them; they navigated only by a dim milky glow which seemed to emanate from Thaga himself. There was no sound but their own footsteps striking the smooth stone floor, echoing off distant walls.

It was to a smaller, more intimate chamber that Thaga brought them at last, throwing open a door and leading them into a room bright with firelight. There were sheepskin rugs on the floor and tapestries in brilliant colors on the walls.

But Sindérian experienced an unpleasant shock of surprise when the Lord rose from his seat to greet his guests. It was not the man she had expected to see, not that doughty old warrior, Goslin of Saer, who had visited the Scholia on Leal twice during her lifetime. This was a much younger man, elegantly dressed and graceful in his movements, with butter-yellow hair and pale green eyes.

And seeing that Sindérian and the others were taken aback (but *not* her father, *not* Faolein, as she would remember later), he smiled a sad and gentle smile. "No one told you of my kinsman's death?"

"Perhaps we left Leal before the news arrived," said Faolein, neither acknowledging or denying. "But—when and how, if one may ask?"

"This winter just past. As to how—" The young Lord Saer made a little movement with his shoulders, not quite a shrug. "He was past eighty and in very poor health. His physicians and Thaga did all they could. But age and a lifetime of trouble and grief at last defeated them."

This is not a man we know, Sindérian thought with a sinking sensation, *not the unshakable friend and ally we expected. What will Faolein do now?*

But what her father did, without any sign of dismay or surprise, was to present each of his companions in turn, and briefly explain something of their predicament.

"Whatever you require; whatever comforts we can provide for the rest of your journey: horses, food, wine, pack animals, pavilions—a litter, perhaps, for the Lady. Ask and it is yours," said the new young Lord, his clear eyes shining with sincerity. Nothing could be more bland and amiable than his expression. "In return, I ask only this: that you accept my hospitality for the evening."

He seemed harmless enough, Sindérian decided, if somewhat affected—and more than fond of the sound of his own voice. She felt her doubts ease. As Goslin's kinsman, he would have the same grudge against Ouriána of Phaôrax. What reason had they *not* to trust him?

"Noble and generous," said Faolein, inclining his head. "We accept with thanks."

At a signal from Saer, Thaga withdrew. Minutes later, a horde of attendants entered the room, and began to lavish their attentions on the travelers. Suddenly realizing that accepting this stranger's hospitality also meant being separated from her friends, Sindérian experienced a sharp return of her former misgivings. The men went one way, she another, surrounded by a flock of chattering young women.

But this was the way that things were always done in a noble household; she had no grounds to refuse. She could only give a last forlorn glance over her shoulder as Faolein and the others disappeared around a corner, and the young women led her off in the opposite direction.

Much to her relief, they did not take her far. In another beautifully appointed chamber, they offered her water to wash with, soap and heated cloths, oils and perfumes. They removed her cloak and her boots and her gown. All her things had been snagged and torn by branches and brambles; they were stiff with dirt and sweat. It would be good to be clean again. Suddenly yielding to the exhaustion of five hard days and as many restless nights, Sindérian allowed the women to wait on her.

At last, blissfully clean, clad in a fresh linen shift, she sat on a stool by the fire, drying her hair, while one of the maidens combed out the tangles, exclaiming over the length and texture.

Every now and again she thought she detected an undercurrent of fear under their gaiety. There were uneasy glances, an occasional unintended clumsiness where something fragile fell and broke. The chatter of the maidens was at times a little too shrill. But that might only be her own presence among them: the stranger, the sorceress. To women who rarely if ever left their own valley, Leal and its school of wizardry must seem a world away.

When they brought her a gown of rich wine-colored velvet with sable at the hem and on the long, hanging sleeves, Sindérian shook her head. "I will wear the poorest and the plainest gown you can lend me," she said, suddenly oppressed by their too-generous, too-effusive hospitality, "so long as it is something more suitable to a woman in mourning."

But "*no, no, no,*" the maidens answered her, fluttering about in their agitation, their voices even shriller than before.

"We are just out of mourning for Lord Goslin," said a pale blond girl. She sounded more breathless than the occasion warranted. "And our new young Lord—he has no wish to be reminded of past sorrows. Having banished all signs of bereavement, having arranged a feast in honor of your father, Lord Dreyde would not like to see you or any other guest appear at his table . . . *all in black*."

So again Sindérian could not refuse. She allowed them to lace her into the gown, wondering all the while if the brightly colored dress was meant to set her apart from their dull greens and browns. They brought her shoes of soft red leather lined with fur, and they placed a girdle around her waist: a length of plaited silk hung with many rows of tiny golden medallions that chimed together softly when she moved.

Belled like a cat, she thought, disgusted with herself and her situation. But that was unworthy of the kindness they had shown her so far, and she began to feel slightly ashamed.

In that same hour, in another part of the fortress, Prince Ruan and Faolein were dressing, too. Ruan could not be sure exactly where and when, but Aell and Jago had disappeared. Someone had spirited them away when the Prince was not looking.

When he asked where the guardsmen had gone, a haughty-looking youth in Saer's color replied very coldly: "They have gone to the barracks. Lord Dreyde thought they would prefer to dine with men of their own sort."

Ruan opened his mouth to say something, but intercepting a glance from Faolein, he swallowed his words. There was simply no protest that he could make and still maintain the pose of a minor nobleman, so he shrugged a shoulder and went on dressing.

He had already allowed this swarm of attendants to strip off his armor and padding; that was simple hospitality, and he could not refuse. But now that he was washed and wearing clean linen, he made up his mind to accept no more, steadfastly turning aside all offers of silken tunics and fur-lined robes, declaring he would have his own light mail and leather instead.

Much to his relief, no one pressed him; they did not insist. One of the pages even brought back his blue wool cloak, which someone had brushed and cleaned. The truth was, no one seemed greatly interested what Ruan did or did not do; most of their attention revolved around Faolein.

They think me a nonentity compared to the wizard, he thought, amazed.

It was a novel sensation. All of his life, those who had not reacted in some way to the High King's grandson had been curious or repelled or uneasy in the presence of the half-breed. But there was nothing of that here. An anomaly on Thäerie, a half-blood Faey was apparently such a commonplace in Mere that no one took notice, no one even bothered to wonder who he might be.

Across the room, he caught sight of a slight, silver-haired figure in among the other squires and pages. A pair of wide golden eyes glanced in his direction, then turned away. Here at least was recognition, hostile as it might be. No one here had seen a Ni-Féa before, they had no way of knowing the difference—only the Ni-Ferys squire, who felt it instinctively.

⸺

At length, Sindérian's attendants swept her up and carried her along to the dining hall. It was a room nearly as vast as the hall of pillars, though brilliantly lit, with an entire pine tree blazing away in a great fire pit. Long, colorful banners hung from the high ceiling, and a row of windows along one wall looked out on the valley. Someone had thrown the heavy casements open, letting in the fragrance of meadows and night, and the banners overhead moved with every shift of the air.

Faolein sat at the High Table along with Lord Dreyde and his household, at Saer's left hand, but Sindérian was allotted a place farther down, sharing a cup and a plate with Prince Ruan.

Dreyde had commanded an impressive feast on such short notice: gleaming platters of freshwater fish and feathered game, delicately cooked and spiced; sausage hedgehogs bristling with almonds; immense wheels of cheese like harvest moons; bowls filled with grapes and apricots and plums; a cool yellow wine with the flavor of honey. Musicians played, acrobats tumbled, while those who sat at the long oak tables ate and gossiped.

Straining to hear what passed between the Lord and her father, Sindérian paid little heed to the food and wine. Though she ate and she drank, hunger had long since died; she hardly tasted or cared what passed between her lips.

Saer was vague, but from hints and innuendoes Sindérian gathered he was not best pleased with the Duke of Mere. He seemed to belong to a faction that shared his displeasure. For a moment, the conversations to either side of her died down, and she could hear Dreyde's voice, soft but clear:

"If Thäerie and Leal looked kindly on us, we might do much. Then the Alliance would be healed, and all as it was before."

He must be very confident of his people to speak treason so openly, Sindérian marveled. Either that, or he was a fool. And somewhat unreasonably, she felt a great sense of relief wash over her. She ought not to feel comfortable, she knew, in the hall of a man plotting treachery against his overlord—yet *now* she understood the warmth of their welcome, the reason behind such pressing hospitality.

He had Saer, but he wanted more. *The appetites of ambi-*

tious men are never sated, she thought. *The more they have, the more they want. He or some friend of his would like to be Duke of Mere, and he thinks that Faolein can help him to achieve this. We might just as well have risked Prince Bael—*

As for Faolein, he listened to Dreyde with a grave, kind, courteous attention that agreed to nothing but seemed to promise everything. Perhaps by morning Saer would realize that the wizard was not going to help him, perhaps by then he would be less generous with his offers of horses and supplies. But until then, Sindérian thought, she and her companions ought to be safe. Dreyde was too caught up in his own concerns, his own schemes, to think of meddling with *them.*

All this time, she had scarcely been aware of Prince Ruan, though he sat beside her, though they shared the same plate and cup. As the meal concluded, she felt a hand grip her arm, and the Prince leaned so close that his fair hair brushed against her face. His own face was pale with excitement and suspicion.

"That hedge wizard of Saer's never made an appearance during the feast," he hissed in her ear. "But one of the servants just came in, reeking of smoke and banewort, and signaled to his master from the foot of the dais."

Sindérian felt a sharp pang of fear, and her stomach clenched in a hard knot. For the plant anciently known as *ylls-yllatha*—more commonly goblin's-weed or banewort— has very few uses and none of them good. The wicked and the ignorant were frequently drawn to it, black magicians, country witches, and village necromancers; but no wizard would touch it or smell it, much less make use of it.

But it may not have anything to do with us. In truth, why should it? Saer was plotting against the Duke. For all that, she took a handful of salt from the table and concealed it in the palm of her hand.

Up on the dais, Dreyde rose to his feet, and everyone else followed his example. Prince Ruan offered Sindérian his arm, which she accepted, and together they edged toward Faolein.

But a mass of bodies moved between them and the wizard. Sindérian lost her hold on the Prince's arm, and was suddenly engulfed in a tide of young women. They swept her away from the tables and toward one of the doors. "You must—you must—you *must* come with the other maidens, Lady," they murmured in her ear. "It is only right."

The people of Saer swarm like bees, she thought, exasperated. They were like a cloud of gnats, impossible to shake off. Taller than any of her companions, she stood on her toes to look over their heads. But Faolein was already gone; she did not even know which door he had left by. She could not find Prince Ruan, and now it occurred to her, for the very first time, that Aell and Jago were missing, too.

Resisting those who urged her toward the doorway, she sent out a thought in search of her father. She found him striding down a long corridor in company with Dreyde. Her mind touched his briefly, drew back at his answer, so harsh and peremptory: *Not now.* Her heart sank, for it was the second time that day he had rebuffed her. Something was very, very wrong.

One thing only was clear: Faolein expected her to act as though nothing were amiss. Knowing this, she had no choice but to do as the maidens bade her. She allowed them to usher her out of the room, along a narrow corridor, and up a flight of stairs.

———

But climbing the stairs she had a prickly sense that someone was following her and the other maidens, someone whose whole mind was bent on *her*. Could it be Thaga? They left the stairs and proceeded down another cavernous passageway. When the trailing hem of her wine-colored gown caught on a projecting bit of stone and she stopped to free herself, Sindérian took the opportunity to glance back over her shoulder.

She caught the barest glimpse of someone—a pale-haired figure in a sky-blue cloak, as lithe as a cat—moving in the shadows along one wall. Her fingers tightened around the handful of salt. Whatever occurred, she was not without resources.

Up a long ramp, through a series of archways and gates, up flights of stairs as steep as ladders, the young women took Sindérian into a part of the fortress much older than any of the rooms she had seen before. Two of the women carried burning torches, one an oil lamp that smoked whenever they encountered a draft from one of the shafts that brought down air and moonlight from above. They hurried her around so many turns, whisked her around so many corners, Sindérian soon lost all sense of direction, had no idea where she was heading.

And she did not like this place, less and less she liked it. There was an unhealthy feel to these rooms and corridors, as though the very atmosphere was tainted. The air seemed to slide over her skin like oil, leaving an unwholesome residue behind.

Entering another shadowy passageway, she felt the panic rising again. Blood pounded in her temples, her heart leapt against her ribs; every sense screamed warning. The muscles in her legs locked, and she could not or would not move.

But someone thrust a hard hand between her shoulders, forcing her to stumble forward, one step, two steps. She felt an intense heat, a giddy faintness, many times worse than the head injury had been. Then the bottom fell out of the world, plunging her into chaos.

11

*

Sindérian stood in the heart of the vortex, in the eye of the storm. Colors whirled madly around her: bold crimson, tattered yellow, scintillating blue-green, a purple so vibrant it made her eyes ache. Thunder roared in her ears. Struggling against the shifting tides of magic, she used every ounce of will she possessed to fight her way free of the spell that held her. Raising her arm with an effort, she tossed her handful of salt into the maelstrom.

Abruptly, the tumult ceased; the air cleared. Yet she was still a prisoner, still bound, trapped inside a circle of blue flame. The other women, the ones who had lured her into the trap, had all disappeared; she thought she could hear their retreating footsteps echoing all down the corridor back the way they had come. They had dropped one of the torches—it was just sputtering out on the floor—and farther down the passage she saw a little pool of burning oil that the blond girl had apparently spilled in her haste to be gone.

The women were gone, but they had been replaced by two armed men who stood as if on guard just outside the fiery circle. They had bright two-handed swords, which they held unsheathed, and though they did not speak, their eyes followed Sindérian's every movement.

They do not like what they have been set here to do, she thought, *but they will do it.*

She took a step forward to test the spell, but the flames leapt up like a row of bright spears, and the heat was intense, forcing her back again.

The taste of despair rose bitter in her mouth, yet she could not—must not—accept defeat. She swallowed several times, dredged up all the reserves she still possessed, and squared her shoulders.

Suddenly remembering Prince Ruan, Sindérian wheeled around, searching the passage from one end to the other, hoping to find him somewhere nearby. The shadows along the walls were so deep, she could not penetrate them, but she did hear a very light footfall, and a moment later had a strong sense of Ruan's presence.

She turned her attention then to the pattern etched into the floor at her feet: the source of the fire and the binding that held her. It was a maze, a knot, one of the old Earth Magics, remnant of an earlier time that had likely waited harmless for centuries until someone (undoubtedly Thaga) had activated the spell.

She drew in a long breath to steady herself, to focus her will, and cried out:

ALꟙALÜꝒANACꟛ Séo CꝒÜANꟛ.
ALꟙALÜꝒANACꟛ Séo LLEOꝒION.
ANéSAOACꟛ ꝒꟛIOO OIOꟛA SINOéꝒION.

There came a clap like thunder, a flash like lightning. The fire wavered and almost died, but then it sprang up again, even hotter than before. She felt the sweat start out on her skin, could smell the fur at the hem of her gown beginning to singe.

One of the men took a step in her direction, menacing her with his sword, but he stopped outside the circle, helpless to do more. The fire kept the men out as effectively as it kept her in, and even afforded her a kind of protection.

She tried her spell again, this time with an even greater effort of will. *"Anésadach rhiod dioha Sindérian."* The flames turned from blue to gold, but that was all.

Putting her hands to her aching skull, she struggled to concentrate. *Think—I must think.* How *have they done this?* A series of scenes flashed through her mind—the stairs, the ramp, the series of passageways. And then she knew: the path she had followed to get here, crossing and recrossing her own footsteps, was a part of the spell. Like a fool, she had helped to create the charm that bound her, the great labyrinthine knot, more complex and powerful than the thing on the floor. But what she had made, she could unmake again.

Tracing the pattern with her fingernail on the palm of her hand, Sindérian watched the blood well up, the figure she had drawn begin to glow with a faint silvery light. *"Anwaetha séo whath!"* she commanded. *"Séo lledrion oma andéinath!"*

A great gust of air blasted through the corridor and extinguished the flames.

The guards stood as men stunned. Before either had time to react, she stepped outside the figure and in the same moment Prince Ruan leapt from the shadows, sword in hand.

Ruan's blade flashed, and a body fell to the ground. The other guard turned, flung up his sword to parry the next blow, but Ruan's blade beat it down and somehow kept on going. There was the dull, sickening sound of metal striking flesh, a spurt of red blood, and another body collapsed on the stony floor.

"We may need a light," said the Prince. There was blood on his hands and on his cloak, but his voice was steady. He picked up the torch, lit it again in the pool of flaming oil, and resheathed his sword. Then, without another word, he reached out and took Sindérian firmly by the wrist and started down the corridor at a brisk pace.

She allowed him to lead her tamely enough, back along the passageway and down a steep flight of stairs, through room after room. She was spattered with blood, dazed and shaking with reaction. They went so swiftly, she hardly had time to catch her breath.

But after a time, her steps lagged, and she held back, dragging on his arm. "Where are you *taking* me?"

"To find Aell and Jago, then out of this place by the quickest way possible."

Sindérian braced her feet against the floor, refusing to take another step. "No, no! We must find my father, even before we look for the others." She struggled against the grasp of his strong, slender fingers. "He may—he *will* be in terrible danger."

"You were able to defeat their spells, and without much effort that I could see. Why shouldn't Faolein do the same?"

"Thaga and Dreyde thought that they took my measure, but they were wrong," she explained breathlessly. "What do they know of me, after all? But they won't make the same mistake with a Master Wizard. Whatever they have planned for Faolein, it will be many, many times worse."

"I wish to speak with you apart," said Dreyde of Saer. "I have things to say that are not for all ears."

Faolein walked a few steps behind him, allowing the young Lord to lead him down one echoing dark corridor after another. He thought: *You have already said quite enough to put your head in a noose if any hint of your plans came to the Duke at Clowes—why turn discreet now?*

Yet the wizard made certain that his face gave nothing away. What more he thought he kept to himself; he simply let Saer lead him wherever he wanted to go, knowing that no good would come of it.

Because Faolein was fey, moving, speaking, feeling as one under a compulsion. His mouth was dry with fear, his heart ached with the knowledge that was in him, yet it was too late to change course, even if he would . . . and he knew that he would not.

Before the gate, he had seen a vast array of possible futures play out in his mind and from them he had chosen his path. It promised him little but suffering and grief, but every other alternative that he had seen was infinitely worse.

They came to a door: solid oak planks and ornate iron hinges, no different from a hundred doors they had already passed. Saer produced a large brass key from somewhere about his person and fitted it into the lock. The door swung open, and they walked through, began to climb a winding stone staircase, lit every fifteen or twenty feet by torches. On the first landing, Faolein thought he heard the door below slam shut, the rattle of another key in the lock.

No matter. A locked door was nothing compared to the tangled web of deadly circumstance that held him now, both like and unlike the *aniffath* he had tried to unravel so many years ago, which had claimed Nimenoë. Perhaps this, too, was a curse, one he could by no means escape, once he had willingly walked in. Very well, then. A wizard had always one last recourse, if he could bring himself to accept the necessity.

Saer threw open another door, and they came out on a wall-walk, behind the jagged line of battlements encircling the fortress. It was so dark that Faolein could scarcely see two yards in front of him, as though a mist or a cloud obscured the moon; but he could smell the air, feel the night around him.

"You hesitate to commit yourself or the other Masters of Leal," said Saer. They had reached a round open place, surrounded by a crenellated parapet wall and walkways radiating out in all directions, and there they paused. "I have letters, documents to show you," said Dreyde. "If you will deign to examine them."

Documents, here? He is not a very good liar. But Faolein was scarcely listening anymore. There was a distraction, a disruption in the flow of energy along the ley lines. He glanced around him, looking with his inner Sight.

The source of that disruption was a great unworked stone set into the tower wall. Roughly triangular in shape, it glimmered faintly in Faolein's mind; not as though it *reflected* light, but as though it deflected it, turned it aside. And cold, bitter cold seemed to flow from that stone.

This *is the reason the fortress was built,* he realized. *Not to protect. Not to preserve. But to guard and contain whatever is prisoned inside that thing.* Yet all this time, Dreyde seemed unaware, he continued to babble on, about plots and incriminating letters, as though he never guessed that the stone was there, as though he never thought that Faolein would sense anything amiss. Because he could not feel the power himself, he imagined that the wizard could not either.

There was a shriek like metal against metal; a flash of deep indigo light split the fog. Faolein instinctively turned away, gathering up the skirts of his robe to flee; though his course was set, some things there are that flesh and blood do not willingly endure. Yet even as he took the first step the trap was sprung.

One—two—three—four—*five* rainbow-hued flames rose up in swift succession. Lightning forked from tower to tower, leaving behind shimmering lines of pure force, forming a gigantic five-pointed star. And Faolein stood frozen in place, completely immobilized, trapped inside the pentagram. His hand lost its grip on the staff, which clattered at his feet, and Saer, with a look equally compounded of malice and fear, kicked it aside.

The fog was rapidly dissipating. From the corners of his eyes, Faolein could see most of the trap that held him. Dreyde could apparently see it, too, though he had been blind and deaf to the stone, for he gave a triumphant laugh and stepped easily outside the pentagram.

"Had I thought it such a small matter to trap a Master Wizard, I might have better enjoyed my dinner."

As the last flags of mist faded, Thaga appeared on one of the walkways, just outside the lines of the figure. In the waxy moonlight, his face was as pale as death, and his hands worked nervously. "We cannot hold him so forever," he shouted across at Saer. "Look at his eyes. Though he doesn't speak, doesn't move, already he is working a *lledrion* to free himself."

Dreyde took several more steps along the wall-walk. His face, which had seemed so pleasant before, was distorted with fear and something even uglier. "But *can* he free himself? You told me the pentagram would be effective!"

Thaga's nervous hands caught at his hanging sleeve, began to twist the silk. He seemed overwhelmed by what he had done already and terrified of what he had to do next. Almost, Faolein could find it in his heart to pity him. "It is the Great Pentacle—harmless to ordinary men, but potent against even the greatest wizard. It will hold him long enough."

Young Saer took another involuntary step, putting more distance between himself and Faolein. "But why do you delay? You promised me—"

"These things require time, they require—certain instruments. One such instrument is being prepared as we speak. To kill a Master Wizard with or without magic, is no small task, and it is dangerous, *dangerous*." Thaga spoke in short, panting breaths. "There are only a very few ways that the thing can be done at all, and each of them carries its own risk.

"Have patience, Lord. It will soon be over. Then we can send word of our success to our noble visitors."

It was a maze; it was an endless labyrinth of rooms and corridors, of chambers, halls, passageways, and closets; it went on like a nightmare, forever. Sindérian had known that the fortress of Saer was old; now she had a confused vision of workmen laboring under the hill for centuries upon centuries, burrowing in the earth like moles.

She and Prince Ruan had been prowling through the castle and that part of the fortress that was under the hill for some interminable period, the Prince stalking on ahead with his lighted torch and Sindérian following, haggard and spiritless, reeling with weariness.

Thanks to Ruan's keen eyes and ears they had so far avoided any encounter with the inhabitants. There had been several close calls and moments when she was absolutely certain they would be discovered, but always they managed to pass undetected.

Nevertheless, their efforts to find Faolein and the two men-at-arms had so far proved fruitless. *And sooner or later,* Sindérian reflected hopelessly, *we will make a mistake, blunder into a room full of people.*

Prince Ruan touched her lightly on the arm, cocked his head as though he was listening to something only he could hear. Then he extinguished the torch, and she was able to see a faint ruddy glow in the passage ahead of them.

Moving even more cautiously, they approached the source of the light: another low-ceilinged corridor that met the one they had been following at right angles. Now Sindérian could smell smoke and just make out faint voices around the corner, a conversation that came to her in fragments:

"... gives me the creeps, that wizard up there. And whatever *devilry* our Lord and that blasted *Thaga* are planning—"

"—had a notion you'd not be able to stomach it. Well, I think it uncanny, too. I've brought something to put a little courage into us all."

Peering around an edge of rough stone, Sindérian saw five guardsmen camped outside a door at the far end of the cross corridor. They were warming their hands at a small charcoal brazier and passing a wineskin between them. She thought she had never seen men look so panicked, or so determined to hide it.

The earth rumbled under her feet, and Sindérian caught at the wall to keep from falling. Around the corner, faces blanched, and the man who was holding the leather flask dropped it. There was another jolt; a wooden doorframe groaned and splintered, and a stone cracked. But it was only a stronger version of the tremors they had all been experiencing for days.

"Full moon," said one of the men, picking up the wineskin, and they all laughed uneasily.

A third shock followed, and a little rain of dry sand dribbled out between stone blocks, where their grinding together turned mortar into dust. Then there was silence.

Sindérian glanced back over her shoulder. By the set of Ruan's jaw, the way that his fingers strayed to the hilt of his sword, she realized he was about to try something heroic, something foolhardy. "No," she whispered. "Do *nothing* so reckless. I beg you, Prince Ruan, *leave this to me*."

He turned on her an incredulous look, as if to remind her of who he was, that he was not accustomed to take orders from anyone. So they stood for a moment, eye to eye, equally stubborn, both of them determined, but Ruan gave in first, shrugging.

Sindérian closed her eyes. It would not be easy at this distance to put a spell on the wine, but she thought that she could manage it. Wine made men sleepy and stupid; it was only a matter of increasing its natural properties. She mumbled the words hastily under her breath, picturing the leather flask in her mind, focusing all of her will on the task.

Yet she felt a twinge of guilt doing so. She had been making sleep charms since she was a child, but she had never witched wine before, and to put men under a spell of sleep for any purpose but healing or relief from pain was coming unpleasantly close to a *waethas*, a sorcerous binding. *But I intend them no actual harm*, she told herself. *And surely it is, it must be, pardonable on* that *account*.

She felt the spell take hold. Opening her eyes, she edged back to the corner, and watched as the wineskin passed from hand to hand. It made one circuit, then another, amidst increasing merriment.

Ruan drew in a hissing breath, she could hear his restless movements in the shadows beside her. Sindérian herself was painfully conscious of the passage of time. Had her spell been enough? Should she have done more?

But as the wine went around for a third, then a fourth time, the guards went from boisterous to muddled and silly. From there, their descent into drunkenness was gratifyingly swift. They giggled, they slurred their words, they made foolish jokes. And then, one by one, they began to slump or topple to the floor.

The last man standing remained on his feet for almost a minute, staring down at his comrades with a puzzled expression. Then his face relaxed, his knees buckled, and he fell down across the inert bodies of his friends.

Up on the moonlit battlements, the same young servant whose signal to Lord Dreyde had alerted the Prince earlier appeared out of the night, carrying in his arms a long awkward bundle wrapped up in scarlet silk.

"Ah," said Thaga, as the youth shuffled in his direction, along the high walkway. "Here comes my apprentice, his task complete."

Dreyde had retreated from the round tower where the wizard was bound, in order to join Thaga on the wall-walk. He lounged against the embattled parapet, feigning a confidence he did not feel.

A moment later the boy was beside them, laying his burden at the magician's feet. Thaga bent down, threw off the scarlet covering, and opened the lid of a long ebony box banded in iron. Very carefully, he removed two objects, handling them reverently. One was a silver bow strung with silk, and the other a long crystal arrow, the shaft inscribed with geometric figures and hieroglyphs, the barbed head covered with a pungent oily substance. He spoke in a breathless whisper. "Prepare to see what few have seen before: the destruction of a Master Wizard."

But just as he spoke, the earth trembled, and the walls shook; the walkway heaved under their feet. The apprentice scuttled away sideways, not wanting to turn his back, yet not wishing to see what was about to happen. At the next jolt, the boy lost his nerve altogether and bolted. Down in the stable yard and the sheep pens, all the animals set up a commotion at once, wild with fear.

"Is this his doing?" asked Saer sharply, jerking his head in Faolein's direction.

"Perhaps he encourages it," said Thaga, with a nervous shift of his eyes. "But if he had the ability to bring down the walls, I can assure you, Lord Drcyde, he would have done so by now."

He fitted the arrow to the bow, aiming the point directly at the wizard's heart. The sorcerer began to chant. His spell hissed and mumbled; the air around him grew heavy, leaden, sickly. The moon overhead turned a dull red, like an old wound.

"*Andeissach séo feilh oewislin,*" cried Thaga, drawing and loosing the crystal arrow. "*Om yffran dioha Faolein.*"

Perhaps his hand was unsteady, perhaps the earth gave another slight imperceptible shake; however it was, the missile did not fly true. The arrow streaked through the air and buried itself in the wizard's side, under his ribs.

A shudder passed over Faolein, a shivering across the skin.

His face contorted in agony. All the air around him seemed to shatter, then flesh and blood began to fray, to dissipate like smoke, but just as the last faint traces threatened to disappear entirely, they began to take on substance again, a boiling cloud of matter writhing and spinning in the air, as if struggling to assume its accustomed form.

All at once, the five colored lights on the towers went out, and the lines of the pentacle faded. Where Faolein had been, chaos shaped itself into a great bird of prey, an immense sea eagle. With a cry that rent the night, it spread its wings and rose high into the air. Light blazed up again, but this time it was golden and pulsing with life.

Thaga gasped and fell back against the parapet wall, but Dreyde stood rooted to the spot. The eagle was beautiful and terrible, all silver and gold, its talons swinging like scythes overhead. The thunder of its wings seemed to rock the towers anew. Light poured from it like water, spilling from its feathered wingtips and setting the night on fire. The sorcerer shaded his eyes; Saer covered his with both hands.

Then, suddenly, the eagle's light was extinguished; a cold wind blew across the battlements, across the tower roof. With another shrill cry, the great raptor launched itself into the sky. For many minutes more, they could hear the mighty strokes of its wings, like a gigantic heartbeat, as it flew off into the night.

For a time, neither man spoke, neither moved. Then Thaga rose unsteadily to his feet, dusted himself off. Dreyde uncovered his eyes, passed a hand across his forehead, which was drenched in sweat.

"It is done," said the magician, in a shaken voice.

But the Lord of Saer ground his teeth and gnawed on his lower lip. "He isn't dead. He ought to be dead."

"He is as good as dead," said Thaga, in a dull, flat voice.

"He is trapped in that shape more effectively than in the pentacle; he will never escape it. And the change will drive him mad. Either he will fly until his heart bursts from exhaustion, or he will freeze to death in the upper air."

———

Two flights below, Faolein's daughter and the Prince crept out from their place of concealment and approached the sleeping guards.

Ruan was all for cutting their throats while they slept, but Sindérian threw out a hand to stop him. "No. I *can't* permit you to do that."

He bridled again, gave her another black look under his silvery eyebrows. "Lady, we are surrounded by enemies."

"But these are helpless."

"We may encounter them again when they are *not helpless*. And we have already been betrayed. These people," he said, with a sudden intensity, "these people may have injured you even more than you know."

Sindérian drew in a breath. She could guess what he meant: that Faolein might be dead, or hurt in some way that she could not heal. "For all that," she replied in a voice shaking with outrage, "I did not render these men helpless so that you could slaughter them like sheep!"

The earth rumbled again; the fortress rocked like a ship in a storm. There was an underground concussion like a clap of thunder, which stunned the ear. But the foundations held.

Sindérian could see the hunger for revenge in Prince Ruan's face, the Ni-Féa compulsion that burned so fiercely within him. For a moment, she was afraid that he would kill the men in spite of her. But he only swore under his breath and rammed his dagger back into its sheath. Then, bending down, he began to search the fallen guardsmen, one by one, until he found the key to the door.

He fitted the key in the lock, and the door swung open with a grating sound; something had settled during the earthquake. Sindérian could see the foot of a stone staircase curving upward into shadows. Prince Ruan led the way, and she followed after him.

"You thought me a fool back there," she said as she climbed.

Ascending three steps ahead of her, he shrugged his shoulders but did not look back. "I have heard it said that wizards are overscrupulous. Now I see that it's true."

"Wizards must needs be overscrupulous—and princes, too. It is far too easy for us to become tyrants, arrogant and merciless!"

He glanced back at her then, a quick look under his long eyelashes, not without irony. "I might take that to heart, Lady, if there were fewer than a dozen kinsmen between me and the throne."

At the top of the stairs, Sindérian felt a sudden urgency. Possessed by a reckless feverish haste, she pushed past the Prince, threw open the door, and slipped on through. She came out on the walkway behind the battlements, with a clear view in all directions.

The moon shone down, huge and horrible, almost as bright as day. Sindérian set off walking, following the parapet wall, going as fast as her legs would carry her, until she came to the flat roof of the round tower, where Ruan finally overtook her.

"Take care," he warned, catching her by the arm. "I sense a trap."

She shook him off, took another two steps. Something

brittle crunched underfoot. She could still sense the lines of force from tower to tower. They left a smell like lightning on the night air, and the stones continued to sizzle with energy. Something had drawn on the power here, on the wards and the ley lines. When she closed her eyes, it was as if she could see a faint residue of the pentagram lingering on the air, but rapidly fading. "A trap has already been sprung!"

She opened her eyes. Catching sight of something at her feet that glittered in the moonlight, she bent down and picked it up. It was a splintered shaft of crystal about as long as her hand.

As she realized what she held, her fingers suddenly went slack, and the crystal shaft dropped at her feet. Over by the parapet she caught sight of the silver bow, gleaming with a sullen light, where the magician had cast it aside.

With a wrenching cry of despair, Sindérian threw herself down on her knees. "There are not many ways to destroy a wizard like Faolein, but they have found one—they have found one!" She beat both fists against her knees.

Never there when I am needed, she thought. Tears ran down her face and her breath came out in great tearing sobs. *Why will they never let me stand with them and die?* She bent almost double, and pain shot through her entire body.

He had no right to leave me, she raged into the night. *He had no right!*

"Is he dead, then?" said Prince Ruan, sounding bewildered.

Raising her head, Sindérian was surprised to see him kneeling there beside her, one hand extended, as if uncertain whether to offer sympathy or not. She gasped for breath, gazed up at him with red-rimmed eyes. "If he's not dead now, he will be soon." She shoved a fist into her mouth to stifle the sobs.

Yet she was a wizard and a healer, trained since childhood in a hard, hard school to put grief aside and do whatever had to be done. She might wish to stay there and wail like a lost child, but she knew that she would not. Too much depended on her— too much depended on whether she could think clearly, and make the right decisions. She had all her life before her to grieve for Faolein's death.

Wiping her eyes on her sleeve, she put back her hair with both hands. "Do you see—this was not the work of a moment, or even an hour," she said hoarsely. "The preparations necessary for casting the Great Pentacle take an entire day, and to hallow and prepare the crystal arrow takes even longer. Beyond all doubt, we were *expected* here!"

At that moment, there was a clatter and a rush of footsteps along the walls. The Prince sprang lightly to his feet.

"We have been spotted," he said, catching her up just behind the elbow and forcing her to stand. She stumbled, tripping on the hem of her gown, and would have fallen except for his painful grip on her arm.

Recovering her balance, she allowed him to pull her behind him, back the way they had just come. Men shouted, a gong somewhere began to sound, and an arrow flew past Sindérian's head, so close that she could feel the feathered fletching brush against her cheek. She saw Ruan duck his head just in time to avoid another.

At last they reached the doorway and passed on through. Ruan pulled the door shut behind them and slammed the bar into place.

12

*

The last red light of sunset burned on the water, reflected off brass-plated figureheads, as a vast fleet of black ships, powered by great banks of oars, rounded the point at Apharos, glided past the last of the nine grim fortresses guarding the harbor and the bay, and came out on the open sea.

Standing on the foredeck of his flagship, which alone bore Ouriána's likeness cast in solid gold, Prince Cuillioc gazed out across a seemingly boundless expanse of fiery ocean, and for one moment it seemed that all the world had turned to blood and flame.

Then the water began to swirl and shimmer with a sorcerous light. An almost impossibly beautiful vision appeared on the surface: Ouriána, her face pale as pearl, her eyes as deep and dark as the night sky, her ruddy hair stretching out across the sea from horizon to horizon in burning streamers of crimson and gold. The night fairly swooned with her presence, like heady incense.

He saw her red lips move, heard her voice chiming like crystal against crystal inside his head: *Do not fail me. This time, do not disappoint me.*

Cuillioc's mouth went suddenly dry; he clutched at the rail, his pulses quickening. For a brief time more she was there, filling the night; then her image faded, and the sea went dark and empty. The Prince released a long slow breath, and his shoulders sagged.

This time, do not disappoint me. It was, he knew too well, meant for a warning as much as a command. If Mirizandi did not fall; if he did not return to Apharos in the autumn, his ships richly laden with silks and perfumes, gold, gemstones, jade, and rare spices; if instead of the fabled wealth of the southern continent he had nothing to lay at her feet but another tale of misfortune and miscalculation . . .

Ouriána had excused much in the past simply because he was her son, yet she was not, as a rule, either patient or forgiving. The thought that he might spend the rest of his days banished from her presence, crushed by the terrible knowledge of her implacable displeasure—Cuillioc felt a familiar pain twist inside him, and it was almost too much to bear.

The sun went down beneath the water, and a young moon painted the sea in shades of silver. It was after midnight before the wind freshened, the sails were set, and the Prince abandoned his vantage point on the deck for his cabin and his narrow bed, hoping to catch an hour or two of sleep before sunrise.

But his mind was overwrought, his nerves unstrung with anticipation. And every time he closed his eyes, he could feel the horror of the nightmare pressing down on him; all his hopes and fears chased each other through his brain. He tossed and turned, threw off his silken comforters, and beat at his goose-down pillows, until finally the very effort to rest exhausted him, and he rose from his bunk, cold and haggard in the chill grey hour before the dawn. Dressing hastily, he returned to his place beside the rail just in time to see the first flash of gold on the eastern horizon.

———

For more than a fortnight the armada continued south and east, between the scattered islands of the central archipelago. Depending on the wind, they rowed or sailed: past lonely islands where primitive villages straggled along ivory beaches or huddled under shiny black cliffs; past islets clothed in trees, and atolls occupied only by multitudes of seabirds.

A hundred miles from the southern continent, where a chain of rocky islets so small, desolate, and uninhabitable they did not appear on any map jutted out of the sea, the galleys each dropped anchor, small boats were lowered from the sides, and slaves rowed the various dignitaries from their respective vessels to the Prince's flagship, there to take part in a final Council of War before the invasion.

The priest Iobhar was the first to arrive, pale and unnatural in his scarlet robes, but soon the deck was aswarm with the richly clad nobles, each apparently intent on outshining his fellows.

Their meeting was brief but decisive. Elaborate plans had been laid before leaving Phaôrax, and no one, least of all Cuillioc, saw fit to alter those plans in any detail. Having arrived at an agreement with remarkable dispatch, everyone then took part in a meal laid out by the Prince's servants for the Prince's guests under a crimson silk canopy.

Whatever his faults, none could deny that Prince Cuillioc was an excellent host, and his flagship had embarked fully provisioned. Moreover, there were those in attendance that day who, for all their gaudy display of velvets and embroidered silks, were accustomed to regard themselves as purse-pinched if not absolutely indigent—they were therefore more than happy to dine at the Prince's expense, on mussels simmered in white wine and artichokes steeped in butter; on salads of cress and sharp green lettuce, poached fish of all sorts, eel pies, and soft cheeses; to nibble on candied fruits and sip a cool sweet wine flavored with anise.

While these noble gentleman inclined to linger long over the sugared figs and dates, there were others who wandered off together in smaller groups, seeking such privacy as the limited space provided. The furiádh Iobhar and a certain Lord Cado made up one such cabal, and were, in fact, the first to excuse themselves.

They retreated to the tiny afterdeck, where they were deep in conversation when the priest startled his companion by interrupting himself in midsentence and diving behind a pile of rope and tackle. There he engaged in a brief brisk scuffle with some unknown person and emerged a moment later dragging behind him a scrawny small boy, rather grubbily attired as a page in soiled silks and rubbed velvets.

"Now, whose spy are you, little rat?" hissed Iobhar, holding both thin wrists in an iron grip that the child could not break for all his squirming and his frantic struggles. When the boy refused to speak, the priest heaved him up off the deck and dangled him over the rail.

Suspended some fifteen feet in the air with nothing between him and the dazzling surface of the water, the urchin very wisely went utterly limp and still.

"Is it mute, do you suppose?" asked Lord Cado, viewing the proceedings with a dispassionate eye.

Ignoring his question, Iobhar spoke to the boy in a threatening growl. "I don't suppose you know how to swim, little rat. I have only to open my hand and you'll sink like a rock, never to be seen again."

"Your pardon," said a cool voice behind him. "But that disreputable object belongs to me. If he has done anything to annoy you, I can only apologize, but unless one of you has a burning desire to spend the rest of the voyage acting as my body servant, I urge you to return him to me. A comely child he is not, but he is the only page I've brought with me."

Iobhar dropped the boy unceremoniously on the deck. He landed with a soft thud, scrambled to his feet, and scurried below. The priest and Lord Cado acknowledged Prince Cuillioc's presence with stiff bows.

"Great Lord," said Iobhar, slipping his hands into the hanging sleeves of his scarlet robe. He bared his yellow teeth in what might have been intended for a conciliating smile, their color a startling contrast with his dead white skin and hair.

It was unlikely he had ever been a good-looking man, with his sloping forehead and weak chin, but of all the Furiádhin there was a particularly loathsome quality about him—one that never failed to raise the fine hairs at the back of Cuillioc's neck. It was said that no man knew the precise nature of Iobhar's deformity, but he walked with a slight limp, and sometimes there was a little scaly rustling sound under the long train of his robes. Next to Goezenou, the Prince hated him most of all.

"I had no idea I was meddling with your property. The boy was insolent; I will say no more than that. No doubt you will wish to deal with the matter yourself."

"No doubt I will," Cuillioc replied agreeably, baring his own even white teeth. "As well as any other displays of—insolence—I might chance to encounter."

Hostility flared, briefly, between the Prince and the furiádh. But then, with an effort, Iobhar remembered himself. "I am duly reprimanded," he murmured, making a deeper and more reverent obeisance than before. "But surely the son of the Goddess knows that I am his to command."

Cuillioc shrugged. "That goes without saying. As for the boy—I will make certain that he doesn't annoy you again."

The visitors returned to their ships soon after, and it was time to pull up anchor. With a stiff breeze bellying their sails, the Prince's armada left the chain of islands behind and looked fair to reach the Bay of Mir before many more days had passed.

They had strayed into waters where no man of Phaôrax had ventured for more than a hundred years. By night, clouds of stars whirled overhead in strange constellations. So alien were these stars that Cuillioc could never quite make out their patterns; as soon as he thought he detected a figure, it somehow seemed to shift. By day, a hot southern sun beat mercilessly down, turning the waves the color of molten gold.

Once, a school of whales swam by in the middle distance. With water pouring off their blue-grey flanks, they sent up columns of wild white spray. Another time, the Prince's galley passed by a solitary beached leviathan, dying on a rocky shoal. Staring into the tiny sunken eye of the half-dead whale, Cuillioc felt a shiver of fear pass through his stomach at the ill omen.

It soon proved accurate. The fleet was spread out over a half mile of ocean, already within sight of land, when a great storm roared in from the east, bringing with it a pelting rain and waves of such enormous size they seemed likely to swamp some of the smaller vessels.

Cuillioc arrived on deck, caught hold of a mast to keep

from being blown away, and peered out across the water. Visibility was so poor that most of the fleet was already hidden behind inpenetrable curtains of rain, yet it was impossible to mistake Iobhar standing at the rail of the nearest ship, his red robes flapping, his silky white hair streaming on the wind, as he shouted out spells to quell the blast.

Whether by chance or design, his sorcery took effect too late to prevent the Prince's ship being separated from the others and blown back out to sea. Driven by fierce winds, pounded by colossal waves, the galley was soon swamped. The Master stood on the afterdeck bawling out orders that no one could hear, and even the Prince and the gentlemen of his household took their turns at the pumps. By dint of furious pumping and bailing, they managed to keep afloat—though how long they might be able to do so was anyone's guess.

For a day and a night, the storm continued. Cuillioc was often on deck, lending a hand wherever he could, feeling the agony of the ship as though it were his own, as she was pounded by the wind and tossed from wave to wave. His face lashed raw by the gale-driven rain and his eyes streaming with salt tears, his voice grew hoarse and his lips chapped, yet he continued to work right alongside the other men. Again and again, he felt the ship raised high by a monstrous grey wave, then dropped through the air to hit the sea with such force that the galley shuddered from stem to stern. It hardly seemed she could continue to suffer such abuse without breaking up.

Then, just as suddenly as it had sprung up, the storm died. The clouds parted, flooding sea and sky with warm amber light. Wind and wave subsided; air and water went utterly still.

Rolling a red-rimmed eye at his nearest companions, Cuillioc went below, cursing his luck. First storm-tossed, now becalmed. He began to doubt whether he would ever see Mirizandi at all.

Meanwhile, with the sails hanging slack and the ship floating motionless on the sun-shot face of the water, the Master gave orders to break out the oars. Down in his cabin, the Prince heard the by-now-familiar rattle and thump of oars slipping into place. Then the drum took up its monotonous *thud-thunk*, like a weary heartbeat.

The slaves kept at their backbreaking labor for hour after hour in the relentless heat, faces red, muscles straining, skins slick with sweat, until word came down from Prince Cuillioc to drop anchor and give the men a rest.

A short while later, the shipmaster, going in search of the Prince and finding him sprawled, sick and exhausted on his bed, was moved to protest. "Great Prince, there was no need. It's not my place to question your orders, but in all truth the men were good for a long time yet."

Cuillioc put his hands behind his head, scowled at the man across the candlelit cabin. "We'll not reach Mirizandi any sooner by killing the oarsmen."

The Master shuffled his feet. "They're able to do more than you may think. And even if we lose a man here and there, I promise you, Great Prince, it will hardly matter. The ones that survive can be urged on to greater efforts, being that much stronger."

"In common humanity, then. And in recognition of their mighty labors working the pumps during the storm."

The man goggled at him. "In common hu— The oarsmen are *slaves*—criminals snatched from the *gallows*."

But Cuillioc had made up his mind. He had seen what happened when galley slaves were pushed too hard, the way the bodies of the dead—and sometimes of those too weak to continue rowing—were commonly thrown overboard to lighten the load. He had no wish to leave a trail of waterlogged and fish-eaten corpses behind him, all the way to Mirizandi.

"We will wait here until sunset. If the wind doesn't rise, the men can row all through the night, when it is cooler."

Shaking his head, the Master withdrew. The Prince rolled over on his side, pulled a pillow over his head, and lapsed into a restless doze, from which he woke a short or a long time later, trembling, sweaty, and hagridden.

He reappeared on deck just as the sun was hovering on the horizon, about to dip into the ocean. A large flock of seagulls flew overhead, heading for the land. Cuillioc leaned over the rail, watching them grow smaller and smaller until they finally disappeared in the dusky air. A waxing moon was already high in the sky.

Just as the sun went down, a stiff breeze sprang up. There was activity in the rigging, the sails were set, and soon the galley went skimming across the water far more swiftly than the men could have rowed her.

Cuillioc went up to the afterdeck, where he stood sniffing the air. There was, he decided, a distinct scent of sorcery on the wind. Nor had he any doubt as to the origin of this highly convenient change in the weather. His heart swelled within him.

Looking in the direction of Phaôrax, he folded his arms and bowed his head in the ritual salute accorded the Empress. "Thank you, Mother," he said under his breath.

And feeling that he had somehow been unaccountably returned to favor, he turned around and went below with a light step and a satisfied smile on his face.

13

✳

The cell where the two guardsmen Jago and Aell languished was in a dungeon buried deep beneath the hill. How deep it was impossible to say, for the way they had been hustled—and sometimes carried when they refused to walk— had involved many long flights of stairs, spiraling down and down, to the very bowels and fundament of the earth it seemed.

But perhaps that perception was exaggerated. Jago had an idea that his own furious attempts to break free, and the rough handling these had provoked, had greatly prolonged the journey. After a while, someone or something had hit him over the head, sending the man-at-arms into peaceful oblivion . . . until he woke in this place with an aching skull and Aell stretched out beside him on the dank stone floor, looking as bruised and battered as he himself felt.

The charity of their captors had been scanty enough: two squat tallow candles, one wooden cup, and an earthenware bottle half-full of water. No other refreshment was offered, though hours passed.

But at least, Jago recalled, *there was beef and ale in the barracks before some mysterious order came down—before we were attacked and taken prisoner.* He wondered where the Prince was, and the two wizards. Dead, maybe, all three of them. Even the powerful could be taken by treachery; no one was immune to *that,* perhaps the wizards of Leal least of all.

In Jago's experience, two sorts of men were most vulnerable to trickery: those who were treacherous themselves, and those so honorable that they never dreamed of betraying a trust. The middle sort like himself, essentially honest but highly practical, tended to see the world as it was, for whatever good that was likely to do them, being sworn, as often as not, to serve one or the other of the other two kinds and share in their troubles.

The cell in which he found himself now was rough, unfinished stone, smelling of earth and stagnant water: more cave than cell, except for a stout wooden door with a barred window and some rusty iron chains dangling from one wall. Otherwise, there was not a bone or a rag to tell about previous prisoners. Even the rats had abandoned this place, even the spiders. Perhaps it had not been used for a long, long time.

On waking, Jago and Aell had pulled themselves up off the floor, and they sat huddled together on a rough cot on which someone had placed a musty old mattress stuffed with moldy hay. It seemed warmer so, sitting back to back, or at least more companionable. But after a while the cold of the place wearied the soul, it sapped the spirit. Seeping past iron rings and padded jacks, it crept into the very marrow of the bones, turning the blood to ice. And they were already using the second candle. Soon, even that tiny spark of light, that meager warmth, would be gone.

"I wonder," said Aell, "if it might be morning yet—and of what day?"

Jago nodded morosely. All hours were the same here.

Sometimes, they could hear the echo of footsteps a long way off. But it was as difficult to judge distances as it was the passage of time; sound bounced off walls, repeated itself again and again and again. And whenever he or Aell left the cot to pace the cell, walking from one end to the other with restless, impatient movements, their own footsteps seemed to die underfoot, as though the floor absorbed them. "This place is uncanny. Why don't they just kill us and be done with it?"

"We have a duty to live and to reach that place we were going to—if we can," said Aell.

Jago pondered that for a while, sitting with his chin in his hands. "Perhaps we do," he replied at last. "Though what we expect to accomplish there without the great ones to speak their piece and do all the persuading, I don't know."

They both knew they stood very little chance of finding out. Barring the survival of Ruan or one of the wizards to effect a rescue, their own prospects looked dim.

Whenever an earthquake struck and the walls shook, Jago wondered idly whether he and his old friend would live to be murdered on purpose, or maybe were fated to be buried alive accidentally.

"This cell has been here for hundreds of years, and Saer has been shaking like this every month since the world Changed, and maybe before that," said Aell, as if sharing the same thought. "I don't see us being entombed alive, I really don't.

"*Not,*" he added, shifting his position so that the cot creaked, "not that this isn't a regular burial vault. I suppose if they just abandon us here, it will come to much the same thing."

Jago rubbed his eyes with the heels of his hands. "It will be quicker and more merciful, though, if the hill falls down on us."

Perhaps their voices covered the sound of approaching

footsteps. When a key scraped in the lock, that was all the warning they had. Aell sprang up at once, and Jago (larger, heavier, and always a bit slower) lumbered to his feet an instant later.

So they were standing braced for battle—prepared to sell their lives dearly, weaponless though they were—when the door slowly swung open and a willowy pale-haired figure strolled into the cell carrying their swords. With a brief courtly bow over the hilts, he gestured toward the open door, as though inviting the astonished prisoners to step through.

"And who might *you* be?" asked Aell, hanging back with a suspicious look. But Jago, ever the more impulsive, reached out and retrieved his weapon, fastening the sheath to his belt.

"I am the one who is going to lead you and your friends to safety, the Fates willing," said the stranger. He looked to be about nineteen and was dressed as a squire or a page in Saer's livery, yet his hair, which he wore in a long braid down his back, was purest silver in the flickering candlelight. Though not much taller than Aell, he gave the impression of being long-limbed and peculiarly supple.

The men-at-arms exchanged a bewildered glance. They were not so gullible as to accept this astounding offer at face value, though cudgel their brains as they might, neither man could come up with a single reason why the offer should be made at all if not sincerely.

"You've been overlooked so far," said the stranger, cocking his head and watching them slantwise out of luminous yellow eyes. There was something about him that reminded Jago of Prince Ruan—and a great deal not. "But when Dreyde and Thaga get over the fright they have given themselves dealing with the two wizards and finally remember your existence, I fear that things may go very badly with you. Do you mean to

stand there and stare at me forever, or will you allow me to rescue you?"

Aell reached out and took his sword, drew it from its
sheath. He inspected the blade carefully, then nodded, one
short, quick movement before heading for the door.

"Oh, we'll allow you to do it," he flung over his shoulder
as he left the cell. "But perhaps you won't take offense if we're
just a little uneasy accepting your help, under the circumstances."

<hr/>

Sindérian and the Prince had somehow managed to elude their
pursuers. But the fortress was so vast and so complex, and parts
of it were so long-abandoned and empty, it was no difficult task
to lose someone or something, or to become lost oneself.

In order to avoid a meeting with Dreyde's guardsmen, they
had descended several flights, scraping their heads passing
through a low doorway all but hidden in the shadows, then
stumbled down a long limestone passageway into an uninhab-
ited part of the castle. Once she was certain that no one was following, Sindérian dredged up the strength to conjure a little
werelight: a lighter-than-air sphere of blue-grey phosphores-
ence that promptly attached itself to the hilt of Ruan's sword,
as the nearest bright object.

And there it had remained, providing very little in the way
of illumination, though it seemed to be enough for the Prince,
who could apparently see like a cat, so long as there was even
the tinest glimmer of light. He moved ahead with a long, confident stride, and Sindérian trailed obediently behind him:
through ancient dining halls and pantries and sculleries,
through a sour-smelling room full of wine casks turning to

vinegar—too heart-weary and sick to challenge his leadership or ask any questions.

Until something about the pattern of cracked tiles on the floor in one of the greater rooms struck her as somehow familiar, and she glanced up and said with a frown: "We have been this way before!"

"Yes."

Sindérian shook the hair out of her eyes. "We have been walking in circles for some time."

"Yes," said the Prince, resting one hand on a harp that was strung with cobwebs. "I am afraid we are lost."

Nevertheless, they had no choice but to continue on.

At the next place where two corridors met, Ruan chose to turn right where he had gone left before, which brought them into a series of abandoned bedchambers and wardrobes, where doors hung loose on broken hinges, where great four-poster beds clothed in embroidered hangings were mildewed and rotting, and everything lay under a thick pall of dust.

Sometimes, they passed below an air shaft, and a rumor of distant voices came down to them, faint and echoing. Sometimes they entered a room where the walls had been plastered and frescoed, though the paintings, whatever they were, had long since been obscured by woodsmoke and patches of damp. Once, they stopped to catch their breath in an old armory, where knives and swords and hand axes still hung in rusty ranks upon the walls.

"Saer," said the Prince, looking pensive in his circle of dim blue light, "must have housed a vast multitude of people, once. Before the catastrophe, perhaps as recently as before the war. It must have been like a small city here, above and below the ground."

Sindérian nodded wearily. Now it was like nothing so

much as a catacomb, a great tomb, if not full of moldering bones, at least full of dead hopes and dead dreams. Goslin, she remembered, had lost both his valiant young sons and all three of his brothers in the war with Phaôrax. Undoubtedly, much else had been lost as well.

Ruan reached out and, with a light touch on her arm, directed Sindérian down another passageway. His manner toward her had been stripped of all arrogance and grown strangely gentle—though there were bruises on her wrists where he had held her before, rough in his haste and his concern for her safety.

Is this pity? she wondered dully. If so, she did not like it, did not want any part of it, yet she was much too tired to resist it actively.

Her eyes burned with tears and sleeplessness. Sometimes she walked in a daze, mindless, empty, beyond grief. Sometimes she remembered; then rage and hatred flared up, filling her emptiness with a single purpose:

If it should be that Thaga crosses our path, I will kill him.

"This way, I think," said the Prince. They had stopped, indecisively, at the foot of a broad staircase, the first stair leading *up* that they had seen in a long time.

Sindérian gathered up the heavy skirts of her wine-colored gown and followed Ruan up two flights of shallow stairs, then through a soaring archway.

They came out into a wide lofty hall, its distant ceiling upheld by massive white pillars that glowed with a faint pearlescent light. On the farthest wall there was a line of tall windows in deep embrasures, looking out on the night.

No, not the night but the morning, Sindérian realized when she drew closer to the windows. The moon had set, the stars had faded, and the sky was all purple and gold with dawn.

Prince Ruan unlatched one of the leaded-glass casements,

threw it open, and stood looking out. He remained there so long that Sindérian grew curious. She joined him in the alcove, leaning out across a windowsill wet with dew.

These windows overlooked the road leading up from the valley. Even so, it was a long way to the ground. By craning her neck, she could just see a section of the ramparts as well as the gatehouse.

"Had we a rope," said the Prince, mentally calculating the distance to the road, "we might perhaps descend."

Sindérian blinked at him incredulously. "And be shot at by Saer's archers while we dangle in the air?"

Ruan merely shrugged. It was a moot point; they had no rope, and no way of getting one.

They heard voices down below, a jingling of harnesses in the courtyard, and the noise of many men riding in company; then the gates swung open and a large party rode out. From their vantage point at the window, Sindérian and the Prince had a clear view of the horses and their riders: about a dozen men in dull black cloaks, some of them armed, and two in heavier mantles of scarlet brocade, who rode with their hoods thrown back and their white hair streaming behind them in the morning breeze.

"Furiádhin!" Ruan hissed between his teeth.

Sindérian's heart gave a painful leap. The breath caught in her throat, and for a moment it seemed she would pass out with the intensity of her emotions, the hatred and loathing that welled up inside of her.

One of the priests was slight and bright and flamelike. Dainty ivory horns grew from his brow, and he sat easy and graceful in the saddle. Yet he was not effeminate; his boyish face was ascetic, and the ardor of a fanatic burned in his strange silver eyes.

Beside him rode one whom it was *impossible* not to notice: in Sindérian's eyes, everything about him spoke of wounded grandeur, the ruin of something high and splendid, a great man, a great mind degraded. He was tall, very tall, with a lean, powerful face, its inherent nobility marred by a look of ineffable sorrow. One of his hands was withered to a claw, but the other, which held the gilded reins, was beautiful, with strong bones and long, tapering fingers. In the pearly dawnlight his skin and hair glowed softly—somehow, there seemed to be more light about him than any of the others.

Her lips moved, but she did not dare say the names out loud, hardly dared to think them: Dyonas. Camhóinhann. No sign of Goezenou.

Realizing that they risked being seen, she and the Prince drew back into the embrasure, and Ruan silently closed the casement.

"They have ways of speaking with each other across great distances," she whispered. Edging out of the alcove, Sindérian rested her head and shoulders against the wall between two windows. "Goe— the one that we saw in Tregna must have told those down below that we were heading this way. They came here for the express purpose of instigating Dreyde's treachery, and he—either for fear or a desire to please—was ready to be of use to them. But what can it mean: *three* of them traveling through Mere?"

"Have we not already guessed where they are going, what they intend? And they are likely to arrive long before we do. Even when we find our way out of this hellish maze—"

Just then, they heard footsteps crossing the hall, echoing off the vaulted ceiling. The Prince bit back the last of his sentence, and he and Sindérian dived back into the embrasure.

There they waited breathlessly, wondering whether they had already been spotted.

As the sound of boots hitting the polished floor came even nearer, accompanied by a low murmur of voices, a rattle of spurs, Ruan's right hand went to the hilt of his sword. He drew it out so slowly that it slipped almost silently past the silver guard at the top—only a whisper of metal against metal.

The voices and footsteps came louder and closer. Ruan's fingers tightened on the hilt of his sword—then he relaxed his grip and most of the tension flowed out of his body. He knew those voices.

Two men walked past a stone column and into view: one short, dark, compact, and vigorous; the other taller and sturdier, with streaks of grey in his brown hair and beard. But the Prince stiffened again when a third figure entered his line of vision and he realized that Aell and Jago were not alone.

Ruan's sword flashed up, light from the windows glancing off the blade as it descended in a perfect arc—stopping scant inches above the stranger's head when Aell cried out, "A friend. *He is a friend*, Lord Prince. A friend."

Ruan's sword hovered in midair.

"One of your own people," Jago insisted earnestly. "Hear him out, I beg you, Lord. He says he can be of use to us."

Reluctantly, the Prince lowered his sword. Still glaring at the Ni-Ferys squire, he drove the blade back into its sheath. "Not one of *my* people," he said under his breath. "But I will hear him. We have need of friends in this place, I suppose—*even such friends as this.*"

The stranger smiled, a wry little smile, and a challenging look passed between him and Ruan.

"Gilrain Worricker of Airey," he said, with a flourishing

bow. "You do have friends in this place, as well as enemies. Or at least, there are those here who have no wish to serve Ouriána of Phaôrax in any way, and who would be glad to do her an ill turn. If you will permit me, I will show you the swiftest and fastest way out of Saer."

Sindérian hooked a long strand of sweaty dark hair behind her ear. "And why should we trust you, having already been betrayed by Lord Dreyde?"

"Discounting the assistance I have already given your friends? I venture to say that you have little choice. The luck has been with you so far; you have been very fortunate to elude capture. But how much longer do you suppose your luck will continue? Yet I know this castle as few others know it; I can guide you to safety by secret ways."

Aell and Jago became vociferous in support of their new friend, but the Prince remained hostile.

"If it will aid you in making a decision," said Gilrain, "I will tell you that the treachery at Saer goes farther—and yet began closer to home—than you may imagine. Those who loved Lord Goslin have no cause to love Dreyde."

Sindérian passed a hand over her face. White-lipped and red-eyed, she swayed where she stood, and Ruan threw out a hand to steady her. Her face was streaked with tears and smudged with dirt; her hands shook with fatigue; yet there was something indomitable about her.

"I say let us accept help when it is offered," she said in a cracked voice. "Let us be out of this place as soon as possible."

The Prince shot the stranger another burning glance. "Very well," he said, the words forced out between clenched teeth. "Take us out of this place, and swiftly."

They followed Gilrain out of the hall—first the Prince, then Sindérian, then the men-at-arms. Moving at a breathless pace, the Ni-Ferys took them through a doorway, down a short corridor, and up a wooden staircase, to the chamber where they had first met Lord Dreyde. There he flung aside one of the tapestries on the wall, exposing a hidden door.

"Quickly now," he said, throwing the door open on a dark passageway, motioning the others to pass through. "The light is growing. I can take you past the walls without being seen, but if Dreyde sends men out into the countryside looking for you, they will have no difficulty tracking you down by daylight."

The Ni-Ferys took them by way of a series of tunnels and cellars, by a passage so low that they were forced to crawl through the filth and the stench of what must be a drain or a sewer, and finally out through a narrow culvert and a rotting iron grate— to a wooded glade beneath the northern wall. They had come (he said) to the other side of the hill from the gatehouse, to rising country above the valley.

There appeared to be adequate cover in this direction, but the morning was by then so far advanced and the light so broad, they would have to go quietly and cautiously, and trust to their guide to lead them aright. Somewhere along the way— the Prince was not sure exactly when, or how it came about—it had been tacitly agreed that Gilrain would continue to show them the way, even though he had only promised to see them beyond the walls.

They followed a narrow path between the trees. After the long night of heartache and peril, it seemed very peaceful, very safe, in the bright wood. The growth there was mostly oak and ilem and beech, dappling the ground with lacy patterns of light and shade. The canopy of green-gold leaves rustled with wings; and every now and then there came a trill of birdsong.

They kept on at a steady pace for perhaps another two miles, until Gilrain indicated it would be safe to stop and rest for a bit. Sindérian threw herself down in the soft leaf mold under a great oak tree, and the others did likewise.

"There is a village called Brill, little more than a league and a half from here," said the Ni-Ferys, "where I am known, and the people are trustworthy. There we can get horses, food—whatever we need."

Sindérian knit her fingers together, rested her forehead on the back of her hands. "If you know someplace closer where we can lie hidden until nightfall, someplace we can rest . . . ? If any of Saer's men should overtake us between here and this village of yours, what could we *do* as we are now?"

The Prince opened his mouth to protest, but the words died on his tongue. For himself, his Ni-Féa pride said to keep on going, show no weakness, but his half-Human flesh *was* weak, and almost fordone.

He looked at each of his companions in turn. Aell and Jago were wan, shadow-eyed, exhausted. As for Sindérian, if she could even stand again and try to stagger on, that was a wonder.

He had a dim memory of Elidûc saying once, in a time of crisis, that he was borrowing strength from the next fortnight. Whether the wizard had meant this literally, or whether he was being facetious, Ruan had an idea that Sindérian was drawing on resources better left untapped. Every step she took now, every effort expended, would have to be paid for later.

All this being so, only a fool would insist on continuing for another four or five miles.

"I know of a place," said Gilrain. "A cave in these hills. But if we decide to go there, I think we should go at once."

Slowly and reluctantly they climbed to their feet and plodded on. Gilrain took them through a cleft between the hills,
past a rocky ravine tangled with blackberry bramble and shep-
herd's ivy, and at last to a ferny green dell with a swift-running
stream, a deep black pool, and a glittering waterfall.

Without a word, they all fell down on their knees by the
stream, dousing faces and hands in the cool clear water, bringing up double handfuls to drink, and to drink again.

They drank their fill, then washed away as much of the dirt
and the sweat as they could. With a sigh, Sindérian sat back
on her heels, pushing damp tendrils of hair back from a white,
glistening face. Droplets of water glimmered in Jago's brown
beard. Everyone turned toward Gilrain, waiting for further in-
structions

"Behind the falls," he said, "there is a cave. Very few people
know of its existence. And as there is only a single narrow way
in, it ought to be highly defensible. If one of us keeps watch at
all times, we should be safe enough there."

He showed them how they might enter: standing with his
back to a wall of sun-warmed stone, and edging sideways along
a mossy shelf until he passed behind the waterfall. Following
after him, the Prince and the rest soon found themselves in a
damp cool place, where the clamorous voice of the falls was
very loud, and only a dim misty light filtered in through the
veiling water.

There they cast themselves down on the rough cave floor,
and disposed themselves to rest. Ruan himself had no intention
of sleeping—he meant to spend the next few hours gathering
his strength, and covertly watching their new friend. But the
cave was spinning around him, his eyelids were very heavy, and
the dark tide of sleep was not to be resisted; despite his struggles to stay awake, it carried him off into oblivion.

14

※

Sindérian woke on the floor of the cave, every muscle and joint aching after so many hours on that stony couch. It was a struggle even to sit up, she had grown so stiff. She sat for a long time with her knees drawn up and her head in her hands, taking short shallow breaths, until she finally summoned the will to stagger to her feet.

A little red sunset glow came in through the waterfall, and she saw that Gilrain had already been out to gather windfall and kindle a tiny fire at the back of the cave. Joining the Prince and his men, she held her stiff white hands over the little yellow flames, cherishing the warmth. That offered scant relief against the ache and the chill, but frozen muscles gradually began to thaw, and the pain subsided to a dull throb.

As soon as the sunset faded, Gilrain stamped out his fire. They left the cave, feeling their way in the dark along the slippery ledge under the waterfall, and came out into a bright moonlit night.

For Sindérian, trudging along at the tail end of the party, the five miles they walked to the village of Brill felt like a hundred. The previous night she had been alternately numb and terrified. Now she was thoroughly alive to the shock and the pain of Faolein's death, the grief every bit as fresh and sharp as it had been when she first held the crystal arrow in the palm of her hand and knew how it had been used.

Her thoughts were a tangle of regrets and resentment: *My father who I never knew or understood as I ought, fool that I was—gone now, and I can never make it up to him. My gentle, kindly father, who loved me much better than I ever deserved— We needed more time, more time!*

All the while, her joints still ached. She might have managed a *shibéath* to ease the pain, but she lacked the strength to help the others, too, and she made up her mind it must be all or none. Miserable as she was, she pitied the men in their armor, which must torment them a hundred different ways, they had been wearing it and sleeping in it for so many days and nights. Well did she know how it could chafe and pinch and gouge, having treated such hurts during the war in Rheithûn. They must be cursing its weight and the discomfort it caused with every step.

Meanwhile, her own discomfort continued to increase. The soles of the dainty red leather shoes she had been given at Saer were full of holes; they were worn to rags, worse than useless. The fur lining chafed at blisters on her heels. With a grunt of disgust, she dropped down suddenly to the ground, tugged off the shoes, and threw them under a bush. Then she stumbled back to her feet and walked on barefoot.

She had long since discarded the silken belt with its chiming golden medallions; dropping it down an air shaft while she and the Prince were still prowling through the fortress; now she wished she might be rid of the heavy, impractical gown as well. It had an annoying tendency to catch on rocks and twigs and trip her up. Again and again she tore herself loose from a bush or a branch, reckless of the fine velvet, the rich sable trim. It had been ruined anyway, she reflected sourly, when she crawled through the drain.

They came down out of the hills and into a flat, wooded country. A narrow road led through the forest and straight on to the village, said Gilrain. The road was of hard-packed earth, less rocky than the ground they had been walking for the last three miles, and far kinder to Sindérian's bruised feet.

They had not gone far when Ruan cried out that he could hear hoofbeats on the road behind them. Caught without a plan, they scattered in five directions, and took cover in the bushes under the trees.

Sindérian lay with her face pressed against the damp, leafy earth. Twiggy branches tangled in her hair; thorns scratched her bare feet. A large company of mounted men rode by at a brisk pace not ten feet away, and the ground shook beneath them. A momentary panic took her. She closed her eyes, breathed in and breathed out, struggling for control. She had supposed she was beyond feeling fear, beyond caring what happened to her, but why then this sick excitement, this trembling in every limb?

As the clatter of the horses and riders gradually died, everyone slowly emerged from hiding. Prince Ruan brushed leaf mold off his cloak. He had blood on his face, Sindérian noted, and Jago's hands were badly scratched. She had not been the only one to take refuge in a thornbush.

"There is a fork in the road a little farther on," said Gilrain. "Let us listen and hear which way they go."

To Sindérian's ears the night was silent, except for a whisper of wind in the trees, the pounding of her own heart. But the two Faey stood alert and listening.

"North," said Ruan, after a moment. "They turned north."

"And the village lies east of here," said Gilrain. "Let us continue on."

Sindérian fell into step beside him. She felt strangely exhilarated after her recent fright, more alert to her surroundings, the woodland sounds and scents—more aware of her companions, too.

She had thought when she first met Gilrain that he was a full-blooded Faey, but now, walking beside him shoulder to shoulder, she realized that could not be true. He was not so tall as Prince Ruan, not even as tall as she was, but tall enough at least to betray Human ancestry. Nor was he quite so graceful in his proportions as the Ni-Ferys she had seen at Tregna.

Half-breed like the Prince, she thought. *Maybe even less.*

And for the first time she began to wonder what helping them was likely to cost him. "What will happen to you after we part company at Brill?"

He hesitated, gave her a sidelong glance out of his yellow eyes. "I have friends I can go to. Or, if you wish, I might continue to guide you. I am much older than I appear." He flashed her a smile. "A trait hardly likely to raise comment in *this* company. And I am well traveled. I know all the back country of Mere and Hythe and Weye, the best roads through the Cadmin Aernan. The high passes will be open this time of year, and you would not find it a difficult or a dangerous journey with the proper guide."

Sindérian drew in her breath, felt a butterfly pulse of fear in her throat. "Why should you think we are heading for the Cadmin Aernan?"

"You need not worry. Your business in the north was not known at Saer. But that you and Dreyde's visitors from Phaôrax are all heading north and east—to Skyrra, perhaps, or Arkenfell—that much is evident. Also that some great matter hangs on who should arrive there first. With me to guide you it is not too late, *you might still win that race*. Will you have me?"

She was much inclined to accept this offer, but she shook her head. "It is not for me to decide . . . or not me alone. I will speak with Prince Ruan, though I am very much afraid that he won't like it."

The village of Brill is a scattered settlement, which has stood for time out of mind at the edge of the Foweraker Wood. Cottages of stone and slate, of wattle and daub, of wood and thatch, cluster on either side of a trickling stream, straggle for a half mile down the road, and encroach on the forest. There is a small village green with a well and a fountain, where geese and smaller fowl drink and dabble during the day, and in addition to these amenities, Brill boasts a smithy, a craft hall, and an ancient temple to the Seven Fates. In those days, there was a high earthen dike on the eastern side, and a low thorny hedge surrounding most of the houses. That was all the defense that they had.

It was to the blacksmith—the headman of the village and its most prosperous citizen—that Gilrain meant to appeal for aid. While the others waited in the darkness under the trees, he went on ahead to the forge. Sindérian could see him quite plainly in the pale moonglow, moving toward a square two-story building, with that light feline step that reminded her so much of Prince Ruan.

She saw him raise his hand and knock on the door, but the sound was absorbed by distance and a rustling of leaves over her head. A door opened, letting out a beam of yellow firelight; a shadowy broad-shouldered figure stood silhouetted on the threshold. What words were exchanged, Sindérian did not know, but she saw a large friendly hand come down on Gilrain's shoulder, saw him nod once, twice, then a third time, before turning around and heading back toward the trees.

"Dreyde's men have searched the village twice already," said Gilrain when he drew near enough to speak. "Once at noon, and again shortly before sunset. They are not expected back, and the smith says that he and his people will be willing to help us."

Over his shoulder, Sindérian saw a slender boyish figure slip out through the open door of the house, heading toward one of the smaller cottages. Seeing which way she looked, Gilrain said: "They are going to set a watch on the road in both directions, just to be safe. If someone comes, we'll have sufficient warning."

The smith's house was solidly built of stone, with a slate roof over massive oak beams. They entered to a savory odor of soup simmering in a copper kettle and griddle cakes browning on hot stones.

Once inside, Sindérian was soon seated on a low bench by the central hearth, with a wool fleece thrown over her shoulders and an earthenware mug full of steaming hot broth thrust into her hands by the smith's buxom wife.

Through a door standing halfway ajar, she could see into the forge, with its open furnace, flagstone floor, and hammers and anvils. Otherwise, the house seemed to be all one large room, with a staircase leading up to a loft for sleeping. Windows were unglazed and covered by stout wooden shutters, and there was no chimney, only a round smokehole at the peak of the roof. But the fire burned with a clean resinous smell, and there were tall yellow candles in polished brass holders standing on a table of solid oak. It was clear to Sindérian that she had come to a place of homely comfort.

In addition to the smith himself—with his barrel chest and bristling blond beard—his wife, and the boy who had gone out earlier, there were also three daughters, and a white-haired grandmother in a faded blue dress who sat on a three-legged stool by the fire, mending a man's shirt with a length of linen thread and a bone needle.

It was a goodly family, Sindérian thought. And realizing that she and her companions put all of them in danger, the children and adults alike, she felt a pang of distress.

What *right* had she to claim their help, to imperil their safety? Yet it was hard to think of moving, harder still to do so, when she was finally warm and comfortable.

Meanwhile, three more men in rough woolen tunics came in through the door, and with them two weather-beaten women, of indeterminate age. They all spoke in low voices, solicitous for the travelers, and very eager to offer assistance.

For these people of Brill, as Sindérian soon gathered, were rustic but hospitable. To the memory of Lord Goslin they were fiercely devoted, but Dreyde they naturally distrusted. He had come from *"foreign parts"* halfway across Mere and had done nothing since settling at Saer and assuming the title to win their affection. That it was even his title to inherit there was some reason to doubt.

Gilrain, on the other hand, they knew very well. He was the old Lord's godson and fosterling. And as such, the whole of Brill was apparently ready to do him any and every service, explained the smith's eldest daughter. If they might in the process cause inconvenience to the upstart Dreyde, then so much the better.

But ought *we to believe in the honesty of these people?* Sindérian wondered. Ought they to trust in such ready kindness, such open-handed generosity? An unpleasant thought insinuated itself: these men of Mere were no longer allies. In another few months, they might even be enemies. And the last time she had received such pressing hospitality, it had all gone badly.

Yet Brill seemed an altogether more wholesome place than Saer. Here she detected no undercurrent of fear, no false bright smiles, no assumed gaiety. The villagers were sober and practical, they spoke and acted like sensible people. They knew their danger—in truth, they knew their situation very well—and after taking reasonable precautions, they accepted it.

Sindérian decided to trust her instincts. She allowed herself to relax, to bask in the warmth of the fire, to sip her broth, and listen to the conversation going on around her.

"We knew *why* we were fighting the war," said a hard-faced man with bright red hair. "Men from this village have *been* there. My brother was with the army that took back Ceirduillin, after ten years of Pharaxion rule. He saw the great temple there, the blood on the stones. He saw the sick and the lame starving in the streets, and the granaries full of corn: to be *burned* in honor of the Empress—all for her vanity, while children starved. The Duke did wrong to forsake the Alliance."

So this, Sindérian thought drowsily, was the temper of the countryside. No matter how insincere Dreyde had been, there was ample resentment against the Duke, even, perhaps, unrest in the villages. These people knew, just as she knew, that the enemy only bided her time before sending armies to invade Mere.

Yet if the people rose up against their Duke— She caught her breath at the thought. If the people rose up in rebellion against the Duke, then so much the better for Ouriána of Phaôrax, so much the worse for the people of Mere. A house divided would the sooner fall. Whatever happened, Ouriána's victory was practically assured.

Yet there remained the prophecy and the quest, Sindérian reminded herself, and the success or failure of *that* might yet change everything. If she had momentarily forgotten, Prince Ruan had not. She could hear him bargaining with the smith and another man for horses.

Two venerable geldings and a five-year-old mare— "raw-boned, ungainly, with a jolting gait"—those were all, said the blacksmith, that could be spared.

"We have only a dozen horses in the entire village, do you see? We use oxen and asses for draft animals mostly. And if half of the horses in Brill suddenly disappeared—" He shrugged a broad shoulder. "That might draw the attention of Lord Dreyde's men."

"Very well," said the Prince. "The mare will do to carry the baggage, if her gait is as bad as you say. We can take it in turns to ride the geldings."

When the smith named a price that was ridiculously low, Ruan's eyebrows rose. It must go against his pride to accept what amounted to charity from such simple people. But he clamped his mouth shut in a thin hard line, dug in his purse, and produced the necessary coins.

"It is one thing to pay for the horses, which they can hardly spare," said Gilrain in Sindérian's ear. "Also for the things that you take with you. But do not allow the Prince or his men to offer money for what you eat here. It would be worse than insulting. In this part of the world, hospitality is sacred."

The villagers offered packets of waybread, of dried fruit and smoked meat wrapped up in fresh leaves, some boiled eggs, and a small cask of ale: ample provision for the next fort-night, and longer if they were prudent. To Sindérian, one of the women brought a homespun gown, faded to a butternut brown, and a pair of scuffed boots that she said had belonged to her son who had gone to the war and not come back.

Just when, precisely, Sindérian drifted off, her mind going vague and her thoughts wandering, she did not know. The voices in the room receded to a distant murmur. She came back awake only when somebody stirred the embers under the pot, and the fire flared up. As if in response, angry voices rose and clashed in another part of the room.

She looked over her shoulder and saw the Prince and Gilrain facing each other beside the door. Ruan's jaw was set in a stubborn line, and his arms were folded across his chest. Gilrain's slim body quivered with tension, and his eyes flashed.

Reluctantly, she left her warm seat by the fire and swept across the room, trailing her sheepskin blanket behind her.

"He says he has offered to guide us through the mountains," Ruan hissed between his teeth. "*Surely* you don't mean to accept?"

She felt a flush of annoyance pass over her. "And why not, after all? You don't know the way and neither do I. We would be fools to attempt the Cadmin Aernan without a guide."

"Neither do we know, yet, why this Ni-Ferys is so eager to be of assistance!"

Gilrain put his hands in his belt, stood with his feet well apart. "To spite Dreyde. To spite Thaga. You can understand that, I think. My people may not love revenge as yours do, but *it is* possible to injure us. Goslin was old, but Dreyde lied when he told you that he was ill. I am not the only one convinced that his sudden death was caused by Dreyde and his tame sorcerer; it came too pat, it was far too convenient. And he lied about something else, too. Whatever he said to the wizard, he is the Duke's man. Dreyde came to us from Clowes, with the Duke's blessing, and Thaga came with him."

He lowered his voice. "And when Thaga was at Clowes, they say he was always at the Duke's side whispering, whispering in his ear. I do *not* think it was simple cowardice, *'simple prudence'* as Dreyde would have it, that caused the Duke to desert his allies. I think he was corrupted, somehow, and that Dreyde and his hedge wizard were a part of that, too."

Sindérian rubbed at her eyes. She would rather not think about Thaga, but she supposed that she must. "Not a hedge wizard, or a simple country sorcerer. I begin to suspect that Thaga must be an Otöwan magus, though probably not of the highest order. The magi, they say, practiced many of the old Earth Magics, as well as their own spells, which were wholly of the Dark. I sensed *both* kinds of magic at Saer."

The two Faey looked at her doubtfully. "But the magi were destroyed," said Ruan. "We were taught the story as children: a thousand magicians died in a single hour, and the world was Changed."

"A thousand magicians died, but a handful may have survived. Some of them *must* have lived to pass on their arts to men like Thaga. Didn't he tell us as much himself?" she asked. "Not of our order on Leal, he said, but educated at a school in the east, no longer in existence. Ouriána may have found him when she was in Otöi, and sent him to Mere to spy and work mischief."

Ruan uncrossed his arms. "There is more than one kind of spy, more than one way to work mischief. I don't trust this half-blood Ni-Ferys, and neither should you."

She was suddenly aware of a hush in the room. Everyone was listening to their dispute. No one spoke, no one moved. With a sigh and an apologetic glance for Gilrain, Sindérian invited the Prince to step outside and discuss the matter privately.

He went out before her, his sky-blue cloak swinging and

his head very high. The wind had risen, sending rags of cloud sailing across the face of the westering moon.

They stood just outside the light from the open door and conversed in low voices. "Has it never occurred to you," said Ruan, "to wonder why he only bestirred himself to befriend us *after* your father died? If he wanted to help us, why didn't he try to save Faolein first?"

Sindérian ran a tired hand through her hair. "Perhaps— perhaps he believed, as you did, that Faolein could look after himself. What was reasonable for you to think could hardly be suspicious in him."

The Prince stiffened, as though hearing himself and the Ni-Ferys mentioned in the same breath was highly offensive. Sindérian struggled to master her own impatience. But she had felt too much in the last day and two nights; her nerves were unstrung. She answered with more heat than she intended: "Whatever there is between his people and yours, we can't allow it to influence our decision. We can't—"

"My *people*," he said, a flush creeping up to his cheek-bones, "are the Men of Thäerie. You know nothing about me if you think otherwise. But at least admit that I know more about the Faey than you do!"

She leaned back against the side of the house. "And what do rivalries and prejudices among the Faey matter to us now? This Gilrain is just as much a *Man* of Mere as you are of Thäerie. What can you possibly say against him, except that you do not like him?"

The Prince shook his head, unable to reply, though the set of his jaw and his rigid, angry posture were argument enough.

And somehow that aroused as much resentment in Sindérian as anything he had said. "*Tuillo* died. *Faolein* died, to bring us this far. We can't allow their deaths to mean nothing, or throw aside this chance my father bought for us and paid for so dearly."

Now Ruan looked bewildered. It was his turn to slide his hands through his hair, to draw it back from his face. "Chance? What *chance* did Faolein buy us with his death? When you speak in riddles, how am I to understand you?"

Sindérian caught her breath sharply. She had not known this thing herself until the words came out of her mouth unbidden. "Do you think that Faolein walked into that trap at Saer without even suspecting?" she asked fiercely. "Do you imagine he couldn't see into Dreyde's mind, into his rotten black heart, within moments of meeting him? My father knew long before that. He knew when he stood before the gate that he was in danger—he saw his peril, but he knew also that we would pass through the fortress unscathed. For our sake he gave himself up."

The Prince gave a short, harsh laugh, astonishment melting into disbelief. He walked to the door, but then he turned back again. "When we might just as well have avoided Saer altogether? That makes no sense at all!"

She clenched her hands, so that the nails drove into her palms. "And what chance do you think we would have had, on foot in the hills, in country that even Faolein did not know well, with Dyonas and *Camhóinhann* hunting us, and Goezenou following right behind them? Whereas now we have horses, supplies, and a guide, if we will accept him, and most likely the Furiádin believe we are *dead* or prisoners at Saer—or else they would never have left the fortress when they did. They will be *miles* away by now, and unlikely to spare us another thought."

He looked her over in frowning silence, his handsome face very pale, his silvery eyebrows coming together. "And you think that his Foresight revealed *all of these things* to Faolein?"

he said at last. "You think that he knew exactly how it would be? Even for a seer like your father, that would be a remarkably detailed prediction!"

Sindérian bit her lip. "Not exactly how it would be, no. He could hardly have seen everything. Just enough to choose his path and know that it was right."

The Prince, who had been about to leave again, stopped with one hand on the doorframe and a suddenly arrested look on his face, as though considering her words, considering them deeply. "That much I can believe. I have known Eliduc to have such inexplicable insights. To know what needed to be done, without knowing *why* it was right—or even how he knew it. It might have been the same with Faolein."

And then he capitulated all at once, with a twist of a smile and a low graceful bow, so that Sindérian wondered if he might be mocking her. "If Faolein's daughter says that it *was,* it must be so. Very well, then, let it be as you wish. The Ni-Ferys shall be our guide. After all, he need not be entirely trustworthy in order to be of use. And it may be as well to have him travel beside us, where we can keep an eye on him, instead of following behind us, unseen and uninvited."

They went back inside the house and told Gilrain, Aell, and Jago of their decision—an arrangement that seemed to find favor with the men-at-arms. With that matter settled, Sindérian gathered up the dress and the boots she had been given earlier and went up to the loft with two of the smith's daughters to change her clothes.

The older girl, Brielli, unlaced the wine-colored gown, and Sindérian shrugged out of the soiled velvet. It fell at her feet on

the plank floor, and she stepped away with a shudder of dis-
taste, glad to be rid of the thing and the memories it evoked.

"I will burn it, after you are gone," said the younger girl,
picking up the gown, wrinkling her nose. It still reeked of the
sewers at Saer.

But Sindérian shook her head. "Better to bury it under the
midden, and leave it there to rot," she said, thinking of the
stench it would make when the fur began to scorch.

She reached for the homespun gown, slipped it over her
head and shoulders. As the loose-fitting garment settled into
place, Brielli gave her a worn leather belt to cinch it in. The
dress had obviously been made for a woman who was shorter
and a good deal heavier than Sindérian; the hem just skimmed
her ankles, but the skirt was very full. Paired with the boots, it
would make a suitable costume for riding and walking.

Brielli handed her a pair of long woolen stockings, and she
sat down on a cot to pull them on, one after the other. Then she
took up one of the knee-high leather boots and worked it on
over the bulky stocking.

A dog barked somewhere outside; the geese set up a terrible clamor. Everyone in the room down below went suddenly
silent. Sindérian stopped with one foot shod and the other boot
still in her hand. She listened, over the hammering of her heart,
as the door opened and closed when someone went out.

"It's nothing," the younger sister assured her. "Just someone going to the well for water, or to fetch in some firewood."

For all that, she tugged on the other boot as quickly as she
could, jumped to her feet, and stood poised for flight—until
the door finally creaked open again, and a voice down below
was heard to announce that all was well.

Possessed by a sudden urge to be off, a nervous pounding
in her blood, Sindérian plaited her hair, her hands grown sud-

denly clumsy with haste, and tied the end with a bit of ribbon provided by Brielli. Then she ran downstairs to rejoin her fellow travelers.

They were already preparing to leave, gathering up the things so generously provided: besides the food and the ale, there were blankets and fleeces to serve them as bedding, and a fine yew bow and a quiver of arrows with grey-goose fletchings, which Gilrain slung over his shoulder.

"You ought to be gone before the sun comes up," cautioned the redheaded man. "You will want to be well on your way, with Dreyde's men out searching the countryside."

"We will hear them long before they hear us," said Gilrain, with a thin smile. "Especially if they travel with such a noise as we heard before."

"I have it in mind," said the smith, rubbing his stubbled cheeks with thumb and forefinger, "that very few of the men of Saer have their hearts in this hunt. Only the men that Dreyde brought with him from Clowes. The rest obey him only because they fear him."

Gilrain nodded. "I think the same thing. So for *their* sake as much as our own we ought to be off."

———

When the others went out, Sindérian was impelled by a sudden impulse to enter the forge. A bucket of water stood by the cooling furnace. She stooped low, scooped up water from the bucket, and dribbled it in a circle on the flagstone floor. Then she traced a symbol in the center of the circle.

Drying her hands on her skirt, she turned toward the furnace. Drawing the runes *hwela, chymís,* and *theroghal* in the feathery grey ashes, she chanted a simple charm: that all things made and mended there might be well made and give faithful service. The signs she had drawn glowed with a pale green light, then faded. She felt the charm take hold.

It was a minor spell—any village witch or warlock might have contrived it, any hedge wizard or cunning-man—yet it cost Sindérian a considerable effort, left her breathless and weak in the knees, at a time when her hands were still inclined to tremble and her sight to blur.

But this much, at least, we owe them in gratitude, she told herself. It was what Faolein would have done in her place; she knew that, too. Aside from simple gratitude, simple decency, there was a danger, an imbalance, in leaving an obligation behind—particularly in what might soon become hostile territory. Wizards had been tripped up that way before, had trapped themselves in complex patterns of cause and effect that they could not escape.

But then—remembering the arrows at Gilaefri—she made a sign, unthought and reflexive, invoking the Light, and she sent up a sort of prayer: *May the Fates forbid that any weapon forged here should be turned against my friends.*

When she rejoined Prince Ruan and the others, they had already saddled and loaded up the horses, and were drawing lots to see who should ride first, who should walk. Learning, to her dismay, that one of the riding horses had been reserved for her use, Sindérian indignantly insisted on taking her chance with the rest. The lots fell to her and to Aell.

"But *can* you ride astride?" said the Prince, suddenly realizing that neither saddle was made for a lady. There was probably not such a thing as a sidesaddle in the entire village. "Or will you ride pillion behind one of us?"

She gave a humorless little laugh and tossed her braid back over her shoulder. "Let us not overburden the horses! I can ride like a man when the need arises." To prove her point, she gathered up her skirt, put a foot in the stirrup, and swung up into the saddle. The Prince, who would have assisted her had she permitted it, stepped back with a shrug and a faint curl of his lips.

They set out from Brill just as the moon was setting behind the hills. Gilrain, as their guide, naturally took the lead, and Sindérian urged the chestnut gelding forward to walk beside him.

"You told me," she said, bending low over the horse's neck in order to speak in his ear, "there was still a chance we might arrive in the north before Ouriána's messengers. But I don't see how."

"Because they are so far ahead of us, so much better mounted?" It was so dark that she could barely see him, though he walked quite near. Yet he seemed to navigate as surely by starlight as he had by moonlight. "There is something you may not know. There is a barrier in the Cadmin Aernan, a great wall of magic, ever since Éireamhóine killed three Furiádhin there. Whether or not it was the wizard's intention, or something he created accidentally, no evil thing or servant of Dark powers can pass that ward.

"Ouriána's creatures will have to turn back and spend almost a month returning to the coast, or else go north through Hythe and Weye. But they can hardly ride openly through the coastal principalities as they've ridden through Mere. If they choose to ride north, it will have to be through the wilder country of the foothills and the backlands, where the roads are few and not very good. And even after they've passed through Prince Bael's territory and Prince Gwynnek's, they will still have to face the dangers of the burning lands and the great northern woods.

"Whether or not these things will slow them *enough* I can't promise you, but there is a chance, a good chance, you may arrive where you're going first."

Sindérian sat up straighter in the saddle. She released a long, heartfelt sigh. "Even a small chance is more than I dared to hope. If you . . . if you can guide us swiftly and safely, Gilrain, there may be *many* who will thank you later."

His light, bell-like voice came to her out of the darkness. "I can lead you over the mountains as well or better than anyone. But what you will find on the other side, that I can't tell you. They say it has finally come to open war between Skyrra and Eisenlonde, that King Ristil and his men are hard-pressed. The entire north may be at war by the time you come there—or it may all be over, and the barbarians victorious."

Her stomach clenched; images of fire and sword leapt in her brain. It was true she had been halfway expecting this news all along, yet she had also foolishly continued to hope that war in the north might be miraculously averted. There were already too many battles being fought in the world, there was already too much death.

A shiver passed over Sindérian's skin, a premonition of evil to come. She thought, *If we come to Skyrra too late, if we find Winloki dead, a victim of the war—or even unwilling to leave her adopted people, when they have such need of healers—then everything we have done, everything we have lost or will lose along the way, will all be for nothing!*

15

✳

And far away, far away to the north and east on the spacious plains of Skyrra, it was as Gilrain described it: a state of open war. Horns were blowing; villages burned, sending up clouds of sparks into the night; armies of horsemen and foot soldiers met on the plains under the stars and clashed, staining the long grass with their blood. Behind a veil of smoke and flying ash, the face of the moon turned red.

———

Midmorning found King Ristil's capital at Lückenbörg in an uproar. Shortly after sundown, young Prince Kivik and his kinsman Skerry had ridden through one of the gates with a war-weary troop, bearing messages from the marshals fighting in the east: they needed more men, more supplies, more healers—more of everything.

"We had thought to win this war in a matter of months, our numbers being so far superior, but there are more of *them* than we ever imagined," Kivik had said when he arrived at the Heldenhof, the King's great house, sweaty, dusty, and trembling with exhaustion, but in such a fever to deliver his news that he turned aside all offers of food and drink, and flung himself through doorways and up long wooden staircases, heedless of the guards who rushed forward to demand his business (then recognizing him, stepped back again), until he came at last, breathless and emphatic, into the King's very presence.

Ristil signed to the guards, to his companions of the hour—his Jarls and Thanes, his trusted counselors—and they all fell silent, so that the Prince might be heard.

"Again and again we're obliged to revise our ideas about their numbers. We won two great battles at the beginning of spring, and we thought it was practically over. Yet a fortnight later they met us with forces even greater than before. We somehow prevailed, and again we thought the war was effectively ended, until eight days ago when we learned to our cost that it wasn't so. We kill them, and there are always more of them. . . . How can this be? How can the rocky wastes of Eisenlonde produce such an army?"

There was a confused muttering throughout the room. That the barbarians had even been able to produce an army worthy of the name—that had come as a shock at the very beginning, when Ristil's commanders were still expecting the usual rabble of horse thieves and raiders. But an army that grew and grew, and continued to grow beyond all reasonable bounds or expectations, that was even harder to grasp.

"Where do they come from?" asked Kivik. He shifted his shoulders, where the weight of mail and padding had become almost unendurable. Half a hundred candles burned in the room, reflected off a floor of polished dark wood, glanced off the gilding on elaborately carved beams overhead. In that clear light his dirt and dishevelment were the more obvious: a mud-spattered cloak and boots; light brown hair plastered to his forehead.

"The conclusion is inevitable: *they're not all Eisenlonders!*"

There was a collective gasp, followed by a feeble stir of protest among the King's aged counselors. They looked at Kivik askance, not even trying to conceal their dismay, their reluctance to credit a word that he said.

"Impossible," said one, the ancient Jarl Vetr. "Eisenlonde signs no treaties, maintains no alliances. They are so isolated there at the edge of the world, such a poor nation, what benefits could they possibly offer to potential allies?"

"It may be blackest magic," another greybeard rasped out. "The barbarians have sorcerers, shamans they call them. They create phantom armies out of the air to confuse you."

"It's entirely possible," answered young Skerry, who had arrived in Kivik's footsteps, "that there are illusions in with the rest. It seems very likely. But illusions don't set fire to the fields, they don't poison wells, or rape our women. You can't *capture an illusion.* We have taken prisoners who were strangely garbed, who bore strange weapons, men who could not understand our questions nor we their answers."

Vetr locked his gnarled hands around the stick that supported most of his weight when he walked. "There are so many different clans and tribes in Eisenlonde, there may be one living out at the very edge of the edge of the world, whose dialect is unknown to us."

"We think otherwise," said Kivik. "We think there are foreign mercenaries along with them—a great many mercenary soldiers perhaps."

And when the entire group assembled around the King began to protest, all the old men and hoary-headed counselors, he cried out: "We don't know, we don't *know* how the Lords of Eisenlonde are able to pay them. But these men we are fighting, they aren't like the cattle thieves who make raids across the border after a bad year. These come to destroy rather than to steal. They've burned villages and crops throughout the Haestfilke, set fire to our forests. They slaughter our herds, then leave them to rot. The worst of it is, they can slaughter and burn far more than they ever carried off. But what do they gain by it? If they mean to expand their territories, claim herds and farmlands to feed their people, then why this wanton destruction?"

He turned toward the King, spoke with all the force and weary desperation that was in him. "Whatever we've been holding back, assuming that victories would come easily, it is time to throw as many men and horses into the field as we possibly can."

King Ristil looked to Skerry. If that generally cool-headed and admirably reasonable young man came in all haste and added his voice to the vehement protestations of the more volatile Kivik, then Ristil was doubly willing to listen.

"It's as my cousin tells you. We need more men, at least another two thousand. Three thousand if you can find them. Meanwhile, we need to arm and fortify the Westvalle, Herzenmark, and Autland. The Eisenlonders may come that far. We may not be able to hold them. As for our people in the farms and villages to the south, they might be wise to come together and repopulate some of the old cities, which are at least defensible." Skerry threw a corner of his tattered green cloak over his shoulder, and took a step toward the King. Where Kivik was slender, he was stocky, with that raven-black hair uncommon in the northlands. It was ruffled now like the feathers of some storm-tossed bird of ill omen.

He lowered his voice—but not so much that the others could not hear him. "It might even be wise to consider the same thing yourself, to remove the court from Lückenbörg to . . . Kuningskallin."

At this, there was an even louder protest than before. The town of Lückenbörg, which is built up around the venerable old timber fortress known as the Heldenhof, is the ancient seat of the Lords of Skyrra, but thirty miles to the south lies the vast stone city of Kuningskallin, where Kings of Skyrra reigned in great splendor for nearly two hundred years. Half of that city lies in ruins, devastated by one of the immense destructive shocks that passed through the earth when the moon changed course in the sky. The King then reigning fled from Kuningskallin along with the surviving members of his court, and neither he nor any of the heirs who followed after him had ever returned.

For that city—and others like it—was raised in part by wizardry, in the days when men of the north pledged friendship with the Empire of Alluinn. Since Alluinn's fall, the great cities of stone, and the arts which had built them, had come to be regarded as presumptuous and unchancy by the men of these northern realms—Skyrra, Arkenfell, and Mistlewald. Let those in the former Empire lands do as they would, let them try to rebuild their mighty fortified houses, let them attempt to reclaim all that had been lost or broken by the catastrophe—the Northmen returned to older ways, to ancient traditions, which suited them better. They had never, perhaps, been entirely comfortable in the cities, anyway.

"Your Majesty," said Vetr, with a hooded glance under wrinkled eyelids, "let us decide nothing in haste. These young princes, noble and valiant as they are, have ridden far on short rest and short rations, as it is readily apparent. In a state of exhaustion, a man is inclined to paint things much blacker than they actually are. In the morning, they may offer more reasonable advice, or at least give a less incredible account of events to the east."

Kivik flushed to the roots of his hair. He glared at them, all the old men with their long grey beards and spindle shanks, their weak eyes and withered hearts.

Men grown coward with age, he thought, *grown complacent and foolish, sitting at home by their own hearths.* He opened his mouth to say so, but Skerry restrained him with a look and a touch on the arm, reminding him that these were also old men who had spent too many days and weeks in the saddle when they were younger, too many long cold nights patrolling the border. Scars shone white on many of their faces; others had wounds that still ached in damp weather. Peace they wanted now, and the world as they knew it—but peace was exactly what they could not have, and the world was changing.

"If you had been where we have been, Jarl Vetr, and seen what we have seen," Skerry said evenly, "you would not doubt the truth of anything we tell you. You would hardly think *any* tale we brought you too incredible."

He bowed to the assembly, deeply, ironically. It might have meant many things, respecting their relative ranks and ages; it might have been youth bowing to experience; it might have been deepest insult. No one mistook the gesture; bloodless faces went even whiter, thin lips grew even thinner.

"We don't doubt you. *I* don't doubt you," said Ristil peaceably. "Why should I question messages from my own marshals, carried to me by my own son? That *would* be incredible." His fingers curled around the arms of his chair, and he sat for a long time with his golden head bowed, profoundly in thought.

At last he looked up. "In this matter of removing to Kun-ingskallin, I must consider a while longer. But if Prince Kivik tells me that more men are needed to fight in the east, then more men he must and will have. Everything he asks for will be provided. Let it be done at once."

By an hour after sunrise, the muster had already begun, for the King's messengers had been busy all during the night.

Men and horses from the manors and farmhouses sur-rounding Lückenbörg came in through both gates, followed by wagons and sledges. Pigs squealed in their pens; ducks and geese pecked at each other and flapped their wings. Every forge in the town had been fired up since midnight, the swordsmiths and armorers hard at work. Elsewhere, fletchers, bowyers, coopers, chandlers, and bootmakers plied their separate crafts; sergeants and quartermasters reckoned men and materials on tally sticks; and in the mews at the Heldenhof, the King's fal-coners debated which of the remaining hawks were best suited to see immediate service as messenger birds. Young men were hunting up and polishing their fathers' and grandfathers' swords, as well as odd bits and pieces of antique armor that had been in the family so many generations people had stopped counting; meanwhile, their wives and sisters and mothers were shaking the dust out of banners and surcoats rich with devices lovingly embroidered over the years. It took the efforts of many to get an army on the move, well armed and well vict-ualed.

"Three hundred men will be ready to leave with you to-morrow," King Ristil told Kivik, when he met him walking with Sigvith the Queen in her garden, among the neat rows of pansies, marigolds, and rampion, between the beds of new veg-etables.

"Five or six hundred by next week, perhaps a thousand

more by the end of the month. After that, it becomes difficult, if we don't wish to leave the south and the west undefended. But I am sending an embassy to Arkenfell and another to Mistlewald, asking that they lend us what help they can. They have troubles of their own, as I know well, but we must make them understand: if *we* fall, can invasion of *their* lands be far behind?"

"But will they believe you, will they understand the need? When we could hardly convince those of our own jarls and thanes who offered their counsel?"

Ristil clapped his son on the shoulder, a rough touch but affectionate. "It is the nature of counselors to be cautious, to temporize, just as it falls on kings and princes to be decisive, most particularly during perilous times. Halfdan and Saerid are not fools; neither do I imagine they mistake me for one. They will send us as many men as they can—let us hope that will be as many as we are going to need." He turned and strode out of the garden, with his head high and the weight of a kingdom on his shoulders.

Kivik and the Queen exchanged a rueful, affectionate glance.

They were much alike, brown-haired and hazel-eyed, with the same fine fair skin, alike in mind, too, though she had learned to moderate her impulses, to think before she spoke, which was a hard lesson. They looked enough alike to be brother and elder sister, not mother and son. She was not, in fact, his mother, and Kivik had been a boy of seven when Sigvith married his father. But she had haunted the royal nurseries for six months before that, a mournful young creature with a tragedy in her past she could neither remember nor entirely escape, quick to apply healing poultices and kisses to bruised shins and skinned knees, or to rock a little boy in her arms when he woke in the night weeping for his dead mother. Even when Ristil made her his queen and she began to bear children of her own, the bond she had formed with her three stepsons remained strong. Yet always there remained that elusive sorrow behind her eyes.

Now she brushed her fingertips across Kivik's face. "Dear heart," she said, "you must make up your mind to come back, whatever happens. We have lost too much already, how could your father and I bear it if we lost you, too?"

He took her soft hand and raised it briefly to his lips, then turned on his heel and followed the King out of the garden.

When the Prince left the Heldenhof, crossing one of the wooden bridges over the stream that divided the fortress from the town, he headed for the market at the center of Lückenbörg. On a patch of open ground between the market square and the guildhall, an area generally set aside for cattle and horse trading, someone had raised a banner, the golden oak of Skyrra on a green field, and they were recruiting men there. It was Kivik's intention to handpick a dozen riders to add to his own troop.

The houses he passed along the way—of timber, or stone, or undressed logs—were of no great size, but they gave that illusion with roofs steeply pitched to shed snow during the winter. They all had brightly painted wooden shutters, decorated with an entire menagerie of fantastical beasts, lions and camel-leopards, winged stags and unicorns, along with objects both mundane and mysterious: hearts and hawkbells, leaves and acorns, the moon and the stars, the sun in glory—clan badges and family emblems many of them, but the symbolism of others was harder to trace. The householders repainted them every third or fourth year in the exact same patterns and colors they had used before. At this season, with the paint on many of them still fresh, the figures shone out brightly: red, yellow, blue, and green.

As Kivik neared the marketplace, following a narrow, unpaved lane scarred with wagon tracks, his cousin Winloki appeared out of a side street, and fell into step beside him.

"You leave at dawn?" She sounded breathless trying to keep up with him, though she was a tall girl, with a stride nearly as long as his own. Her grey silk gown, belted with a chain of bronze links shaped like crescent moons, showed dirt about the hem; her thick red-gold hair seemed to be working loose from a long, careless braid; and it was evident to Kivik she was in a passion about something.

He nodded, one short, preoccupied jerk of his head.

A stain of crimson flooded into her cheeks; her chin came up defiantly. "I want to go with you—why not?" she asked, forestalling a protest she obviously expected. "You asked for more healers."

Kivik stopped at the edge of the square and spun to face her. At nineteen, she was inclined to be headstrong and impervious to argument, but even he (who thought her a little spoiled) was not immune to the charm and high spirits that sooner or later won all hearts to her. He ran a hand through his hair, rifled through a hundred disorganized thoughts, searching for the right words to say.

In the end he decided he might just as well be blunt, for he had nothing to tell her that she wanted to hear. "I asked for more healers, but my father has said you're not to be one of them. Winloki, I have a thousand things to attend to today—"

"It's *folly* that the King has forbidden me to go," she

flashed back at him, not to be deterred by his other concerns, his other preoccupations. "Other women will be going—others have gone before—girls much younger than I, and less powerful for healing. Why should *I* alone stay behind, like some bauble made of glass wrapped up in wool for safe-keeping?"

"That," he answered, as patiently as he was able—though not without a sidelong glance at the men congregating in the field across the square, "is for the King to decide, and not for me. If it were my decision, you would certainly come. I would gladly take you, we have such need of healers."

But as soon as the words were out, Kivik knew he had spoken amiss. He saw her lovely face radiant, the leap of hope behind her grey eyes. And much as he hated to dash that hope, it had to be done. "If you might go with the King's blessing, not otherwise," he said sternly. "Not otherwise, Winloki!"

An hour later, she was pleading her case to the King, in the great audience chamber with its beautiful embroidered banners and tapestries, where he listened to petitions twice every fortnight. Knowing what she meant to ask him, what was likely to follow, Ristil sent his attendants away with a motion of his hand and a nod.

"I *know* why you keep me here," said Winloki, as soon as the others filed out. "You do so against the day when some unknown kinsman arrives to claim me. But Uncle, Uncle, that day may never come. There may not *be* anyone living who knows my real name or to whom I belong."

She dropped to her knees on the steps below the dais, urgent, vehement, trembling with the force of her desire. "And in the meantime, what must people *think* of me, when their own sons and daughters go to war, while I stay here in ease and comfort?"

"They will think what they have always thought: that you are a brave heart and an ardent spirit," he answered—not unkindly, not unmoved by her plea. "They will understand that it is your duty *to me* that keeps you here."

Winloki covered her face with her hands. "And would they understand the same thing if Kivik stayed behind . . . or Aesa, or Sigfrid, or Arinn?" she asked, envying her cousins and her brother their masculine privilege, their uncontested right to risk all in defense of their people.

She lowered her hands, looked up at him pleadingly. "Why won't you allow me to do the work I was born to do? Why deny me, as you would never deny your own sons, my fair share of the danger?"

"My dear child," said the King, reaching out to touch her bright head. "My beloved niece in all but blood, there may be peril in your future, and great deeds, too. But not in Skyrra. Your Wyrd—your fate for good or ill—is in the south."

She sat back on her heels. "You know who I am," she said softly, wonderingly. "You know more about me than you ever told me!"

And she remembered, suddenly, the southern wizard, Aethon, who had come during the winter, asked so many questions, then, abruptly, departed. "You have reason to believe that someone is on their way to claim me even now!"

Ristil shook his head; yet he looked troubled, uncertain. "I have no way of knowing when the summons will arrive, or how it will come, only that when it does come you must be here. I have promises to keep, and you have a duty far beyond Skyrra."

But by then she was well and truly frightened. The King

might not know anything about this Aethon, his reasons for coming to Skyrra; but that part of her which sometimes gave warning of things, the mysterious intuitive gift that was somehow tied up with the secret of her birth, *did* know.

Winloki rose slowly to her feet, her brain awhirl with wild surmises. They were coming for her, those unknown kinsmen who haunted her dreams, they would take her away from everyone and everything she loved, claim her at a time when the need for healers grew daily more desperate.

A cold stab of fear went through her; Winloki struggled for control. She had to think and to think clearly; she would *not* sit and wait with folded hands for events to sweep her away. She wondered, *If I'm not here, how far would they go to seek me out? Into battle? Into danger—when they were content to forget me for so many years?*

She made up her mind that they could wait a little longer.

If they come to Lückenbörg looking for me, she resolved, *they can* stay *at Lückenbörg, while* I *go to war.*

⊢———⊣

Visits to the Jarl Marshal, to several of the elder healers, and to the Queen were no more satisfactory.

"I don't understand what you expect me to do," said Sigvith, looking up from the fine needlework with which she beguiled her afternoons. "Do you think the King could possibly be made to accept my judgment in place of his own?"

Winloki sighed. It was only a variation on what she had been hearing all day. Still, there was that nervous beating in her blood, that pressure around her heart urging her so insistently to be gone.

She went in search of Skerry, finally running him to earth

at the stable where he kept most of his horses. Kivik, she immediately realized, had already warned him; he greeted her appearance with something less than the ardor that might be
expected of a young lover.

"What is it you want of me?" Skerry asked with a wary
look, as he closed the gate of the stall that housed dapple-grey
Grani and stepped out into the aisle.

She drew a long breath, inhaling the dusty sweet scents of
wheat straw and oats, the earthier odors that came of the
horses. "A place among your riders, disguised as a man. It
would work. I am tall enough, and I ride well enough."

"Madness," he answered, latching the gate behind him.
"Utter madness. You'd be discovered at once, if not much
sooner. And how would we ever explain our disobedience to
the King?"

She gnawed on her lower lip, clenched her hands into fists.
"You were not so ready to bow to tyranny three years ago
when we exchanged tokens!"

"We were children then, selfish and heedless. What we mistook for your uncle's tyranny was merely his kindness . . . and
his very good common sense! I hope that we're wiser now."

Winloki felt the world close in on her, a lump rise in her
throat. Sensing her agitation, the horses grew restless in their
stalls: grey stallion Grani, gentle mare Gisl, chestnut Arvak and
his half brother Bavor, stamping their heavy hooves and whickering in protest. As they sensed her anger, Winloki knew their
distress.

"Do you regret it, then, that secret pact we made between
us?" she asked, stiffly, angrily, feeling betrayed where she had
placed the most trust. "Do you wish we had waited for the
King's consent?"

"Do I regret pledging myself to you? No," Skerry said emphatically. He reached out to lay a placating hand on her shoulder, but she shrugged it away. "But this that you ask of me now—I can't and won't!"

She wanted to cry out: *And what becomes of us if they take me away? Where is our pledge* then? But that was the one argument she was too proud to use against him. She could only look at him, bewildered and angry. "I never took you for a coward, Skerry."

Another man might have taken offense, but he knew her temper of old. He knew how it flared up suddenly and passed almost as quickly—that she did not hold grudges or take petty vengeance—but while the mood was on her there was simply no reasoning with her. He did not even attempt it; he merely folded her hands between both of his and turned on her a deep, clear glance.

There they stood for several long minutes: Skerry patient, silent, waiting her out; Winloki seething, and nursing her anger. She knew when she was being managed. In truth, they knew each other far too well, she often thought. This time she was determined not to yield to his wordless influence.

She snatched her hands away with a violent motion and turned her back on him. "If you have any respect for me at all—" she began.

"No," said Skerry, gently but forcefully. "I do love you, Winloki, but I won't go against the King in this, scold how you will."

※

And so, after all, she was forced to take matters into her own hands. With a plan but half-formed in her mind, Winloki headed for the Healers' Hall.

It was a large house three stories high, of split logs on a stone foundation, with runes of great virtue carved above the door. There as elsewhere, the activity was frantic: simples being brewed, herbs being ground up in mortars or dried in ovens, powders and compounds and salves sealed up in glass bottles or earthenware jars with blots of red wax, then packed away in chests to be transported in the morning.

She felt a brief twinge of guilt as she slipped past the still-room, knowing that she ought to be in there helping. It was because she was expected to be with the healers that she had been able to move so freely all day, without her usual flock of attendants.

I have other business that is even more vital, she reminded herself, as she climbed two flights of narrow wooden stairs to the top of the house

In one of the dormitory bedchambers under the eaves, Winloki found Aija, the youngest healer, nervously packing for her journey on the morrow. "So you, too, are going. Every healer in the hall but the old, old women—and me!"

"There will be a need for healers here as well." Aija looked up from rummaging through a clothes chest at the foot of her bed, where she had been sorting through woolen stockings, linen shifts, and bright woven hair ribbons. "Children will be sick. Women will deliver babies—"

"And there will be nursemaids and midwives to attend them," Winloki finished for her, sitting down on a bench by an open dormer window, where the late-afternoon sun came through in a golden bar.

It was a long room, bright and airy, with five low wooden beds lined up in a row, a chest at the foot of each bed, and a beautifully carved clothespress of solid oak opposite the window. But Aija had it all to herself now; the other healers who used to sleep there had left with the army months ago.

"What *use* am I here," asked Winloki bitterly, "making charms for colicky infants and hysterical mothers, when men are *dying*—men I might save?"

Aija found the thing she had been so desperately looking for: a little triskele amulet carved of ivory on a thin leather cord. She slipped it on over her head. "You could have my place in one of the wagons for all of me," she muttered. "I'd trade places with you a thousand times over."

But then—glancing up to see her companion glowing, triumphant—she cried out, "No, no, I didn't mean that. Besides, my lady, you know that we can't. They would *never* allow it."

On Winloki's face, the bright look died. "Yes, I know," she said, with uncharacteristic meekness, as she left her seat on the bench and began to help the other girl pack up her things. "But it's very hard luck for the colicky infants. You were always much better with them than I was."

"Bad luck all around," said Aija. Her breath came quickly, and she seemed close to tears. But when the princess commented on her agitation, she passed it off with a wave of her hand. "It's just excitement, that is all that it is."

In the evening, Winloki sent a message to her servants at the Heldenhof, telling them that she meant to spend the next few days working with the healers. No one would be surprised, no one would think anything amiss if she did not come back to her rooms during all of that time. There was work in plenty to be done in the Healers' Hall, and after the coming morning very few hands to do it.

Then she went into the stillroom, knelt by the hearth, where the coals were still red, and stirred up the fire.

That was a pleasant room, fragrant with the herbs that hung drying from the ceiling, cluttered but still orderly, even after the recent spate of activity. As the flames rose, there was dazzle of light off of bottles on the shelves, crystal and alabaster and dark green glass; off jars of salt-glazed clay, and off boxes of cedarwood, ebony, and brass. There, too, were piles of brittle old papers or parchments bound together by cords or string, antique scrolls stored upright in brown jars, codices bound in crumbling leather: compendiums of herb lore and spells for healing, learned treatises writ down in *Niadhélen*—all of the books and most of the writing that remained in Lückenbörg. Books were a part of that discredited past abandoned along with the cities. Very few people could read anymore and fewer write—only the healers, the King and his family, and a handful of officers in Ristil's army who sent messages back and forth, laboriously inscribed.

But Winloki had no need to consult those tattered old volumes. She knew what she had to do, and she had to work swiftly, lest anyone come in to ask awkward questions. She moved quickly around the room, gathering up the things she would need, trying not to drop or break anything in her haste.

Returning to the hearth, she heated milk in a pannikin over the fire. When it was warm, she poured it very carefully into a beaten copper cup with a wooden handle. With shaking hands, she took a small staghorn flask off one of the shelves, unstoppered it, and let three drops of a clear amber liquid fall, turning the milk a deep buttercup-yellow and scenting the air with honey and spring flowers.

"To help you rest—you'll be calmer and stronger tomorrow, if you can sleep tonight," she said a short while later,
standing by Aija's bed with the cup in one hand and her heart
rattling against her ribs, wondering if such a transparent device
could possibly succeed.

She thought she might compel Aija's cooperation if the
younger girl balked, her will being so much stronger—only
that was a magic she had never tried, to enforce her desire on
the mind of another. It was also a line she was reluctant to
cross.

But Aija was caught up in her own fears, her own dread of
the night still ahead, and of all the days and nights to follow.
She accepted the potion with a grateful look. "I'm to rise before
dawn," she said, sniffing at the cup. "If I were to oversleep, to
have trouble waking—"

"I measured it out with the greatest care. But if you would
like—" Winloki pretended that the suggestion had suddenly
occurred to her. "If you would like, I will sit by your bed, stay
with you until the rest of the house wakes, make certain that
nothing goes wrong."

Aija lifted the cup and swallowed the potion in three
short gulps. "You are kind, Princess. I don't know how to
thank you."

Taking back the cup, Winloki put it down on the chest at
the foot of the bed. She reached out to take the other girl's
hand, gave it a reassuring squeeze. "As to that," she said, with
the faintest blush, "I am doing no more than I ought. Rest now,
my friend, and fear nothing."

Already, Aija was growing drowsy; it seemed she could
hardly hold her eyelids up, they had grown so heavy. She
yawned, sat down on the bed. Without undressing, she laid her
head down on the coarse woolen blankets and was almost im-

mediately asleep. Winloki watched the hectic flush fade from her face, then bent down and loosened her laces and removed her shoes, that she might rest more comfortably.

True to her word, the princess remained by her friend's bedside for many hours. But when the other healers in the house began to stir just before dawn, she did not wake Aija. Instead, she lit a stub of wax candle and stood over the bed, watching the other girl's slow, steady breathing. She had indeed measured the potion most carefully. Aija was certain to sleep all through the day and into the night, nor was anyone likely to disturb her in this great empty house.

Moving swiftly by candlelight, Winloki bound up her red-gold hair and pinned it in place. She donned Aija's cloak of plain brown wool, pulled the hood well forward. Then she took light from the candle into her hands and deftly shaped it into a mask to cover her face and blur her features. It would serve only so long as no one looked at her too closely or too steadily.

It was the simplest of spells: something she had been forced to teach herself as a child, finding no worthy teachers among the runestone readers and healers of Skyrra. She had employed it then to escape from nursemaids and servants, to slip out of the Heldenhof unattended, but never recently, thinking herself too old to play tricks on her attendants, accounting it a subterfuge unworthy of a princess.

But this was different. *I am stronger than Aija,* she reminded herself, *and more fit for the work.*

Picking up the bundle at the foot of the bed, Winloki extinguished the candle with a thought and went downstairs in the other girl's place. But she paused on the threshold under the lintel inscribed with the runes, before going out to the yard where wagons were waiting.

She glanced up at the sky, sniffed at the wind, gathering omens. The stars were already fading, they told her nothing. But a breeze from the east smelled heavy with moisture, and if that was not precisely an omen, at least it was a very good thing. It would be foggy before the sun was well up, and the mist was an ally that would help to conceal her. She could hardly have arranged things better herself.

16

✳

All day and into the evening the army was on the move. *Bump, bump, bump* went the wagon in which Winloki and some of the other healers traveled, and *creak, creak, creak* went the wheels, but the sounds came muffled and dreamlike in the heavy fog. So also the slow, steady hoofbeats of the broad-backed draft horses, the low, growling thunder of some six hundred warhorses to the front of the column (at least two for each man, and more for the officers), the light, quick canter of the smaller and fleeter steeds belonging to the scouts and the messengers, who went back and forth constantly between the mounted troops and the long train of wagons and carts—all subdued, all sounding hollow and distant, even when one of the couriers rode by like a shadow in the fog only yards away. Sometimes the mist thinned and gave a promise of daylight ahead; but that promise was never fulfilled, and the air soon became thick with cloudy moisture again.

For Winloki, perched atop a wooden chest full of medicines in one of the wagons, the day dragged on as pure misery. Aside from the boredom, the damp, and the all-pervading chill, she had never dreamed there could be such jolting discomfort as she was experiencing. To ride in a wagon was not *in the least* like riding on horseback. In the saddle, one learned to fall into a harmonious rhythm, to move as the horse moved, so that the two became one. A wagon offered no such harmony, no such communion. As she pitched and tossed on her uncomfortable seat, she could never quite gain a dependable feel for the road. A bump would come, and Winloki was all unprepared. It rattled her teeth, jarred her very bones, and if she was not careful she would bite her tongue, filling her mouth with the taste of blood.

Much of the time, she suffered from motion sickness, her head swimming and her stomach roiling. She would have gladly climbed down and walked between the wagons like some of the other women, but she feared recognition. On foot, some of the scouts might try to talk to her, as they did speak from time to time with the girls who walked. So long as she remained, clammy and miserable, on the coffinlike box of herbs and salves, with her head bowed and Aija's brown cloak wrapped tightly around her, everyone apparently thought it kinder to leave her alone.

This is the price that I pay for my deception, Winloki told herself. *It is all my own doing, and I must bear it.* That was hardly a comforting thought, but it was all she had to keep up her courage.

After hours of such misery, the mist began to grow greyer and darker, a sign that night was finally descending. Some of the riders lit torches, which glowed like small suns in the fog, casting haloes of light about the men who carried them.

Only when it was truly dark did they stop and begin to set up camp, on land that had once been good for grazing before the movements of armies had wounded and trampled it. It was long before the last of the wagons rolled into camp. By that time the tents were already up: pavilions of silk or canvas for the nobles and officers, smaller and ruder shelters for the healers, but many of the other women—the wives of common soldiers, as well as the less respectable camp followers who drove some of the carts—found their way into both sorts of tents.

Winloki shared a lean-to stitched out of hides with two of the healers, Thyra and Sivi, and with a weather-beaten woman and her sixteen-year-old daughter, who had *somehow* insinuated their way in. Winloki at least was not minded to turn them out. In the chatter and confusion of so many settling down to rest in the dark tent, she was able to go unrecognized for at least one night. That was reason enough to be grateful for their presence.

But she slept very ill with only a bedroll between her and the cold, hard ground, only a single blanket and Aija's cloak to cover her—she who had never slept but on a goose-down mattress, with a feather pillow and an eider-stuffed quilt and fair linen sheets. She woke in the morning with a stiff neck and a mood of the very blackest, which had not improved in the slightest by the time the tents were lowered and bundled away, and the women returned to the wagons.

That day was as murky and obscure as the day before. Winloki took a seat in a different wagon this time, on top of a grain sack, wedged between a bushel of apples and some rough burlap bags with an earthy smell that *might* contain turnips.

Like a farmer's daughter, she thought. Which for all she knew, she might very well be: a poor man's child with a gift for magic, sent north because *someone* felt threatened by that gift. Yet she did not think she was a farmer's or a herdsman's daughter: all of her dreams, the good and the bad alike, were of palaces and temples and other such marvelous places.

On the evening of the third day, Winloki's wagon, as one of the heaviest and slowest, arrived in camp long after nightfall, when the fires were already lit and the supper cooking. She had dozed off earlier on her sack of grain, but she woke when the wagon creaked to a halt, to a fragrance of woodsmoke, the sound and the scent of sausages and onions sizzling in a pan. Her stomach had still not settled, and she felt too weary and ill to move. She merely curled up again in her uncomfortable nest, and slept for the rest of the night.

But waking both hungry and parched to the braying of horns at dawn, she rubbed the sleep from her eyes, climbed over the side of the wagon, and set out in search of water. She could smell the horses all around her, hear the stamping of their heavy feet, their soft whickering, and she could also hear the gurgle of a stream running over stones somewhere nearby. She felt her way through the gradually lightening mist, past wagons and tents, past cookfires being lit and men arming up and belting on their weapons, moving always toward the sound of running water.

She fell in with a party of women on a similar errand, some carrying buckets and some carrying pans. Before she had gone more than a few yards in their company, she heard a clink of metal, and two men in steel hauberks appeared out of the fog, one of them carrying a lantern.

"Orders," he said. "No women to leave camp without an escort. We're in dangerous territory now."

So . . . they had left the frequent villages and wide, culti-vated fields of the Herzenmark for the more sparsely settled Haestfilke, far too close to the border and Eisenlonde. With this realization came an unhappy stir among the females, an exchange of wide-eyed, nervous glances. Some hung back, but Winloki went on ahead with the men, and soon she could hear the others following behind.

Reaching the banks of a shallow but swift-running stream, they found a party of scouts already before them, watering their horses and simultaneously receiving orders from a stocky young man in a long green cloak. Winloki paid them scant heed, intent as she was on washing and drinking.

Kneeling on wet grass at the edge of stream, she splashed water on her face. It was shockingly cold, but the sound and the scent of the water so near made her thirst nearly unbearable; she bent lower still, and scooped up a handful to drink. It tasted of minerals washed down from the mountains, and it was by far too chill for her empty stomach. A sudden sharp pain took her breath away and doubled her up on the grassy embankment.

She unbent with an effort, reciting a charm to ease the cramp. But as she straightened, the hood of her cloak slipped off; the hair tumbled down over her shoulders in a mass of red-gold tangles. Somewhere behind her a familiar voice uttered a cut-off obscenity and called out her name.

With a jaded and weary glance back over her shoulder, Winloki spied Skerry striding in her direction, his dark hair bristling and his green cloak flapping behind him. Knowing that the time for concealment had well and truly passed, she resigned herself to the coming unpleasantness. Nor could she even *hope* to put Skerry off with her tricks or her spells—for one thing, he knew them all.

By the time he arrived at her side, she had already scrambled to her feet. Determined to brazen the thing out if she possibly could, she greeted him with her chin held high and an imperious little gesture. "You'll not tell anyone that you saw me here!"

"I?" said Skerry, between gritted teeth, as he reached out and took her firmly by the arm. "I won't say a word. What I *will* do is take you to our cousin, who can say to you the things that only a king's son may say to a princess!"

And he led her, whether she would come or not, up the bank from the stream, between two lines of picketed horses, and finally to the Prince's great tent of dew-drenched green silk, where she received a far from cordial welcome.

Kivik turned an ugly shade of white; he shot Skerry an incredulous glance. Receiving a tight-lipped shake of the head in response, he sputtered out an oath. "It wanted only this! What are you doing here? No, don't bother to answer, for it's plain enough. You are a wicked and willful girl—and what I am to *do* with you only the Powers and the Ancestors know!"

Winloki had nothing to say, now that the reckoning, which she had always expected, had finally come. Wisely, she kept her thoughts to herself and her eyes on the ground, while the Prince tore her character to shreds and cursed the day he had ever met her. Finally, he choked out another oath and fell ominously silent.

That silence continued so long, stretched on past the point where curiosity got the better of her, that she dared to raise her eyes and study the faces of both her cousins. Skerry was grinding his teeth and snorting like a warhorse in a very bad temper, while Kivik had gone from white to red, and all but breathed fire.

"Too late," he said, with a simmering glance in her direction, "*by far* too late to send her back. We can't spare half our army, which is what it would take to do it safely, when the enemy might just as well be behind as ahead of us—and the scouts are practically useless in this foul mirk. She will be safer with us for the time being."

"So it would seem," replied Skerry. "But let us hope that the King doesn't suspect us of abetting her from the very beginning."

At this, Winloki abandoned her resolution to suffer their displeasure in a dignified silence. "Do you think I would allow you to take the blame for what *I* have done?" she asked indignantly. "Do you imagine I have no more pride, no more honor, than—"

"We don't think anything of the sort. Nor does my father!" Kivik retorted. "Which is why, no matter how you protest our innocence, he will *never believe you.*"

With a sinking sensation, Winloki realized that what he said was true. A wave of contrition swept over her—not quite sufficient to cause her to question her motives or regret her behavior, but it was an unpleasant feeling nevertheless.

"I will try to be as little trouble to you as I possibly can," she offered meekly. "I will continue to ride in the wagons with the other women and live in all respects as poor Aija would, if I hadn't taken her place."

"Which is exactly what you *can't* do, nor I allow, now that I know you are here," snapped Kivik, far from mollified. "I will assign four trusty men to guard you at all times. And if— if!—you really mean not to make any trouble, you will accept that arrangement with all good grace, and do *nothing* to evade their watch."

It hardly seemed an auspicious moment to argue that point, or indeed any at all. So Winloki merely nodded in wordless agreement and resolved to bring up the matter of the guards again later, when Kivik should be in a more equable temper, and Skerry—Skerry was acting more like himself.

As if she had expressly ordered it (and perhaps she had), the fog burned off before noon that day. Riding along between the wagons on a chestnut mare belonging to one of the scouts, with her escort of four riding ahead, behind, and to either side of her, Winloki felt remarkably conspicuous crossing that wide, rolling landscape in the broad bright noontime, the only female on horseback among three hundred riders.

And yet she was glad to give up her uncomfortable place in the wagon, pleased and excited to be in the saddle enjoying the spring sunshine, enjoying the constantly changing scenery of this pleasant green country. Up ahead, banners snapped in the wind; bronze helmets and shield bosses shone in the sun; over all stretched a shining sky of brilliant blue. It was simply not in her to be less than blissfully happy on such a day.

Haakon, the youngest of her guards, nudged his rawboned piebald gelding a little closer, so that they were riding almost knee to knee. The gelding was an ugly creature of no particular breeding, but very strong and a good deal faster than anyone might think, or so the youth had confided to her earlier. Lif was its name, and he had raised it from a foal on his father's farm. Haakon also appeared long-limbed and gangly, though he possessed a face of such singular beauty as a girl might envy. He seemed heartbreakingly young to be going to war, even to Winloki, but, just like poor Lif, there was more to Haakon than met the eye. Skerry had praised him as a fierce fighter who had already distinguished himself in battle.

"I wouldn't look quite so blithe, were I you, the next time Prince Kivik comes by," said the boy, lowering his voice, but giving her a quick conspiratorial smile under his dark eyelashes. "They say he's still in a terrible rage."

Winloki shrugged. She did not fear Kivik, and was capable, if she chose, of matching him temper for temper. Besides, Kivik had other things on his mind, compared to which, her presence here was an entirely minor and trivial matter.

Because of the fog, they had veered many miles north of the place where they were to meet Hialli and Eikenskalli and the other marshals. They could change their course, make it right again, now they could see the way, but they could not make up for lost time, not with the wagons, and the day they had agreed to meet had already come and gone. And when Kivik sent scouts ahead to the appointed meeting place by the River Nisse, they had ridden back two hours later to say that the marshals and their armies were not there, nor seemingly had ever been. How could they mistake the signs of such a large encampment, so many thousands of men and horses?

Of course, it was altogether possible that the marshals had also gone astray in the heavy mist. As for the other armies, they might only be five or ten miles off in any direction, just out of range of the scouts. Anytime now, one or two riders might come hurrying back with the welcome news that a great mass of Skyrran cavalry had been spotted over the next hill.

But for the first time, when Winloki thought of those foggy days just past, the mist did not seem so friendly. What if it *had* served her own purposes so admirably? There might well have been another will behind it, one that wanted to sow confusion among the armies of Skyrra.

At that idea, a cold shiver ran down her spine and she felt a cold, heavy feeling in the pit of her stomach. The mist had seemed wholly innocent, wholly natural, but what did she know of these things, truly, with her little knowledge and her untrained talents? That, too, was an uneasy thought. Winloki had always considered herself equal to or better than any person or situation she might chance to meet—but supposing there was someone nearby working magics, someone who knew more, and understood more, and could do more than she? Someone beside whom she and her fledgling gifts were negligible?

She suddenly began to doubt herself in other ways, to realize that perhaps she had never been nearly so brave as she imagined. Perhaps what she had mistaken for courage was only arrogance and ignorance. It is easy to be fearless when you think no one can best you, no one can harm you.

To banish those thoughts, she turned to Haakon, searched her mind for something she might say to start a conversation, anything to distract her from her fears, these disturbing revelations of her own character.

"You were born near here?" she ventured at last. "My cousin said that he thought you were."

"Some twenty miles to the north," the young man replied, gesturing. "But I've been all over this country." And he proceeded to regale her with stories of his youthful adventures in this wild land.

He was in the midst of a hair-raising story when his voice suddenly died, and he reached out to take the mare by the bridle. Winloki turned on him a startled and angry look, but he shook his head and advised her to listen.

She did listen, and now she could hear it, too: a rising murmur among the riders up ahead, followed by the clatter of hooves as two of the scouts came riding at great speed back toward the wagons.

"Eisenlonders," shouted one, as he rode past Winloki and her guards. "A great many of them."

What happened next was pure chaos and confusion in Winloki's eyes, though those around her seemed cool-headed enough and to know exactly what they were doing. Amidst a great deal of shouting and backing of horses, the wagons changed course, heading toward the rising, more defensible, ground to the north. Reluctant to follow, in sudden doubt as to what was expected of her, Winloki hung back. "If there is going to be a battle, they will need healers."

"The healers come in *after* the fighting," said Haakon, taking the reins out of her hands. "Princess, begging you're pardon, you'd only be in the way."

Yet Winloki remained uncertain, until she saw that the older, more experienced healers were going, too. Then she consented to be led.

It was a hard pull up the hill for the heavier wagons. Axles groaned, and wheels found little purchase, but the stolid draft horses caught some of the tension and made a valiant effort, straining at the traces with their big heads down. At last they were all there at the top of the rise, in a great loose circle two wagons deep. The drivers unhitched the horses and led them into the center for their better protection. At the same time, some of the other females hastily began to unload bales and barrels and cords of firewood, piling them up in the gaps between the wagons, forming a solid barrier. Two companies of riders had detached themselves from the rest of the army and stationed themselves outside the circle, waiting with their swords drawn, in case the enemy should try to storm the hill. Some of the drivers carried bows and arrows with them, to defend themselves at need, and those few quickly armed and clambered up onto the barricade.

Winloki urged her mare through a noisy ferment of women and horses, edging toward a better vantage point, where she could look down on the battle. By that time, the Eisenlonders had come into view: a great mass of riders, too many to count, and hundreds of foot soldiers, carrying axes and spears that glittered in the sun.

"I didn't think they would be mounted. At least not so many of them," she said, catching her breath at the sight. She had expected a ragged barbarian rabble, not these well-armed men in armor of leather and steel, and certainly no cavalry worthy of the name.

"They are great horse thieves, the Eisenlonders," answered one of her guards, a man called Arvi, curbing his dancing black stallion. "They've been carrying off the pick of our herds for years."

Down below, trumpets sounded, swords and spears and axes clattering against shields as both lines spread out. A loud cry went up from the ranks of the Eisenlonders, a bestial howling, and Winloki saw that there were uncanny wolflike creatures among them, rising on shaggy grey haunches, almost like men, and clashing their yellow teeth.

As if in response to a common signal, both armies swept forward at once. The thunder of that charge caused the very air to vibrate; the world seemed to tilt. Watching them, Winloki felt a flush of triumph, a thrill of pride, for it was a lovely thing to see: all the bright banners flaming out on the wind, green and gold, blue and red; the beautiful, spirited horses stretching out from a canter to a gallop, with their silky tails streaming behind them, and the grass bowing in the wind of their passage; the sun reflecting off iron-bladed spears and long, slender swords.

But then the two lines came together with a roar and a clash of arms, a shock that reached all the way to Winloki up on her hilltop. Shields and lances met and shattered. Horses screamed and reared up, fighting the air. Horns blared. Men cried out in agony.

At first, it was difficult to sort out her impressions—it was all just hideous noise and turmoil, the smell of blood on the wind. But as more and more men and horses went down, she began to feel their pain and terror battering at her in great waves, to hear their dying screams ringing inside her skull. She covered her ears, bowed down over the horse's neck, and screwed her eyes tightly shut; but it was no better that way. Empath and healer as she was, the horror was *inside her* as much as without. Bile rose in her throat, almost choking her, and sweat broke out all over her skin.

Winloki raised her head. Fighting for breath, she opened her eyes. A red mist obscured her vision. All around her was a seething mass of skittish sidestepping horses, of women weeping with fear and excitement. Down below, metal hammered against metal, against flesh and bone, and men were dying in their own blood. Arrows flew. Horses threw their riders to the ground and bolted. She saw some of the fallen stagger to their feet, catch hold of dangling reins, and heave themselves back up into strange saddles, but many more were crushed and mutilated under stamping hooves.

Gradually she became aware of little whirlwinds of movement between the men and horses, of threads and tendrils of shadow that flowed and crept across the ground. They weaved in and out among the combatants—apparently unseen, as no one reacted to them—but every now and then a tentacle would break away from the central mass, rear up, and take on an almost-shape of man or beast that would strike out against the men of Skyrra with the rude beginnings of a hand, or a claw, or a taloned foot.

Watching the shades was like looking at something out of one eye. They had no depth, no dimension. Being shadows, they had no shadows themselves; they seemed to have no sides, only surface; they were almost impossibly thin and tenuous.

Yet if they had hardly any substance, they had power and will and the strength to do harm. They did do harm. Again and again Winloki saw them overwhelm men and horses, who fell and never knew what struck them.

Sometimes it happened that one of the shadow things was trampled under the hooves of a warhorse, or a warrior caught one on the backstroke of his swing, or an arrow meant for the Eisenlonders struck one. Then that shade would dissipate and fade like smoke. But how were men to defend themselves effectively against things they could neither see nor sense?

Meanwhile, Winloki's guards watched the battle with eager faces and burning eyes. They seemed to understand it all far better than she did, for several times they raised their fists and shouted. Perhaps, in spite of the shadow-things, her countrymen were faring much better than she thought.

"Are we winning?" she asked faintly.

"Aye," said Arvi grimly, "though with heavy casualties on both sides."

But then the tide of battle shifted; Kivik's line broke and scattered. There was fighting at the very foot of the hill. Winloki saw a man beheaded, and another impaled. She saw werewolves attacking the horses, pulling them down. She saw shadows engulf the fallen riders, swallow them up, and drain them of life.

Watching these things, she felt crushed with horror. She had imagined that she was strong, had honestly believed herself accustomed to the ugliest sights, having treated wounded men, set broken and shattered bones more times than she could count. But she had never seen blood pumping from an open wound, never seen swords hew living flesh, or arms and legs and heads hacked off before her very eyes. Once, she had even helped to amputate a leg below the knee when the patient was sedated with syrup of poppy, dazed with mandragora—that had been soul-shaking enough, but nothing to compare with this, this carnage, this *obscenity* of men being butchered by other men.

And this *is war,* she thought. Behind all the tales of glory and heroism, this was the reality: this din, this chaos, this filthy, bestial, *wanton* waste of life. Why did they do it? What could possibly be worth it?

As though sensing her thoughts, Haakon spoke somewhere behind her, over the hoarse shouts of the fighting men, the shrill neighing of the horses. "We didn't start this, my Lady. We're only defending our own lands, our own people. We never wanted it to come to this."

She looked back at him over her shoulder, bewildered and only half-comprehending. "*They* started it? It was none of our choosing? But even so, why would they—?"

He shook his head, reached down and patted his shivering piebald gelding. "Rightly speaking, I don't suppose they started it either. Someone has been inciting them. They've always had nasty habits, the Eisenlonders, but they were never like they are now: raping and burning, consorting with skinchangers." On the field below, Kivik stood high in the stirrups, brandishing his sword and calling out to his men, rallying them. "Nor were there ever so many of them, or so well armed."

It was too much for her to take in; it made her head ache just to think of it, let alone try to understand it. "But *why?* What could anyone have to gain, sending them out to slaughter us, to be slaughtered themselves? Who could possibly hate us so much?"

He shook his head again. Her questions were simply unanswerable, yet the proof of his words was there on the battlefield before them, living and dying in a welter of blood and a cacophony of human misery.

17

✳

Faolein is dead. That was Sindérian's first thought on waking—as it had become, almost invariably, her last thought at night. There had been a time, not so long ago, when she woke to painful memories of Gilaefri's fall, of Cailltin's death, but now it was Faolein's loss that greeted her each new day. As she propped herself up with one elbow on the stony ground and rose from her uncomfortable resting place, this third day of traveling through Hythe, she wondered if that was how she would reckon her life in after years, with a growing litany of her dead.

Shivering in the half-light of dawn, she rolled up her blankets and bound them securely, then joined the others for a hasty cold breakfast: goat cheese and dry, gritty seedcake, a mouthful of ale. As they saddled up the horses and broke camp, thunderclouds, violet and gold, lay heaped on the eastern horizon; a chill wind came whipping down from the north, smelling unseasonably of snow.

"Queer weather this time of year," said Aell, narrowing his eyes against the stinging gale.

"Curious weather whatever the year or season," Sindérian muttered under her breath as she swung up into the saddle.

The others mounted, too. One of the first things they had done on shaking off the dust of turncoat Mere was to buy more horses in one of the border towns, so that no one need walk. That should have made for swifter travel, had it not been for a long series of mishaps and near-disasters that had plagued them along the way. Too many such mishaps, Sindérian considered, *by far too many* all to be happenstance.

They set off along the same road they had been following for days: that straight road which arrows through the countryside from Dacre on the border to the rocky foothills of the Cadmin Aernan. Before they had gone more than a mile or two, the rain came down, swift and cold. Thunder pealed in the distance, and branched lightning lit the sky: white, blue-white, blue-violet.

Trees creaked in the icy blast; leaves and branches tore loose and whirled in the air like bats. Jago's grey, Gilrain's black mare, both reared up, raking the air.

"This," said the Ni-Ferys, shouting to be heard over the tumult, "is no ordinary storm."

"No," Sindérian answered, breathless after a tussle with the chestnut gelding. The hood of her cloak had slipped back, and her hair was streaming with water. "This is Thaga's doing."

To her wizard's sight, the very landscape seemed perilous, full of dark omens. In the straggling woods to either side of the road, uncanny lights, violet and indigo, danced from branch to branch and tree to tree. Hungry mud sucked at the horses' hooves, and the wind raged at them with shrieking maledictions. "Just as the bridge that began to collapse under us yesterday was Thaga's work. And the fire in that cottage where we stopped two nights ago— Dreyde's men wouldn't dare to follow us across Prince Bael's lands, but the mage's spells respect no borders."

There came another violent crash of thunder directly overhead. The air crackled with electricity. "Lady, is there nothing that you can do?" shouted Prince Ruan.

Sindérian turned an angry white face his way. He had scarcely deigned to speak with her these last several days, and typically, she thought, he broke his silence only to give her an order. "I am doing more than you think. We would all be dead by now if I had done nothing. It's no easy thing," she added, with a curling lip, "to deflect lightning from those of our party who ride about dressed in *iron.*"

They rode for several miles more in the drenching rain, with water down their necks, soaking through their heavy garments. The horses plodded on with their ears laid back, with draggled manes and tails, looking utterly miserable. Clouds boiled overhead, and lightning struck on all sides. First one, then another of the horses would refuse to go forward, eyes rolling white, fighting at the bit until the foam flew.

Exhausting enough, Sindérian reflected wearily, *just trying to sit upright in this battering wind, without contesting for every yard of the road as well.*

An oak ripped up out of the ground and crashed into the road ahead of them, setting all the horses bucking and dancing. Almost simultaneously, a vivid bolt of lightning struck a beech less than twenty yards away. It burst into flame, showering sparks like a torch in the rain.

"Is there no place where we can take shelter?" growled the Prince, curbing his dun stallion with a heavy hand.

"There's Kemys just over the hill and beyond the wood." Gilrain blinked back the water that was running down his high white forehead and dripping into his eyes. "A den of thieves by reputation, though in my experience they're more likely to cheat—" The rest of his sentence was lost in another rolling chord of thunder.

Sindérian gritted her teeth to keep them from chattering. There was sleet mixed in with the rain, and it grew steadily colder. Her hands on the reins felt numb and lifeless, her feet, in the well-worn boots, like wooden blocks. "Then *take* us there. If we've a roof over our heads, walls around us, I can set wards."

Gilrain swung the black mare's head around, skirted the fallen tree, then urged the mare off the road and up a steep slope, following a trail so faint that Sindérian could barely make it out in the sheeting downpour. Pulling up her hood, she leaned forward in the saddle to avoid as much of the wind as possible, and muttered a *béanath* under her breath.

The village of Kemys was a labyrinth of slatternly old timber houses and squalid little beehive huts, all packed together inside a stone wall rotten with time and neglect.

Scant welcome and even scanter hospitality our travelers had there. Stabling for the horses and shelter for themselves, all crowded together in a hut with a leaky roof, this they obtained from the village headman in return for a handful of copper coins; and the other villagers sold them firewood and cider at extravagant prices.

Inside the hut, Sindérian made a little blue-grey bubble of werelight to work by, and everyone was busy for a time, unsaddling the horses and rubbing them down.

Then, while the men hung up their sodden cloaks to dry, shook water out of their hair, and emptied it out of their boots,

Sindérian set her wards. As she felt them take hold, some of the tension in her neck and shoulders relaxed. There, at least, was safety, no matter how temporary.

Meanwhile, Gilrain had succeeded in coaxing a fire from the few sticks of uncured wood the villagers had sold them. Even a wizard might be hard-pressed to start a blaze under such conditions: the wood green, and damp at that. Was this simple woodcraft, Sindérian wondered, or some fairy spell?

The Prince was right: I know less than I should about the Faey, she thought with a lump in her throat.

The sad truth was, her ignorance in *many* areas was likely to get them all killed, now that she was the wizard the rest depended on. Her whole life up until then began to feel like a fraud and a waste. Had she spent the last six years studying on Leal, instead of mending broken bodies in Rheithûn only to send them out to be slaughtered more efficiently the next time, she might *almost* be fit for the task before her.

It should be Faolein here now, she thought miserably. *Why was it my father who died and I who lived? Either the Fates are against us, or they've gone mad and senile.*

But that was a thought too impious even for her, and she felt an immediate twinge of remorse. Perhaps the Fates were simply punishing her for her crisis of faith. Yet Faolein would say that Servants of the Light did not mete out punishments, that they were wholly beneficent and kind, though their ways were often mysterious. Of late, they had been far too mysterious for Sindérian.

Making supper under such damp, crowded conditions soon became an adventure. The horses' hooves and tails seemed to be here, there, and everywhere; among the two-footed, knees, ribs, shins, and elbows appeared to exert a magical attraction, with many bumps and bruises resulting. The small smoky fire went out twice and had to be rekindled.

And when Jago jostled Gilrain's arm, tipping a cauldron of broth into the flames, Prince Ruan gave a snort of disgust, left his seat on the ground, and stalked outside.

"Much good a warding spell does us, when we insist on inviting ill luck inside with us!" he said over his shoulder, as he passed through the doorway.

Bristling up, Gilrain scrambled to his feet, but Sindérian threw out a hand to restrain him. "Please do not," she said. "You've no need to defend yourself. No one, not even the Prince, really blames you for our bad fortune."

The Ni-Ferys settled down again with a rueful look. "I shouldn't allow him to provoke me. Nor should I find so many ways to provoke him. It is a curious thing: the Prince and I were both raised among Humans, and as a general rule we consider ourselves Men rather than Faey; I have even heard it said that Ruan is entirely estranged from his mother's people; but throw us together in the same company . . ."

He smiled and shrugged. "No doubt to you our two tribes are practically indistinguishable; but believe me, we are no more alike than chalk and cheese. We regard *them* as insufferably proud and high-handed, and they see *us* as sly and insinuating. Perhaps there is fault on both sides."

Sindérian shook her head wearily. "Who am I to judge the Ni-Ferys and Ni-Féa, when Men have been at war my entire life? Some of the grievances between Thäerie and Phaôrax go back for hundreds of years, when the truth is they are kindred peoples, who ought to live together like brothers and sisters. But the years pass, and still we go on slaughtering each other."

Gilrain sat gazing into the fire for a long time before he spoke. "It may not be a war of Men only—or of Men and half-Men like myself and the Prince—for much longer." In the pale firelight, his eyes were luminous like a cat's, and his fair hair tinted with all the colors of the flames. When he spread his hands, there was a thin, translucent webbing between his third and fourth fingers, which Sindérian had noticed before. Another hybrid anomaly that was, like the color of Prince Ruan's eyes.

"The world is in flux," he went on, after another silence. "*Silüren uilédani amffüriandem*—isn't that what the wizards say? All things under the moon are changing. It's been true for more than a century, but it seems to be more true now, and even a half-blood Ni-Ferys like me senses this increasingly."

In his words, Sindérian caught an echo of her own worst fears. And she wondered what perceptions the Faey had to know these things, what knowledge and powers that even wizards lacked. Faolein might have known the answer to that, but she did not. One thing she remembered that her father had said, back at Tregna: *It is bad enough when our enemies take us by surprise, but when it is our* friends *who prove unpredictable and untrustworthy—*"

Sitting back on her heels, she said with a sigh: "If Prince Ruan dislikes and mistrusts you, he seems to like me even less. I'm afraid that I said things back at Brill that he will never forgive. I would set things right if I could, but I fear the breach is already past mending."

Much to her surprise, Gilrain began to shake with silent laughter. "To do the Prince no more than justice," he said, his voice colored with amusement, "I think you are wrong. You are merely the victim of Prince Ruan's peculiar idea of chivalry.

He thinks it proper to keep you at a distance. Have you never considered the evils of your situation, now that your father is gone? A lone female, traveling with a party of men—

"But I see that you have not," he added, when her eyes widened and her jaw dropped. "Your pardon, Lady Healer, if I've made you uncomfortable. Perhaps I should never have mentioned it."

She felt the hot blood rising in her face, and not because of the fire. "I'm well able to defend my own honor, should it come to that," she replied stiffly. "In any case, there are far more important things I should be thinking about now. I can't allow myself to be distracted by what you call *'the evils of my situation.'*"

"Yet Prince Ruan seems to be able to think of little else," said Gilrain, with an odd little smile. "I wonder why that is?"

———

They rode out the next morning in a fine, misting rain, with a cold wind blowing in their faces. The worst of the storm had passed; but as Sindérian sniffed the air and tasted the wind, she was keenly aware of ripples in the world of matter, of currents and eddies—the aftereffects of Thaga's spell. Power, restless and chaotic, shimmered on the air, and a whole series of tiny vibrations moved like ants across her skin. The horses seemed to feel it, too. Prince Ruan's dun trembled and fought at the bit, and the chestnut gelding blew out a nervous breath and shied at nothing.

That wretch Thaga's unseasonable thunderstorm, Sindérian thought. *It will be muddling up the weather in Hythe and Mere for the next half year. Not to mention what it might do to all the fertility spells and birthing charms of all the village midwives and wisewomen between the border and the mountains.*

And who would suffer if the crops rotted in the fields, if the flocks dwindled? Not the likes of Dreyde and his tame sorcerer, certainly. It was the ordinary people in tiny villages like Brill and Kemys, in towns like Dacre: they would suffer, they would do without, their children would go to bed hungry.

It filled Sindérian with an impotent rage just to think of it, the more so because she felt partly responsible. She and her companions had come into the region like a wandering curse, and who knew how long afterward the suffering and the hardship they left behind them would last? How could people who already lived in such appalling poverty as they had seen in Kemys survive a bad season, when they could hardly scrape out a miserable living as it was?

"Are we really so different from Ouriána and those who serve her?" she wondered out loud.

"I would hope," said the Prince, startled into answering, "that we are as different as night and day."

Sindérian bit her lip. If only it could be that obvious to her! "Don't both sides use people like counters in some horrible game, gambling castles and cities and kingdoms, hazarding lives and futures on the very narrowest of chances, rationalizing it all in the name of some distant—and possibly unreachable— higher good? Who decides when the cost is too great? Who reckons up the value of a life lost now against lives spent later? Wizards? Princes? The Fates? Or that vast and incomprehensible power the Fates are supposed to serve, that Men call the Light?"

To this Ruan had no answer; he could only shake his head. Yet she knew what Faolein would say, if he were there.

Our lives are the clay the Fates use to shape a better world. Only Faolein was *not* there, nor would ever be again, and so far as Sindérian could see—for all that she had done and experienced so far, for all the myriad questions that swarmed in her brain—the world became more and more a perilous place to live in, and one harder and harder for her to understand.

But then, all at once, she was furiously, breathtakingly angry with herself.

Sitting up straighter in the saddle she took the reins more firmly in her hands. *What gives you the right to self-pity? You ought to be ashamed! You may be orphaned, but you're young and strong and whole, which is a good deal more than many can say. And you have a home to return to, when there are thousands left homeless by the war.*

How dare *you even begin to feel sorry for yourself.*

18

✳

As if in sympathy with Thaga's distant spellcasting, it was raining on Phaôrax, too.

For three days and two nights there had been a thick, slow, persistent rainfall over the capital. It drummed on slate roofs, leaked under wooden shutters, filled all the gutters and cisterns to overflowing. It turned narrow, dirty streets into sluggish brown rivers, polluted with garbage and drowned cats.

Lightning flared and thunder rumbled; the slate-grey waters of the bay turned a burning sulfurous yellow. Sometimes a bolt struck one of the dagger-pointed obelisks, or a belfry at the New Temple—then there would be smoke and a sizzle, followed by a rain of dead bats in the courtyards below.

At Ouriána's nine-towered palace on its rocky promontory, the gargoyles and serpentine drainpipes were spouting like fountains; the hideous lead statues on all the lower terraces stood knee deep in water. Inside the looming black stone structures, gusts of wet air blew open the heavy, iron-banded doors, then slammed them shut again; rain came tumbling down the chimneys, putting fires out; and the Empress was in a perilous temper.

When messages had arrived earlier that day by way of a draggled rain-drenched crow, she had closeted herself in an upper room with two of her priests and her Lord Chancellor. And there she remained, pacing the floor with a restless, uneasy step, brooding over the news from Mere.

⁂

"This Sindérian, the daughter of Faolein—who and what *is* she, to have made such a fool of Thaga?" Her voice vibrating with passion, Ouriána turned a fierce, green-eyed glance on the two priests, Vitré and Scioleann.

Standing together by the door, gaunt and wraithlike in their damp crimson robes, they could only look bewildered and shake their heads. She had called them away in the midst of their fortnightly sacrifices, and they still smelled faintly of blood and smoke. While they understood her anger, her impatience (anything in the way of incompetence always incited her wrath), they could by no means comprehend the scope of her dismay.

"I've never thought much of that scheming mountebank, Thaga," Vitré declared, with a slight grimace. "A second-rate magician from a discredited tradition! Are we really to be surprised if, after first disposing of the Master Wizard, he has allowed himself to be bested by the daughter—a mere journeyman wizard of no name or reputation?"

He made a dismissive gesture with one lean, spidery, six-fingered hand. "And even if she did make a mockery of the magus and his spells at Saer, can we doubt there will be a *very different* outcome, should she manage to overtake Camhóinhann and the others, which is unlikely in itself, and attempt to hinder them in any way?"

Scioleann murmured his agreement, but Ouriána was less than satisfied. Her fingers closed, reflexively and unthinkingly, around a small object she carried in one hand. Somehow—she could not say how or why, yet the feeling was unmistakable— she had a strong presentiment that something had gone *seriously wrong*, something far more important than the escape of an inexperienced young wizard and her equally insignificant companions from a fortress in Mere.

Abruptly, she shifted her gaze to the fourth person in the room: a little old man, so bent and crabbed with age that the braids of his long, white hair and beard swept the floor when he hobbled across to stand at her feet.

This was Noz, the onetime court jester, the onetime spy— Noz, the grotesque one-eyed hunchback with the bandy legs and the battered face, who had tumbled and leapfrogged over so many other ambitious and determined men, rising first to the office of Chamberlain, and at last to Lord Chancellor, the most envied—and therefore the most hated—man on Phaôrax. The Furiádhin, in particular, loathed and despised him, which she knew very well, but they had better sense than to protest his presence.

"What can *you* tell me about this young woman?" she asked, going back to her brooding and pacing. "Surely our spies have mentioned her at one time or the other, surely there is something written about her in that great book of yours?"

The old man cleared his throat. He wore a red leather patch over the empty eye socket, but his remaining eye was a bright hazel, curiously young and alive in his damaged face. He had a remarkable memory, was known to carry around a vast and comprehensive library of information inside his head, and though he kept careful records of everything, every last scrap that her spies brought in—maintaining, for instance, a thick ledger full of detailed notations on the Scholia and the wizards on Leal, including family trees and much else besides—he was seldom obliged to consult his written archives.

Nor did he find it necessary to do so on the present occasion. "She has, in truth, a formidable pedigree. Sindérian Faellanëos, sin Faolein Faellanëos ei Shionneth Eäldridhin—descended, according to my best recollection, from at least seven generations of wizards in both the paternal and maternal lines. Despite which," he added, "she seems to be nothing more than a particularly gifted but innocuous young healer. Perhaps we should not make too much of the fact that Thaga's bindings could not hold her. With such a father, it is no wonder if the young woman is armed with any number of counterspells for her protection. But more than that—?"

Noz scratched at his beard with a long, yellow fingernail, hooked like a claw. "Yet I do recall one thing. It may mean much, it may mean nothing at all."

Again Ouriána experienced that little chill in the blood, that inexplicable intimation of trouble. "What have you remembered?"

"Only that she spent two or three years in the household of the Princess Nimenoë. But at such a tender age, it's unlikely she acquired much of your sister's craft. However, she would have been there, along with her father, when the Princess gave birth."

Self-proclaimed goddess though she was, the Empress felt a purely mortal dew start out on her skin.

It *ought* to mean nothing—a child healer present at a difficult and ultimately fatal birth; a little girl rendered helpless by reason of her youth and inexperience, as much as by the effects of Ouriána's own curse; and forced thereby to watch and do nothing while a foster sister came into the world, a foster mother left it. And if Nimenoë (who *must* have known that she was dying) had tried to protect her babe by linking the infant's destiny to that of another, then surely, *surely* she would have chosen one of the older, more powerful wizards who were there at the time.

Ouriána's restless movements took her over to one of the tall, arched windows, where she paused, watching the rain sheet down the diamond-shaped glass panes, listening to the roar of surf on the jagged rocks below. Lightning flashed out over the water, and the concussion that followed rattled the windows.

Suddenly remembering that her hands were not empty, she glanced down at the slightly sweaty object she held in her left palm.

It had arrived with the letters from Dreyde and the magus: a little packet wrapped up in silvery fish skin to protect it from the weather, then bound to the crow's leg. The contents—a slender coil of weather-roughened dark hair, and five short woolen threads—she had originally mistaken for some rustic charm or fetish, for there was still much of the village warlock about Thaga.

But the hair was Sindérian's, obtained (according to the magus) by one of the maidens who had helped her to dress before dinner, and the threads, which were stiff with blood and sweat, had come from the gown she was wearing when she first arrived at Saer. *"These I send you,"* Thaga had written in his bold, uneven hand, *"in case you should find use for them."*

Ouriána permitted herself a brief, grim smile. Whatever else you could say about Thaga, the wretch was at least resourceful. She could not imagine, for instance, any of the Furiádhin condescending to bribe or bully a lady's handmaids in order to get at her blood or hair. And yet some of the old

Earth Magics—the magic of bone dust, spittle, nail clippings, and the like—could be surprisingly potent. Particularly when one wished to harry or curse a person one had never seen or touched, who just at the moment was many hundreds of miles away.

"I think," she said at last, "that we should not dismiss this Sindérian too easily, just because we know so little about her.

"The girl is probably nothing in herself, but she may be a part of something greater."

Behind the building that housed the mews there was a narrow stair, seldom used, which wound up and up to a lonely turret and a barred door, overlooked by a particularly repellent screaming gargoyle.

No one but the Empress ever took that stair. No one but Ouriána herself would have dared to do so. Even to stand on the lowest step and breathe the malign atmosphere seeping down from above would have tested the courage of even the hardiest. As Faolein had discovered at Saer, there are *some* things a healthy mind utterly rejects, from which the body instinctively recoils.

To the alley behind the mews, and to that stair, the Empress went on that same day, after sending the priests Vitré and Scioleann back to their bloody duties at the New Temple and releasing the Lord Chancellor to the dusty pleasures of his musty archives. She left a shivering and unhappy mob of attendants waiting for her in the muddy, drizzling, twilit courtyard, and began her solitary climb.

With her own white hands she removed the heavy bar and pushed open the massive door. A rank, nauseating odor flowed

out to greet her, so that for a moment her head spun, and her
stomach roiled.

It would have been difficult to describe that smell. Remi-
niscent of graves, sickrooms, torture chambers, it was literally
the odor of fear itself, and therefore suggestive of all that inspires it: the sour smell of rodent; the tiny electric tingle of spiders across the skin; plagues, tombs, winding sheets, fear of live
burial.

The low, round chamber, already close and breathless, became more oppressive still when she shut the door behind her.
A faint light came in through a small window of cloudy green
glass, but not enough to illuminate the room. The green glass
shone like a jewel in what was otherwise total darkness.

And she could hear queer, disquieting noises in that darkness: the piteous mewling of sickly infants; a consumptive rattle like air passing through a pair of diseased lungs; a wracking
animal cry of terror and agony; an insane babbling that went on
and on and on.

With a Word, Ouriána ignited a branch of candles on a
stand by the door. The noises rose to a feverish pitch—and then
died down.

Twenty-one iron cages dangled on chains from the great
oak beams that held up the ceiling, twenty-one cages contain-
ing an equal number of tiny monstrosities.

They were something like rats and a good deal like mon-
keys. They were no two exactly alike: They were horned,
winged, taloned—several were armed with vicious stingers at
the end of long reticulated tails. When they skinned back their
wrinkled black lips, they showed double rows of sharp brass
teeth. A few were covered in shaggy brown hair, but most were
naked.

Those who lived in the palace at Apharos grew accustomed

to the ugly, the deformed, the grotesque, but even Ouriána's household monsters (the Furiádhin, for instance, or the dwarfish Noz) would have flinched at the sight of *these*. They were nightmare incarnate: the malicious imps who carry bad dreams, who bring hallucinations to feverish minds, and horrors and delusions to drunkards and drug-fiends.

As befitted a goddess, the Empress, of course, was quite immune. With a firm step, she crossed the room and opened one of the cages, allowing the grey-skinned nightmare inside to leap through the air and land on her shoulder.

At once, all of the others set up a piteous plaint. There was a rattling of leathery wings, and a whirr like a thousand insects. Inside their iron cages, the imps flinched, jittered, and chattered their teeth, as if to show that even *they* were troubled by their own presence, or at least by the proximity of so many of their own kind.

Ouriána ignored them, her mind on other things. "For you," she said, reaching up to stroke the shivering and excited nightmare balancing on her shoulder, "I have a most important task. Seek out the one to whom these belong—" She held up three of Sindérian's hairs, and the imp reached out and snatched them with its tiny shriveled hands. "You will find her traveling through Hythe or Mere."

The nightmare hissed in her ear, sidled down her arm, and settled on her wrist, where it sat fanning its double pair of wasplike wings and swinging its barbed prehensile tail, as if eager to be off. Perhaps its most disquieting feature was a pair of milky blue eyes, innocent and pure, particularly startling in that depraved little mad-monkey face.

Ouriána held it on her wrist for several minutes longer, savoring the moment. Then she swept across the floor with a determined step, and threw open the door. While she had lingered in the room, the last light had faded from the sky. Torches flared down in the courtyard, and the wind brought in a strong whiff of smoke along with the rain.

Like an austringer loosing a favorite hawk, she tossed the nightmare softly into the air, and watched it take wing. "Sindérian Faellanëos," she called out, by way of farewell. "Bend her or *break* her."

19

*

Toward evening the road began to climb; in the distance, Sindérian thought she could just make out the dusky outlines of the foothills. Then the wind blew rain into her eyes, momentarily blinding her.

Blinking the water away, she saw something dark flying high overhead, just under the clouds. It was impossible to see clearly in the failing light, the falling rain, but she had a vague impression of immense size and a tremendous wingspan.

Wyvaerun? she wondered. But she knew that the creatures generally traveled in flocks. It was unusual to see one flying alone, unusual, too, to see one flying in the rain. Only when Ouriána or the Furiádin sent one out to spy or to carry messages. When that happened—

She felt a prickling of gooseflesh across her skin, and her mind began to whirl with endless possibilities, of defeat, of disaster; above all, of *failure*, which was unacceptable, considering the price they had already paid.

Don't borrow trouble, she told herself. *You didn't see anything, not really, so don't conjure up dangers that aren't even there. More than that, you are a wizard: be careful what you think.*

———

Morning brought a welcome break in the weather. The clouds parted and a little silvery sunlight shone through. By midafternoon, the land was unmistakably rising into foothills, a bleak country of basalt and limestone, heather and sage. It was a hard-knuckled land of knife-edged ridges and stony valleys, of chasms half sunlight and half shadow, where noisy waters flowed down from the mountain heights.

Treacherous and unchancy country it might be, but Gilrain seemed to know it well. He could find a path through a bramble thicket in a gully where even Prince Ruan's sharp eyes failed; he could lead the way after dark or in a fog past pitfalls and landslips innumerable, and never once come to grief.

Somewhere nearby, Sindérian decided, there must be hidden bogs, a whole network of secret waterways, breeding midges and mosquitoes. Though she never saw so much as a puddle of standing water, each night when she drifted off to sleep it was to a low whine as of myriad insect wings sounding in her ears—and once it seemed that *something* bit her, a deep venomous wound just over the large vein in her left wrist, which itched and burned throughout the night.

Only perhaps she had dreamed or imagined that after all, because when she examined the arm in the morning, there was no swelling, no redness. Staring at the unbroken skin, she shook her head, questioning the evidence of her own eyes. The pain had seemed so *real*, yet her memory of that pain was interwoven with fragments of nightmare.

Three days passed, each as uneventful as the day before.

Sometimes they encountered traces of previous travelers—a circular fire pit filled with ashes, a horseshoe and an earthenware bottle left behind—but they never overtook any other party along the way, nor did anyone overtake them.

Late on the third day they paused at the crest of a hill, and saw stretched out before them a broad, wooded valley of unknown depth, and on the other side, marching along the horizon from north to south, the terrific masses of the Cadmin Aernan, ranged peak above peak, precipice beyond precipice—showing here a glittering tracery of ice-blue glacier, dropping there a slender thread of silver waterfall, yet still rising up and up to unguessable heights, white with snow and purple with shadow, in ever more fantastical shapes: spires, columns, tusks, battlements, scimitars—the legendary mountains they had yet to cross.

Gilrain named the great peaks, pointing them out one by one: Pennsligo, with his head above the clouds; Gwinémon; Min Odëlüen, of evil name; Min Ogra. And farther to the east, barely seen in the misty distance: Mineirie, Penadamin, Dain Aerum.

As he spoke, Sindérian saw something that made her heart jump and the cold sweat start out on her skin: a bird the size of an eagle or even greater, sailing high overhead with odd uneven wing strokes, weaving back and forth across the sky, as though searching for something—or someone—below.

Seeing which way she looked, Gilrain shaded his eyes with one hand and stared out across the distance. "Have you spotted our wyvaerun, then? The creature has been following us for many days now, yet it never seems to come within range." He motioned toward the quiver of arrows he carried on his back. "If ever it does, be sure I'll be ready for it."

Taking up the reins, the Ni-Ferys urged his black mare

down a steep, rocky trail, and Prince Ruan, Aell, and Jago rode after him in single file. But Sindérian continued to watch the wyvaerun for many minutes more, before giving the chestnut gelding its head and following the others down.

"How long—how long till we reach the barrier you spoke of before?" she asked Gilrain, when she reached the bottom and found the others waiting for her. "The one that Ouriána's servants can't cross?"

Gilrain gave the very faintest of shrugs. "A week or ten days, if this weather holds."

Sindérian winced inwardly. A week or ten days—it seemed an eternity. Too much could happen during that time, too many mischances could slow them down.

And again, reality tangled for a moment with nightmare.

She had dreamed of traveling through a horribly animate landscape, the very outlines of the hills, the contours of the land, suggesting monstrous figures struggling to emerge out of solid rock, shapes of giants, behemoths, leviathans, lying just under the surface and waiting to be born in some future cataclysm.

Caught up in that memory, she glanced back at the hill they had just descended, and thought with a shiver, *Those rocks might be the spine, that formation the head— Is it possible we have been passing for days through a nursery of monstrosities? That horrible things are incubating under the very ground where we sleep?*

Then reason asserted itself, and she made an effort to shake off her fears.

You have enough *to worry about,* she scolded herself, *without populating the landscape with imaginary terrors.*

They began their ascent of Gwinémon, following a winding path through a lightly wooded country of beech, chestnut, and silver pine, where primrose and lady's slipper grew in the shady places. As they continued to climb, the character of the forest changed, became darker and denser. The trees were fir, birch, alder, and fragrant spruce. Branches blotted out the sky, and the paths through the wood became more and more tangled, like witches' knots.

A maiden moon as slender as a needle rose in daylight and set before midnight; Ouriána's power would be at its lowest ebb. With the waning of her influence, the wyvaerun was seen no more. Perhaps it had lost them under the trees; perhaps it had never been following them after all. The men were inclined to think so, anyway.

But Sindérian did not, and Prince Ruan—watching her grow more and more colorless and silent as the days went by—began to doubt, also. That she still grieved for her father he knew, but he feared there was more eating at her heart than that.

He knew, at least, that her nights were disturbed, that she slept very ill. Often, he heard her tossing and turning, muttering in her sleep.

And late one evening, when they had accepted shelter for the night in a woodman's hut, as the Prince was standing watch at about the hour for which he was named, she started up from her bed on the floor, sweating and shivering. She called out in a voice that jarred at his nerves: "The earth is breeding monsters. How can we hope to prevail against so *many*?"

The fine hairs prickled at the back of his neck. He stood there listening to his heart beat three more times, waiting for her to say more, before he realized that she was dreaming, that she spoke to someone other than himself.

Then she dropped down again with a soft little sigh, curled up on her side, and lapsed into a deep and peaceful sleep that lasted, if not through the rest of the night, at least until the end of his vigil, when Aell took over.

Ruan said nothing of her outburst then or later, neither to Sindérian nor to the other men, but he began to observe her even more closely than he had done before. He saw how she rose each morning wan and listless, how that remarkable face of hers, which had once been a mirror for a hundred different emotions in an hour, had taken on a stony stoicism.

He found the change distressing, and in more ways than one. The King and his Council at Baillébachlein had chosen Faolein and his daughter to make this journey for very specific reasons, and Ruan had an idea that once they reached Skyrra—if ever they did reach Skyrra—it would be impossible for him acting on his own to convince King Ristil of *anything*, let alone that he should yield up his adopted niece to the protection of strangers, that he should send her hundreds and hundreds of dangerous miles away to Thäerie, all for the sake of a prophecy that would certainly mean nothing to him. Any hope of success would *surely* depend on Sindérian's presence, her eloquence and conviction, speaking not only on behalf of the wizards on Leal, but as Winloki-Guenloie's foster sister.

He told himself that without Sindérian, the quest must fail.

The land became rougher and craggier, the paths steeper; the forest straggled to an end. Now there was only clover and hawkweed growing in the thin soil, monkshood, blue nettle, and thistle rooted in the scree. The last of the hunters' and woodsmen's cottages receded into the distance, and the travelers camped each night under the firefly stars.

Here there were freakish winds that seemed to blow in all

directions at once, winds that threatened to lift them right off the mountain and dash them on the jagged rocks below. As soon as the sun set, the nights were filled with high, wailing voices, with deep, booming laughter, with an incredible cacophony of growls and squeals.

The wind, said Gilrain, that was all it was: the wind blowing through the stacks and chimneys of rock, down narrow gullies, through cracks in the mountainside.

———

Night after night, the voice of the wind entered into Sindérian's dreams. It was the same nightmare that had plagued her ever since leaving the lowlands, but each time it came the terror increased.

Dark forces tore at her, winds of sorcery railed in her ears. Her father, Prince Ruan, and the others had abandoned her; she was lost and alone in the wilderness, defenseless in the howling gale.

A storm of birds descended: rooks, blackbirds, crows, ravens. They raked at her with bloody talons, fastening their claws like hooks in her flesh, flaying skin, muscle, and sinew until nothing was left but hollow bones. The wind whistled in her empty rib cage; voices chattered and raved inside her fleshless skull.

For years beyond counting, for centuries upon centuries, she felt her bones disintegrating. At last, worn away by the relentless, scouring blast, they were reduced to sand and blown away on that dark wind.

It seemed that where the wind went, Sindérian went, too—bodiless, bereft, yet keenly—even agonizingly—aware. All about her was the stink of corruption, the corrosive taste of ruin. In the heavens, the snake that was a galaxy of stars devoured its own tail; the moon was a loathsome, putrifying mass, raining down poisons and dark sorceries on the earth and the ocean. The earth itself was a foetid womb, breeding its own destruction.

Some part of her knew that she was dreaming, and struggled to wake. Yet she was helpless, bound and ensorcelled; a pitiless universe held her in thrall.

So she could only watch as a vast figure rose up, blotting out the stars: a giantess beautiful and terrifying at the same time, who stood with one foot on Phaôrax and the other on the continent, straddling the sea between. Her gown was made of rushing waters, her cloak of wind. A crown made of bone rested on her high, pale brow; twelve silver bracelets glittered on her bare white arms.

When she raised her hands, rain fell like scalding acid, scoring the dust below. When she spoke a Word, lava seethed under the skin of the earth. Mountains belched fire; ice caps melted; great landmasses crumbled and slid beneath the sea. Wearily, hopelessly, Sindérian watched as the waters boiled, as the oceans dried up, until all the world was a vast wasteland of crawling muds and choking ash. Then there was not even that—only Darkness, between an infinitude of dead stars.

But it was then, when her dreaming mind felt the greatest despair, when she had no hope, that the nightmare took a surprising turn and carried her where she had never gone before.

In the manner of dreams, she was suddenly transported to a great cavern inside the earth. All around her there was a red glare, and a mighty clamor, like a mill and an armory and a battle combined. Despite the desolation above, the secret fires were still burning.

"They are forging a New World," said a voice, infinitely

sweet, infinitely gentle, infinitely seductive. "This is the furnace, this is the smithy, where a new age will be born."

And gradually, she became aware of titanic shadowy figures wielding colossal hammers. Something that shone like a star went into an enormous vat of water—there was a mighty hissing and steaming.

With a thrill of mingled terror and delight, Sindérian realized what the giants were doing. They were beating out new suns, new stars, in magnitude many times brighter than any that had existed before. They were creating new races, new species to inhabit the world that was to come.

"You *could* be a part of all this," the beguiling voice whispered, just before she woke.

"Forsake the old myths, repudiate the lies taught by senile old men and women on Leal. If you choose, you *shall* be the midwife of the new age—"

Sindérian started awake, sweating and breathless, and lay there for a long time, sick and terrified. Even when the sun rose and the day began, even when she and her fellow travelers broke their fast, saddled up, and continued on their way, the images of the dream ran in her brain.

This new turn had made it all very clear: these were not ordinary dreams, but something evil, something insidious. The Dark was wooing her. It almost took her breath away even to think such a thing, yet it was unmistakable.

Which fault of mine, she wondered, *what taint, what sin, has opened the way for this to happen? Is it because of impious thoughts? Is it because I've asked questions I had no business asking?*

Perhaps I have always been vulnerable, she thought miserably. Perhaps it had only been her father's wide knowledge and exemplary goodness, the counsel of wizards older and wiser than she was, that had shielded her before. That was a particularly lonely and terrifying thought. And if it was true—

If it was true, without Faolein, without Níone, Sindérian very much feared she was inadequate to save herself.

20

✳

For days they followed Gilrain over steep-sided ridges, across ledges, and up trails that were breathless and dangerous, often leading to the edge of some fall or landslide. Then their guide was forced to turn the black mare around and lead them some other way.

"Another dead end. Is it possible we're lost?" Prince Ruan challenged him on one such occasion. His temper was even more explosive than usual, because earlier that day he had caught Sindérian standing heedlessly balanced on the very brink of a sheer precipice, looking down with the slack expression and dull, unseeing eyes of a sleepwalker. When he gently and wordlessly reached out and led her away, she had not even reacted to *that*—which was so unlike her, it unnerved him more than anything.

"Things change here in the heights; it is never the same two years in a row," Gilrain threw back over his shoulder. "In the winter there are avalanches; in the spring, mud slides. I haven't been this way for many seasons. But if you think you can lead us better than I can, you're welcome to try."

Sindérian watched this exchange with a listless eye. More

and more she felt detached from the others, isolated by her own misery.

On Midsummer's Day, the hinge of the year, they passed by the site of Éireamhóine's now legendary battle with six of Ouri-ána's warrior-priests.

Ascending by a parallel trail, Sindérian looked out across a great gulf of air and shadow to a sheer rock wall, riven with thousands of fissures and crevices, where half the mountainside had been ripped away. There was a jagged ridge above, like rotten teeth, and an immense cairn of shattered stones below—beneath which, she imagined, the bodies of the three Furiádhin who had perished were buried so deep the survivors had not even attempted to recover them.

Riding through the magical barrier was like passing through a sheet of cold water; it made her flesh tingle and her vision blur. At the same time, the ward seemed to shatter into a rainbow of brilliant colors: vivid blues and violets; stormy greens; yellow, vermillion, and tangerine; a deep, pulsing crimson.

It was light, she realized, light so pure and intense that creatures of the Dark could not pass through. The few minutes that it took the chestnut gelding to cross were agonizing and exhilarating at the same time. She felt all of her petty faults and doubts and fears exposed, all artifice, all pride stripped away; she felt as naked as an infant fresh from the womb, and as helpless.

And then it was over, she had reached the other side, feeling alive in a way she had not felt since Saer, drawing deep breaths and trying to regulate the thunderous beating of her heart. Looking around at her companions, their dazed faces, the sidelong glances they exchanged, she knew that they, too, had experienced something profound.

It was an unusual ward that affected the unmagicked. She wondered what Éireamhóine had been thinking when the avalanche came down. What was in his mind, there at the end? She knew that a dying wizard could sometimes seize the moment, could twist events in such a way that his or her death might serve some good or useful purpose. But *this* could hardly have been Éireamhóine's intention, as vast and beautiful and miraculous as it was. Warding the Cadmin Aernan could have been no part of his plan—far less could it have been the intention of the three dying Furiádhin.

Summer awaited the travelers on the other side of the mountains: a summer gracious with wildflowers in the windy meadows above the pinewoods.

They were still many thousands of feet above the plain, on the shoulders of Mineirie, and they had still a long way to go before they reached the lowlands. Yet east of Gwinémon the sunlight had a different quality, being warmer and brighter. Even the air smelled fresher and felt softer on the skin.

And though Sindérian's nightmares continued, they were every night less vivid, less intense, and she found it easier and easier to forget them during the day.

They were dreams, that was all. And whatever their origin, they could not *make* her do anything she did not want to do. Anyway, it was dreadfully presumptuous to imagine that *she* had been singled out.

It came as an ugly shock, then, to look up and see the black wings of the wyvaerun darkening the sky once more.

It can't be the same, she told herself, as the creature wheeled and dipped in the thin air. No spy sent by Ouriána could possibly cross Éireamhóine's ward.

But *two* wyvaerun, solitary, searching, each met by pure chance in the wilderness? That was too much coincidence; it was simply impossible.

Her horse stumbled in a rabbit hole and almost went down. Sindérian tore her eyes away from the sky, tried to focus her attention on the trail ahead. She reached out and gave the gelding an absentminded pat on the withers, but her brain continued to worry at the problem.

Could there be a second spy, she wondered, *waiting for us on this side of the barrier, ready to take up where the other wyvaerun left off?*

Her head began to ache with all of the dire possibilities *that* opened up, and the mountain air felt a little colder. Supposing that every move they made, every decision they reached had been anticipated in advance? Supposing that their enemies knew exactly what they would do, long before they did it? And for the first time, when she thought of Gilrain an unpleasant doubt insinuated itself. What if he was not as friendly as he seemed? What if Prince Ruan had been right from the very beginning?

But that was sheer nonsense. The Ni-Ferys had had ample opportunity to betray them before this.

I said I would never let Prince Ruan's prejudices influence me, she reminded herself. *And I would be a fool to break that promise now. And yet—and yet Gilrain was suspiciously eager to attach himself to our party. We never asked him to guide us through the mountains; it would never have occurred to us to do so. He was the one who* offered, *and in such a way that we could hardly refuse.*

The sun was declining in the west, and a cool wind was blowing when Sindérian and her companions came to a place where the path descended in wide stony ledges like a broken staircase. They dismounted and led the horses down. On reaching the bottom, they found themselves in a hollow fringed with dark pine, where the grass grew long and green, and water pooled in a little rock cistern among mosses and ferns.

Though it was early to set up camp, the place seemed so sheltered and welcoming that Gilrain proposed they make an exception, and the others agreed. They unsaddled the horses and left them to graze in the sweet grass, while everyone hunted up deadwood and pinecones to make a fire.

As the men began preparing supper, Sindérian wandered over to the tarn to bathe her hands and face.

The water was deep and cool and mirror bright, reflecting the light-drenched white mountain peaks behind her, a bright blue sky with scarcely a cloud in sight. But there was something else in the water: a face so coarse and sallow, a person so altogether unkempt, ragged, dirty, and wild that it took her several moments to recognize her own reflection.

With a gasp of dismay, she bent closer to the glittering water, staring at the unwelcome image—that thorny, *disreputable*-looking female, with her thin face, broken fingernails, and ragged dark hair—worse: the creature had a sly, unsteady, almost *wicked* look about her that filled Sindérian with despair.

Did you really think Éireamhóine's barrier would wash away ALL *your sins, you who have failed everyone you ever loved? And what little remains to you, you'll lose that, too. Have you not seen it? The end of the world you know, and the triumph of Ouriána—where we all take new bodies and grovel in the dirt at her feet.*

Was it even worth living in a world like that?

And yet there were so many ways that offered release: the pool, the knife—and a healer knew just where to strike—she could even halt her own heartbeat with little more than a thought, though that would be a perversion, before which, even in her present state, she quailed.

The pool? To slip quietly down beneath the cool waters and be gone before anyone missed her; it would look like an accident. Only perhaps one of the men would notice after all, and pull her out too soon. It seemed that the Prince, in particular, was always watching her, always spying on her.

The knife, then. It would be swift and certain.

With a wondering terror at her own resolution, she was sliding the blade out of its sheath on her belt, when something else about the reflection in the water drew her attention, distracting her from her purpose.

It was the wyvaerun, flying lower than she had ever seen it before. Even worse, it was the *same* wyvaerun, the one that had followed them all of the way from Hythe, for it was impossible not to recognize that slightly erratic flight, one wing stroke shorter than the other.

And now that she saw the creature so close, she could see the reason for that peculiarity: under the left wing, where something was lodged, something that might have been the shaft of an arrow, or a bolt from a crossbow, except that it glittered almost like glass—

A sudden rush of blood to her head made her all but swoon. The world turned dark for a moment, and all she knew was the loud hammering of her pulse.

And when her vision cleared, when she turned to tell the others what she had seen, Sindérian saw something else, something that sent a cold jolt of panic right through her: Gilrain fitting an arrow to his bow, pulling it back to full draw, aiming—

"Hold! Hold your fire!" she cried springing to her feet, giddy with joy and sick with apprehension all in the same moment. "*Don't* loose that arrow, whatever you do."

⊢⊣

To Prince Ruan, watching her cover the distance between the pool and the camp at a dead run, then arrive flushed and breathless to hang on Gilrain's arm, her eyes blazing with excitement and her whole body shaking with the wildest agitation, it seemed that Sindérian had lost her mind.

"Your sight is much keener than mine," she panted, looking from the Ni-Ferys to Ruan, then back again. "Tell me what you see—" She swallowed hard, struggled to catch her breath, and went on, "—tell me what you see, in the hollow under the left wing."

The Prince tilted his head back, shaded his eyes with his hand. At first, he saw nothing remarkable. But then, as the wyvaerun turned in a wide arc exposing its breast to the setting sun, something dazzled his eyes with rainbow colors, refracting the sunlight like a shard of glass or—

"The shaft of a crystal arrow . . . it *might be*," he said, beginning to catch a little of her excitement.

The words were scarcely past his lips when Sindérian dropped Gilrain's arm and was on the move again. Flinging herself back toward the path they had so lately descended, she began to scramble from ledge to ledge until she reached the top.

Once there, she ran out along a rocky outcrop, gathering up her skirt and plunging fearlessly ahead, stopping only when she came to the very brink.

And there she stood, with her dress, her cloak, and her dark hair all in motion, dangerously balanced at the windy edge, utterly reckless of her own safety. She called out in a high sweet voice that seemed to echo from mountain to mountain:

Bρeισeρ-αnασαn, ɦαŁésαρ ɲéα Sιnσéριαn.
ASI éɱα ɲésασα esoρα,
ɲéɱα oɱαρ ɲé ғαoŁeιn.

Watching and listening down below, the Prince hardly dared breathe. If she was wrong in what she had guessed, the great raptor could easily swoop down and tear her to shreds before anyone else could come to her rescue. If she was right . . . But it hardly seemed possible that she *could* be right.

The wyvaerun was circling again, it was coming back. Now it descended in a terrifying rush of oily black wings and gleaming scales, its snakelike tail curled over its back, its knife-like talons extended. But it stopped just inches from her face, batting wildly.

The air around the bird shimmered and the wyvaerun disappeared: in its place, a blue-grey peregrine falcon hovered on the lucent air. Then, as lightly as thistledown, as gently as a breath, it landed on Sindérian's outstretched arm and tucked in its ragged wings.

21

*

It was a bright day of wind and sun when Prince Cuillioc's reunited armada sailed into the Bay of Mir—Mir of the sapphire waters and fragrant breezes, of the palm trees and the silvery white beaches—Mir, the gateway to the mines and the cities of the interior, and all their riches.

Cuillioc stood on the deck of his flagship surrounded by the knights of his household, his jeweled armor glittering in the sunlight, and watched the approach of a floating delegation from Xanthipei, the great city on the bay.

As he waited, he had not a shadow of a doubt how this parley would go. First the Mirazhites would demand to know whether he came in peace or in war. When he told them he had come to conquer them and to collect tribute in the name of the Empress, there would be a polite exchange of threats, rapidly degenerating into open hostility, whereupon the ambassadors would retire in a state of high indignation to communicate his demands to their countrymen.

With all this settled in his mind long in advance, he welcomed the envoys on board with his usual grave courtesy, stifled a yawn, and waited for the questioning to begin. Much to his astonishment, they seemed already to know his intentions. More than that, they were ready to comply, ready indeed to welcome him and his armies into their city, even to provide hostages—in token of their respect for the Empress—as a pledge of their good behavior—whatever the Great Prince Cuillioc should decree.

Cuillioc felt the deck dip violently under his feet; the world spun around him. He hardly knew how to reply, this was so unexpected. To prepare for this campaign, he had spent many months pouring over antique papyrus scrolls and wax tablets, studying the languages of the east. He considered himself reasonably proficient, yet he feared that he made—he *must* have made—some odd errors in translation.

They could not *possibly* have said all that he *thought* they had said.

Searching for some excuse to temporize, he sent for Iobhar. But the furiádh, his curiosity aroused, appeared rather sooner than might reasonably have been expected, arriving all in a hot impatience to learn more, and a rowboat manned by two of his acolytes. Though he reacted with surprise and no little wonder when Cuillioc explained the situation, the priest made a swift recovery and proceeded to ask a number of shrewd questions, the answers to which at least made the matter somewhat easier to comprehend, if no less remarkable.

It developed that the oracles, haruspicers, soothsayers, and prophets of Xanthipei had, every one of them, *foreseen Cuillioc's coming, to the day and hour.* More, they had predicted his *ultimate and bloody victory* in the event of a battle. Therefore, the great men of the city had agreed to follow the only course which prudence dictated—an immediate and unconditional surrender, thereby avoiding the tumults and alarms of a futile resistance and the resulting bloodbath.

The Prince looked from Iobhar to the noblemen of his household, and back again, still scarcely able to believe what he heard. Never before had he met with people so willing to rely wholly and utterly on the advice of their seers. Yet it seemed that he had no choice but to accept their surrender, accept, too, the offered hostages, and prepare himself to enter his newly conquered city.

He watched his fighting men disembark first, shipload after shipload. When he had seen them safely landed, he, Iobhar, and all the Pharaxion nobles brought their households ashore. Once on land, Cuillioc was escorted to a seat in a howdah on an elephant—a creature he had hitherto considered unlikely, if not strictly fabulous—then, with his senses all awhirl, carried amidst great pomp and gaudy celebration to the great palace, or Citadel, at the heart of the city, where he was soon comfortably ensconced in a suite of sumptuous rooms.

Many days passed, in which the men of Phaôrax sampled the varied delights of that remarkable city. The nights were long and languorous, the wines heady, and the women supremely skilled in the arts of seduction.

While the others caroused, Cuillioc remained always on his guard. He, whose life had been one long series of misfortunes and cruel, unexpected turns, must naturally suspect the ease with which he had taken Xanthipei, the good fortune by which he stood perfectly poised to conquer the interior and make himself master of all Mirizandi.

For many days he hardly dared venture outside his luxurious residence in the Citadel, content to receive visitors and grant audiences, to spend hours in the vast treasuries selecting suitable gifts and tribute to send back to the Empress, or wandering through the shady porticoes and pergolas of the palace, the collonades and the sanctuaries—all built of cool green marble, with a well, a cistern, or a fountain in every courtyard and garden.

"The great men of Xanthipei smile and smile," he said to Iobhar, "but you have only to look at the faces of the people in the streets. We are not welcome here, we are not wanted. I fear we have walked into a trap."

Iobhar shrugged. "I have deployed my spies throughout the city—as you no doubt have deployed yours, Great Prince, and the other Great Lords theirs—and not so much as a hint of a whisper of sedition has reached my ears. It seems that the Goddess Ouriána inspires fear and worship even here. It is that fear, I believe, that has influenced the masters of Xanthipei, for all their talk of seers and predictions."

Cuillioc tried to believe him. He *wanted* to believe, and was well on his way to doing so when an incident occurred that reawakened all of his former doubts. Quite by accident, he learned that the hostages he kept under constant guard in an isolated wing of the palace were not, as they had been presented, the sons and daughters of noble families. They were, in truth, foreign slaves decked out in the cast-off finery of their young masters and mistresses.

As word of this deception spread through the Citadel, the Pharaxion nobles were soon in an uproar, gathering in the corridor outside the Prince's chambers to express their dismay. Lord Cado and his brother Armael waxed particularly vociferous.

"They must be taught to fear us utterly. They must tremble at the thought of our just retribution," said Armael, in his pompous way. "Let those responsible for the imposture be taken and executed; let others be arrested as well, to serve as an example."

With an effort, Cuillioc managed to keep his temper. All along, he had expected these parasites of the court to seize on some such opportunity to cause him embarrassment, but this passed all bounds. "Arrest and execute men who have welcomed us here with elephants and processions? What sort of *example* would that be?"

"Yet they have deceived us in the matter of the hostages," Cado protested. "Worse, they have made fools of us. What more proof do we need that they have intended treachery all along?"

Oddly, it was Iobhar who stepped in to conciliate the two sides.

"Let new hostages be taken from among the great families, now that we know who they are," said the priest. "Let Lord Cado and his brother do the choosing, but let the noble lords of the Prince's household make the arrests, so that all may be done fairly and honorably."

Though Cado and his faction continued to protest, they did so in an undertone, and Prince Cuillioc himself, try as he might (he could never quite trust the furiádh), could find no fault with his plan. He immediately ordered that it should be so, and soon had the satisfaction of seeing it done.

‹——›

Once he determined to leave the palace and become better acquainted with the life of the streets, Prince Cuillioc spent his first weeks in Mirizandi overwhelmed by the sights and the smells, the colors, and the sounds, at the same time equally intrigued and appalled by the unabashed hedonism of the Mirazhite nobles.

The Goddess knew he was no stranger to luxury, nor to the reckless extravagance of a royal court. And yet—and yet at home in his mother's capital city there was always a *somber undercurrent*, a sense that every pleasure would eventually have to be paid for with prayers and penances. Temple spies were everywhere, and just retribution seemed always to be lurking around the next corner, so that even the most dissipated, no matter how reprehensible their lives in between, always turned up sober and subdued for the principle religious festivals.

In Xanthipei, there were no such mitigating factors. Those who could afford to do so reveled in pleasure, became resoundingly drunk, ate until they vomited, gambled, whored, spent a king's ransom on clothing and trinkets—all with a thoughtless abandon that was as foreign to the Prince's nature as it was to his experience.

Here, he had seen noble youths, for mere sport, cast pearls into wine, wagering on which vintage would prove the more efficient solvent. In the schools attached to the playhouses, he was told, they castrated young boys to keep their voices sweet. In the gambling houses, they kept a ready supply of comely young virgins for the amusement of their patrons.

He became wary of the food on that memorable day when he discovered that the sweets he was happily devouring were actually a confection of beetles drenched in honey and stuffed with spices. It seemed there was *nothing* these people did not dip in honey or roll in sugar: fruits, flowers, dragonflies and honeybees, powdered gemstones; the tongues of nightingales and the hearts of hummingbirds. Some things were to be eaten, and some to be sniffed and tasted, as actual consumption was likely to prove harmful and others simply to be admired and wondered at.

The streets were full of fire-eaters, snake charmers, and sword dancers; of beggars juggling delicate glass .balls that flashed in the sunlight; old women who cast knucklebones or read portents in wine or water.

Beyond the ten square miles of gardens and ornate villas surrounding the Citadel, there were miles and miles of little clay houses and an infinity of small temples and crazy leaning ziggurats, each with its own mummified deity: a cat or a crocodile, a river horse, a two-headed calf, or a rat with seven tails.

After a time, Xanthipei began to have a strange effect on Cuillioc. There was something in the convoluted patterns of the city, in the teeming life of the slums, in the fantastical architecture of the Citadel, which—when he was under the influence of too much wine or other intoxicants—suggested immensities of time and space, power and possibility, hitherto uncontemplated. At other times, times of greater lucidity, it was simply a place of great squalor and disorder, grotesquely mixed up with luxury and debauchery, like the spiders and winged insects inside their sweetmeats.

Oddly and disturbingly, in both states he was often irresistibly reminded of things he had seen in the cluttered attic of the mad astrologer in Apharos: Maelor's curious arrangements of bones and potsherds; the symbols he had drawn in ochre and chalk and charcoal. Had the old man ever *visited* this city? Had his eyes been opened here to Mirazhite mysteries and labyrinthine secrecies he was still pursuing?

Or was it simply that all madmen dreamed alike? In sober truth, his entire sojourn in Xanthipei had many of the qualities of a fever dream.

Of Maelor's warnings he remained ever mindful. The dan-

ger of poisoning or drugging was ever-present, the opportuni-
ties endless. But against the stealthy assault, the knife-wielding
assassin, the betrayal that came in the form of a smothering pillow, a fall from a balcony, a slip at the top of the stairs—against
such perils as those, Cuillioc was always on his guard. If he distrusted the Mirazhites, still less did he trust the majority of his
Pharaxion nobles. Though dazed by splendor, giddy with so
many new experiences, he was well aware of the plots and
whisperings, the secret meetings, all taking place *inside* the
Citadel.

Accordingly, he was not to be seduced by the dubious
pleasures of the wine shops, hashish dens, and brothels. He
confined himself solely to those diversions he might more
safely enjoy in his chambers at the palace, surrounded by a
handful of trusted friends.

So it came about that he was lying passed out on his own bed,
with one of the palace concubines under him and strong sunlight shining in through his bedchamber window, when his
little spy came into the room with an urgent message. Only half
awakened by the urchin's frantic shaking, Cuillioc rolled over,
opened a bloodshot eye, and mumbled a barely audible obscenity.

But he was suddenly awake and alert, and on his feet
within moments, when he realized what the boy was trying
to tell him. "When? Where?" he asked grimly, reaching for his
clothes.

The page's answer convinced him to cast those garments
aside, catch up a rich brocade covering from the bed, wrap it

around him, and stalk out of the room, bawling out for his attendants as he did so.

On a wide balcony overlooking one of the courtyards, he met with Iobhar. The priest stood gazing down with his white, impassive face at a scene of unbridled carnage and bloodshed. But he turned at hearing Cuillioc's footstep behind him, and regarded the Prince with an enigmatic look.

"It is too late, Great Prince. There is nothing that we can do; the hostages have already been executed. It would appear that the noble lords of your household did their best to prevent it, but they were overwhelmed and placed under bodily restraint."

Cuillioc glared at him. "By whose order? If by yours, or with your connivance, my good Iobhar, do not imagine that those scarlet robes of yours will offer you any protection!"

Sliding his hands into his wide sleeves, the furiádh made a deep obeisance. "Not by my order, Great Prince, I assure you. I suggest you direct your questions—and your threats—to Lords Armael and Cado.

"You may see them down in the courtyard now," he added with a grimace—more for the barbaric crudity of it all than for the violence, Cuillioc assumed, "no doubt admiring their revolting handiwork."

Sick, shaken, torn between anger and revulsion, the Prince went back to his room, where he dressed and armed himself. Then he marched down to the courtyard.

He arrived just as the last of the hacked and mutilated bodies were being removed, to find his attendants—their freedom and their weapons but recently restored to them—burning with indignation at the rough and humiliating treatment to which they had been subjected, eager to assure him they were in no way at fault. Lords Cado and Armael had already departed.

Cuillioc took only so long as it required to determine that the lords in question had in truth ordered and supervised the executions, before leading his grim-faced followers in search of them.

He had no trouble running them to earth as they refreshed themselves after their morning's labors with a light repast under a quince tree in one of the gardens.

At the sight of their smug faces, their air of being totally unconscious of having done anything wrong, a sudden mist rose before his eyes, and the blood roared in his ears. Then his sword was hissing out of the scabbard and flashing through the air.

Cado died almost before he knew what was happening, but Armael had scrambled up from his seat and was halfway across the garden before the Prince caught up to him and struck off his head.

Spattered in the blood of his victims, dizzy and shaking with reaction, Cuillioc stood gazing down on Armael's body. His knees nearly gave out at the thought that he—he! who aspired to chivalry and honor at all times and in all his dealings— had actually executed these men out of hand.

And yet they had impugned his honor, undermined his mission here in other ways, too. He tried to convince himself that he was well rid of them, however it came about.

Could it possibly be over: the plotting, the treachery? Have I convinced the others I am not to be trifled with?

Could anything in his life ever be that simple?

Then he glanced up and caught Iobhar unaware, surprising on the priest's ghostly face a look of unmistakable satisfaction, almost gloating.

Because he thinks my mother will be pleased? Or because he knows I have made some irredeemable error?

22

＊

S indérian climbed down from her dangerous perch, stepping carefully from one rocky ledge to the next. She was flushed with triumph, fairly blazing with excitement, vivid and passionate as Prince Ruan had not seen her since Saer. As soon as she reached the foot of the path, he and his guards swept forward to meet her, showering her with questions, unable to contain their wonder and curiosity.

"And is this *indeed* Faolein?" asked Ruan, scarcely able to believe his eyes. "You told me he was dead!"

Tears sparkled on her eyelashes; her lips trembled. "Had the hand that pulled the bow been steadier, if the shaft had pierced his heart instead of his side, that spell would have melted him like a wax candle. Even as it was, to make a new shape for himself—you can't imagine the strength of mind and will—and then to follow after us all of this time, in pain and confusion—" The words caught in her throat, and she could not go on.

"He came back for *you*," said Jago, with a perfect air of conviction—Jago who had sons and daughters of his own. "It was a father's love that kept him alive, that brought him so far. That was how it was."

And seeing how her face lit up, how her fine eyes glowed, Ruan wished that he had been the one to speak those words.

She turned somber again examining the falcon's injuries. Even the Prince could see that the bird was in a bad way, reduced to little more than bones and dirty feathers. The place under one wing where the crystal shaft still protruded was particularly nasty. He thought he could see maggots moving beneath the skin, and there was a strong odor of rotting meat or mortifying flesh.

Sindérian sat down cross-legged in the grass, cradling the falcon in her lap. "There are medicines in my saddlebags. If someone could get them—?"

Aell immediately went back to the campsite, where Gilrain had prudently stayed with the horses, and returned a minute later with the leather saddlebags slung over one shoulder.

She spent a long time gently removing the arrow, then cleaning out the wound, applying a poultice of herbs, cobwebs, and honey, reciting charms of healing. By the time it was over, she was white with exhaustion, but her eyes were bright, and her hands remained steady and sure throughout.

As she worked, a series of silent messages seemed to pass between father and daughter. "He has been many things since we parted at Saer," she told the others. "An eagle, a gyrfalcon, a hawk, a wyvaerun. He's changed shape again and again, but it doesn't seem possible for him to go back to being Faolein."

"But can *you* change him back?" asked the Prince, kneeling on the ground beside Sindérian. Like the two men-at-arms, he had gained considerable respect for her abilities during the course of the journey.

"Undo a spell that defeats even Faolein?" She sounded incredulous. "I have done all I can; all that I know how to do.

"It's possible, I suppose, that one of the other Masters on Leal can help him," she added wistfully. "But until we come home, we're not likely to see my father as we knew him again."

—

They came down from the mountains and into a land of rolling hills and springy green turf, of flocks and cultivated fields. For a long time, Sindérian was simply content to ride rejoicing in the warm sunlight, with a fresh color in her face, her dark hair blowing in the light breeze, and the falcon perched on her saddlebow.

Her first transports over Faolein's return had subsided, replaced by a more quiet joy. One she had loved and believed lost was miraculously restored to her (albeit in altered form), and it was more than present happiness, it was healing for past hurts, and armor against future pain.

Jago's words continued to echo in her mind. For her sake Faolein had come back; a father's love had sustained him through unimaginable suffering and confusion; and her love for *him* had proved not a curse but a *reason* to return.

As for the dreams that had haunted her all through the mountains? Faolein's return had banished them entirely. She felt redeemed, strengthened. As she had saved him, he had saved her.

Only one thing shadowed their reunion: the wizard had set limits, their communion was imperfect. There were dark places in his mind where he would not let her go, experiences he did not wish to recall or share.

Yet time must dull the pain of memory, she told herself. Surely as the horror of what he had been through began to fade he would finally be ready to confide in her—as she, eventually, would be able to confide in him. It was easy for her to be glad and to believe good things on such a glorious day.

But a little of her brightness faded when Gilrain surprised everyone by announcing that it was time to part company. They had all grown so used to having him with them, no one had remembered he was not to go along for the whole way. No one, that is, but Gilrain himself.

"I have seen you safely through the Cadmin Acrnan, as I promised. Now I need to go home and attend to unfinished business."

"But where will you go? What will you do? You can hardly go back to Saer," Sindérian exclaimed.

"Oh, but I will return to Saer, later if not sooner. I still have questions about Lord Goslin's death, and I don't intend to be put off with half-truths forever . . . or denied my revenge, if what I suspect should turn out to be true," he added, with a sudden fierce smile.

An odd, unreadable look passed between him and the Prince. It almost, *almost* seemed as though they came to some better understanding there at the end.

Still, Ruan said nothing. He watched Gilrain exchange a rough embrace with Aell, another with Jago, and merely raised a gloved hand in silent salute as the Ni-Ferys wheeled his black mare and headed back toward the mountains.

No one spoke for several minutes, listening to the sound of hoofbeats on the road receding in the distance. Perhaps even the Prince felt a little bereft. They were in Arkenfell now, a country far removed from the lands they knew, a place of strange customs. The High King's Ward and Law did not exist there, and whatever knowledge Gilrain had of the people and the land, it was no longer available to them.

"We've come among heathen folk," said Aell, under his breath. "Do they even speak our language?"

"More or less," answered Sindérian. "We may find the accents and the dialects of the north a little difficult at first, but on the whole we should be able to understand them, and they us."

Yet even as she spoke, she wondered if it were true. History, religion, culture: they were as much a part of language as the words themselves. Misunderstandings were practically inevitable; she could only hope that none of them proved fatal.

———

That they were in a foreign country and unwelcome there soon became woefully evident. At every farm, in every little settlement where they stopped to ask directions or to buy supplies, it was the same: dogs barked at them, geese hissed, farmwives shooed them away.

In the late afternoon, when they stopped by one of the turf-roofed farmhouses and asked to fill their waterskins at the well, a stout old man with a forked white beard waved them away. And when Prince Ruan offered a piece of ivory for a loaf of the bread they could smell baking, the old man threatened to set his dog on them.

"I don't understand it," said Sindérian, as they jogged back to the road, with the great villainous-looking hound following close behind and rumbling in its chest. "I've always been told that the men of the north remembered the Old Alliance fondly, that they were friendly to travelers from the west."

"Perhaps they've turned unfriendly to strangers generally," the Prince replied. "Hard times breed hard hearts, so it's said, and these people of Arkenfell strike me as frightened more than anything else."

"Frightened of what?" asked Jago.

It was what they all wanted to know. Though sunlight still shone in the sky, evening shadows gathered in the folds of the hills, and the air was growing chill. No one liked to think of spending the night out-of-doors in unfamiliar country, without the guide who had seen them safely through the mountains, with unknown dangers, maybe, lurking in the shadows.

In the fading light, they followed a beaten path through a cleft in the hills, filled their bottles and waterskins by a shallow stream, and continued north, down a road rutted and broken by the passage of many carts and wagons.

At a place where two roads met, they found a gruesome answer to Jago's question.

There was a gibbet at the crossroads, and the body of some malefactor hung in chains swung gently back and forth in the dusky air. As they drew closer, they saw that the gallows bore even more grisly fruit: all along the oak crossbeam someone had nailed up seven naked skulls in a row, human from the eyes up but with long wolfish jaws and fierce yellow teeth. Beyond the gibbet there stretched a field of corn crushed and trampled into the earth.

"Werewolves," said Sindérian in a tight voice, taking in the bestial heads, the broken cornstalks. "There must have been a skirmish between men and beast-men right here. No wonder the people have grown unfriendly. In their eyes, anyone they don't know could be a skinchanger."

The chains creaked in the slight breeze, drawing her attention back to the dangling corpse. She felt a sudden queasy sensation.

Most of the flesh had been pecked away by hungry birds, but there were still some ragged scraps of dark woolen cloth clinging to the bones, and the scanty locks of straw-colored hair on the withered head were tied up in intricate charm knots. "Or anyone who uses magic a black sorcerer."

Weave no spells, make no signs on the air, said Faolein's voice in her head. *Not even a simple ward or healing. If the people here fear charms and bewitchments, we don't wish to rouse the entire countryside against us.*

23

*

Though Sindérian could not know it, a thousand miles away the powerful, malicious mind of the Empress Ouriána was intent on *her*, and danger of a particularly malignant and personal nature was brewing where she least expected it.

For weeks after dispatching the nightmare, Ouriána had often amused herself by spying on the young wizard's journey across the mountains. In the secret conjuring room and alchemical laboratory where she performed all her most dreadful spells, the Empress had fashioned a crude figure, six inches high: out of tallow and salt and ash, three woolen threads rusty with blood, and other materials far more sinister and arcane.

At that point it was nothing more than a misshapen lump of animal fat and other matter. But when Ouriána worked her spells, the mite took on Sindérian's likeness—perfect to the smudged face and windblown hair, the ragged gown and cloak, and scuffed boots. And whatever Sindérian did, the doll did also: eat, sleep, walk, cry, laugh—though there was little enough of *that*, as time went on.

It was pleasant for the Empress to watch the tiny counter-

feit move about the cluttered table where she first set it down,
to see it try to negotiate pathways through the green glass bottles and silver flasks, between the ancient parchments in gilded
scroll-cases, or to scale great stacks of books, as though they
were in fact the mighty chain of mountains it had to cross.

And it was pleasanter still, as the days and weeks passed, to
see the homunculus lose its color, bite its lip, hide behind a curtain of tangled dark hair as if avoiding the too-familiar, too-
solicitous gaze of unseen traveling companions, or to sit down
at the end of a long bitter day, burying its tiny head in its minis-
cule hands as one overcome by weariness, dread, and remorse.

But most gratifying of all were the unmistakable physical
signs of mental and moral decay: the hollow cheek, the haggard
eye, the increasingly listless manner. The poison injected by the
imp was doing its work so well, Ouriána was convinced that
sooner or later, probably sooner, Sindérian must either destroy
herself in a fit of despair or else repudiate the teachings of the
Scholia, renounce her allegiance to Thäerie and Leal, and no
longer count herself among the enemies of Phaôrax.

In either case, the Empress congratulated herself, the
messy business of killing a wizard of unknown innate power
directly by magic had been neatly avoided.

But then more pressing matters intervened and Ouriána
was forced to give up her new plaything. An entire fortnight
passed during which Sindérian never once crossed her mind.
And even when interest revived, it was only as a matter of idle
curiosity, so confident was the Empress of her own success.

After so long a period of neglect, the homunculus had gone
dormant. When Ouriána opened the little silver casket in which
she had stored it away, she found that it had returned to its former lumpen, shapeless, condition—more closely resembling
dirty candle drippings than anything human.

She sprinkled the thing with water and wine, repeated her former spells, and so, in the course of time, brought the doll back to a semblance of life.

But the moment the effigy climbed to its feet and began to scamper about on the tile floor amidst the symbols and diagrams of dreadful import, Ouriána's alabaster skin went whiter than ever; her green eyes narrowed. Gazing down at the little tallow figure from her superior height, she shook back her fiery hair, ground her teeth, then looked around the room for someone she could punish.

If the evidence of the homunculus was to be believed, a change had come over Sindérian. No longer angry, terrified, and on the brink of self-destruction, she was glowing with life. The face that had been growing every day colder, more sullen and withdrawn, was mobile and expressive again. Either the girl had resources not immediately apparent, or someone or something considerably more powerful must be protecting her.

And it was then that Ouriána remembered her initial misgivings, the presentiment that whatever Faolein's daughter might be, in and of herself, she was almost certainly a part of something much, much greater. For a moment she could almost see a pattern of most subtle design, linking Nimenoë on her deathbed, the child who was whisked away, and this young healer— But no, whatever it was, she had failed to fully grasp it, and it slipped away.

I have been too tender, too merciful, she thought. *Regarding the chit as a possible tool, I aimed to seduce rather than destroy. But no more. No more.*

Yet even now, she reminded herself, it would not be wise to do anything rash, anything too overt. Not while her understanding of the situation was still imperfect.

But then the bolder, more dangerous, infinitely more cunning part of her said, *You know what to do. Against one pattern, create another. Against one web of circumstance, fashion a curse of your own.*

Ouriána hesitated. What that inner voice suggested was a spell born of deepest malice and deepest pain. It could never be created except at great cost. Nor was it anything that, in the normal course of events, she would ever consider waging against so insignificant a figure as Sindérian, daughter of Faolein.

But would you, then, brook defiance of your will—and from such a minor wizard? Make an example of her. Let whoever or whatever is guarding her know: you are not to be balked in even the smallest particular. Work the spell. It may be that her protectors will also be involved in her doom.

Again, Ouriána felt the fury building inside of her. She would *not* be balked. She would *not* allow any wizard, great or small, to live once she had willed their destruction! This girl would be but the first of many.

In a whirlwind of temper, she began to pull energies out of the earth, out of the air, and spin them into filaments stronger than iron, finer than silk. On the table beside her there was a dagger with a slender, wicked blade, all made out of bone. Catching this up, she opened a vein in her arm, tempering the strands with her own heart's blood.

Then she began to weave the *aniffath,* and set Sindérian's name at the center of her spell.

⊢⊣

Two days later, Sindérian and her friends were in the grassy flatlands where the tiny, isolated farms of the hill country gave way to vast herds of shaggy white cattle and sleek grey horses. Sometimes there were orchards, or fenced-in land where sheep grazed peacefully. Sometimes they passed by ancient stoneworks—cromlechs, standing stones, and stone circles so heavy with age they were sinking into the earth.

And sometimes, riding past some barrow or passage grave covered in flowering weeds, Sindérian thought she could see out of the corner of her eye the pale spirits of long-dead kings and warriors: figures of mist and shadow, showing here and there a glittering armring, a jeweled circlet, a glimpse of bare bone.

For Arkenfell (Faolein told her) was a haunted land. Every village had its tutelary spirit, every graveyard and barrow its guardian. Marsh lights appeared where there was no standing water; any traveler on the road after nightfall was likely to see uncanny things. The Men of the north practiced ancestor worship, glorifying their forebears in songs and sagas; they left out offerings of milk and ale for the recently dead; so ghosts were inclined to linger.

That there were more hostile things than ghosts abroad in the flatlands soon became evident. Bandits harried them, skinchangers stalked them, farmers and villagers threw stones wherever they went.

The footpads who attacked on three different occasions were small bands of hungry-looking ragged men who leapt out of ambush, and were so readily discouraged by mounted men with better armor and weapons that Sindérian could only marvel they had found the courage to attack in the first place. She could almost believe that some will not their own was influencing them.

But the skinchangers were a more serious problem altogether. A pack of werewolves followed the travelers for several days, slinking through the shadows morning and evening, often unseen but never quite absent, as the horses could sense them at all times, growing increasingly skittish as the days went on.

Such glimpses of them as Sindérian had chilled her to the marrow. It was odd and disquieting to see the eyes of men staring out of those bestial faces, above those dirty grey muzzles; unsettling to watch them loping along with their unnaturally long legs and their grotesquely clubbed hand-paws.

And if the creatures kept their distance at first—having, it would seem, no love of fire—they eventually attacked in broad daylight, coming in from all sides at once, some on two legs and some on four, hamstringing one of the pack animals and inflicting much damage on Sindérian and the horses before the Prince and his men were finally able to slay the entire pack.

Afterward, winding yards of linen bandage around her own badly bitten and savaged ankle, then hobbling over to see to the injured horses, Sindérian felt her first stirrings of sympathy for the angry, unfriendly farmers and villagers.

Prince Ruan was right, she thought. *Hard times do breed hard hearts, and the people here have good reason to be wary.*

While she tended the surviving horses, the men made a pile of the shaggy grey bodies and gathered wood to make a fire. Horribly, one of the creatures had died in the process of changing, and his corpse was a disturbing mix of skin and fur, beast and man. What patches of skin showed through were very fair, and tatooed with strange patterns in blue and scarlet. When Prince Ruan finally set the pyre ablaze, no one could bear to look at that one body; the idea of watching it burn was simply unsupportable.

The stench of burning followed Sindérian for many days, for the smoke got into her hair and her clothes; nor did any amount of brushing or rubbing with sweet herbs make the least difference. She could smell it on the horses and on her fellow travelers until it nearly maddened her. When she sat down to eat, she tasted it in the food and water they carried with them. She began to wonder if she would ever be free of it.

Meanwhile, the mauled ankle was slow to mend. For all Sindérian's efforts to heal it, the wound wept and throbbed incessantly. One of the horses, less seriously injured than she was, died. It simply stopped in its tracks and fell over, dead as a stone. Though she said nothing to the others, she feared hydrophobia. Healers were not all-powerful, there were *some* things they could not cure, and the bite of a rabid animal was one of them.

There came a night when Sindérian found sleep impossible. Every time she closed her eyes and started to drift off, she thought she could hear voices and movements under the earth. But when she opened her eyes again all was still, all silent.

Finally, she gathered herself up off the ground and limped over to speak to Aell, who had been assigned the first watch. Offering to take his place, she settled down cross-legged by the fire.

There, she spent the next several hours studying the sky, marveling at the changing patterns of the Hidden Stars: a half year's movement, under ordinary circumstances, compressed into a single night. She was still trying to puzzle this out when the falcon fluttered up and landed in the grass by her feet. He, too, was wakeful and anxious.

Tearing her gaze away from the heavens, she caught a glimpse of something moving just beyond the circle of firelight. With a creeping sensation she saw that while she was stargazing a host of pale, insubstantial figures had formed a ring around the camp.

Her own heartbeat seemed to shake the silence. Though the dead seemed curious and watchful rather than openly hostile, she could not believe that their presence meant anything good.

What do they want—do you know? she asked Faolein.

I think, he answered, *that they wish only to speak with us—though why they should single us out I'm not certain.*

Sindérian frowned. These were not the spirits of men who had died in peaceful times, or in their own beds. Their faces were seamed with scars; many were missing arms or legs. Some were hardly more than a collection of blurred and confused features, with bones shining through. Perhaps they had been dead so long, they had forgotten how they looked in life. One wore—in place of his own head—the skull of a horse that had been buried with him.

The falcon took several sideways steps. *I do not think it would be wise to rebuff them—not without learning first exactly what they want.*

Sindérian scowled. Yet her trust in her father was strong. If he said they should speak with the dead—

Nevertheless, this is hardly the place, Faolein continued. *I think we should go a little apart, away from our sleeping friends—what the dead have to say to us may not be meant for their ears.*

Still frowning, Sindérian rose reluctantly to her feet. Limping through the high, moon-silvered grass, she left the circle of firelight far behind, trying to keep pace with the falcon as he swooped before her. The dead followed after, rank upon rank, their numbers seeming to swell the farther they walked from the camp.

At last, in a grassy dell screened from the fire by brambles, the falcon settled on Sindérian's shoulder and the gruesome parade came to an end.

By then there were dozens of them, perhaps even hundreds. They had come in their winding sheets and earth-stained shrouds, their armor and antique finery. Not all of them were men. There were shield-maidens and archers, tall and well formed, carrying long white knives and great yew bows.

The breeze did not stir any of their garments, nor did moonlight reflect from their eyes. They brought with them no taint of corruption, no reek of the grave or the tomb. If the air smelled of anything, it was of green and growing things: pastures and woodlands; hayfields and cornfields under the sun; roots clotted with earth. They had all been dead for so long, their fleshly parts had melted into dust and returned to the soil.

Yet seeing that they had all been so *very* long dead, Sindérian could not help wondering what business they could possibly have with the living—and especially with two foreign wizards, passing as it were by chance through these lands.

As if he sensed her question, the man wearing the horse's head took several steps forward and spoke in a hollow, windy voice. "The world is changing. Things that were bound by magicians of old have cast off their bindings, and the banished creatures of the Dark are beginning to return. Things that have no place in this world are slipping through from Outside. They have formed an alliance with the men of Eisenlonde, and they go to wage battle against our cousins in Skyrra."

Another took up the tale, a tall gaunt man in armor of gilded leather and an iron crown: "Long ago, years beyond counting, we fought a great battle. We won a great victory against the Dark, but only because our kinsmen came from across the channel and fought alongside us, brother to brother. When the battle was over, we swore a most binding oath that we would aid them in similar circumstances. Now we wish to fulfill that oath. We *must* do so, or we will never rest.

"Yet the Necke lies between," he went on. "And the dead who have been buried and returned to the earth have not the power to pass over such a great body of water. We cannot do it without the help of the living."

Sindérian could scarcely credit her ears. "You want *us* to take you to Skyrra with us?"

"Yes. It should not be beyond you, sorceress and wizard. Will you not help us?"

If we were to help you, said Faolein, much to her surprise and dismay, *you would have to swear again, swear no harm to living man or woman. Otherwise, we could not, in good conscience, loose you in Skyrra. Could you keep such an oath?*

One of the shield-maidens moved a step closer. Her hair was the color of ripe wheat: but there was a spear embedded in her chest, and someone had horribly mutilated her face. "We wish only to fulfill our oath, to meet our ancient enemies in battle. What are the battles of the living to us?"

Sindérian turned toward her father. *You cannot truly mean for us to do any such thing.* Sweat was gathering in the palms of her hands, it was dripping down her sides. *Do we even know how? And you said we were not to work any spells while we are in Arkenfell—still less should we attempt what sounds like necromancy!*

Yet none would be bound against his or her will, he answered mildly. *In a sense we would be setting them free—free from constraints that bind and frustrate them.*

Yet still she hesitated. Every instinct urged her against it. So recently and so narrowly had she escaped the seductions of the Dark, she could not trust herself to take part in any such thing and suffer no harm.

Sindérian, said Faolein, *if we don't do this, they may yet find someone else to do it for them. Someone less scrupulous, someone who might set conditions we would not wish to see fulfilled. Do you understand me?*

Reluctantly, she nodded.

I cannot do this alone, he continued. *I know the spell, but I have no hands to make the signs, no voice to say the words.*

Sindérian released a long, bitter sigh. It seemed that all things were in favor of her doing this, save only her fear and revulsion.

But my father has never led me astray, she told herself. *Nor would he—nor would he! He is older and wiser than I.*

"Very well, I will do it," she said at last. "But you must instruct me."

There was a stir of approval, like a gust of wind, from among the ranks of the dead.

You will need a sack or pouch, Faolein told her. *One of the bags that you use to carry herbs will do very well. Empty it out and bring it back here.*

Sindérian went back to the camp, where she found the Prince and his men still sleeping. Trying not to imagine what they would make of this unseelie bargain, she knelt by her saddlebags and rummaged through her packets and pouches of herbs. Deciding that pennymint was the one she could most easily spare, she loosened the drawstring, upended the bag, and watched the dried leaves trickle to the ground.

And again she wondered how Faolein had ever learned any such spell. They did not teach spells like that at the Scholia on Leal.

Yet, she remembered, he had wandered far as a young wizard, and no doubt he had seen and heard many strange things during those years. He might have gone anywhere and done anything—how was she to know? That thought made her father a stranger in a way that his present form never could.

She returned to the place where she had left Faolein and the wraiths, to find that the falcon had been busy during her absence, pulling up the grass with his beak and scratching up the dirt with his talons. He had a little pile of moist earth already waiting for her.

Put this soil in the bag. Enough to fill it nearly full. Then you can conjure the dead inside.

Sindérian frowned at him. *What—all of them?* she asked incredulously.

Yes, all. They could fit into a space much smaller than that, were it necessary.

It took so many hours that the night was nearly over before she was done. Already long before that, she grew hoarse from speaking the words that Faolein had taught her, haggard with lack of sleep. Yet finally the ordeal ended. One last time she recited the verse, conjured one last wraith into the sack.

Sindérian looked around her with a weary and jaded eye. Only she and her father remained of all that multitude. While she was busy the first light of sunrise had appeared on the horizon; the Prince and his men might already be waking. It was time and past time to return to the campsite and tell them exactly what she and Faolein had been doing, during the night while they slept.

And though she dreaded the outcome, she thought with a sigh, there was really no use in putting it off.

24

✳

Winloki woke to a confusion of men and horses milling in the half-light all around her. Her first thought was: *Eisenlonders! We are under attack!* Panic ran like ice water through her veins.

This last week had been one endless heart-wrenching nightmare, as skirmish after bloody skirmish followed the first clash between Kivik's army and the barbarian hordes. There had been ambushes and night attacks as well, so it was natural by now for Winloki to expect the worst. But this time she heard the quiet voices of her guards speaking somewhere to the right of her, and the thunder in her blood subsided, her breathing slowed. If there were any immediate threat, Haakon and the others would have already wakened her and hustled her into the saddle.

Groaning for her stiff neck and dry, leathery mouth, she rolled over on her side, burying her face in the crook of her arm. *It can't be dawn,* she protested inwardly. *Not so soon. Not already.*

And even if it *was* dawn, surely her cousin could not mean

his weary and disheartened troops to make such an early start, not after traveling through most of the night.

Still the noises around her went on: a soft *clink* of metal against metal as men armed themselves; a horse shaking its head and blowing out an explosion of breath; a rattle of pots and pans.

Gritting her teeth against the pain, Winloki sat up and rubbed a sleeve across her eyes. Her head ached; she had that faint feeling of nausea which comes of arduous days and nearly sleepless nights, of rising far too early and unrested. The sky directly overhead was still black, but over to the east it had turned a dirty ashen grey, the color of soiled linen. In the high grass all around the camp, birds twittered their early-morning hymn. As much as she might wish it otherwise, the dawn *had* come.

She pushed back a tangle of red-gold hair with a trembling hand and rose stiffly from her cold bed on the ground. Awkward and half-blind, with her hair tumbling back into her eyes, she stumbled over a tussock of grass and lost her footing, but Haakon was there to catch hold of her elbow.

"It was a cruel hard night for you and the other healers, Princess," he said sympathetically.

"Infinitely harder and crueler for our wounded and dying."

Yet for all Winloki's efforts to put on a good face, she had to admit that she was drained mentally and emotionally as well as physically. First there had been that long, wearisome, interminable retreat ending in the cold small hours, as Kivik sought to evade a battle with superior enemy numbers; then an equally exhausting and harrowing period when she and her fellow healers tried to settle their patients for what remained of the night, doing all in their power (it was pitifully little by then) to make them easy and comfortable after the jolting torture of the long wagon ride.

She ran her fingers through the worst of the snarls, trying to bring a little order to her appearance. She asked herself, *How did we ever come to be hunted and harried like foxes in our own land? And how did there ever come to be so many of them, those barbarians who had never all down through the years managed to muster more than a few ragtag companies of raiders and horse thieves, wholly dependent on surprise attacks and a speedy departure to save their own skins?*

Winloki felt a choking lump of hatred and loathing rise in her throat. She drew in a long, difficult breath, put all her will into banishing anger and confusion. A healer needed a quiet heart, a serenity of mind, lest she pass on her own tumultuous emotions to her patients, who had troubles enough of their own. But oh, some days it was a struggle, one she could by no means always win.

And what, she wondered glumly, *has become of the army we came here to meet, the thousands of mounted troops led by Hialli and the other marshals?*

They could not just disappear, not such a vast number of them—could they? Surely they had to be somewhere in this wide, ravaged land, trying just as hard to find Kivik as he and his scouts were trying to find them.

She ran a coated tongue over dry lips, gratefully accepted the leather flask that Arvi offered her, and took a mouthful of water before passing it on. All the faces around her wore the same grey mask of dust and dried sweat; she supposed that her own looked much the same. Knowing that the water in the barrels they carried in the wagons was running low, she gathered some dew from the grass, and made a halfhearted attempt to scrub at her face with a corner of Aija's brown wool cloak. If she only succeeded in smearing the dirt, in rubbing some color back into her pale cheeks, still she felt a little fresher, and that heartened her.

From the camp adjacent to that of the healers and the wagon drivers, there rose a clamor of bawling, indignant live-stock and squalling, hungry children. In these last five days, Kivik's army had met up with many parties of refugees fleeing before the advance of the Eisenlonders. Women of all ages, young children, men who were too old or infirm for battle, they had gathered up all their portable property in oxcarts and hay wagons, saddlebags or packs, setting out for what they hoped would be safer country, perhaps driving a cow, or two goats, or a half-dozen sheep before them.

Some were traveling west toward the Herzenmark, others north to the mountains. Most continued on the way they were going, but no few had placed themselves under Kivik's protection and attached themselves to the army.

At a sudden pounding of hooves on the road, Winloki turned just in time to see two scouts riding into camp on lathered horses. They vaulted from their saddles to the ground, threw themselves panting at their prince's feet. Though Winloki strained her ears to listen, all she could hear at this distance was a low murmur of voices. She saw one of the men make a wide gesture, motioning toward the east, and by the grim line of Kivik's jaw, the bleak look he exchanged with Skerry, she knew that the news could not be good.

No sooner had the scouts finished their report than it passed from mouth to mouth across the camp: "An army of Eisenlonders, immense past counting, already on the move and heading this way."

Kivik began to shout orders; everyone swung into action at once. Winloki gathered up her bedroll and her other things, stowed them in the nearest wagon. Then she climbed over the side into the straw-covered wagon bed and moved among the wounded men: tightening a bandage stained with fresh blood here, speaking a word of comfort to a man sweating and tossing in a high fever there. She felt a clammy hand fumble for hers in the straw, and turned her attention to a boy who had lost both of his legs.

Of all the youths and men she had tried to help, his condition was by far the most hopeless. Others like him usually died, but for some reason he clung fiercely to life. Not more than fifteen or sixteen, if even so old as that, he had called out for his mother again and again while the healers worked over him, until one of them granted him the mercy of sleep. Now, after two days dreaming, he finally showed signs of waking, fluttering his eyelids and grunting with pain.

He *is going to die whatever happens to the rest of us,* Winloki told herself drearily, touching the bone ring lightly to his damp forehead and watching the lines in his face relax. *But at least he need not* suffer *so much.*

Haakon came trotting up on Lif, leading Winloki's mare on a long rein behind him. She nodded her thanks, scrambled from the wagon to the saddle, and took up the reins. With a sinking sensation, she realized there would be no breakfast, just another long ride on an empty stomach. But far better that than risk a battle when they were so woefully outnumbered.

All the time she was working with the wounded men, others had been busy loading up gear, hitching draft horses to the wagons. Now the drivers climbed to their seats; there was a low groan from the injured men as the wheels began to roll, and the wagons lurched over the bumpy ground.

Winloki urged her mare to the middle of the road, and Haakon and her other guards fell into position around her. Behind them came a straggling train of carts and farm wagons, and finally those who tramped along on foot driving their unruly livestock before them.

The next few hours passed in a blur of sweaty exhaustion. A pale ghost of the sun rose in a hazy sky, and there was not so much as a breath of wind. Winloki's hands grew cramped on the reins; her eyes burned in the smoky, diffuse light. The men rode in silence, too tired for speech, and the wagon drivers sat hunched forward in their seats.

A little before noon, they passed what must once have been a fair orchard, reduced to blackened smoldering stumps. Beyond the devastation of the orchard stood the smoking skeleton of a great house and stockade. There was an odor of charred meat on the air, and as the wagons rumbled by a cloud of ravens rose up, crying out in their hard, discordant voices. Kivik sent out a party of men to search for survivors among the rubble, to burn or bury any bodies they might find.

Those men caught up with the army a while later and rode past the wagons stark-faced with grief and anger. They had found none but the dead, bones picked nearly clean by the ravens and other scavengers: bodies of men, women, cattle, and children.

Hearing of this, Winloki felt the blood drain from her heart. *What manner of men, what kind of monsters are we fighting, that they murder children and leave them for the carrion eaters?*

At last Kivik called for a stop to rest and water the horses. Handing the reins back over to Haakon, Winloki slid down from the saddle, stretched her aching muscles, and eased herself to a seat on a sun-warmed boulder beside the road. Too ill and exhausted to think about food or drink, she closed her eyes against the glare of the sky.

She opened them reluctantly a short while later, when someone offered her a flat loaf of buckwheat bread, a drink from an earthenware flask. A trickle of warm liquid across her tongue was hardly sufficient to relieve her thirst; the bread was dry, sour, and a labor to chew. Still, she made an effort, forced herself to eat and drink, in order to keep up her strength.

Long before she was ready to get back into the saddle, it was time to move again.

For Kivik, it often seemed, there was no rest by night or by day. Whether he was riding in the vanguard, as then, with the sun blazing down on his armor, or sitting up late taking counsel with his captains, there were always so many matters large and small that required his personal and immediate attention that sometimes it was hard for him to keep it all straight in his head.

Of course he must listen to the reports of the scouts and make the best use that he could of whatever information they had to offer. He had to determine when and how often to release the hawks that bore his brief dispatches back to Lücken-börg, though he could expect no reply, so long as his army remained on the move. He had to try and outguess, outflank, and outstrategize his enemies; above all, he had to find ways to avoid them until after his belated reunion with his father's marshals.

Tugging off one of his gauntlets, he passed a hand over his brow, where the light brown hair was plastered with sweat. He had a slight headache, but whether that was the sun, the small amount of sleep he allowed himself, or the ever-present sense that he was on the verge of some monstrous mistake, he did not know. Probably it was all those things, with an empty stomach thrown in for good measure.

Naturally, as a king's son should, he had studied the tactics of war, even though, until the present conflict, there had been no *real* wars in the northlands for more than a century, just isolated skirmishes, the occasional clash with mounted outlaws or bandits. Still, he had applied himself to his lessons: on the movements of mass armies; the proper disposition of archers, foot soldiers, and cavalry; the science of fortification. He had memorized stirring accounts of famous battles. Now it appeared that these studies were not only insufficient, but grossly misleading.

For war, as he was learning, was neither so rational and mathematical as his tutors would have it, nor so noble and glorious as the sagas portrayed. Without exception, both these sources of information had glossed things over: the filth and the muck, the noise and the stench; the slow, frustrating marches and the grinding exhaustion; the blundering stupidity of two or more armies rambling the countryside more or less blind to each other's whereabouts, until opposing forces *happened* to stumble across each other and engage in battle; above all the sheer brutality and the bloody waste.

Scouts could only tell you so much, the study of tactics could only take you so far—after that, it was dumb luck and endurance and maybe being too bullheaded stubborn to know when you were beaten.

In the beginning, Kivik reflected, he and his countrymen had been pig-ignorant, as naive as young boys playing at war with pointed sticks. It was true they had grown wiser during the last half year—experience had proved a stern and exacting teacher—still, the Eisenlonders seemed to understand these things much better than they did.

But why and how? Kivik asked himself, as he had asked so many times before. *Whence this greater sophistication in tactics, coupled with an unwonted savagery?*

A man could drive himself mad with questions like that. As he could also go mad brooding on his own mistakes and miscalculations, because for every one of those mistakes men died, some of them quite horribly, few of them quickly and cleanly.

Then there were the smaller things, where if he fell short the misery of those in his care was thereby increased—not only for his fighting men and wounded, but for the healers and the camp followers, this ragged train of homeless wanderers he had somehow acquired. Latrines had to be dug, water and forage had to be found for the horses—every time he chose a place to camp he must take these into account—disputes had to be settled among the three camps. Most of all, and most importantly, he had to find a way to keep everyone adequately provisioned.

The road they were following narrowed, and what had been a snail's pace slowed even further as the horsemen in the vanguard sorted themselves out. Kivik watched from the side of the road, swatting at a fly that buzzed around his head.

One thing at least his lessons had been good for, he reminded himself. *"Live off the land as much as you can,"* he had been taught, *"and save the supplies that you carry with you for the times when you* can't.*"*

The Eisenlonders burned orchards and trampled over cornfields and gardens, but it was too much trouble for them to destroy all the root crops, so sometimes, when his army came to a burnt-out farmstead, Kivik detailed men to dig for turnips, parsnips, onions, carrots—whatever they could find. When they stopped in the shade of a woodland to breathe the horses, he sent some of the women in among the trees to gather nuts, berries, and mushrooms.

At this time of year the cows, the nannies, and the ewes were all in milk, and most of the hens were still laying. The refugees shared their milk and eggs with the army, and Kivik made certain they received bread and dried beans in return.

Such ordinary, practical things had become his cares, because lives depended on them—depended on *him*, all of these people trusting to *him* for no better reason than because he was their prince, King Ristil's second eldest son—a young man brought up to weapons and horses, music and poetry, the oral history of his people, the manners of the court, the higher policies of kings and princes—sometimes he broke out into a cold sweat under his armor and padding, terrified by his own inadequacy.

Fortunately, he had Skerry and his captains and his scouts to advise him: Skerry with his rational mind, his steady disposition, and the scouts with their knowledge of everyday things. Yet always he was the one who must balance one thing against another and make the final decision.

And whenever that time came, he had to choose right. Kivik, the impulsive, the hasty, the hotheaded, the thoughtless—he had to choose right. Because he must not fail those who depended on him. He would not.

An ominous and oppressive feeling descended on Winloki, a heaviness she could neither wholly understand nor shake off. Even when the warhorses began to prance and shake their heads, even when the plodding draft animals lifted their heavy hooves a little higher, as plain a sign as anyone might wish for that they scented water—yes, even when the rush and gurgle of a stream running swift over stones not far away made it a certainty—the formless oppression remained.

They camped that night within sight and sound of the stream, where they were able to replenish their flasks, bottles, skins, and water barrels; and everyone drank until they could drink no more. Flowing from a source high in the mountains, the water was far too chill for real bathing; even so, Winloki did a more thorough job of washing than she had been able to do in days.

When she climbed into one of the wagons to settle the men for the night, she found that the boy who had lost his legs was cold as clay. Nor could she, for all her desperate and prolonged efforts, bring him to life again.

"A mercy," said Thrya, eldest among the healers. But remembering how the youth had lingered on, how he fought so hard to live, Winloki was suddenly not so sure. Perhaps even maimed he had cared more for life than some who were whole.

The next afternoon, they were surprised by a force of Eisenlonders.

Winloki's guards instantly surrounded her, hurrying her off the road and up a slight incline. The carts and wagons and those who traveled on foot followed. There were too many to make a protective circle of wagons, but the wagoners did throw up a crude barricade and hoped it would not be tested.

Kivik took up a horn from one of the standard-bearers and blew a challenging blast; his men unfurled their ragged banners. From the ranks of the enemy came a braying of horns, and both sides advanced.

As before, the melee was so fierce, the confusion so great, it was impossible for Winloki to tell who had the advantage. For a long time it was all just the clash of iron, the squall of angry horses, a flash of armored bodies falling to the ground. Arrows flew hissing through the air. Under a rain of blows from swords and axes, shields splintered and flew apart, blood spattered in all directions.

And just as it had been in every battle before, shadows swarmed on the field, though only Winloki could see them. For her, they were becoming more and more distinct. This time they had taken on the forms of little misshapen men and women, with thin wiry bodies and enormous splayed feet. Some had heads like birds or beasts. Some had lumpen features and pallid skin. All reeked of malevolence.

She asked herself, *Is it* they *who are changing, so much, so quickly—or is it my Sight that grows keener and keener?*

On another part of the field, all of the horses began to plunge and rear, lashing out with hooves and teeth, striking anyone, friend or foe, who came in their way. Turning her head to see what maddened them so, Winloki set eyes for the very first time on those most terrible of skinchangers: the *Varjolükka*, the Shadow-Beasts, the Man-Bears. Great shaggy ursine creatures they were, with bloodstained muzzles and powerful arms that could snatch up a man and crush him to death before he had time to cry out or attempt to defend himself.

It was impossible for Kivik's horsemen to charge in among the werebeasts. Where the *Varjolükka* went the horses would not go; they panicked and fought the reins until their riders finally had to dismount and fight the creatures on foot.

Even the horses up on the knoll began to grow restless, as if they, too, caught some taint of the beast scent carried on the wind. The chestnut mare rose on her hind legs, trumpeting her distress, her sides heaving, her flanks slick with sweat. Winloki was hard put to keep the mare from jumping over the barricade and bolting. Only by a combination of main strength and a hastily muttered spell did she finally gain control.

On the field below, blood puddled on the trampled grass. Sometimes horses slipped in it and went down; many of them did not get up. Kivik was unhorsed, and none of his men could force a way close enough to bring him a new mount.

As the fighting waxed more furious, Winloki saw Skerry break away from the press of his first foes and rally his men behind him. Then he spurred once more into the thick of the battle, his crow-dark hair ruffled in the wind, and his green cloak flowing behind him.

Miraculously, the enemy lines broke and scattered.

That was not the end of the battle, but it was the beginning of the end. More and more often it was the barbarians who died in their own blood, the swords and spears of Kivik's men that ran red with gore. The Prince himself, still on foot, came in behind one of the werebeasts and hewed off its head. Two more fell with arrows in their hairy throats.

And afterward, inevitably, someone must attend to the terrible and heartbreaking business of searching through the bodies on the field, sorting out the living from the dead. Winloki blinked back tears of shock and horror, forced herself to look the other way when one of Kivik's men cut the throat of a barbarian too crippled to crawl off into the high grass.

She tried to convince herself it was better so. They had too many injured of their own, the healers were dropping from exhaustion, and one had even died. Under the circumstances, it seemed far more merciful to finish these wounded and shattered enemies swiftly. She knew very well the Eisenlonders would never come back for them; that was not their way.

As the day ended, and night crept over the battlefield, Winloki and her fellow healers still worked on. She bandaged bleeding limbs, cauterized wounds, wove charms of sleep and healing, brought water to a dying man—did all that she knew how to do, until her hands went numb, and she could no longer feel her own feet.

Suddenly giddy with fatigue, she stopped what she was doing and struggled for breath. The fire where they kept the irons blurred and grew hazy. Then her knees gave out, the night reached out to take her, and she slumped to the ground.

25

*

Two days later, Kivik's battered army left the grasslands behind, and set off across a rough country of ghylls and crags; of whin, thorn, and sage; rising into gaunt foothills, and eventually to snow-clad peaks.

All along the road they continued to meet homeless travelers. As this was a far less hospitable region, these were poorer people, most often met walking hungry and footsore, carrying no more than a basket or a sack, having less to take with them and far less to lose—yet for all that they plodded on grim-faced, bleary-eyed, sometimes mute with grief at leaving their rocky little hillside villages, their tiny sod houses and meager gardens.

Those who *could* speak and answer Kivik's questions had no news to give him of the marshals. Yet, more and more often, he heard mention of a certain name: Tirfang. The stories of the refugees varied, but all had a common theme: those without kin or clan to the west or the south were slowly making their way toward the Old Fortress, the Haunted Fortress at Tirfang in the Drakenskaller Mountains.

One afternoon, when the scouts were ranging even farther ahead than usual, a group of them came upon three old women, rattling down a narrow, rutted track in a ramshackle cart pulled by a team of six white goats.

Three wilder-looking, uncannier women had seldom been seen: two short and stout, remarkably similar, with twinkling little black-beetle eyes; the other tall, bony, ancient past reckoning, with a mass of windblown white hair, and a face as old as the summer stars.

There was something uncanny, too, about the goats, with their wicked white faces and slotted yellow eyes, their ridged horns and cloven hooves—though how and wherein that strangeness might lie it was difficult to say.

No, said the women, all three, when the scouts stopped to question them, they had no rumors to pass on about the movements of armies. "But if you are, as I think, Prince Kivik's men," added the crone, waving a skinny finger, "it is possible we may be able to tell him something to his advantage."

One of the scouts hurried back to the Prince bearing their message. "They say they are *runestone readers,* going to live with a great-granddaughter or a great-grand-niece who lives west of the Nisse. But they have offered to cast runes on your behalf, if you desire it."

Kivik drew in a quick breath. For the first time in many days he felt a faint stirring of hope.

There had been a time when runestone readers were as common in the north as wizards and mages in the south; now they were a dying breed. A man would be a fool who passed up the opportunity to consult not just one but three old women who claimed to know the art; a man in Kivik's situation who declined would be three times a fool.

"Tell them—tell them that they will be very welcome. Say that they honor us," he instructed the scout. Then he gave orders to set up a temporary camp, erect his green silk pavilion, and assemble such refreshments as might be found suitable for such distinguished visitors.

A wave of excited speculation ran through the army as the word spread. Curiosity was rampant, and many would have given much for an invitation to observe the casting of the runes.

Winloki was one of the envied few whom Kivik summoned. She arrived outside the green pavilion riding pillion behind Skerry, with her arms around his waist and her heart beating fast with anticipation. As she slid down to the ground, landing lightly on her feet, she wondered if these chance-met women could possibly be what they claimed. She knew that fewer and fewer were born to the gift with every passing year, and that even those with extraordinary talents had difficulty finding teachers capable of instructing them.

She thought, *It is likely that Kivik sent for me with just that in mind. He thinks that I will sense their power if they have it, or tell him they are less than they seem, if they don't.*

Then the crowd parted, the goat cart clattered to a stop outside the tent, and the three aged seeresses climbed over the side and lowered themselves stiffly to the ground.

They were ragged and unkempt, there was no denying that. Yet Winloki instinctively sank down into a deep curtsy as the gangling figure of the crone hobbled past, followed by the dark-eyed twins. She was only dimly aware that her legs were shaking, that tears stung her eyes. These women had power—elemental as the powers of the bone ring, and to Winloki just as mysterious.

⊢────┤

Kivik fêted them with the last of the honey wine. Offering them seats on three elaborately carved camp stools in the green shade of the pavilion, he plied them with a salad of crayfish and wild cress, with blackberries and cream, with a cold soup flavored with mushrooms, and boiled eggs served in their shells. It was the best he could do on such short notice, a much better meal than he and his captains had enjoyed for many a day.

But when the meal was over, the oldest of the three women told Kivik that an accurate casting of the runes required that the rite be performed in the open air, under the sky.

"As you wish, Grandmother," he replied politely. Rising to his feet, he offered her his own arm to lean on as he escorted her out of the pavilion, through the curious crowd that had gathered outside, and beyond the camp.

Privately, Kivik thought she was the oddest—certainly the *oldest*—old woman he had ever seen. She was dressed all in rags and tatters, and her hair, which hung down in dirty white elflocks, looked as though the wind had braided it; she brought with her a distinctive odor of rain, woodsmoke, wet earth, and burnt porridge. The ancient twin sisters stumping along behind were just as bizarre, but they lacked her presence and her sharp-nosed, bony, long-legged dignity.

About a hundred yards from the encampment, the women stopped, formed a circle facing each other, and groaning with the effort, all three crouched down in the dust.

The crone spat in the palm of her hand, then drew a wobbly circle and some other signs in the dirt with a gnarled finger. Then, reaching inside her layers of rags, she produced a surprising number of items: a handful of salt, a milkweed pod, a piece of charcoal, a glass bead, a fragment of bone, and a small hard knob of some coarse, dark bread.

"Here is sea, wind, fire, and earth," she intoned, placing each item in turn within the circle. "Here is the flesh that feeds us, and the grain that sustains us." She wove a symbol in the air with a motion of her fingers.

One of the twins passed her a handful of polished pebbles: quartz, amber, obsidian, beryl, and agate. Every stone had at least three faces, and on every face a different symbol had been scratched or painted.

And so began the casting of the runes: the crone threw the stones into the circle; they made little puffs of dust in the air as they landed. She was a long time studying the symbols, the patterns they made, and which of her marks they fell closest to in the dirt. Then, wordlessly, she gathered up the pebbles and dropped them into the open hand of the woman on her right.

So it went for some time, in utter silence; the stones passing from hand to hand countersunwise; the cast, the intense frowning scrutiny; the stones gathered up and dropped into the hand of the next seeress. Kivik had an uneasy impression that not one of them liked what she saw, but it was not until the third time around that he finally realized, with a prickling across his skin, what it was that troubled them.

Impossibly, *the stones fell in the exact same pattern, the same symbols uppermost, every time they landed.*

The crone glanced up, met Kivik's eyes across the circle. She shook her head. "There is some strong magic at work," she said in her cracked voice. "It confuses the signs. Still, if you wish, we will try again."

She rubbed out and redrew the circle and the other marks in the dirt, then performed the same ritual as before, with the charcoal, the glass bead, and the other items. Muttering something under her breath that Kivik could not quite hear, she tossed the pebbles into the still, hot air. When they landed, a glance was enough to tell her that the result was exactly the same as it had been nine times before. With a snort of disgust, she swept the stones into her hand, and passed them over to the twin on her right.

Three times around, and it all happened the same way again. The toss, the scowl, the gathering up, and the passing on.

"It is no use," said the crone, at last. "The barbarians have cast some mighty spell."

Kivik knotted both of his hands into fists; he felt a trickle of sweat go down his side. A man who considered himself of more importance in the world might decide that the whole world was against him. "What kind of spell?"

"It is a spell of confusion and misdirection, my Prince—on you and those with you, most certainly, and perhaps on the friends that you seek. It continually leads you off in the wrong direction; you circle each other and never meet; the roads lead you astray."

Slowly, painfully, she rose to her feet. "While it lasts you will never find each other. At least not so long as you keep moving."

A short while later, Kivik sat in his pavilion, having assembled there the men he trusted most. Skerry straddled an armor chest on his right, while his other captains stood weary and disheartened in their tattered surcoats and their dull, heavy mail, in a semicircle before him.

"If we are to believe what we have been told—and speaking for myself I don't doubt a word of it—our plight is even worse than we imagined," he began. "The question *now* is, what do we plan to do about it?"

There was a subdued murmur, dying away to silence. Kivik

waited for a time, hoping that someone would speak up, either with questions or suggestions, but as it became evident that no one would, he continued:

"We left Lückenbörg with a clear purpose: to bring supplies and reinforcements to the marshals. Much has changed since then. Our numbers are depleted; we have more women and children, old men and wounded, than we have men capable of fighting. Weakened as we are, what help could we bring to anyone? Even if we *did* find Hialli and the rest, which it becomes increasingly plain that we can't."

There was another long silence, everyone standing or sitting with eyes downcast, as if pondering the futility of their situation.

At last Skerry cleared his throat. "The old woman did say that we would never find our friends *while we keep moving.* But if we could find a strong place to hold, send messages to the King, then wait for someone—either the marshals, or the army your father has been mustering since we left—if we could wait for *them* to find *us,* then we might cirumvent this sorcery of the Eisenlonders.

"At the very least, we would buy some time to heal our wounded and train some of the older lads among the refugees."

Several men nodded; there was a slight leavening of the heaviness in the tent. But then one of the captains gave a bitter laugh.

"That sounds very well—very well indeed. Only where are we to find such a place? By all accounts, every town in the Haestfilke has been put to the torch, and even if there *is* a town with walls still standing, even if we could get there, the Eisenlonders would still come along sooner or later and burn us out. We never prepared ourselves for this kind of warfare; we have built all our walls of wood."

"There is—" Kivik began, then stopped. He sat contemplating the toes of his boots for several minutes, then blurted it out all in a rush: "There is such a place, Deor, a place of high stone walls. The refugees have been talking of little else for many days now; some of our people will be there already. The marshals may be there, for all that we know. I never thought to go there, but . . ." His voice died.

He saw the knowledge dawn in several pairs of eyes at once; faces paled, breaths bated. Skerry changed his position on the armor trunk, and Deor gave another incredulous laugh.

"You are speaking of the Old Fortress at Tirfang! With all respect, my prince, shall we make alliance with ghosts and dead sorcerers?"

Kivik sighed. It was true that the fortress at Tirfang had an evil name. It had been built in the days of the legendary Witch Lords, who had ruled over all these lands during some dim prehistoric epoch long before the rise of Alluinn in the south, long before the Three Tribes became three separate nations of Skyrra, Arkenfell, and Mistlewald, and the distant grandfathers of Ristil's people crossed the Necke, settling all the country west of Eisenlonde.

"According to legend," said Skerry, softly, consideringly, "the walls at Tirfang are impossible to breach. They stand thirty ells high on every side—more than three times as tall as the walls of the Heldenhof! There are seven strong gates in seven mighty gatehouses before you even reach the inner courtyards and the great fortified keep. According to legend, it has moats, drawbridges, arrow slots, murder holes: never before or since has a fortress been built so admirably suited for defense."

"And yet, for all these advantages, no one has ever succeeded in holding Tirfang during a siege." This came from a grey-haired veteran of many border skirmishes, by the name of Regin. "Not once in a thousand years, according to legend."

Kivik sat chewing on a broken fingernail, thinking that over. Whether the Old Fortress fell by treachery or some deadly disease that struck down the defenders from within, by some spell of magic gone wrong or through some other mischance, whoever defended Tirfang had always failed. People said the fortress was haunted, that there was a curse on the place, a bane of black misfortune of peculiar strength and malevolence.

And yet it was all so long ago. Who knows, really, how much of that history is even true? Our people had never even seen these lands when those walls were raised.

"How far is it to Tirfang?" he asked aloud. "Does anyone here know?"

"Maybe three days, with the wagons and all," said the chief of the scouts. "The horses would find it a steep pull most of the way."

"I think we would be wise to make for Tirfang," offered the practical Skerry. "These stories we've all heard—nursemaids tell them, and small children allow themselves to be frightened. But if they are not outright untruths, they may be wildly exaggerated." He seemed to gain greater certainty as he spoke. "It *must* be so, if the people who live closest and know it best are suddenly flocking there."

The Prince saw doubtful faces all around him, and some of the men fingered talismans they wore on leather thongs around their necks or set into the hilts of their swords. But these were made to guard against ordinary bad luck; they offered a very frail defense against the ghosts of ancient sorcerers.

He believed that he knew these men well: their hardihood,

their courage, their loyalty. He also knew that it is one thing for a man to show himself fearless facing a foe that he understands, even believing himself overmatched, quite another to face terrors he can scarcely comprehend.

But a place to rest and lick our wounds, to recover our strength . . . That idea was difficult to resist. Kivik himself was bruised in every part of his body after falling from his horse during the last battle, and most of the others gathered in the tent had similar injuries, too minor to take to the healers, too painful to ignore entirely.

Meanwhile, Deor seemed to be reconsidering his position. "Those who built Tirfang were, by all accounts, a wicked, treacherous, and bloody people, but what of that? Most of the homes destroyed by the Eisenlonders were made by honest, hardworking, decent folk, yet that made no difference one way or the other."

"But our people aren't sorcerers," retorted Regin.

Skerry made an impatient gesture. "How long can evil inhabit a place after the people who brought it there are dead and gone?"

But that, thought Kivik, *is just what nobody here knows. In the days when we swore friendship with the wizards of the south, we might have known the answers to such questions. But now there are far too many things we simply don't understand anymore. And that being so, how are we—how am I to make any rational decision?*

"It is growing late," he said, rising from his seat, and shifting his shoulders where the armor lay heavily on bruised flesh and strained muscles. "I see no reason to break camp, only to have to set up again in another hour or two. And if we are going nowhere tonight . . . let us sleep on this question."

There was a mumbled protest here and there, but it lacked fire, it lacked conviction.

He thought, *By morning, the idea will have taken hold with more of them. And those who are against it now, they will be growing used to it. If I make up my mind that we will go there, I doubt anyone will try to persuade me otherwise.*

In the morning, the word went like wildfire through the camp. Kivik had scarcely made his decision before everyone seemed to know of it: "We go to the Old Fortress at Tirfang. That is a strong place, and the Prince is determined to hold it."

Kivik himself was somewhat taken aback by the sudden wave of enthusiasm that spread like a contagion, banishing all misgiving. Any curse that had lasted for more than ten centuries must be losing its strength by now (everyone said); any walls that had stood even longer than that must be strong indeed. They all packed up their tents with unprecedented dispatch and departed in almost a holiday mood.

For a day and a half they followed an ancient track through the foothills, then up to the skirts of the Drakenskaller Mountains.

Once they left the hills behind, they came upon a meandering mountain road that rose gently at first, then grew steadily steeper. The way soon became so narrow and the climb so difficult, the column began to string out. The wagons and those who traveled on foot fell farther and farther behind, until the Prince sent men back to ride as a rear guard, and to urge on anyone who showed signs of flagging.

A damp wind came down the throat of the pass, laden with

scents of pine and cedar, the promise of snow. The cliff wall rose sheer on one side, and on the other was broken by rocky ledges and terraces, by slopes only a little less precipitous, where hardy alpine plants had rooted in the scree.

Kivik thought that country magnificent, but very bleak. From a practical standpoint, it offered little in the way of forage, and he could only hope the stories were true of wide high meadows in the vicinity of the fortress, where the ancient Witch Lords had grazed their beautiful black steeds. But, regardless, he liked to listen to the high, eerie wailing of the wind among the rocks, the sound of stony waters running in narrow channels. There was a grandeur about it that spoke to his soul.

The mountain walls rose higher and higher, blocking out more and more of the sky. By the second night, Kivik could only see a handful of stars directly overhead.

The next day the winds blew shriller and colder, and even those most eager to reach the fortress began to lose heart. Meanwhile, the horses, not accustomed to these ever-climbing roads that twisted and turned up the walls of mountain gorges, had taken up a wearisome, jogging gait, very difficult to endure. It was beginning to feel as though the journey would never come to an end.

26

✳

How do we even know that these wraiths mean to do what they say?" asked Prince Ruan, clearly aghast on receiving the news that Sindérian now carried, on a cord around her neck, a linen bag filled with battlefield earth and spirits of the dead. "And if you take them to Skyrra only to learn that they have very different intentions from what they have promised you, what are we supposed to do *then*?"

"Ghosts are very seldom devious," Sindérian replied—with rather more confidence than she actually felt. "They only remain bound to the earth because of some overmastering passion, some absolutely compelling purpose. That usually fills them quite up, so that they have no room for anything else."

If the Prince was very far from mollified, in the end there was nothing he could do. The wraiths were already in Sindérian's possession, she was determined to keep them, and she had neither asked for Ruan's pardon nor his permission.

As for Aell and Jago, they were no less astonished than they were unnerved, yet they seemed to regard these dealings with the dead as quite within a wizard's ordinary business—or at least, not anything the two of them wished to know about.

To Sindérian's relief, they scarcely spoke a word on the subject over breakfast, and continued silent when it came time to saddle up the horses and take to the road again.

After a few more days of travel, everyone began to smell the sea. Huge flocks of skua-gulls beat white wings in the sky overhead, and the water in all the little streams along the way became increasingly brackish, then finally undrinkable.

On the last day of the month of *Duilligir*, they crested a hill and caught their first glimpse of the bustling seaside town of Aurvang inside its massive timber walls, and of the blue-grey waters of the Necke, sparkling in the distance.

<hr />

All the ways of Aurvang twist and turn, and all the buildings have high-peaked roofs in order to shed snow during the winter. Because of this, many of the courts and alleys near the center of town are dark and overshadowed winter and summer, existing in a perpetual twilight.

In later years, it would become a great center for trade, drawing merchants from ports as far distant as Tirhene and Pehlidor, and if in these days it was far less crowded and considerably less sophisticated than it was destined to be, it was still a busy and colorful place.

"We won't be such pariahs here," said Prince Ruan, eyeing with approval the guildhalls and warehouses, the forges and workshops lining the streets, the market square filled with stalls and carts and wheelbarrows selling such varied items as eggs and live poultry, fleeces, embroidered cloth, lodestone, tin kettles, baskets, pins, and gingerbread. "There are foreigners here every bit as exotic as we are."

In the gathering dusk they rode toward the harbor, where

tall masts of many ships loomed dark against a sunset sky. Gradually, the streets became more and more empty. At last, passing by a humble little inn not far from the water, a spill of firelight through an open door and the savory scent of cooking beckoned Sindérian and her friends in. At the thought of a civilized meal her stomach growled. She felt suddenly faint with hunger and anticipation.

As she dismounted in the inn yard, the falcon, who had ridden on her shoulder since they first entered the town, flapped his wings, soared into the air, and disappeared into the windy night.

I will know where to find you in the morning. It seems I no longer care for roofs and walls and firelit rooms, spoke Faolein in her mind.

Leaving Aell and Jago to stable the horses, Sindérian followed Ruan through the open door and into a smoky room. Ropes of onions and dried apples hung from the beamed ceiling; a side of beef sizzled on a spit inside an enormous fireplace; and something that smelled like mulled wine was bubbling in a cauldron.

Soon, they were all seated at a long, scarred table, squeezed in between two traders from Weye and a party of travelers from Mistlewald, eating pease porridge, mutton pies, smoked salmon, new cheese, and baked pears. After the privations of the road, it seemed like a feast.

As she chewed, Sindérian listened with half an ear to the conversations going on all around her. The babble of different dialects and accents confused her, perhaps because she was more than half asleep. In any case, it all sounded exactly like the type of stories—exaggerated, contradictory, fantastical—one might hear in dockside taverns or hostels anywhere.

I will sort it all out in the morning, she promised herself.

Soon after that, she stumbled upstairs to the room and the bed she was to share with three other women. Slipping out of her stained and threadbare gown, she stood by the open window in her patched linen shift, drinking in the scents of sea and night.

Then she tucked the bag of earth inside the neck of her shift and crawled under the blankets with her already snoring bedfellows. Stuffed with prickly straw and none too clean, the mattress was nevertheless welcome to one whose only couch had been the ground for so many weeks.

Her last thought before sliding into sleep was, *Only a few days more and we will be in Skyrra. The longest and hardest part of our journey is over.*

But it was not to prove nearly so easy, as they learned the next day, and those stories Sindérian had been so ready to dismiss when she heard them recounted in a room reeking of pipeweed and the stale fumes of ale became at once more believable and sinister when repeated on the midday street.

In truth, the whole town was buzzing with tales of sea serpents and giant eels, of ghost ships and maelstroms fifty—sixty—a hundred miles across. As Sindérian and her friends were to learn after tramping for hours upon hours along the docks trying to find a shipmaster willing to carry them across the channel.

"There aren't many reckless enough to hazard that crossing in these times," said one sea captain, a heavyset man with a shock of grey hair. "Most of us think it dangerous enough to sail up and down the coast—and we wouldn't do that if it wasn't our livelihood. No, keep your coin," he added, as the Prince drew out his purse. "Even if I thought it worth the risk, I could never find a crew."

It was the same answer whomever they approached, and that answer was too often accompanied by hard, suspicious glances, or a string of oaths that made Prince Ruan flush to the eyebrows and finger the hilt of his sword.

"Perhaps we will find someone who is willing tomorrow," said Sindérian, as she and the Prince, and the two men-at-arms, returned to the inn at sunset. "New ships come in every day."

But the next morning nothing had changed. By afternoon, they had stopped looking for a ship and were combing the docks for any owner of a fishing boat valiant enough or venial enough to make the voyage.

"We might buy a boat and sail it across ourselves," Ruan suggested at last. He himself had often sailed in his boyhood, while Aell had spent all the years of his youth either rigging the sails or hauling in the nets, on a fishing boat belonging to his father and his older brothers.

"But have we the price of a boat?" Sindérian asked, thinking how carefully Ruan had counted out his bits of amber and ivory last night at the inn. "I must suppose that the purse you had from the High King is not—inexhaustible."

"It is not," said the Prince, a bit stiffly, as though discussing these things went against his pride—as no doubt it did. "Yet what we have left, it should suffice—particularly if we sell the horses. We can walk across Skyrra if we must, but we can't walk there, across the channel."

Yet buying a boat they could sail proved just as impossible as purchasing their passage. Nothing smaller than a carrack, nothing larger than a rowboat would anyone offer for sale, except for one ancient clinker-built fishing boat with a broken mast and so many warped planks that the hull must leak like a sieve.

"It seems impossible there is not even *one* seaworthy vessel in Aurvang that someone will sell," said Sindérian, so tired and vexed she could weep, as they trudged back to the inn. Her ankle was finally healing, but this long day on her feet had brought on a series of tearing pains that often made it difficult for her to catch her breath. "I begin to feel that someone or something has set their will against ours."

That will, though Sindérian could not know it, belonged to Ouriána, as she stood in her secret room among the retorts and alembics, the bottles of inky liquids and the baleful symbols, looking at the tangled pattern she had created, and scowling · most horribly.

Since the first hour of its conception the *aniffath* had grown, in extent, in complexity, as the Empress refined it day by day: adding a knot of difficulty here, attaching a new thread of peril there. By now, it had become a fiendishly deadly and intricate curse.

And yet, as time and again Sindérian found a way to side-step danger—as she survived bandits, werewolves, festering wounds, and even an encounter with the dead—as she caused thread after thread to snap or unravel, and by so doing dealt blow after blow to Ouriána's pride—the Empress became more and more determined to remove this source of irritation, to punish this presumption.

Who *was* this girl, after all, this daughter of Faolein? she had seethed inwardly at each new escape. Who was this Sindérian to challenge the schemes of the Empress of Phaôrax, to flout the will of a *goddess*?

So that now, gazing at the partial ruin of her own artistry, of this complex and marvelous thing she had created with such consummate skill, Ouriána's rage knew no bounds.

All through the night she worked. She sent her spirit ranging through the palace and even into the town below, harvesting the sleeping minds around her for the materials she worked with: spite, envy, brutality, treachery—every last festering resentment or cherished bit of malice that human minds could compass. Out of all these things she spun more and more threads, while the sleepers sweated in their beds and muttered of barbarous sensations and tormenting visions.

"You have survived a great deal, you have endured much," she said with a hiss, as she wove in strand after fatal strand, filament after mortal filament. "You may have escaped dangers innumerable on land. But you won't escape this."

27

⁜

In Aurvang, Sindérian woke to the sound of wings beating outside her window. For a moment, the darkness confused her, until she remembered that the shutters were closed. She threw off the covers, jumped out of bed, and felt her way in the dark until she found the catch and pushed the shutters open. A dim, moist moonlight came pouring in, and the peregrine falcon landed on the windowsill and ruffled up his feathers.

We must leave this place tonight.

Sindérian shook her head, scarcely comprehending. *How shall we leave? And why?*

He tilted his head, fixed her with a fiery golden eye. *The Furiádhin are here in Aurvang. Camhóinhann, Dyonas, and Goezenou: I saw them, but it seems they did not sense me. And if we sail tonight, we may reach Skyrra before they do.*

She yawned and stretched, massaged a cramped muscle in her neck. *I don't suppose Ouriána's priests will have any more success than we did buying a boat or paying for their passage.*

He walked along the windowsill, raised and lowered his wings as though impatient to be gone. *And do you also imagine they would hesitate to use force, or magic, or even theft to gain a ship, once they realize that none is going where they want to go? If we mean to leave Arkenfell ahead of them, we must find a way to do so* tonight.

Yes, I see. Sindérian struggled to retrieve her scattered thoughts. *But are we to steal a boat?*

Not steal. We will buy the one that is available, and make her seaworthy. I will teach you the spells.

She sat down very abruptly on the bed, her hands knotted together in her lap. *You want* ME *to repair the boat—with magic? But I've never done anything remotely like that before. I doubt I am capable. And if my spells fail, then what becomes of us, out on the water in a leaky boat?*

There is some risk, he admitted. *But what else can we do? This thing is not beyond your abilities, it is simply outside your knowledge—and I can provide what you lack.*

Though still unconvinced, Sindérian began to dress.

In any case, she thought, it was altogether likely that the old man who owned the boat would refuse to see anyone at this advanced hour—altogether likely that even if he *did* answer his door, he would refuse to do business. Then she could go back to bed.

But what about the horses? she suddenly remembered to ask. *We had no time to sell them, and we can hardly take them with us on such a little boat. Even without them we are going to be cramped.*

We will have to leave the horses behind. The falcon fluttered up and landed on her shoulder. *That is unfortunate, but it can't be helped.*

At *malanëos,* the darkest hour of the night, Sindérian, Faolein, the Prince, and his men, quietly left the inn by a back door. They stepped outside into a thick, swirling mist. The cobbles on the street were slick with moisture, and condensed fog dripped from the eaves of all the houses.

With the fog muffling their footsteps, they moved toward the docks. In that damp air, the town smelled strongly of fish, rope, wood shavings, smoke, pitch, and seawater—comforting, homey, *civilized* scents that reminded Sindérian irresistibly of Leal.

The air was not quite so thick down by the water. While Ruan and his guards headed for the little tumbledown house of the man who owned the fishing boat, Sindérian and Faolein went on to a narrow strip of sand where the boat was beached.

But as she knelt in the sand, all her former doubts came trooping back. She thought, *How am I to do this thing? And if I can't do it, how will we ever reach Skyrra and Winloki?*

The falcon nudged her gently with his beak. *I will guide you.*

Feeling that she had no choice but to try, Sindérian listened while her father explained the spells, slowly and carefully. It did not *sound* so very difficult, she had to admit. Taking several deep breaths, she rested her hands on the weathered hull.

She began by straightening the warped planks. While Faolein poured the knowledge and the power into her mind, she provided the hands to shape the wood, to draw the glowing runes in the air. These spells, she realized, were not so different from healing, except they did not require the same empathy, or the same precise and sensitive delicacy of touch. It was only a matter of using lines of force to push things back into place, to mold them into a form that she desired—rather than gently pouring strength and intention into living flesh so that it might grow back together, essentially healing itself.

When the hull was sealed and sound, they moved on to the shattered mast. Before long, Faolein withdrew and she continued on her own. All doubt had vanished; she felt an increasing confidence, an almost giddy euphoria.

Exactly when Prince Ruan and his men returned, Sindérian could not be certain, she was so absorbed in the work. She went into the wood and out of it again. The runes she wrought took on a deeper meaning. *Govanidan*—that was the passion of the craftsman. *Theroghal*—that was the yielding of the material. As those mysteries unfolded in her mind, she became one and many: She was the weaver, the loom, the thread, and the shuttle. She was the hand that molded the clay, the clay itself, and the force spinning the potter's wheel. She was the smith, the hammer, the fire, and the metal.

And then it was over. The mast stood strong and whole in the position she placed it; the boat was as sound as ever she could make it. She drew back inside the limits of her own chilled and exhausted body—felt the cold sweat in the palms of her hands, a quivering weakness in her arms and legs, an intense and terrifying sense of her own separate and unique identity.

Yet not the same, she told herself. *Never the same again.*

As the tide took them out, Sindérian sat on the stern thwart and watched Aurvang slowly slip away, its deep streets all but hidden by the fog. From this distance, it looked a wholly different place than the town they had entered a few evenings before.

It occurred to her then, with a pang, that she was more than twice as far from home as she had ever been before, and had still a great distance to go. The world was a much larger place than she had ever imagined.

Yet it was pleasant to be out on the water. All those weeks traveling inland, she had missed the sea. She was satisfied to remain where she was for another hour, drinking in the bitter spray. And when finally she settled down in the bottom of the boat with her head pillowed on one of the saddlebags, lulled by the gentle motion she soon fell asleep.

———

Sindérian woke in full sunlight, with the falcon pulling gently at her hair. With a gaping yawn, she pushed herself up on one elbow and then sat up. It seemed they had only just sailed out of the fog, for the men were still muffled up in their cloaks, and tiny drops of moisture shone in their hair.

The day passed uneventfully. A light wind filled the sail, and the boat sped on through a bright morning, an even brighter afternoon. Sindérian could not help suspecting that sunshine, that silence, that steady progress. The sky was empty of birds, the sea of fish; extend her senses as she might, she could not detect so much as a sprat. She had thought to catch sight of the whales and sea lions who thrived in these northern waters, yet they, too, were absent.

At these latitudes, the sun set very late in summer. For what seemed like days, the curiously empty sea and sky remained bathed in a brilliant golden light. At last, however, it grew very dark. At the same time, the wind died.

Sindérian was of two minds about summoning even the tiniest breeze, for there was no knowing how close the Furiádhin might be following—and they could easily sense a magical wind from many miles off. In the end she decided to wait. Aell took down the sail, lit a lantern, and hung it from the yard.

Sometime in the middle night, she felt a sudden prickling across the skin, caught a nauseating whiff of something foul, something unnatural. Beside her, Prince Ruan abruptly sat up straighter, his fingers gripping the hilt of his sword.

She sprang to her feet, turning her head from side to side, straining to see. In the darkness off to her right, she heard a low sound between a moan and a whistle, followed by a harsh scraping against the hull.

The men, too, had jumped to their feet, swords drawn and ready. Yet the next several minutes were so still, so quiet, Sindérian released a pent-up breath, hoping that the danger, whatever it was, had passed.

Then she heard a loud thrashing in the water on all sides at once. The boat rocked so wildly, Sindérian lost her balance and had to clutch at the mast to keep from falling

All around the small fishing boat, the channel was boiling, seething. Hideous bony heads were thrusting up out of the water as far as the eye could see. Fleshless hands, fleshless arms, grappled the side of the boat; scaly bodies rasped against the hull.

They are the dead that were buried at sea, Sindérian realized with a shudder.

And still they bobbed up in the water, more and more of them, crowding around the boat: young boys and maidens, pale wraiths with long soaking hair and wide staring eyes, animated now by a fearful malice. Galley slaves, rattling the rusty chains that had bound them helpless while their ships went down. Drowned fishermen, nibbled away to naked bones riddled with sea worms or covered in barnacles. Worst of all were those who had made covenants of their own with the Deep, undergoing a fearsome sea change. They had kelp in their hair, and little live crabs and fishes; their eyes glowed a sickly green.

Already, many were pulling their loathsome bodies over the side, sliding over the gunwales, creeping on board. The Prince and his guards put up a desperate defense, hacking and slashing, but they were outnumbered, already hopelessly outnumbered, and more and more of the dead came crawling over the side.

Sindérian drew out her little knife and took a swipe at an advancing skeleton covered in spiny growths. A clammy hand caught at the half-healed ankle, tumbling her down into the bottom of the boat. She bit her tongue so hard that her mouth filled with blood. Somehow, she managed to keep her hold on the knife, twisted around, and aimed a reckless cut. By luck or sheer determination the blade struck true, severing the hand at the wrist.

Over by the mast, she saw Jago fall to his knees under the blows of a dozen assailants. Unable to reach him because of the flailing bodies between, she could only watch in horror as two scaled hands grasped his head on either side, and wrenched it around with a hideous grinding sound until something snapped.

Sindérian felt something tug at her scalp, something dragging her over the planks in the bottom of the boat. She angled her head around, and saw that a great horny claw had fastened on a handful of dark hair, was pulling her inexorably toward the side. She struck wildly at the claw, but the knife blade slid off that thick hard hide. Halfway over the gunwales already, she dug the fingernails of one hand into the wood, while with the other she made a frantic effort, sawing the blade against her own hair in order to get free.

At the last possible moment, the lock parted and she fell back into the boat; the claw scrabbled over the side after her. Prince Ruan rushed in between; blood was streaming from a gash in his forehead all down one side of his face, but his arm had lost none of its strength, his sword none of its edge. He dispatched whatever was attached to the claw, and then took on a skeletal maiden in a garland of rotting seaweed.

Shielded, for the moment, between the Prince and the side of the boat, Sindérian finally remembered the packet of earth that she wore on a cord around her neck. She fumbled for the linen bag and tried to loosen the drawstring.

The voice of the king with the iron crown sounded cool and detached inside her head. *Why do you disturb us, wizard woman?*

We need your help! We will all die here without your help, she hurled back at him.

This battle is none of ours. Our battle is on Skyrra, and we are less than a league from the shore. We can reach land of our own will from here. Your service to us is ended.

Sindérian's fingers closed tight around the mouth of the bag. *But not* your *service to* me—*fair recompense for bringing you this far! Either you will swear to fight for us or I will take you to the bottom of the sea with me, and hold you there a thousand, ten thousand years.*

In the whirl of combat, Ruan had moved on, giving Sindérian a chance to climb to her feet. She staggered to an upright position, wincing at the searing pain in her ankle yet still keeping a firm grip on the bag, so that the wraiths remained sealed inside. A scaly pair of arms enfolded her, surrounding her with a dead-fish stench that made her stomach spasm and her gorge rise, but the falcon came screaming down from above, wings thundering, beak striking, and beat the creature aside.

Do you imagine I cannot do what I say, and you still bound by my spell? Decide swiftly. There is very little time, Sindérian demanded. The resistance of hundreds of minds hit her at once, battering her. She clenched her teeth, felt the sweat slide down her face. *Swear now. There is no more time.*

We pledge to aid you in this battle, answered many fierce voices as one. *Let us go free, and we will fight for you.*

She released her hold, tugged at the drawstring, and something came seeping out through the mouth of the bag: a scintillating blue-green light, tinged with silver. All around Sindérian, wraiths of Arkenfell shimmered into existence, and began to do battle with the dead from the sea. Ancient kings grappled with galley slaves; shield-maidens sang as they drew their long knives and entered the fray; the warrior with the horse's head took on the scaled thing that had killed Jago. Seeing that the numbers were a little more equal, Ruan and Aell began to fight with renewed strength.

Their relief was short-lived. Against the dark southern sky a colossal figure rose up, her hair like scarlet flame rippling across the heavens, burning moon and stars to ashes. Her beautiful pale face was contorted with anger, her vast white hand reached out across fifteen hundred miles of ocean—

Only for a heartbeat was she there, then the lights in the sky shone out again. The next moment there came a loud scraping under the water and the boat shuddered from one end to the other, as the hull hit submerged rocks and cracked open. The sea came rushing in.

When the boat began to break up, Sindérian's spell failed, too. She made a futile attempt to strengthen the charm, scribbling runes on the air, pouring will and intention into the wood, but the pattern she had made had shattered along with the hull. Nor could the old, warped planks long withstand the pounding of the rocks.

Within moments, there was nothing left of the boat but some floating boards, a splintered mast; and everyone, living and dead, went down into the sea together.

28

*

The road, which had steadily climbed for so many days, began to descend, narrowing and becoming rougher and less reliable underfoot until it became a mere rugged path. A little stream, black in the shadow of the mountain wall, trickled along beside the trail for many miles.

It was the afternoon of the fourth day since Kivik had made up his mind to head for Tirfang, and for the first time since he and his army left the foothills and began their slow ascent of the mountain slopes, the Prince saw something that had clearly been created by men: a tall, finger-shaped stone, wondrously carven, though not of the native rock.

As he rode a little nearer and pulled up before the milestone, he could see that the carvings were not the ordinary triskeles, mazes, and cup-and-ring marks, but flowing, sinuous figures, scarcely weathered for all their enormous age, so rounded and smooth-looking he could not forbear to reach out with one hand and run his fingertips over them.

"It is not much farther," said one of his captains. "By all accounts, this stone marks the beginning of those lands anciently known as Tirfang, and from here it's only a few hours' ride to the Old Fortress."

A few miles more and the walls of the mountain fell back; the way before them began to open up, as though they had reached the gate of some high mountain valley. The light grew stronger, the water in the stream began to sparkle, and the wind brought with it a strong scent of green, growing things.

The valley in which the first of Kivik's horsemen eventually found themselves was long and narrow, not even a mile across, though it was impossible to see how far ahead it extended. Long, green grass covered the valley floor, but the steep slopes on either side were dark with forest. The trees were great pines and spruce and firs, and if the height and girth of the largest were any indication, this was a very ancient wood. Crows called out from among the shadowy branches, and every now and then a flock would rise up and wheel in the air like a black whirlwind just above the treetops.

After another few miles, something far greater than any of the trees loomed up in the distance: a castle—no, an immense fortress, larger than any Kivik had ever imagined, all built of shining white stone. Though the dark wooded slopes rose up and up behind a large central mass that must be the keep, many of the towers and turrets rose higher still, until the very highest flamed out white against the pale blue sky. There were so many of those slender, needle-sharp towers clustered together that the fortress—no, this great city—must have housed thousands, even tens of thousands of souls in its time.

"I don't ever remember," said Skerry, who was riding beside him, "that anyone ever told me the place was beautiful."

"Nor I," said Kivik. Yet for all that, it was perfectly true. If some of the towers had lost their roofs, if some of the spiraling

outside staircases ended in midair, still the Old Fortress was ex-
quisite, enchanting, even in decay.

And he thought, *If this is how it looks now, what must it
have been like when it was whole? With banners waving and
trumpets sounding, with statues on some of those empty ledges,
and those faded roof tiles shining out in fresher colors?*

Only perhaps that was the wrong question. Perhaps the
fortress was more lovely *now*, with everything gross, or gaudy,
or commonplace stripped away, until only the beautiful bones
remained.

As he came closer, it was possible to see that the outer walls
were not, after all, the legendary thirty ells high, though still of
a dizzying, impressive height, and that the fortress was indeed
inhabited. Tiny antlike men and women ran back and forth
along the walls, behind an embattled parapet. And while he
could not make out any faces at such a distance, he knew that
they were Skyrran, for the sunlight gleamed off hair that was
every conceivable shade of blond from wheaten pale to golden
brown.

Then, remarkably, the sun went behind a massed bank of
dark grey clouds, the light failed, and snow began to fall. At
first, it was only a scattering of big damp flakes. But the air
went from mild to frigid in the space of minutes, and the snow
came whirling down in ever denser clouds.

"This is impossible," said the Prince, feeling the sting of
ice on his cheek, experiencing a chill that had nothing—and
everything—to do with the sudden bite in the air. "We are *well*
below those peaks where the snow lies unmelted—and even
there I doubt they have blizzards at the beginning of summer!"

Skerry nodded his agreement. "Particularly not when the
weather was so fine only moments ago!"

Even the horses had grown uneasy; some whinnied and

fought the bits until foam flew; they would have bolted if not for the firm hold their riders kept on the reins. Others side-stepped nervously, with eyes rolling, and nostrils flaring.

Then Kivik heard voices of those to the rear rise shrill in alarm—faint with distance at first, but growing louder and louder as others took up the cry.

Pulling hard on the reins to turn the reluctant gelding and see what was happening, the Prince gazed in horror as six or seven gigantic figures came roaring out of the crow-haunted pinewoods, charging toward the back of the line. The reason for this freakish weather was all too apparent.

"Ice giants! They will go right through the women and the children if we can't cut them off!" Whipping out his sword, he began to shout orders to those around him.

Within seconds, those in the vanguard had separated from the rest and were gaining speed in a great wheeling charge, hoping to reach the wagons and those who traveled on foot before the giants did.

◇

Meanwhile, Winloki found herself at the very heart of a whirling maelstrom of men and horses. She had been riding farther toward the front than usual, eager to get a glimpse of the fabled fortress, and now, as one company of riders after another turned their horses and went peeling off, following the Prince, she realized that she was very much in the way.

At the same time, her four guards had gathered around her, shouting something she could barely hear over the uproar. At last Haakon managed to edge in his bony gelding a little closer and catch hold of her chestnut mare by the harness.

"Princess, we must ride on ahead to the fortress," he

shouted in her ear. "This is *just* the sort of situation where Prince Kivik meant us to take you out of danger. And you promised not to resist our efforts to keep you safe."

She was by no means certain she had promised any such thing. Though she had always gone where they told her before, that had always been with the healers and the other women. To desert those same comrades now when they were in terrible danger, to allow herself to be whisked away to some place of greater safety, leaving the rest to be almost certainly slaughtered—that was too much like cowardice. She shook her head emphatically "no."

"Princess—" Haakon was beginning again, when she reached out and struck at his hands until he loosed his hold on the harness, and she was able to haul the mare around and see what was happening behind.

Her first steady look at the ice giants nearly took her breath away. They were manlike in form but many times greater, with skin of a bluish-leaden hue, pockmarked and craggy as mountains. They had eyes like deep black pits. And if their movements were awkward and somewhat slow, still they covered ground with their long, sturdy legs, and their pale hair streamed out behind them like blue flame on the wind of their passage. Each carried on his arm a mighty buckler, set with ice-blue crystals, and brandished an immense war hammer that looked capable of crushing great boulders into dust.

Then one of the giants veered off from the others, heading her way. His empty black eyes met Winloki's across the distance, and she felt a sudden, *shuddering* jolt of recognition.

These creatures will be attracted to me, she thought, her blood turning to ice water and her heart to a frozen lump in her chest. *Just as I am attracted and repelled by them. And if I do*

*not put some distance between myself and everyone else, who-
ever is by me will share my danger.*

Winloki wheeled the panicking chestnut around again, laid
heels to flanks, and felt the mare surge into a dead run. If the
mare was running away with her, just at the moment that
hardly mattered. The gates of the fortress lay straight ahead,
and if someone opened them in time, she might yet be safe. If
not, regaining control of her horse was the least of her prob-
lems.

There came a pounding of hooves behind and to both
sides, and Winloki realized that her guards were catching up to
her on their more powerful mounts. "No," she screamed, as
one of the men drew abreast of her, riding low in the saddle and
spurring his horse along. She did not want to see any of them
die for her.

Then thunderous footsteps sounded behind, and a stinging
gust of snow and wind struck her. The mare, still running hard,
flattened her ears and squealed a warning as a tremendous dark
shadow went hurtling on ahead, blocking their path to the
fortress.

The chestnut would take no more. She reared up on her
hind legs, raking the air and screaming in terror. Winloki felt
herself falling, landing with bruising force on the icy grass; then
all the air was knocked out of her lungs, and for a moment she
saw and felt nothing.

She came back to herself just in time to avoid being crushed
under the hooves of the dancing mare. Though she could still
barely see for the snow and the dizzy grey sparks of light
whirling before her eyes, Winloki managed to scramble to her
feet.

The giant loomed up before her, snarling. His mouth

opened on a row of broken yellow teeth, and a blast of burning cold air hit her so hard that she nearly fell. Then his war hammer passed over her head, only barely missing her. It made the air whistle, and the breath of the nearest horse turn to ice.

I ought not to be still standing after that, she thought, remembering the men she had revived, and the one she had *not* been able to revive, in Lückenbörg. But as she clenched her hands together, Winloki felt the great ring of bone on her right thumb. It was, she suddenly realized, both her peril and her salvation.

Two of her guards hurled themselves between her and the giant, and Haakon was suddenly there on foot beside her. The boy's strong hands encircled her waist, and he was lifting her up to the back of the piebald gelding, which stood solid as a wall while she tried to mount. She reached out, caught ahold of the cantle and a handful of dust-colored mane, then managed to throw a leg over Lif's broad back and settle into the saddle. She saw that Arvi was there on the other side, where she had not been able to see him before, still mounted, and holding the gelding's reins.

He threw her the reins, she nodded her thanks, and a moment later they were riding along, side by side, as fast as the horses would go. Lif, she realized, was every bit as good as Haakon said he was; he moved like the wind, in long, effortless strides.

Just as she saw the massive gates swinging open before her, she could hear the ice giant come loping along behind her. Arvi fell back a little, to defend her at need, and Lif, without any urging, managed an extra burst of speed.

Then she was riding under the arch of the gate, clattering through the dark tunnel inside the gatehouse, then out the other side into an overgrown courtyard, where Lif's hooves struck violet fire from a broken marble pavement. She pulled in and looked back over her shoulder, just in time to see Arvi emerge from the tunnel behind her and hear the gate slam shut. Then she leaned forward, resting her face on the gelding's sweaty, bristly neck, while she struggled to catch her breath.

A moment later there were running footsteps, a babble of voices high and low. When she looked up, the courtyard was a sea of curious faces. A host of ragged men and women had gathered around her, shivering in the chill air and asking excited questions.

"It is the Lady Winloki," panted Arvi. "She is a great healer, but I think—I think she should be looked after herself just now."

She took a great gulp of air and shook her head. "I am well enough."

"No you are not, Princess," he retorted. "You can't see your own face to see what that creature did to you, but look at your hands: they are blue with cold."

Holding up one hand, Winloki saw that he was right. She had not, after all, been entirely immune to the wind of the ice giant's hammer.

As she slid down from the saddle and stood unsteadily on the marble paving, two tall women put their arms around her and supported her across the courtyard, then through another gate. She felt somebody drop a rough woolen shawl over her shoulders.

"Thank you," Winloki whispered, feeling weak tears rise in her eyes at the thought of one of these ragged women sacrificing her own inadequate protection against the cold in order to warm her.

But as she emerged into the next snowy courtyard she could see and feel the shadows all around her: faint and tenuous, yet quite unmistakable, lurking wherever the light was dimmest, prowling in the shrubbery, sliding from one dark alley between the buildings to the next. Fear settled into her bones then, and stayed there.

And she thought, *For all the good intentions of the people here, the kindness of these women—for someone like* me, *the Old Fortress at Tirfang is no safe place.*

29

✳

For Sindérian there was pain—agonizing pain in her head, her shoulder, all down her left side. She felt herself buffeted repeatedly by the waves, beaten against a hard, unyielding surface. Scarcely conscious of where she was or what she was doing, she floundered in the water, swallowed a bitter mouthful of brine, and somehow managed to get away from the tormenting rocks.

Then something heavy struck her, and she felt herself sinking, down and down, fathoms deep in cold green water.

Tangled up in her long skirt, she tried and failed to struggle back toward the surface. In growing desperation, she watched her breath doing what she could not: rising upward, as a series of tiny pearly bubbles.

The farther she sank, the darker it grew. Yet there was something shining in the depths: a pattern wrought in iridescent silver, a phosphorescent spiderweb of eerie light. It was, she realized, all around her—more than that, it was the thing that was pulling her down. She began to struggle even harder, but the strands which appeared so insubstantial were as tough and resilient as rope. She was netted as neatly as a fish—and was likely to die as one, flailing about and gasping for breath. The more she fought the weaker she became, wasting the little air that she had still in her lungs.

Then something burst inside her head, and for a moment it seemed that she was floating in endless light.

So this is what it is to die, she thought, *this vision, this clarity.* Indeed, it seemed that she could see for a thousand, two thousand miles in all directions, worlds within worlds under the ocean.

She saw the gigantic kraken waving their myriad tentacles in a deadly slow dance; the skull of a leviathan so tremendous that whales swam in and out through the gaping eyeholes. She saw the breeding grounds of water dragons and sea serpents, and a clutch of new eggs the color of jade, as large as houses. She saw vast mermaid cities of coral and ivory in the deepest trenches of the sea, and knew that this was where the Sea-People had retreated, into the abyss, to rebuild their civilization farther from the land and the proximity of wizards and magicians fighting their endless wars. She saw hulks of wrecked ships, and towers of drowned cities where the sea had encroached on the land. She saw monstrous great creatures, neither fish nor serpent, armored like dragons, gnawing away at the roots of the islands of Thäerie and Phaôrax.

Most terrifying of all, she saw what might be the type and progenitor of all the dragons: a long, pale, bloated body, as round as an earthworm yet miles and miles across, with spines as high as underwater mountains, all glowing with an unwholesome, nacreous light. It was curled up on the bottom of the ocean as if in sleep, but as Sindérian watched, it slowly lifted its weighty head and met her gaze, looking back at her with Ouriána's face, Ouriána's vivid green eyes.

All this, in a brief bright instant of inspiration, which was gone before she could truly grasp it.

A shadowy form glided past Sindérian, so close that she could almost touch it. With the detachment of despair, she watched it turn and come back, shearing through the gleaming strands that held her. A sleek, muscular body grazed against hers, a hard head nudging her ribs. Then it was underneath her, pushing her, pushing her upward, back toward the air and the pale moonlight.

As soon as her head broke the surface of the water she gasped for air, dragging as much as she could into her lungs. Blinking water out of her eyes, she tried to get her bearings, but the moonlight was fading, the night was closing in on her. Out of nowhere, a thin cold hand reached out and strongly grasped hers.

After that, for a time, she knew nothing at all.

———

When Sindérian next became aware of herself, she was lying facedown in wet sand. She tasted sand in her mouth, felt more of it in her eyes, in her hair, sticking to her face and her arms like a second skin. With a groan, she rolled over on her side. It was early morning, not long after sunrise, if she could judge by the pale pink and gold colors of the sea and sky; but it might as well be noon, so fierce was the glare to her burning eyes.

Squinting to keep out some of the light, she saw Prince Ruan and Aell not far away, sprawled as she was on the beach, where they had all apparently been deposited like driftwood. Her vision blurred again, so that it was impossible to tell if either of them was breathing. She *thought* she saw Aell move.

Struggling to lift her head, the better to see, she felt the world tilt under her, and everything turned grey again.

—————

But the next time she woke, both men had revived. The sky was even brighter than before, and the Prince and Aell knelt in the sand beside her, gazing down at her with looks of grave concern on their white, weary faces.

And no wonder, she thought, *if I look even* half *as bruised and beaten as they do.*

"I thought I was drowning," she said to Ruan in a cracked whisper. "But then you helped me."

"I regret to say that I was unable to help anyone, I was so battered against the rocks," he replied with a shake of his head. His voice was flat and toneless, all of the music gone. "Your Arkenfeller ghosts saved all three of us—with some assistance from Faolein. He was, as I think I recall, a sea lion at the time, though he has since returned to the falcon-shape he seems to favor."

"*Three* of us?" Sindérian asked sharply, then she remembered. "Jago is dead?"

"Yes," said Ruan, and she saw his face suddenly twist in pain.

She tried to gather her thoughts, to think of something she could say—she who had been consoling the living for the death of their friends almost as long as she could remember. Yet this time the words were simply not there.

"Your losses have been very great," she finally whispered, glancing from him to Aell and back again, remembering Tuillo as well as Jago.

"Yes," the Prince answered shortly. And then, with a brief flash of his old arrogance: "The more reason—as you once told me—to make certain they did not die in vain."

Reminded that she had a duty, Sindérian sat up then and tried to struggle to her feet. But the pain in her head was so intense, she could only fall forward on her hands and knees, vomiting seawater into the sand.

A long time later—it *seemed* a long time later, no matter how long it actually was—she sat back on her heels and wiped at her mouth.

"I think you have another head injury," said the Prince. "You look very much as you did that time before."

Remembering how sick she had felt that other time, how long the misery had lasted, Sindérian thought for a moment that death would have almost been preferable.

Only you *don't have that luxury,* she reminded herself, gritting her teeth.

She remembered what she had seen under the water, the web that had entangled her. She knew what it meant and she knew who was responsible. There were only a few people capable of creating such a thing, and only one of those wicked enough to do it.

Many things which had worried and puzzled her before began to make sense: the dreams that had haunted her across the mountains, the perils which had assailed her every step of the way through Arkenfell. None of it was accident; nothing had occurred at random. Somehow, Ouriána knew about *her,* out of all the world Ouriána had singled out *her,* marked her for destruction.

Yet as terrifying as that thought was, against it she could set this new knowledge of herself and her potentialities, of all that she might learn and become under Faolein's continued tutelage. Or might—if her time were not so dreadfully limited, if she were not under this curse! It was a curious feeling, knowing herself to be under sentence of death.

There was a flutter of wings, and the falcon settled on Sindérian's shoulder. A warm, reassuring current of life force flowed from father to daughter, and after a while, though her head still throbbed, she began to feel a little stronger.

"What happened to the wraiths of Arkenfell?" she asked, realizing with a start that somewhere along the way she had lost the bag of earth.

Ruan shrugged. "They have gone on their way. No doubt impatient to attend to their own pressing business, according to your bargain. Even bringing the three of us ashore, they wanted me to know, was a great concession."

She accepted the hand that he was offering her and staggered to her feet. Her gown and the shift underneath were both stiff with salt; she ached in every part of her body. "It is as well that I have a hard head," she said, attempting a smile.

"So it is," answered Ruan, with a flash of his teeth. "They chose well on Leal. As much for your strength as your impressive stubbornness."

———

It was already well after noon when they left the beach behind and started walking inland, through acres and acres of coarse sea grass, past the occasional stretch of reeking green bog. Aell went first, then Sindérian, then the Prince.

"We have no horses, no food, and very little money," she said, making an effort to hold up her head, to put a little iron into her backbone. "At least we have reached Skyrra ahead of the Furiádhin. I suppose we should be grateful for that."

"We aren't nearly so destitute as you seem to think," said the Prince. "When we come to a town, I will sell my brooch or my torc. The brooch alone should provide for our needs as far as Lückenbörg."

If and when we come to a town, she thought grimly. There was no telling how far these marshes extended. It might be five miles, it might be a hundred.

As she walked, more and more of her undersea revelations returned to her. She told Faolein of the creatures she had seen undermining the islands, expecting him to be as shocked and horrified as she was. Tens of thousands of people lived on Thäerie and Phaôrax, and if those islands were swamped, the death and destruction would be—unthinkable. *We thought we had years, even decades, to set things right. Now it looks as though we can measure that time in months or weeks.*

I must admit, he answered calmly, *that I had some inkling of that at Saer.*

And yet you never told me? she asked, bristling up with indignation.

No more than you intend to tell Prince Ruan or Aell. You should know that as soon as a seer shares his or her vision with others it alters the world in mysterious ways.

Sindérian bit her lip. It was true there were things she had seen that she was not yet ready to share even with him. She could not even be sure of what she *had* seen, or what it might mean. Sometimes the line between revelation and hallucination was very thin, and parts of what she had seen came uncomfortably close to her nightmares.

Although a woman who might measure the time remaining

to her in heartbeats ought not, perhaps, to worry overmuch about the future.

She gritted her teeth against the pain in her head. Well then, what if she *was* doomed? At least knowing that, she had a chance to make her death matter, a chance to choose the time and the place, perhaps even the manner.

They walked on until sunset, without coming to any houses. At last, feeling unable to take another step, Sindérian threw herself down on the soft grass on a little hillock, looking back the way they had come. The sky overhead and to the west was like a stained-glass window, in gorgeous shades of orange and red, fading into a transparent violet and a faint, luminous turquoise.

After it turned completely dark, there was a rain of shooting stars falling into the sea. Her sight still blurry with the concussion, Sindérian tilted her head back to look at the stars directly overhead.

She could not be certain, but it seemed to her that there were strange new signs in the heavens, omens and portents of things amazing and terrible and wonderful to come: unknown constellations rising, in colors as vivid as the sunset, among the Hidden Stars.

30

*

Fumes of mandragora, hellbore, and *ylls-yllatha* hung heavy on the air. The fire hissed like a basilisk.

The chamber where Ouriána stood feeding the fire had twelve walls, one door, and no windows; it was paneled in ivory. Nine torches burned in sconces around the room, and nine faint shadows fluttered on the walls. On the floor was enscribed a hexagram: two triangles overlapping to form a six-pointed star.

Ouriána had positioned herself at the center of the star, and they were her shadows that danced on the walls. She wore a slithery grey gown made of snake skins, sewn together with silver wire. Her auburn hair was bound back by a silver fillet, enriched with pearls and deep purple amethysts; silver, too, were the bracelets she wore on her shapely white arms. At her sandaled feet, an iron brazier on a curious goat-legged brass stand was responsible for the sluggish wreaths of faintly purple smoke that scented the air, causing her to feel slightly giddy.

She threw more herbs on the fire. The flames pulsed, and there was a little flurry of white sparks when leaves caught fire. Around the room, the nine shadows took on fantastical shapes:

images of Ouriána as a siren, a lamia, a sphinx, a harpy, and creatures stranger still.

She muttered certain words, spread her palms wide, and something began to form in the heavy air. Chaos boiled and smoked between her hands; it changed color from palest lavender to a rosy red, and finally to a deep crimson. Chanting a verse, she divided the whirling mass into nine parts, then named each one.

As she spoke a name, a single ball of matter would wink out, and a scintillating cone of light would materialize, either at one of the six points of the star, or at an intersection where two lines met. At first thin as smoke, it gradually took on the lineaments and the apparent solidarity of a gaunt man in robes of scarlet.

Some appeared to her in the elaborate vestments they wore to celebrate her rites in the temple; others came booted and spurred for travel, or sweaty and bloodstained, as if fresh from battle; they stood with their salt-white hair billowing and their red cloaks flaring, as though on board ship or standing in a high wind; they carried flails, or heavy iron maces, or long-bladed spears. They came to her with their twisted limbs, damaged faces, and other deformities; Scioleann and Vitré; the warlike Graelent, Ganhardin, and Náoiss; the subtle Iobhar; Goezenou of the heavy jaw and barren eyes; slender Dyonas, with the neat ivory horns shining on his brow; Camhóinhann, who alone matched her in stature, overtopping the others by at least a head.

The nine phantom priests waited silently for her to speak. So real did they appear, so immediately present, that their flat metallic eyes even reflected the red glow of the coals, the flickering torchlight. Yet three points of the star remained empty, signifying the three Furiádhin who had perished.

"Camhóinhann, Dyonas, Goezenou—you are not to go to Lückenbörg after all," she commanded. "I have learned that this mysterious niece of mine is to be found much farther to the west, traveling with the armies of Skyrra in the Drakenskaller Mountains. Go there immediately."

Those she addressed bowed low before her.

"And if," she went on, a little archly, "if it should chance that anyone tries to interfere with your business in Skyrra, kill them without hesitation. *Whoever* they might be, high or low. Do not, this time, think to delegate the task, as was done at Saer. One of you must attend to it *personally*."

The three priests exchanged questioning glances, not absolutely certain whether she meant a reproach, or wherein they had failed. Nor did she deign to elighten them, or to mention Sindérian by name, so confident was she that the young healer had been—or soon would be—utterly obliterated. The *aniffath* could not fail.

Indeed, in that moment, Ouriána's confidence was very great. Drugged with the fumes, she felt big with the future, pregnant with possibilities. A bitter chill crept into the room, so that the flames seemed to exude cold, not light, and she felt the Darkness unfold within her.

Her green eyes turned black, and her pale face blanched whiter still, the skin pulling thin and taut over the bones of the skull. An ageless evil surveyed the Furiádhin out of the fathomless dark eyes. Then the illusion—if that was what it was— passed, and her beauty blazed up again, more vivid than before.

"Soon you will be at your full strength, the full complement of twelve once more complete," she proclaimed, in a low, excited voice. "Three of your acolytes have gone into seclusion; the change burns in their blood. It cannot be long, now, before they are judged ready and worthy to take the final vows.

And behold: as I foretold, as I have promised you, the twelve will be invincible!"

A tremor passed through the entire edifice of the palace, soundless, but nevertheless thrilling. Náoiss's pale wings flexed, unfurled, showing transparent in the yellow torchlight. Shadows played across the elegant, commanding planes of Camhóinhann's face, noble and eloquent even in ruin.

"Thäerie will fall, and the cities of the coast," she continued. "We will paint the stones of the Great House at Pentheirie with the blood of the Pendawers. We will raze the walls of the Scholia on Leal and harry the Master Wizards across the face of the earth. As we move north and east, we will extend Our empire as we go."

As the Furiádhin prostrated themselves in token of their obedience, she broke the spell that held them in thrall. The nine phantoms vanished, more suddenly than they had come, all of them gone in an instant.

Yet in her mind's eye she could still see them: plying the seas, riding out like thunder across the land, laying waste to vast kingdoms. She could hear the hoofbeats of their mighty steeds, the crack of shattered stone as city walls crumbled, the roar of flames reaching up to the sky.

"The new age will come," she cried out, to the Night, to the Universe. "In fire and in torment, perhaps, but it *will* come!"